CROCKETT felt a great fear welling up within him, but not a natural, rational survival mechanism type of fear. It was a mindless, xenophobic cringing from a sight that was utterly alien.

Below him, wrapped in a shifting, glowing mist, stood a very tall, excessively slender figure. After a few seconds, Crockett realized the figure was male, dressed in an elaborate armorial garment. The colors red and blue predominated. The long limbs were covered by a pattern of iridescent, interlocking scales.

A crest of golden feathers topped the elongated, narrow skull and ran down the back of the cranium. The face had a subtly reptilian cast—broad, prominent cheekbones and a pronounced brow ridge. Crockett saw no ears.

Projecting out and down from between the brows was a nose resembling a small scythe—extremely thin, sharply ridged, curving toward a lipless mouth like an eagle's beak. The large, almond shaped eyes stared blindly, black vertical slits centered in golden, opalescent irises. They were animal eyes, the eyes of a predator.

Long-fingered hands were crossed over the chest-plate and the thumbs were tipped with curved talons, like a gamecock's spur.

He tried to back away, but the Brigadefuhrer put a hand against his back to keep him in place.

"Nothing to fear, Colonel." The man's quiet voice purred with amusement. "He can't see you."

Fenris reached up and snatched away the sunglasses from his face. His eyes were narrowed in amusement. Black, vertical pupils bisected golden irises. "But I can."

Published by Fortuna Books ~ 48 Bedlow Avenue, Newport RI 02840

Cover art and design by Melissa Martin-Ellis
Fortuna logo design by Michael Hudson

ISBN-10: 061569781X
ISBN-13: 978-0615697819

THE
SPUR™
LOKI'S ROCK

by

Mark Ellis

As always, to and for Melissa

From Colonel Quentin Crockett, RE: LOKI MISSION

So, here's how it was explained to me, more or less—

About four hundred years ago, after several Third World powers engaged in a limited nuclear exchange, multi-national corporations took over the division and parceling out of Earth's resources. Good old Earth became a very small commodity, so the corporations and conglomerates had no choice but to look for profits offworld.

For everyone else, the priorities were different—the ultimate issue was the survival of mankind and to ensure that, we needed new places to live.

Nippon International constructed a permanent mining outpost on Luna and the terra-forming of Mars began by Creations Unlimited. Hiflite Industries developed the first Bussard Ramjet space vessel that achieved a maximum velocity of one percent of light speed.

When Nippon International discovered a field of asteroids rich in rare ores and minerals, hostilities broke out among several corporations in a dispute over ownership. When the struggle among the industrial giants threatened to leave Earth's foothold into space a floating mass of radioactive rubble, the hostilities were quelled by the formation of the Sol 9 Commonwealth.

An international governing body descended from the old United Nations, the Commonwealth called for the peaceful and cooperative exploration of the Solar System.

The spirit of peaceful cooperation didn't last long—it never does when there are conflicts of interest. In response to Commonwealth edicts, most of the corporations formed their own private security organizations and the clashes of interest extended from boardrooms to back alleys. By the end of the 22nd century, three industrial empires dominated almost all trade in the Solar System: Nippon, now calling itself Nippon Interstellar, Taktron and Utopia Import.

Also around this time, GenTek Industries achieved a breakthrough in genetic engineering—they developed the TH-1 series of synthetic TransHumans.

The TransHumans were just the first example of all sorts of biological products created by GenTek. Many others followed over the decades, including the Mnemosyne Line—essentially organic computers in human form.

Hiflite Industries patented the ion drive which powered ships to a maximum velocity of 20 percent of light speed. One technological breakthrough led to another and then another. The expected slow, gradual expansion of human exploration became a human explosion across the system, then into extrasolar space.

Throughout the Orion Spur, dozens of worlds and moons were found to be perfectly suited for habitation and colonization. On some of those Spur worlds, the explorers found the first evidence of the so-called Imperator Tyranny.

Exoarcheologists theorized that the technologically advanced Imperators had ruled and colonized many planets in the Orion Spur thousands of years ago. All they left behind were ruins, myths and fragments of artifacts. Based on the architecture, scientists speculated that the humanoid Imperators might have been a strong influence on early Earth cultures such as Sumeria.

Corporations continued to plant colonies on Spur planets, in defiance of the Commonwealth Colonization Board edicts that all worlds had to be first searched for Imperator relics or tech. If the corporations found anything of the sort on planets they claimed, they kept their discoveries closely guarded secrets.

Over the next century, the Sol 9 Commonwealth lost most of its governing influence as the corporations relocated their central industrial operations to The Spur.

The outer rim worlds of The Spur—known derisively as "Rowel Planets"—were frequently settled by outcasts and a lot of "ists"—religious and cultural separatists, cultists, militarists, alienists, political extremists, and even fringe research and development departments of certain corporations that wanted to keep their tinkering as far from the mainstream as possible.

One such Rowel Planet was designated Loki, because of its history as an exceptionally unpredictable, hostile and tricky world.

Although the biosphere was Earth-like in many ways, weather changes were as dramatic as they were disastrous. Its sun—13 Orionis-was wildly variable in regards to the heat it produced and most of the habitable land was restricted to a single supercontinent known as Midgard. Here could be found deserts, jungles, mountains and even three-thousand mile long rivers. The indigenous life forms, although different from those on Terra were still close enough to the familiar so they didn't seem completely alien.

In a less than decade after its discovery, Loki became more of a refuge than a colony, a planet sized Hole-In-The-Wall, a hideaway to where criminal organizations, fringe groups and religions that had worn out their respective welcomes on Terra fled to start over. Loki was a new world and on a new world there are always many beginnings.

The new colonists brought everything they could for a fresh start—building materials, seeds, animals such as cows, horses and even certain kinds of birds and bees so an ecosystem comparable to Earth's could be created. Terraforming projects met with varying degrees of success.

The Commonwealth Enclave monitoring outpost reported that most societies formed on Loki were of the rough-and-tumble frontier type, scrambling after scarce trade goods, competing fiercely for natural resources, battling over everything from water to hunting grounds. Different settlements were at each other's throats half the time.

But a little under a century after Loki opened to colonists, a series of catastrophes laid much of the planet to waste. The magnetic centers shifted and the great glaciers at the poles withdrew toward new positions. Convulsions shattered mountains and rivers became inland seas.

No one was really sure what happened, but the general consensus of opinion was the long-term and poorly executed terra-forming program triggered the geological cataclysms.

Commonwealth statisticians speculated that less than 20 percent of Loki's population survived. But since the monitoring outpost on the Midgard continent was apparently destroyed along with most of the surrounding regions, no one could be sure of anything about the conditions of the planet, or those who had colonized it.

Besides, after 188 years, nobody cared about or even really remembered the remote Rowel Planet. On the star charts, Loki became an insignificant speck, one among thousands.

It remained a speck until the office of Offworld Operations was formed and the newly-named director, Judge Jonathan Blake, came to me.

For seventeen years, I'd worked as the chief Commonwealth law officer on the Outland asteroid mining station. I wasn't in the employ of the mining companies and I didn't act as a liaison with corporate security services, either. I enforced Commonwealth law, not company policy. Eventually I earned the rank of Colonel in the Commonwealth Marshal Service.

I wasn't popular--no lawman ever is--but when there was trouble, I was the first man they looked for and the last man they wanted to meet. After I lost my wife Laura Lee and the full use of my left leg in the Tantalus Ring Incident, it became a very lonely job. I did it the best way I knew how and sometimes that way wasn't particularly diplomatic.

Most likely, a lack of diplomatic training combined with my age and perceived infirmities were the main reasons my contract wasn't renewed. As a concession to my years of service, I was offered a substantial severance package when the new executive board took over. I accepted it, but for the first time in many years I had no idea of where to go or what to do next.

I hadn't even finished packing up my office when Judge Blake asked me to lead a team of investigators to Loki and make a legitimate attempt at separating fact from speculation.

Loki was a big X, an almost total unknown—except to the people who still clawed out an existence there and they weren't providing information. What little Intel had leaked out since the Catastrophe of two centuries before had to be assembled like a jigsaw puzzle with most of the pieces missing.

During the official OWO briefing, the mission statement Judge Blake laid out for me seemed straightforward enough--to assess the extent of the geological changes on Loki, take a stab at gathering information about the flora and fauna and salvage what could be salvaged in the Enclave monitoring outpost... providing I could even locate the damn place after all of these years.

He also said, "Secrecy sometimes has to be imposed and though I wouldn't call this a secret mission, the OWO would prefer it was secure. But just so you won't accuse me of holding out on you later, the major part of your assignment is still under wraps. You'll get full encoded instructions once you've landed on the planet—or, depending on your report, you'll be pulled out and that will be all there is to it."

I didn't like the idea of being kept in the dark, but I liked the idea of forced retirement even less. Besides, even though the reasons for the sudden renewed interest in Loki weren't shared with me, I made a fairly educated guess—corporations control far too many Spur colonies and dole out their resources in the time, manner and volume they see fit. Most of them are locked in power conflicts with one another. The result is millions of suffering people on Terra and other Spur worlds.

In times of fierce competition, even Rowel Planets increase in value.

I also had the suspicion—which I kept to myself—that something else had been found on Loki, something the corporate elite either feared very much or wanted very much.

So, the OWO decided one man was needed to take charge of the Loki situation—one man who could act fast, decisively and brutally if he had to. I assumed that if I accepted the job, I would be gambling my neck and could very likely lose it.

I didn't think about the offer for very long. I took the job and pretty damn quickly understood that although I have a hand-picked team of specialists to rely on, nothing has changed all that much.

When there's trouble, I'm still the first man they look for and the last man they want to meet.

CHAPTER ONE

Loki: Western Quadrant of Midgard—The Hellgrounds

Crockett figured it was one degree shy of being hotter than Hell. He dragged the back of one hand across his perspiration-filmed forehead and surveyed the terrain with stinging eyes. The country stretched away flat in three directions--so flat that he judged the haze-gray low mountain range rising from the horizon to be a good thirty kilometers away.

Squinting, he tried to see beyond the shimmer of heat waves. Although he had rolled the sleeves of his faded khaki shirt all the way up to his biceps, the relief was minimal. Dark half-moons of perspiration showed under the arms. The fabric was sweat-pasted skintight against his back.

The old, unpaved roadway on which he stood lanced directly through the serrated range, twisting between hills of barren rock, deeply eroded by the ages. Crockett hoped to find cooler temperatures and green grass in the higher country, but he didn't trust Loki to grant even the smallest wish without demanding some sort of payment—most likely in blood.

Rangy of limb and standing six feet four in his thick-soled jump boots, Quentin Crockett looked like he belonged in the wastelands of Loki—his bronzed, weather-beaten face was turned unflinchingly toward the blue canopy of the sky. His eyes, faded to the pale gray-blue color of old steel, slitted against the unremitting glare of 13 Orionis. The faint breeze stirred his blonde hair, so sun-bleached it appeared almost white. He rested his right hand on the walnut-handled butt of a Hawken Big 50 in the battered leather holster low on his thigh.

The only spot of color anywhere about him was the small yellow-red-and-black insignia patch positioned high on his right shirt sleeve. Shaped like a stylized sunburst, the letters OWO were stitched in yellow thread against a black background.

Although he didn't care for the heat, Crockett wasn't intimidated by the parched, rocky terrain stretching away in drifting dunes of ocher and saffron. Compared to the stark, ice-rimmed asteroid mines of Io, the so-called Hellgrounds seemed almost lush. At least he had enough oxygen to keep alive, even if every breath felt like inhaling a blowtorch.

Just to be contrary, he took a slim cigarillo from a shirt pocket. From the other, he removed a stick match and set it afire with a flick of his thumbnail. The air was so dry, he was a little surprised the sulfur hadn't ignited spontaneously. Lighting the cigar, he relished the bittersweet smoke, blowing a stream of it in the direction of the sun.

The air was oxygen/nitrogen in a rich 75/23 proportion. Trace elements made breathing it a healthier practice than inhaling the industrialized soup that passed for Terra's atmosphere. The irony that his Earth-made cigar polluted the clean air of Loki didn't escape him.

From a clip on his gunbelt he took a set of microbinoculars. Raising them to his eyes, he peered through the ruby-coated lenses. He swept them over the hills, noting how a jumble of rubble atop a distant knoll resembled the ruins of an old building--a watch tower, maybe.

He saw a sand-colored lizard sitting sleepy-eyed in the miniscule shade offered by a rock not much larger than a loaf of bread. Crockett examined all the shadows cast by rocks but he didn't see another living creature, not even an insect. The terrain lay dust-silent under the unremitting assault of the sun.

Lowering the binoculars, he glanced behind him at the dark shape bulking up from the ground. *Ambler's* idling engine hit high notes of strain as the air-conditioning system worked overtime to keep the interior from turning into an oven.

The massive APC rested on eight huge tires. Gun ports, missile pods and machine gun blisters perforated the sleek armor plate sheathing the vehicle.

Forty feet long and weighing in at fifteen tons, *Ambler* started life as cargo hauler in the mines of Io. Completely refurbished and updated, the vehicle was state-of-the-art with computerized controls energized from small but very reliable onboard generator units. Powered by a six-hundred horsepower drive train, the APC was designed to withstand nuclear, biological and environmental threats.

Crockett hadn't bestowed the name *Ambler* upon it, but Dr. Alexis Elgin-Jones of the Scientific Intelligence Network tended to personalize everything. As long as her habit didn't interfere with the mission, Crockett didn't mind indulging her. Still and all, he found the SIN officer's formal mode of address to the Mnemosyne more than a little silly.

Gusting out a sigh, he unclipped the insulated canteen from his belt, thumbed up the nozzle and took several long swallows of thankfully cool water.

"Don't drink so much," warned Quanah Parker from behind a boulder on the roadside. "You'll founder."

"Mind your own fluids," Crockett snapped. "That's why we stopped in the first place."

"Yeah, well...maybe you don't get tired of peeing in a can." Quanah Parker strode quickly from around the boulder, zipping up his fly. "I do."

"They're not cans—they're chemical toilets. We have other options, you know."

"I won't wear those biodegradable diapers Mr. Syne prefers."

Crockett scowled in his direction. "Mr. Syne? Now Jones has got you calling him that, too?"

Quanah shrugged. "Jones also suggested we all wear diapers when we can't change out the cans—I mean the toilets."

Crockett rinsed out his mouth, spit and returned the canteen to his belt. "I think this conversation has officially bottomed out. Let's go."

Stubbing out the cigarillo against a boulder, he turned back toward *Ambler*. He heard a sudden distant racket and he whirled, his hand making a reflexive move toward the butt of the Hawken. He leaned in the direction of the sound, listening intently to the cacophony of high-pitched, piping shrieks.

He said flatly, "I don't like the sound of that."

"You shouldn't." Quanah inclined his shaggy, black-haired head to the west. The red bandana around his forehead was already dark with sweat. "Sounds like a swarm of shreekwings. Maybe stirred up by the engine."

"Shreekwings?"

Quanah nodded. "You know what they are?"

"What they're supposed to be, anyhow. Don't know how much to believe."

"Believe what I tell you...I was born only a hundred klicks away, over in Comancheria." A lithely built man of medium height with anthracite-black eyes and a ruddy complexion, Quanah Parker wore a lightweight white shirt and brown leather vest. A pair of boot moccasins encased his feet to mid-calf. "If we're hearing the shreekwings, they're already too close and we need to find cover fast."

Crockett looked at the flat curve of roadway behind *Ambler*. According to the records, the road had been named Perdition Highway a couple of centuries before and he couldn't deny the name was well-chosen. A hundred yards away, on the far side of the road, he barely made out the figure of Alex standing in copse of scrub. She intently examined a shrub, peering at the leaves through a small magnifier. Crockett guessed she spoke into her ever-present pocket recorder and hadn't heard the high-pitched whistling shrieks floating up from behind the hills.

Crockett grimaced in exasperation. At the insistence of Alex and Quanah, the APC had stopped so the team could stretch their legs and take a whiff of unrecycled air after a nonstop ten-hour drive. Crockett assumed Syne was still inside the vehicle, monitoring the on-board systems. At least he hoped so.

Quanah jerked his thumb back toward hills. The Comanche medic's lips set in a grim line, his obsidian eyes narrowed. "The shreekwings will be on top of us soon."

Crockett and Quanah returned to the APC at a trot, casting watchful glances over their shoulders. They still saw nothing, but the cacophony of eerie cries grew louder by the second.

"Jones, get back aboard!" Crockett shouted toward Alex. "Shreekwings! On their way! *Jones!*"

Syne pushed open the side door panel. A wave of wonderfully cool air touched Crockett's face. The slender, hairless TransHuman stared impassively at Crockett, and then asked mildly, ""Where are the shreekwings, Colonel?"

Crockett gestured back toward the hills. "Hear 'em?"

Syne angled his head, turning one small, delicately shaped ear toward the sounds. His round blue eyes closed in concentration but his paper-pale face did not change expression. After a second, he opened his eyes. "I do indeed. Rather a sizable swarm, judging by cries"

Crockett cupped his hands around his mouth and bellowed, *"Jones!"*

When no response was forthcoming, Quanah made a move in that direction. "I'll go get her."

Crockett checked the move by stepping in front of him. "Stay put. Get inside and button up."

He turned to Syne. "Kill the engine."

The TransHuman obeyed instantly. As the rumbling engine fell silent, they heard the rustling of hundreds of wings interwoven with the weird shrieks.

"Can't we outrun the damn things?" Crockett asked.

Quanah shook his head. "Worst thing we can try. Shreekwings can't spot live prey unless it's moving. If we aren't rolling before the flock gets here, we've got to stay put.

Leastways, that's what I'm told."

Crockett nodded and unleathered his pistol. He ran across the shoulder of the road, down a gentle slope, and blundered through the sparse undergrowth growing among the rocks. He sprinted with an almost imperceptible limp, favoring his left leg. He glanced back once and glimpsed a dark, twisting mass uncoiling from the far side of the hills, silhouetted by the lowering sun.

From what he knew, shreekwings were rare, even in the Hellgrounds region of Loki. Crockett certainly hadn't seen one in the three-plus weeks since coming planetside, but he had read hundred year-old reports about isolated settlements being completely wiped out by ravenous hordes of the winged predators. One witness compared a shreekwing flock to a huge school of piranha with wings.

He ran through waist-high weeds and tangled brush, heedless of the thorns snagging his clothes and tearing his skin. He continued shouting Alex's name. He reached a small clearing in the vegetation, just as the slim woman appeared on the opposite side. Like Crockett and Quanah, the SIN officer wore clothes of tough khaki but she had unbuttoned her shirt and tied the tails beneath her breasts for some relief from the heat. Her *café au lait* skin glistened with perspiration. She carried a sample case slung over a shoulder by a nylon strap.

Relief welled up inside Crockett but he didn't allow it to be heard in his voice when he snarled, "You weren't supposed to wander so far, goddammit."

Alex ran a hand through her sleek black hair pinned up at the back of her head. Small twigs and leaves were snarled in the plaited strands that had come loose. "Sorry, Colonel. I'd hoped to find some sort of edible berry in this wasteland. It would add to our database about how colonists survived out here." She spoke with the burred enunciation of a Scotswoman.

"Let's hope our visitors don't have your sweet tooth," Crockett said.

Alexis crooked an eyebrow at him. "Pardon?"

"Shreekwings. A swarm is on its way."

"You're joking."

"Not today, Jones."

"I thought they were myths."

They heard the beat of wings, and Alex's face registered sudden fear. Her deep brown eyes widened. She murmured, "I suppose I thought wrong."

"We're not going to be able to make it back to *Ambler*," Crockett said tersely. "Don't move unless you have to--stand stock-still and hope the shreekwings will pass us by."

Alex opened to her mouth to reply, and then she wrinkled her nose. "You've been smoking again. I'm sure Dr. Parker can prescribe plenty of medicinal herbs that are just sedative as tobacco and not as obnoxious."

"Stop talking, Jones," Crockett growled.

The two people stood back to back. Crockett faced the way he had come, holding the Hawken Big 50 in a double-fisted grip, the eight-inch long barrel pointed upward. Within seconds he caught his first glimpse of the shreekwings.

Several black shapes held aloft by furiously fluttering wings darted above the overgrowth, dipping and banking and diving. Crockett tried to keep them framed within his field of vision, but it was nearly impossible. The speed and maneuverability of the creatures appeared little short of supernatural.

Crockett stopped trying to follow their blindingly fast movements and concentrated only on staying as motionless as he could, breathing very shallowly.

A shreekwing landed on the upraised barrel of the Hawken. He felt Alex's body tense at his back, her muscles tightening like bowstrings.

Barely six inches long, the shreekwing had a wingspread of over two feet. Its lean body coated in a pattern of overlapping black scales. A pair of leathery, talon-tipped wings continued to beat the air with a sound like a violently shaken cloth. Long claws curved out from the hind toes. The reptilian head appeared to be little more than a maw full of needle-tipped, razor-keen teeth.

A slime-coated tongue whipped out and retracted between its jaws. A small thorn of bone or gristle sprouted from the damp tip.

A whip-like tail lashed tightly around the gun barrel as it sought to secure its perch. Unblinking eyes, like chips of polished onyx, glared into Crockett's face and then moved on, uninterested. He received the distinct and uneasy impression that the creature hunted a very specific prey.

Crockett had seen a few of indigenous animals on Loki such as the quadrupedal rhinothonium, but he had never seen one that looked like predatory death stripped down to its bare essentials. He wondered if the shreekwings were some species of hunting bird that had regressed to their reptilian roots.

According to the report he had read, the shreekwings possessed no conventional organs of hearing, but relied on a supersensitive nervous systems to detect sound vibrations in the air and ground with their entire bodies, and with their acute vomeronasal sense and a favorable wind, they could sniff out carcasses up to ten kilometers away.

The creature continued to cling there, turning its head jerkily back and forth. Crockett saw its rear claws score small scratches in the finish of the Hawken. It took all of his willpower to hold the weapon steady. He had no idea if a shriek from the thing would draw the flock to the clearing, or if it would decide to take an experimental bite out of his hand.

The shreekwing repeatedly opened and shut its jaws with a clashing of teeth. The sunlight glinted on a tiny speck of metal affixed to the roof of its mouth. Crockett narrowed his eyes, trying to ascertain its shape. Then the creature launched itself from the barrel of the pistol, the point of its tail brushing the tip of Crockett's nose, a puff of air fanning his cheeks.

The shreekwing flew in a rapid circle around the clearing, and then flapped from sight.

Crockett exhaled in weary relief, lowering his arms. He heard the shrieking and leathery slap of wings from the road, and an occasional muffled thud as if the little demons were trying to batter their way into *Ambler*.

Since the APC carried three-inch-thick armor plate, he doubted the shreekwings could inflict much damage but he didn't care to give them the time to find the vehicle's vulnerable areas—if there were any to be found.

Alex blew out a sigh. "I'm glad that's over, although I found the creatures to be fascinating...I wish we had a sample to study."

"Careful what you wish for, Jones," Crockett retorted.

Then, over the shrieks and flutterings, came the staccato hammering of Quanah's pulse rifle. Alex's hand went to the small TX-5 rail pistol holstered at her hip. "They may need our help."

Crockett nodded curtly. "Let's move, but try not to draw attention to ourselves."

The two people ran as quickly as they dared through the underbrush, eyes scanning the area all around and above. When they reached the perimeter of the brushline, they sank to their knees.

The surface of *Ambler* crawled with scaled black bodies, snapping teeth and beating wings. Although the engine had been silenced, the little predators had still zeroed in on the vehicle as the source of the vibrations. Another group swirled, swooped and circled above it.

Quanah opened one of the shuttered gun ports just enough to accommodate the barrel of his pulse rifle. He fired it in short bursts, not really aiming. Some of the creatures fell with thrashing thumps to the road, where they were set upon by other members of the swarm. Their long tongues flicked out, barbed tips plunging into the entrance and exit wounds.

A shreekwing soared toward Alex, gliding on the air currents. She didn't cry out, but she recoiled. Crockett brought the Hawken's heavy barrel down on the top of the creature's skull, knocking it out of the air. Metal met bone with a loud crack.

It had time to voice a thin scream before hitting the ground.

Drawn by the sound of pain, a clot of shreekwings detached themselves from the main mass orbiting the APC and fluttered in the direction of Crockett and Alex. Crockett deftly thumbed the ammo selector switch on the backstrap of the Hawken and squeezed the trigger.

An explosion of 18-gauge buckshot ripped a hole through the swarm.

Small bodies rained to the ground, blood and viscera spraying in all directions. The survivors swerved away and rejoined the rest of the circling flock.

Alex toed the body of the creature Crockett had struck with his pistol. Distractedly, she said, "The bone structure resembles Archaeopteryx...the earliest known ancestor of the Terran bird."

Bending down, she gingerly picked up the corpse by the tail and dropped it in the sample case. Just for an instant, Crockett caught the gleam of metal inside its broken skull.

"The Archaeopteryx was believed to have feathers," Alex continued. "These things are more lizard than bird."

"Reptile or bird," Crockett replied dryly, "they've got us outnumbered."

The corners of Alex's mouth quirked in a smile. "I have doctorates in exobiology and xenosociology. Quanah is a physician and Mr. Syne possesses an organic computer for a brain which processes information at least a hundred times faster than our own. I'm confident that one of us can figure out a way to outmaneuver these little bastards."

"You didn't mention my qualifications, I notice," Crockett commented, still studying the flock circling above *Ambler*.

Alex nodded to the pistol in his hand. "You're holding yours."

Crockett declined to respond. He quickly considered and discarded several plans. Even if he and Jones braved their way through the gauntlet of deadly demons and got back inside the APC more or less intact, the single-minded predators might very well cling to it forever, or until they died of starvation and dropped off. The best option seemed to be waiting them out, hoping the shreekwings would tire of trying to chew armor plating and seek out more palatable prey.

Then another possibility arose. In the near distance, a blur of motion caught Crockett's attention. He stiffened, staring in silent incredulity at the naked woman.

CHAPTER TWO

Crockett raised his binoculars, peering through the eyepieces. Under his breath, he murmured, "Now *that's* something I didn't expect to see today."

"What?" Alex asked, sounding peeved and puzzled.

He didn't answer, tightening the focus. Alex followed his gaze and caught her breath in surprise. The view through the binoculars confirmed Crockett's first glimpse. The woman—a young one—ran very swiftly, with the smooth, ground-eating stride of an Olympic champion. Her gamine-slim legs pumped effortlessly, carrying her over the rock-strewn ground without a misstep. She ran from the direction of the hills. Droplets of perspiration sparkled on her bare limbs, glistening between her breasts.

Her complexion was a uniform matte-tan with no hint of reddening from exposure to the sun. To make the scene even more surreal, silver and turquoise jewelry glittered at her wrists, fingers and ankles. Her short-cropped, feathered hair glowed a cerulean blue in the sunlight.

Although it required some effort, Crockett slid the lenses from the girl's body and scanned the area from which she ran. Far in the distance, he saw a black, dragonfly-shaped speck outlined against the cloudless sky, but he couldn't make out details.

"Where the bloody hell did she come from?" demanded Alex, shading her eyes with her hands.

Crockett shook his head. "Wherever it was, she's not dressed for this place."

"She's definitely dressed for the shreekwing's dinner," Alex said grimly. "They haven't seen her yet, so perhaps—"

She broke off when reflected sunlight blazed from the woman's jewelry in prismatic fragments and shimmered briefly over the surface of the APC.

"Oh—*bugger*," muttered Alex.

With a piercing collective shriek, all of the shreekwings flung themselves from the hull of *Ambler* and into the air. Like a cloud of black smoke, the flock rushed away, drawn toward the running woman.

Crockett got to his feet and ran to the APC, Alex at his heels. As they climbed inside, he glanced down the long flat ribbon of roadway. The woman continued to sprint in their direction. Over her head dark shapes fluttered, like bundles of dirty cloth unfolding and folding in the air.

Quanah said sourly, "Lucky break for us."

"Bloody unlucky for somebody else," Alex commented, leaning forward to stare through the front port. "We drew those monsters out. Now that poor girl is paying for it."

Even as she spoke, a shreekwing made a darting pass at the woman, striking her on the shoulder. The woman stumbled and staggered, paying no attention to the laceration on her right shoulder that painted her upper arm scarlet. The shreekwings circled her, their keening cries even audible through the body-work of the APC.

Crockett eyed the grade of the road and said to Syne, "Put us in neutral. Let's see how far we can roll without turning on the engine."

Immediately Syne engaged the gears and the vehicle slowly moved forward. Peering out the viewport, Crockett kept his eyes on the woman. Her gait slowed as she swatted and batted at the winged demons. She bled from dozens of fang and claw inflicted wounds. A stone turned beneath her foot and she lost her balance, staggering for several yards before she fell. "Syne," Crockett directed, "when we get abreast of her, just tap the brakes. Don't stop."

"What're you planning?" Alex asked, a line of worry appearing on her brow.

"I'm going to get her inside. Give me gloves and a blanket."

Quanah opened an overhead storage bin and removed the items. Crockett took a pair of goggles from a hook under the main control console and fitted them over his eyes. After slipping on the heavy work gloves and draping a blanket over his head and shoulders, he crouched by the passenger door, holding the handle.

"I'll need both hands free," he said to Alex. "Keep me covered."

Alex moved directly behind him, her pump pistol held at the ready.

"Almost there," Syne said.

"Keep the door open a crack and keep *Ambler* moving. I don't plan to be out there more than thirty seconds."

"Touching the brakes," announced Syne.

In two smooth motions, Crockett slid open the door and leaped out of the vehicle. Since it wasn't traveling more than five miles per hour, he hit the turf running. He silently endured the spasm of pain flaring up and down his left leg. Quanah pulled the door to, but didn't shut it.

The woman lay on the ground, adding her shrieks to those voiced by the darting, slashing, biting creatures, but her screams were not of pain but rage. Two shreekwings sank teeth and claws into her back. Another clung to her right calf, fangs tearing at the flesh, gnawing at the bone, its tail coiled around her ankle. She kicked frantically at it with her left leg while she rolled over the ground, seeking the crush the monsters on her back.

Because of the blanket hooding his head, Crockett's peripheral vision was obstructed and he had no idea if any of the shreekwings turned their

18

attention to him.

Even as the thought registered, he heard the sharp double snap of Alex's pistol.

A limp object landed on his right shoulder, then fell to the ground at his feet.

Not bothering to look down, Crockett kept his eyes on the blood-streaked woman thrashing over the rocky soil. He reached her in two long-legged bounds and snatched one of the little demons from the woman's head.

It came away clutching little hanks of blue hair, yowling in protest and pain. It sank needle teeth into the thick leather of Crockett's glove, and though the points didn't penetrate, he felt the pinching pressure. He snapped its neck with his other hand.

At the same time, the woman stopped rolling and struck with a balled fist at the devil-beast tearing at her leg. The rings of thick silver on her fingers shattered bone and blood spewed from the creature's maw amid a few broken fangs. She looked up at Crockett and her cries of anger became a wordless call of astonishment. Although it was hard to tell with her features streaked with blood, she looked very young.

Crockett threw the blanket over her body and then pulled the woman to her feet. She was smaller than he had originally guessed, but very solidly built. For a second, she went limp in his arms, and then managed to straighten up. She didn't speak, but her eyes, the color of old pewter, sought out Crockett's. She nodded in wordless acknowledgment of his help.

The two people ran back toward *Ambler*, which had progressed only another fifty feet down the road. They loped across the shoulder of the road, ducking as several winged shapes swooped in front of their faces, tails lashing for their eyes. A tongue struck out at Crockett's face, leaving a wet smear on the right lens of his goggles, the barb scoring the polymer.

Quanah and Alex slid the door open just as Crockett and the woman reached it. They leapt into the APC, and Quanah slammed the door shut behind them, the edge clipping Crockett's boot heel.

The woman lay on her right side, gasping hoarsely, her eyes closed. Quanah kneeled on the deck beside her, pulling aside the blanket. He peeled back her left eyelid and said, "Out of it. Pain, shock and exhaustion."

Crockett pulled off the goggles and wiped at the sweat filming his face. "Heat stroke, too, maybe."

Quanah shook his head, reaching over to tug out the first-aid kit stowed beneath the front passenger seat. "Don't think so...she's not the slightest bit flushed."

"May I start the engine now?" Syne asked. "We have reached the bottom of the grade and can go no further on our own momentum."

Trying to regain his wind, Crockett dropped into the passenger seat. "Go ahead."

Alex unfolded a jump seat from the bulkhead and settled onto it. "What do you make of that jewelry she's wearing, Quanah?"

"I don't make anything of it, yet. I'm a doctor, not a fashion consultant."

Alex nodded, trying to repress a smile. "So noted. I forgot the extreme limitations of your fields of expertise."

Syne keyed the engine to rumbling life, threw the vehicle into gear and sent it rocketing up Perdition Highway. Everyone lurched backward. Quanah, who was trying to swab away blood from the woman's face, swore explosively.

"My apologies," Syne said."

"Just keep this thing steady."

Stripping off the work gloves, Crockett watched Quanah methodically clean his patient's wounds, swab away the blood and check her vital signs. For the hundredth time since the Loki mission officially began, he thanked the twist of fate that had planted the Comanche medic on his team.

Quanah Bartholomew Parker was not only a medical doctor, but he had been born on Loki thirty-five years ago, in a region settled by descendants of Native Americans who called it Comancheria.

His family killed by a mysterious epidemic that often swept the outlands of Loki, ten-year old Quanah was found wandering the plains by one of the fact-finding teams infrequently dispatched by the Commonwealth Colony Board.

Adopted by a distant relative on Terra and sent to medical school, Quanah specialized in microbiology and exomedicine. Crockett met the man during his time as a medical researcher on Io, studying and treating the effects of low gravity on human health. When he accepted the Loki mission, Quanah was the only person he felt had the necessary qualifications to serve as both his resident medical officer and his second-in-command, although Alexis Elgin-Jones carried more rank as a SIN officer.

But Alex was young and Loki her first offworld duty assignment. Although they had been travelling together in the cramped confines of *Ambler* for the last three weeks, Crockett didn't know her much better than the day when they had first met in the OWO facility on Luna Base.

So far, Alex had proven herself to be professional, considerate and fairly personable. The fact she had scored exceptionally high during the firearm certification made him disposed to allow her more rein than he would a typical SIN officer. Most of that type he had met in the past were middle-aged, humorless bureaucrats who had no real talent beyond creating spread-sheets.

Alex's field of specialty lay in sociology, history and the study of the various cultures and groups that had settled Loki nearly three hundred years ago. She spoke a variety of languages and dialects. Crockett hadn't yet seen her display those skills but he had no reason to doubt her. He did not feel the same way about the Mnemosyne the OWO insisted was as standard a part of their ordnance as the APC.

Neither androids nor cyborgs, the Mnemosynes were products of GenTek, one of the most powerful but secretive corporations of the past four hundred years. Their "Building a Better Humanity" motto had been challenged by various human and artificial intelligence rights groups for decades, but other than paying a few fines for unlicensed experimentation, GenTek went right on creating everything from antibiotics to synthetic organs.

Named after the personification of memory in Greek myth, the Mnemosyne Models were synthetic humans, modified by a combination of organic and cybernetic technology. Designed to be walking, breathing and interactive computers, they possessed simplified digestive, circulatory and nervous systems. Their brains operated on nanocarbon modeling in order to mimic human synaptic function but the speed by which they processed and accessed information was vastly superior to that of the most brilliant Homo sapiens.

The Mnemosynes physically resembled humans in that they were bipedal with five fingers and five toes, but their appearance looked oddly unfinished. They reminded Crockett of statues as crafted by minimalist sculptors. They were less than six feet tall and excessively slender. Their high, domed craniums rose above faces that seemed all cheek and brow, with little in between but a snub nose and round, blue eyes.

As far as Crockett was concerned, the Mnemosyne assigned to his team wasn't much different than an animatronic machine shaped like a person to facilitate easy access. Although Mnemosynes were essentially genderless, Alex insisted on addressing it as "Mister" which made Crockett feel distinctly uneasy for a reason he couldn't identify.

"This is odd," declared Quanah, his tone puzzled.

Crockett swiveled the chair around. The woman still lay unconscious on the deck, covered by the blanket. Although her face had been wiped clean of the blood, Quanah held up her beringed left hand, gazing at it with narrowed eyes.

"What's odd?" Alex asked.

Quanah turned the woman's hand slightly toward her. Visible in blue ink right below the wrist were four letters: ZED-A.

"Zeda," said Alex. "Could that be her name?"

"That doesn't seem likely," Syne stated. "A scientific or military designation is more probable...Zee A. Zed Alpha."

"Perhaps," Alex admitted. "But the style of jewelry she's wearing fits what we have on file for Gypsies. We do know that a revival of the Romani culture settled here."

"Did Gypsies go in for piercings?"

Alex frowned. "Earrings and such, I suppose. Why?"

Quanah tapped the back of his neck. "She's got a little silver stud right back here."

"I wouldn't think that's the usual place for studs," Alex said after a thoughtful moment.

Quanah grunted and went back to cleaning the woman's wounds.

Crockett turned the seat around and peered through the dust-powdered forward ob port. He saw nothing in the sky but an expanse of blue. "Looks like we've lost our aerial escort."

Alex leaned forward, following his gaze. "That *is* strange. The shreekwings should be all over us since we restarted the engine."

"You're right." Crockett tapped keys on the scanner board and a panel slid up, revealing a small round radar screen. The computer-generated simulation of the terrain registered no hits anywhere ahead or around them, but pinged softly when it detected an object five point three kilometers to the northwest, at the extreme limit of the sensors.

Crockett read the specifics aloud. "Height, two hundred and two meters, traveling at an airspeed of about 185 klicks per hour. Ten meters long by five wide. Definitely an aircraft."

"Who would have an aircraft out here?" Alex demanded.

Crockett shrugged. "I spotted an object in the air earlier—my guess is it's an old VTOL airship, dating back to the settlement days—they were called Skeeters a couple of hundred years ago."

Alex pursed her lips. "I recall seeing a few of them listed among the cargo manifests of a couple of the corporate expeditions."

"Do you remember which corporations?"

Alex shook her head, and Syne said smoothly, "Two corporations were recorded as owning such machines: Terro-Venusian Metals, a mining concern and the Ahnenerbe Foundation, a research and development branch of Gen-Tek. Neither T-V Metals nor the Foundation are extant at the present time. Nor have they been for nearly a century."

Quanah said sarcastically, "That's all very not fascinating, but we've got other things to worry about. Like this woman."

"Do you need help moving her into a bunk?" Crockett asked.

"It's not that. Her wounds are superficial...they look worse than they are. Her secondary epidermal layer is very dense. The bleeding has stopped. It's almost like some kind of autonomic sealing off of blood vessels occurred. I don't think she even needs bandages."

"All of your patients should be so considerate," said Crockett dryly.

Quanah shot him an irritated glare. "You're not getting this...her skin has an additional layer of tough tissue that protects her both from heat-stroke and minor wounds. The soles of her feet don't have any abrasions on them, even after she ran over rocks."

Frowning, Alex leaned forward, staring at the woman. "It couldn't be an adaptive trait, could it? Developed by the colonists due to the conditions here?"

Quanah shook his head. "That would be an extreme evolutionary spike in less than two hundred years. Not very probable."

A groan from the woman commanded his attention. He said quietly, "My patient is coming around. Maybe she can answer some questions."

CHAPTER THREE

The woman propped herself up on one elbow, made a tentative move to touch her head, though better of it, blinked around, licked her full lips and said in a faint, but melodiously accented voice, "Sastimos."

"Sastimos yourself," Quanah replied with a smile. "Before you ask, you're not hurt too badly. A few contusions and abrasions, a few more lacerations, but they're all superficial."

"She spoke Romani," said Alex. "She said 'good health' to you, which is a greeting to strangers."

Crockett asked, "Can you speak her Gypsy lingo?"

"No need," said the woman, slowly hiking herself up into a sitting position. Her jewelry jingled. She seemed totally at ease with her nudity. "I speak your tongue."

Quanah handed her a bottle of water and she drank from it greedily, gulping mouthful after mouthful until he laid a hand on her arm. "Not so fast... you'll make yourself sick."

She lowered the bottle and peered at Quanah suspiciously, her gaze flicking over his brightly beaded necklace and silver pendant.. "You talk like Drabarnia...a healer."

"I am."

"But you look like hair-lifter." She mimed holding a blade at her hairline, making a back-and-forth sawing motion.

Quanah scowled. "I guess I'm that, too. But not lately. What's your name?"

The woman scanned the faces of Crockett, Alex and Quanah and fixed her gaze on Crockett. "Those shreekwings nearly chewed me to pieces. You got 'em off me?"

"Yeah," Crockett answered. "It was the only fair thing to do since we stirred them up."

"Accidentally," Alex interjected. "The vibrations of the engine disturbed them."

She made quick introductions all around, but the woman didn't seem inclined to identify herself, nor did she appear too surprised by the presence of Syne.

"Where are you from?" the woman asked.

"Far and away, hither and yon," Alex replied with a smile.

"Never heard of them places," the woman muttered.

"We're still waiting to hear your name," Quanah reminded her.

Impassively, she said, "As am I."

"What?"

"I don't know my name," the woman said impatiently. "Is that all right with you, hair-lifter?"

Quanah raised an eyebrow. "Not really...selective amnesia is usually the result of a head trauma but I didn't find any sign of it when I examined you."

"Where are you from?" Crockett asked.

"Don't know that either."

Crockett's eyes narrowed. "How'd you end up naked being chased by shree-kwings?"

The woman ran her fingers through her hair, looked down at herself and said, "I'd like to know that myself, big man."

Although the light was dimming, Crockett gave the woman a closer inspection. No longer daubed by blood, she looked very healthy. The bold-nosed, full-lipped face she lifted to Crockett held a defiant, wary expression and her slightly tip-tilted gray eyes surveyed him with a frank appraisal. Her body was strong-limbed and firm-breasted. Her fingernails, although short, weren't dirty or ragged. Nor were the soles of her bare feet overly callused. He gauged her age at either late teens or early twenties. He couldn't help but note that her hair was the same blue tint everywhere on her anatomy.

"Well," ventured Alex, "if you don't know your name, would you object to us giving you one for the time being?"

She eyed Alex distrustfully. "Like what?"

Alex pointed toward the woman's wrist. "Like Zeda. Who knows, perhaps that *is* your name."

She glanced down at the letters imprinted on her flesh and her face twisted in momentary surprise and even fear. "I—I don't think—I didn't put that there..."

She trailed off and bowed her head in resignation. "That is as good a name as any."

Quanah patted her shoulder. "It's just until we find out your real one. C'mon, let's get you up and find you some clothes."

Her mouth creased in a wry smile. "I'm getting used to not wearing any."

Quanah held out a hand to her. "But we're not."

After a second's hesitation, she took his hand and allowed him to pull her to her feet. He directed her toward a clothes locker down the narrow, grille-floored passageway.

"Nothing fancy in there," he said, "but it'll do until we find something better suited for you."

She strode toward the locker, her body movements fluid and graceful.

Crockett couldn't help but admire the firm rondure of the rear end she turned toward him. He affected not to notice the sour glance Alex directed at him and he swiveled his chair back around.

"Find us a place to camp for the night," he said to Syne. "Preferably one that's well off the trail. This is Indian territory, remember."

Syne nodded, engaging the gears. "The Lakota to be precise, but we're very far from worthwhile hunting grounds. Only desperation would send them out here."

Ambler went up into the foothills. Beyond them towered the black-cut higher peaks. The vehicle rolled steadily along a rocky rampart as the sun began to sink. Within a few minutes, they came across a few scattered trees. The first hints of twilight deepened around the vehicle, a sea of russet and indigo flowing from the western sky. The ridgeline debouched down into a rugged path that swerved around rock formations and dipped into shallow gullies.

Syne suddenly leaned forward, hands on the wheel and said, "Ah."

Turning the wheel to the right, the Mnemosyne steered *Ambler* through a few scraggly bushes. An old, almost completely overgrown gravel path stretched through the underbrush. The APC followed it slowly.

As the vehicle rolled farther down the path, the brush became greener and thicker, the trees more frequent. Branches whipped at *Ambler's* sides, dragging along the armored hull. Crockett looked out the ob port, his eyes straining to see through the greenery ahead.

Gazing between the tress, he saw the surface of a river winking in the fading sunlight. The rushing water foamed white around boulders. From bank to bank, the river spanned fifty meters. Syne braked and sat with his hands on the wheel. He glanced at Crockett. "I believe this place meets your specifications, Colonel."

He nodded in approval. "It does. Well done. Everybody stay put until I do a recon."

Crockett climbed out, hand on the butt of his weapon. Under the trees, the air was considerably cooler. He walked close to the river's edge. Judging by its lack of odor, the water wasn't contaminated. He determined to test the water's quality and if it passed, to refill the APC's supply tank before setting out the next day.

Carefully, he strode onto a flat rock ledge projecting into the river, extending outward toward the opposite bank. He guessed it was the remnant of an old dam, made of concrete and stone slabs.

He waved toward the APC. "Looks all right. Let's set up camp."

Everyone disembarked. Zeda wore a shapeless olive-drab coverall and oversized, unlaced combat boots. She didn't look particularly happy about the ensemble. Still, she scrounged for firewood and found enough dried twigs and sticks to provide tinder. Crockett set up the portable security sensors, surrounding the campsite with an invisible barrier. Alex built a small fire and balanced an aluminum cooking pot over the flames.

Quanah mixed tidbits from their six month supply of MRE packages with water to make a nutritious but not particularly flavorful stew. Syne brought out bedrolls and folding campstools. He arranged them in mathematically precise, equidistant positions from one another. Watching him, Crockett tamped down annoyance.

As the stew warmed and the sun set completely, Zeda stalked around the camp-site, whispering words in Romani, staring at the opposite bank of the river.

"I know this place," she declared positively. "I have been here before."

"When?" asked Alex.

Zeda opened her mouth to reply, then her face screwed up in frustration and she shook her head. "I do not remember. I remember wagons here, fording the river. The horses did not like."

"Gypsy wagons?"

Zeda shook her head again. "Maybe yes. Maybe no."

She gave Alex a sideways stare. "You talk funny. You are not from here."

Alex smiled. "None of us are...and your accent sounds as funny to us as ours do to yours."

"No—only *you* talk funny. The Colonel and the healer...I have heard men who talk like them before."

Alex arched an eyebrow. "But you don't remember."

Zeda sighed. "I don't remember."

Quanah clanged a ladle against the pot. "Soup's—or whatever the hell it's supposed to be—is on."

Syne accepted a small mug of the stew and sipped at it delicately, although Crockett suspected he did so just to be polite. His metabolism was such that he needed very little bulk matter to sustain him. Zeda, however, filled a bowl to the brim and spooned the stew into her mouth with a single-minded intensity. With a short-bladed knife taken from a cutlery box, she hacked off chunks of bread and used them to sponge up the liquid.

"That girl hasn't eaten since her last meal," Crockett sidemouthed to Quanah.

Alex pushed her stool against the trunk of a tree and leaned her back against it. She picked at her food, more interested in watching Zeda eat. Night fell swiftly. Loki had a small moon that cast only a feeble light, so the night outside the perimeter of the campfire became extremely dark extremely quickly. Starlight filtered only dimly down through the trees. A few insects trilled and chirped in the underbrush.

When Zeda finished the stew, she swept the bottom and sides of the bowl clean with a piece of bread, and then popped it into her mouth. Silently, Alex handed Zeda her own bowl, and she took it without a word of thanks, as if she and Alex had made a prior arrangement about the disposal of extra food.

Afterward, she dragged a sleeve of the coverall across her mouth, belched and said, "Kushti."

"That means 'good' in Romani," observed Alex wryly.

Quanah feigned relief. "Phew. And here I was all jittery she wouldn't like my signature dish of *cuire à swill*."

Zeda regarded Alex suspiciously. "How you know my language?"

Alex shrugged. "Part of my training."

"Training for what?"

Alex gestured to the woods around them. "Training to explore this world. That's why we're here....to learn what we can and report."

Zeda's eyes flicked from Alex to Quanah to Crockett to Syne, her eyes uncomprehending. "Report to who?"

"Not who," Crockett said, placing his bowl and spoon at his feet. "Whom. Actually, we report to a what. The Office of Offworld Operations."

"Offworld?" Zeda echoed incredulously. "You're offworlders?"

"Not me," Quanah said. "I was born here." He saluted the air in a southerly direction. "About 100 klicks thataway."

Zeda nodded. "Comancheria. But the rest of you—not born here? Where are you from? Oldworld?"

Alex said, "Oldworld is the common vernacular for Earth. Yes, that's where we came from."

"Why? Why not stay there?"

Alex, Syne and Quanah glanced expectantly at Crockett. After a couple of seconds, so did Zeda. After clearing his throat, Crockett stated, "It's our mission, our job to find out what has been happening on Loki since the Catastrophe."

Seeing her confused expression, Crockett asked "You don't know about the time when your world shook and split?"

Zeda's eyes widened in understanding. "We call that the Megasnuff. All the weak and weak-minded died. Only the smart and strong survived. Happen a long time ago. Only remember stories."

"How can you remember stories and not your name?" Crockett demanded.

"That's why it's called selective amnesia, Colonel," put in Quanah dryly. "The key word is 'selective.' "

Crockett removed his half-smoked cigarillo from his pocket and lit it with a piece of firewood. He exhaled a plume of smoke skyward. "I'll try to explain. What you call Oldworld, we call Earth or Terra. It's the planet where all the people of Loki can trace their ancestry. About three hundred years ago, your great-great-great grandparents and a lot of other folks' great-great-great grandparents came here from Terra to build a new world."

"Why?" Zeda asked bluntly. She tossed the short-bladed knife idly from hand to hand.

"Not to put too fine a spin on it, the original colonists weren't exactly the gentry. They were misfits, cultural throwbacks, political separatists, religious nuts and cultists. They didn't like Earth and the feeling was mutual, so they came here, to this planet in the Orion Spur. Of course, it didn't take long for the misfits to start fighting other misfits. The whole planet eventually was divided up by a lot of different societies, most of them ruled by petty tyrants."

"How many societies?" Zeda asked, sounding very intrigued.

"We don't know," answered Alex. "That's why we're here...to find out."

"There are reports," put in Syne, "of societies based on dead cultures of Terra such as the Xian Empire of ancient China, the Osirian civilization of pre-dynastic Egypt, and even revivals of Sparta. But we really do not know for certain."

"The Catastrophe wiped out the monitoring station," said Quanah. "It stopped transmitting reports nearly two hundred years ago. We're hoping to find it. If we can, we might be able to salvage the data."

"Catastrophe?" Zeda repeated, balancing the blade on the back of her hand. She tossed it up and caught it expertly by the hilt, then repeated the motion, this time catching the knife by the blade.

"What you call the Megasnuff," replied Alex. "Apparently it was caused by global tectonic plate slippages and volcanic eruptions, which in turn caused a shifting of the magnetic poles. Massive destruction. Whole populations were wiped out in a heartbeat. The few cities that had been built in the previous hundred years lay in total ruin. Science, technology, books, manufacturing facilities and what passed for civilization here were mostly destroyed.

"It took nearly another hundred years for the destructive aftershocks to settle into a period of relative calm. By then, Loki had transformed itself into a world not even your ancestors would recognize or want to set foot upon."

"Then why now?" challenged Zeda. "Why did you come back now after all this time? Why not keep ignoring us?"

"You weren't ignored," Crockett said, tossing the stub of the cigarillo toward the fire. "Loki is a rim world, at the far edges of the Spur. There are many other more populated planets in the Spur with far more desirable natural resources. All Loki had going for it was a lot of unpredictable people and some unpleasant indigenous lifeforms...like the shreekwings and something else called the Deadie Bug. You were just basically forgotten."

Zeda swiftly snatched the smoldering cigarillo from the edge of the campfire. She planted it in the corner of her mouth and grinned at Crockett. "We were lost, yes?"

"No, just not remembered...at least, not remembered clearly or fondly. There were a few Commonwealth ship stop-overs in the last fifty years or so, but not frequent enough to matter. But someone or something is suddenly interested in Loki and the OWO gave us the job of finding out why—and also to get an idea of what's been going on here for the last 188 years."

"How long you been here?" inquired Zeda, puffing on the cigarillo in her mouth while absently flipping the knife into the air and catching it by the blade. The firelight gleamed from the dull metal of the blade.

"A little over three weeks," answered Crockett. "We were dropped in an area to the north known on the old maps as the Low Steppes. We've been traveling ever since, looking for settlements that, according to the original reports were built along our route. In the old days, it was called Perdition Highway."

"Did you find any?"

Alex fanned the air in front of her face, but voiced no objection to the malodorous tobacco smoke. "Not yet. Only some ruins. I hardly feel I'm earning my pay."

"However, we *did* glimpse curious examples of flora," Syne put in, "Such as a pack of dire wolves and even a herd of woolly mammoths."

"What's so curious about that?" inquired Zeda.

"For one thing," Syne said, "they're extinct. For another, they're not native to Loki. No reports from the original colonists or the monitoring station ever mentioned their existence."

"Indians hunt the mammoths," Zeda said, spitting the cigarillo stub into the fire.

"We saw a Lakota encampment from a distance," said Quanah. "We figured it best not to introduce ourselves until we learned a little more about their dispositions."

"Do you know of any settlements in the Hellgrounds?" Alex asked.

Zeda started to shake her head, and then she closed her eyes. "The river..."

"What about the river?" Crockett asked irritably.

"It is called Rio Loki." Her accented voice held a faraway hush. "If you follow it to the source, it will take you to Loki's Rock. Go the other way."

Zeda fell silent, eyes still closed. Her lips stirred as if she were whispering.

Alex and Crockett exchanged baffled glances. Crockett lifted a shoulder in a shrug. Leaning forward, Alex said loudly, "Zeda!"

Whipping her head around, Zeda's eyes opened wide. Alex bit back a startled cry. The woman's eyes were no longer the hue of pewter but colored like moonstone, milkily translucent. In the instant Zeda gripped her with that fixed, blank stare, Alex felt a sudden, painful pressure in her mind as of a fist tightening around it.

Then Zeda snapped her right arm forward, hurling the knife directly at Alex's face.

CHAPTER FOUR

Alex had no time to react other than to lean frantically away from the knife flashing her way. It passed so close to the left side of her head, the hilt brushed the lobe of her ear before thudding solidly against the tree trunk.

Alex threw herself sideways, dragging the camp stool with her to the ground. At the same time, Crockett jumped to his feet, reaching for the pistol at his hip. His hand closed around it, then he froze, staring in silent astonishment at the knife and the creature pinned to the tree by its blade.

The insect impaled by the knife held the general contours of a scorpion-- a black shiny carapace, long foreclaws and a stinger-tipped tail that curled and quivered over its segmented back. But the resemblance ended there. Nearly eight inches long with a cluster of four eyes atop its streamlined body, the creature's clawed legs kicked convulsively.

Quanah came to his feet in a lunging rush, blurting, "Deadie Bug! Its poison is a hundred times more deadly than a scorpion!"

Alex swiftly crawled away from the tree and stood up, her breath coming fast and labored. She put a trembling hand to her throat "I didn't know it was there."

Zeda slowly arose. Her eyes had lost their pearly luster. Stepping over to the tree, she grasped the knife by its handle, whipped it loose from the bug and when the creature flopped to the ground, she stomped down hard on the body. With a snarl of satisfaction, she twisted on the heel of her combat boot, grinding the insect into the soil.

"Hate these fuckin' things", she spat. "Always have. They lay eggs in your ears."

Then she calmly handed the knife to Quanah and walked past him to her bedroll. Wincing, she rubbed the back of her neck. When she noticed Quanah gazing at her, she smiled wanly and said, "I'm tired."

Syne tilted his head back, peering upward at the boughs of the trees overhead. "It must have been up there in the limbs...that's why it didn't trigger the alarms."

Crockett frowned. "Great. Now we have to worry about poison insects dropping down on us while we sleep. Hope you don't breath through your mouth, Jones."

Alex affected not to have heard the comment. She leaned over the creature's fluid-leaking body, hands on her knees. "It looks related to a scorpion, so it's most probably an arachnid, not an insect."

"That makes me feel a whole better," retorted Crockett sourly. "Syne, is it possible to recalibrate the perimeter sensors to register hits from overhead?"

Syne nodded, walked over to the one of the sensor units resting on its tripod at the edge of the camp. "Very possible. I'll take care of it."

"Thanks," said Crockett automatically, without thinking about it.

"You're welcome, Colonel," Syne responded crisply.

Hands on his hips, Crockett swept his gaze over the area, wondering if it made more sense to order everybody to sleep aboard *Ambler*. Zeda was already snuggled into her sleeping bag, snoring loudly.

"She's had a busy day," Quanah commented, absently tapping the knife blade against the palm of one hand. When he realized the steel was smeared with dark, sticky ichor, he dropped it to the ground and snatched a napkin from the food basket. He industriously dry-scrubbed his hand.

"Did you see Zeda's eyes?" Alex asked quietly, stepping up beside Crockett.

"I did."

"It's almost as if she entered an altered state, both mentally and physically. She somehow sensed the Deadie Bug behind me. She saved my life."

"Seems that way," agreed Crockett, apprehensively glancing up into the trees. "Let's hope she can sense more of those things—"

He broke off, staring at a small flash of light overhead, bright against the indigo sky. The light flashed green, red and white. Quanah and Alex followed his gaze.

"An aircraft," Quanah said tensely. "Definitely hovering."

"I don't hear any engine sound," pointed out Alex.

"It's quite some distance away," Crockett said. "Besides, if it's a Skeeter, then it's equipped with bafflers."

Quanah squinted upward. "Somebody is definitely curious about us."

"Or one of us," Alex commented, nodding meaningfully toward the slumbering Zeda.

Even as she spoke, the light inched across the sky and disappeared.

Syne announced, "I've finished recalibrating the sensors. Everyone should be able to sleep easy tonight, but I don't mind standing watch."

Quanah eyed him suspiciously. "Don't you need sleep?"

Syne nodded. "Yes. But I require far less than you to remain alert."

Crockett opened his mouth to ask him how much less, thought better of it and decided to address the subject another time.

Everyone retired to their bedrolls. Crockett, as tired as he was, found sleep elusive. His mind toyed with images of the day's events, including Zeda's cryptic words and even her blue hair. Like Alex, he felt she was one of the Romani. He knew from the fragmented reports filed since the Catastrophe that many of the nomadic cultures which settled Loki had actually thrived in the chaos.

That included the various Native American tribes who had asserted claims over huge regions of land, like Quanah's birthplace of Comancheria.

Crockett finally fell into a fitful sleep, dreaming of a great bat-winged evil hovering overhead, of something as mysterious as the land they traveled across. It was a dream of flight and pursuit and grinning, demonic faces.

The brief trilling of a songbird awakened him at daybreak. He blinked up at a sky gray with the oyster-shell hue of false dawn. He knew it wouldn't last long. 13 Orionis rose very fast. Zeda still snored loudly and Quanah lay with a fold of blanket draping his face. Syne sat on a campstool on the far side of the site, backbone straight, hands resting on his knees, but with his eyes closed.

Moving quietly, Crockett tightened his bootlaces, took his gunbelt and softfooted behind the APC to relieve himself. Zipping up, he peered around the vehicle to see if Alex was still asleep. She was gone, her sleeping bag open and spread out on the ground.

Crockett made a quick visual circuit of the perimeter of the camp, but saw no sign of her. He knew, as uneasy as his sleep had been, the slightest odd sound would have snapped him awake. He saw by the lightening sky a few footprints in the earth around her bedroll which led toward the riverbank.

Crockett walked quickly in that direction, gunbelt thrown over his shoulder. He pushed through the underbrush and came to a sudden halt. Alex's clothes and boots lay in a neat pile on rock overhang extending out into the river.

She knelt in the shallow water, wearing only her undergarments. Her dark hair hung in loose plaits and glistened with droplets. With a cloth, she washed her arms, face and body.

For a moment, Crockett found himself watching the sensuous play of muscles beneath the smooth skin of her back. He wondered if he should clear his throat, turn around or just leave. But Alex cast him a glance over a bare shoulder and smiled. "Good morning."

Crockett backstepped, murmuring, "Sorry, Jones—I didn't know the river was taken."

Alex stood up in the knee deep water and chuckled. "No need for the false modesty, Colonel. Last I looked, we're both adults—one of us more than the other—and we've both been married."

"But not to each other," Crockett replied, trying to match her amused tone. "At least you had enough sense to keep your underwear on."

"I prefer not to run or fight in the nude if I have the option."

Crockett strode out onto the ledge. He noted that with her wet brassiere stretched taut across her breasts and her equally wet panties outlining very fold and crease, she might as well have been naked. Alex's mane of hair tumbled artlessly over her shoulders. Her slim body was long-limbed, with no trace of softness underlying the curves. With a distant sensation of shock, he suddenly realized what a beautiful woman she was.

"Even so," he said, striving to sound stern, "you shouldn't be out here alone. There are reports of river monsters big enough to swallow xenosociologists whole."

Alex waded atop the overhang, wringing water out her hair. She reached for her clothes. "I read those reports. Folktales. Besides, I couldn't face the day with yesterday's accumulation of grit still all over me."

Shrugging into her shirt, she studied him carefully, with feigned disapproval. "You could do with a bit of scrubbing yourself."

She stepped close. With the tip of a forefinger, she touched the stubble on his jawline, producing a sound like sandpaper rubbed against a rasp. "Not to mention a shave."

Crockett maintained a non-committal tone and expression. "Can't argue with that. But I'll wait until I don't have to share my bath with a folktale."

Alex flashed him an uncertain grin as she pulled on her pants. "What do you mean?"

He nodded toward the river. "Only that."

She turned just as the surface heaved and a spray of water and slime spumed into the air. A huge, rubbery-lipped maw with a shovel-shaped head arose from the river and the underjaw opened with a liquid, slurping gasp. A fluked tail threshed the water into a white froth. The creature looked to be a minimum of ten feet long.

"What the hell—?!" Alex staggered backward and would have fallen if Crockett hadn't caught her.

"Don't worry," Crockett said calmly, steadying her. "It's only a folktale known as the Muckslogger. It's apparently a lungfish of some sort."

Like a sail unfurling, a serrated dorsal fin unfolded vertically from the creature's back. Crockett pulled her backward a meter or so. "The Muckslogger's fins eject a neurotoxin—according to folktales."

"Give it a rest, Colonel," Alex said gruffly, pulling away from him. "I stand corrected."

The Muckslogger silently sank back beneath the roiling, bubbling surface. Alex quickly buttoned up her shirt and stepped into her boots, staying well away from the water's edge. Kneeling, she laced them up with sharp, impatient movements.

"You're rather smug sometimes, Colonel," she said. "Not a particularly endearing quality."

"And you're rather reckless, Jones. Not a particularly safety-conscious quality."

Alex stood up and gazed unblinkingly into Crockett's face. "If I were safety-conscious, I wouldn't be here. None of us would."

Wheeling around, she marched back toward the camp. Crockett easily kept pace with her, trying to minimize his limp. He asked, "How did you know I'd been married?"

Alex arched a quizzical eyebrow. "I read your personnel file...how else? Didn't you read mine?"

"Just your qualifications. I skipped over the personal parts."

"Why?"

The bluntness of the question caught Crockett off-guard for a moment and he fumbled for a response. "They didn't seem relevant."

A hard, stitched-on smile tightened Alex's lips. "I have a feeling that's your entire philosophy of life. The personal parts aren't relevant." She increased the length of her stride, pulling out ahead of him. "You and Mr. Syne are far more alike than you think."

Crockett didn't try to catch up with her. By the time he returned to the camp, 13 Orionis had climbed well above the horizon and washed the area with a brassy brilliance. Everyone was awake and stirring. Zeda munched a protein bar and silently endured Quanah's quick examination of her pulse and the whites of her eyes. Syne deactivated the sensor web and began packing up the units.

As he did so, he said, "I took the liberty of analyzing the river water. It contains trace minerals in similar proportions to that of Arctic glacier meltwater. I have already refilled *Ambler's* reservoir."

Alex fetched her sample bag from beneath *Ambler* and uttered a short exclamation of disgust. She held it away from her with one hand, pinching her nostrils shut with the other. "Ew. That is *foul*. I forgot I put a shreekwing in there for examination."

Quanah fanned the air in front of his face, waving away the effluvium of decomposition. "I didn't need to eat breakfast anyway. Dump it out downwind of here—please."

Holding the case out at arm's length, Alex walked into the treeline. When she reached a point a hundred meters away, she opened the case and turned it upside down. Crockett kept a discreet eye on her, expecting her to return to the camp very quickly. Instead, she stared down at the ground, where she had dumped the winged corpse.

In a strained but eerily calm voice, she called, "Colonel Crockett, Dr. Parker—I think you might be interested in seeing this. Please join me."

Quanah glanced at Crockett who shrugged. The two men did as Alex requested. The fresh breeze from the river blew away the worst of the stench, but the dead shreekwing still exuded a nauseating odor. It lay flat on the ground at Alex's feet, bat-wings folded beneath the body.

"Okay," said Quanah impatiently. "Now what?"

She pointed. "Take a look at the head, please."

Quanah and Crockett gazed down at the creature's skull, battered out of shape by the Hawken's heavy barrel. Red-stained metal threads gleamed just beneath the cranial bone.

Quanah uttered a muffled exclamation and dropped to one knee. With a forefinger he gingerly pushed the creature's head back and forth. "Looks like a SQUID network"

"A what?" demanded Crockett. "Is that a cybernetic implant of some kind?"

"Not exactly. SQUID stands for superconducting quantum interface devices. The thing's brain is so intertwined with the circuitry, I'd guess it was there since the embryonic stage. This shreekwing is the product of genetic engineering. Has to be."

Carefully, Quanah pried open the creature's jaws. Sunlight glinted on tiny metal dot inside of its maw. Inhaling sharply, Quanah said, "There's a mate to that doohickey attached to the back of Zeda's neck."

"You said it was a Gypsy piercing," Crockett challenged. "A stud."

Quanah pushed himself up. "I thought it was," he said gruffly. "I stand corrected. Sir."

Alex turned. "Let's see if Zeda will allow us a closer look—"

She broke off, hand reaching for the pistol holstered at her hip. There came the stealthy sound of feet treading on leaves and dry twigs. Crockett drew the Hawken instantly, assuming a combat stance, holding it in a double-fisted grip.

A black-and-white pinto pony stepped lightly from the underbrush at the western perimeter of the campsite. Astride the horse's back was a slightly built but lithe-looking Lakota warrior. He wore a fringed buckskin hunting shirt and leggings. His black hair flowed freely down his back, and red hawk feathers were pinned to the back of his head. His face, though unpainted, was a mask of restrained ferocity.

The warrior could have stepped from the nineteenth century or an old Western vid, except for the automatic shotgun cradled in his arms. His sharp, dark eyes closely examined the faces of the people spread out in a semicircle around him, finally resting on Quanah.

Having picked up a smattering of the Lakota language, Quanah said, *"Hou le mita cola."*

The warrior's grim slash of a mouth twitched ever so slightly at the flawed pronunciation of "Hello, my friend."

"Good afternoon," he said in perfect, unaccented English. "I am Sky Wolf. The *wasicun* call me Sam."

Noticing that the pistol bores pointing at him hadn't wavered, he added, "I mean no harm. I assure you I'm alone."

Crockett slowly lowered his weapon, and Alex followed suit.

"I see you survived the shreekwing flock," Sam said, nodding toward the creature's body.

"You know about that?" Alex asked.

Sam snorted. "Of course. This is my country, even if it is a bit off the usual trails of my people."

"Where are your people?" Crockett inquired. "If they're nearby, you're all invited to our camp."

Shifting position on his saddle blanket, Sam replied, "This isn't a social call. What are you Oldworlders doing here?"

"How did you know we're Oldworlders?" Alex demanded.

"I didn't," Sam shot back. "Until just now. Why are you here?"

"Exploring," answered Crockett casually. "We're hoping to make contact with the people to let them know that the government of Terra—Oldworld—hasn't forgotten about them."

Sam scowled. "The people you might come into contact with in the Hellgrounds are definitely best forgotten about."

Alex said, "I don't follow you."

"You don't know about Loki's Rock?"

"You mean there *is* such a place?" Quanah asked.

"There is, and if you value your lives, your spirits, you'll give it a very wide berth." Sam gestured toward north, away from the river. "Go that way. Leave now."

Crockett's eyes narrowed. "That has the sound of a threat in it, Sam."

"I don't intend to threaten you—only to warn."

"You're being very cryptic," Alex said. "Inscrutable, even."

Sam smiled. "In which case I'm living up to my stereotype. Very well. I'll speak with a blunt tongue."

Saluting the area around them, he said, "This land once belonged to the Cheyenne, the Lakota, the Crow, and even the Comanche. All of us revived and revered the old ways. When Megasnuff came, we believed it was a time of deliverance for our people and divine retribution against the evil that had reigned here. This region was known as the Hellgrounds for more than one reason. We hoped the evil here was destroyed forever. Unfortunately, evil has a way of returning... or, in the case of the masters of Loki's Rock, never truly going away."

"You said you were going to speak with a blunt tongue," Crockett reminded him.

Sam's eyebrows knitted at the bridge of his nose. "I'm speaking with as blunt a tongue as you will understand. If you travel to Loki's Rock, then you'll learn the truth of my words. By then, it may be too late for all of you."

Reacting to the pressure of Sam's knees, the pony turned and walked back into the brush.For a long moment, no one spoke. Then Crockett turned to Alex, "Well, Jones...you said you wanted to interact with the natives. In the last eight hours, you've gotten acquainted with Zeda, Deadie bugs, Sam and shreekwings. You feel you're finally earning your pay?"

Alexis Elgin-Jones kicked dirt over the shreekwing's body and turned away. "As a point of fact," she declared, "I do."

CHAPTER FIVE

For five hours *Ambler* had rolled down a stretch of Perdition Highway that barely qualified as a footpath. The roadbed was cracked, split, furrowed, wrinkled and overgrown with scraggly weeds. On either side rose wide featureless expanses of dark earth. Far ahead, the dome-shaped peaks of the Midnight Hills shouldered the sky. Rising above them was the snow-capped Mount Maleficent, its peak the highest point in the Hellgrounds.

The relatively smooth surface of the road had deteriorated with every mile they logged. After fording the river, *Ambler* rumbled along steadily for most of the morning, following the waterway. Then the road dipped down into canyons that gashed through the foothills. Crockett, at the wheel, swore as the APC pitched, yawed and nearly dumped him out of his seat.

More than once he had been forced to engage the ACP's front-wheel drive to get them over sections of canyon floor that had completely caved in. Everyone was jounced, bounced, tossed and thoroughly pummeled. Not for the first time it occurred to Crockett that all the old maps the OWO provided them were virtually of no use. The Catastrophe had completely resculpted most of the continent. New mountains had appeared almost overnight, long-dormant volcanoes had erupted and earthquakes had shaken hundreds of thousands of square miles with cataclysmic tremors and aftershocks that lasted for decades.

Crockett glanced over his shoulder at Zeda, strapped into a jumpseat. She didn't appear the slightest bit dismayed by the rough travel. He asked, "Does any of this look familiar to you?"

She started to nod, then her brow furrowed in thought. "I keep thinking it should. If we're not on the road to Loki's Rock, then we're on the way somewhere."

Seated beside her, Alex laughed. "Can't find fault with that logic."

Zeda didn't so much as smile. Before embarking that morning, Quanah had asked to examine the stud at the back of her neck and she vehemently refused. They argued about it, with both people becoming heated and vociferous until Crockett put a stop to it. Due to the intensity of her refusal, Crockett suspected there was something about the nature of the stud she didn't want either disturbed or exposed.

Quanah suddenly leaned forward, peering through the ob port. "A sign post up ahead, looks like."

Crockett relaxed his foot's pressure on the accelerator. "It's about damn time we found out where we're going."

A wooden post rose ten feet from the ground on *Ambler*'s left side. A dead man hung head down from a crossbar. A chain bound his crossed feet at the ankles. He had been suspended there for a very long time. The desert climate had dried every drop of moisture from his naked body, leaving it in the condition of shrunken, creased leather. The lips were peeled back over his discolored teeth.

Nailed to the post just below his head was a square placard that read: This Way to Loki's Rock—Go the Other way. A red arrow pointed straight ahead.

"Not very encouraging," murmured Syne.

"I agree," Quanah said. "If you look close, you can see that the man was eviscerated…his internal organs were removed and his body cavity sewn shut."

Crockett narrowed his eyes and saw the long cicatrix scar extending from the corpse's pelvis to just below the sternum. "Why would that be done?"

"Perhaps he was stuffed with preservatives and other chemicals to hasten mummification," Syne ventured. "If the body was intended to hang here for a long time, then such a practice would be pragmatic."

Crockett and Quanah exchanged a long look and Quanah remarked, "Pragmatic is not the word I would choose."

The vehicle began to move again. Just past the sign post stretched a path that at first glance was no more than a shallow trench raked through the dirt. Crockett turned the ACP onto it. It was a rugged, rocky hellway surrounded by bare, castellated hills. The suspension of *Ambler* creaked and groaned so loudly that Crockett wondered if the vehicle could take the roughing.

The narrow road swerved around rock formations and dipped down into gullies. The area looked like Hell with the fires out. An ancient seabed of clay strata worn by aeons of frost and flood had been shaped into forms resembling colossal pagodas and pyramids. Throat and eye-burning vapors arose from burning coal seams in the ground, cloaking their surroundings with a noxious fog.

"The name of this place—Loki's Rock—might have some significance," Syne said.

"How so?" asked Alex.

"In the Norse myths, after the gods held Loki responsible for the death of Baldur, he was bound to a rock with a venomous snake over his face. From its fangs, poison dripped. Loki's wife Sigyn held a basin beneath the venom, yet when the basin became full, she carried the poison away and drops fell on Loki's face. He writhed with such violent pain that all of the Earth shook, resulting in what became known as earthquakes."

The path swung down into a dry arroyo with a lazy serpentine motion. Pebbles rattled noisily beneath *Ambler's* wheels and chassis. The winding course twisted through a jumble of outcroppings and house-sized boulders. It looked as if this particular part of the Hellgrounds had been the playground of gargantuan children and they had left the place as it was after particularly protracted tantrums.

Crockett stated grimly, "Looks like Loki is *still* writhing."

"Severe tremors here," Alex said. "The area is probably geologically unstable."

Crockett suddenly slowed the vehicle to a crawl, hitting the brakes and downshifting.

Early afternoon sunlight slanted through the dust. Children played in the warmth, mothers lay upon old mattresses on the ridge, mongrel dogs yapped and bounded all about. The children, unnerved by the lion roar of the ACP's engine, ran squalling up the sides of the bank. Their mothers beckoned to them and stared at the vehicle with a combination of fear, hostility and wonder.

"I think this is the place," Quanah said.

Crockett drove the vehicle another two hundred feet into the arroyo and braked. The mothers and children stood above them on the edge of the ridge and stared down.

"Not very outgoing," commented Crockett.

Alex unbuckled her seat belt. "Want me to get out and talk to them?"

"No, I'll make the contact," Crockett replied. "Keep the engine running and your fingers on the triggers."

Zeda blurted, "I don't have a gun."

"That's right," retorted Crockett. "We'll keep it that way until you remember if you know how to use one."

Opening the driver's side hatch, Crockett stepped out, hands held well away from the butt of his pistol. One of the women stood closer than the others. Barely out of her teens with an unruly mop of red hair, she wore only a ragged shift with the hemline at her upper thighs. A little naked boy tried to crawl up one of her slim legs.

"Afternoon," said Crockett, pasting a friendly smile on his face.

The woman only nodded.

"Is this the way to Loki's Rock?"

She nodded again.

"How far?"

She parted her pale lips. Her voice was creaky, as if she were unaccustomed to using it.

"Half a mile. Less."

"Thanks. Who's in charge there?"

The woman's small eyes suddenly narrowed. "You never heard of Django?"

Before Crockett could answer, a whip-*crack* split the air, and a fountain of dirt erupted from the arroyo floor a foot in front of him. Even as the dust spurted, Crockett lunged backward against the APC, the Hawken springing from its holster into his hand.

To jump back inside *Ambler* would require a couple of seconds, an eternity in which he would be exposed to bullets. Crouching behind one of the armored flanges protecting the front wheel wells, Crockett peered up at the lip of the ridge. He saw the woman and children scuttling away.

The gun ports clanked open in the APC, and he heard the passenger side door handle turning. "No," he commanded. "Everyone stay inside."

A second shot winged past, buzzing like a furious bee. Crockett looked over the wheel well, tracking for a target. A third steel-jacketed bullet spanged off *Ambler's* heavy metal hide, leaving a shiny smear on the bodywork to commemorate its impact.

"Hey, you're ruining the paint job!" Crockett shouted. "I'm not impressed!"

He heard rustling from the brush at the crest of the arroyo's bank, and a hoarse male voice inquired, "You armed?"

"Of course."

"What are you doing here?"

"We don't mean any harm. We're from Terra."

"What's that?"

"The Oldworld."

There was a long period of silence, and then Crockett heard faint whispers. The voice shouted, "Okay, stand up-- your blaster by the barrel."

The six-inch barrel of Quanah's pulse rifle protruded from the gun port over his head, and Crockett heard him say, "Got in 'em in my sights. Three men with rifles."

"Keep watching them."

"Plan to."

Crockett stood up slowly, holding his pistol by the barrel. As if waiting for a cue, three men broke out of the shrubbery at the lip of the ridge. Their beards and long hair were matted with dust and twigs, and they wore the ragged remnants of shorts. Battered leather sandals and moccasins covered their feet, and though their rifles looked as if they had seen better days, they used them carefully to cover him and *Ambler*.

A burly man with a mass of dark hair confined by a rawhide thong leapt down the bank, cradling an old bolt-action rifle in his arms. Though he grinned, his eyes held the alert, wary look of a half-wild animal.

He dropped lightly onto the arroyo's floor and approached Crockett, the wide grin never faltering. He looked over *Ambler* and said, "Nice wheels. Where do you find the gas for it?"

Crockett shrugged. "She runs on different fuels, depending on the circumstances and environment. Mind if I put my hands down now?"

The man responded to the question with one of his own. "Who are you?"

"Crockett." He turned slightly so the man could see the insignia patch on his sleeve. "Colonel Quentin Crockett of the office of Offworld Operations."

The man nodded. "Commonwealth law dog. Django said somebody like you would show up one day soon. Yeah, you can put your hands down."

Crockett did so, but he didn't leather the pistol. "What's your name?"

"Phil. The other two gentlemen are known as Barbie and Ken."

"Who's who?"

Phil indicated the tallest of the pair. "This is Ken."

If Ken had ever introduced a drop of water to his face, he might have been fairly handsome. As it was, his skin was almost black with encrusted dirt. Straight raven hair was gathered in a knot at the base of his neck. A cloud of gnats hovered around him.

"This here's Barbie."

Barbie was short and fair-complexioned, and he was one of the ugliest mortals Crockett had ever seen. The left side of his face was covered by a red, puckered weal, a badly healed scar that lifted his lip on that side in a permanent grin, revealing brown, cavity-speckled teeth. His hair was shaggy and dirty, and at one time might have been blond. The irises of his eyes were a yellow-brown.

"Barbie ain't got no tongue," Phil went on. "Had it shot out of his head by a Comanche. Can't talk, but Jesus God, is he mean."

Barbie looked at Crockett with his yellow eyes and grunted. Saliva dripped from his lip on the left side of his mouth. He knew that sooner or later, he would kill Barbie or Barbie would kill him.

"Yeah, a real nice set of wheels," Phil said, walking around *Ambler* and kicking the front tire. "What would you trade for it?"

"Not in the market."

Phil grinned wider. "We could just appropriate it, if you don't want to bargain."

"I suppose you could try. I should point out that at least four guns are pointed at you from the inside." Crockett lifted the Hawken, but didn't aim it. He gestured negligently. "Not to mention the one out here. I doubt you small-timers could take all of us."

Barbie made a slobbering sound. Crockett smiled coldly, knowing that the three men would either start a firefight they couldn't win or knuckle under.

Phil continued to grin, but there was a trace of uncertainty in his eyes. "Don't get fragged, man. You say you're from Oldworld?"

"That's right."

"Come on into Loki's Rock, then. Strangers are always welcome."

He turned and began trudging down the arroyo. Barbie and Ken lingered behind. When Crockett made a move to open the driver-side hatch, Barbie jammed the bore of the rifle into his spine.

Over his shoulder, Phil said, "You walk with us. Your pals are less apt to get nervy with their blasters if you're on the road with us."

The rifle barrel prodded Crockett's kidney, and whirling quickly, he back-fisted the length of steel away. "Step off, doll face."

Barbie growled and lunged forward, swinging the rifle, trying to shatter Crockett's profile with the wood-grain stock. Crockett dropped to the ground, knocking the man's legs out from under him with a swift leg sweep. Barbie went down heavily on his back with a crunch of gravel.

Springing erect, Crockett put the bore of the Hawken on Ken and booted Barbie expertly beneath the chin with his right foot. The man's head snapped back and met the arroyo floor with a thud. Crockett kicked the rifle from his slack fingers, and it clattered across the rocks, tumbling end over end.

Phil stared at him, wide-eyed. His grin had been replaced by an O of surprise. He looked at Barbie, dazed and twitching in the dust, and said faintly, "I hope you didn't kill him."

"I don't think so. I'm riding into Loki's Rock in my vehicle, with my people, you three will lead us. You try to run, you try to take us into an ambush, I'll put six bullets up and down all of your backbones. Acceptable?"

Phil nodded. He and Ken helped the groggy Barbie to his feet.

Crockett climbed into *Ambler* and said. "I guess we've been formally welcomed."

As they rolled down the arroyo, six men, all of them uniformly big, wearing leather belts studded with cartridges and pistols, stepped out into the open. The mirrored lenses of their sunglasses masked their eyes. Small red tattoos resembling the stylized letter A stood out starkly on their right cheeks. The men stared suspiciously at *Ambler,* but Phil gestured and they moved aside. Crockett looked past them and saw deadfalls of high-stacked boulders on either side of the arroyo. He guessed that it wouldn't take much to start an avalanche and either bury or disable an interloping vehicle.

"Any of this ring a bell, Zeda?" he asked.

The blue-haired girl's answer was curt and brooked no debate. "No. Stop asking."

After less than a mile, the arroyo opened into a wide flat plain with cultivated fields. The crops were wheat, corn and beans. Beyond the fields lay the town of Loki's Rock. In the near distance glimmered the ribbon of the river.

The overall design of the settlement was a confusing mishmash of architecture—big tents, geodesic domes, Quonset huts and even metal cargo containers that resembled ancient box-cars from the railroad era. The main part of the town looked like a standing set from an old Hollywood western movie, partly due to the number of horses and mules hitched to posts.

Ambler wheeled up the main thoroughfare, following Phil, Barbie and Ken. Loki's Rock looked to be great open market, where nearly anything could be bought or sold.

Shops and stalls were brightly painted. Vendors with wheelbarrows cried out the merits of their wares, merchants were shouting "today only" special deals and wandering musicians played a discordant variety of tunes, few of them recognizable.

Men and women on old hover cycles roared up and down, back and forth along the streets, throwing clouds of dust into the air. Crockett noted that all the cycles looked exceptionally well cared for with fresh paint, highly polished chrome and the sounds of healthy engines. He recognized the models as "bullet bikes" and guessed they were a minimum of two hundred years old.

A large number of people wandered everywhere, a conglomeration of all sexes and ages, dressed and undressed in every imaginable fashion. Girls wearing colorful flowered skirts and bright head-scarves stared at them from open doorways. Silver jewelry winked from their fingers and throats.

Syne said, "Gypsies have a presence here, apparently."

Alex asked, "Zeda, do you—"

"—No," the girl interrupted. "I do not recognize anyone here."

Crockett easily differentiated between the citizenry and Loki's Rock security. They wore mirrored sunglasses and were festooned with weaponry, ammunition bandoliers crisscrossed over their chests with foot-long Bowie knives and big, showy handguns at their hips. Small triangle tattoos in red ink showed on their faces.

Most people on the street shuffled, stumbled or lay about, busily doing whatever occurred to them at the moment. One girl, completely naked except for looping whorls of blue paint, danced alone atop the rusting, wheelless husk of an old vehicle, moving in time to the soundless music of invisible instruments. The hot metal of the roof had to have been burning her bare feet, but she didn't seem to notice.

"Laid back place," Quanah muttered sourly.

"Lilies of the field," Alex said. "They toil not, nor do they spin."

The dusty avenue went past hovel and tent and crude shack, until it opened up in a large central square. Phil stopped in the middle of the street and pointed to a three-story wood frame structure, the only building in the square. A sign painted in red and yellow ran the length of the façade. It read The Bitter End.

Phil said matter-of-factly, "Django needs to look you over before any other business gets done."

Climbing out of the APC, Crockett asked, "Who is he again?"

Phil blinked, confused by the question. "Django Bonner. Django is Django. You answer to him. *Everybody* answers to him. He decides if you earn your keep or have to roll the bones."

They disembarked. From a hook on the interior bulkhead, Quanah took his broad-brimmed black hat and settled it carefully on his head. Responding to Alex's quizzical glance, he said, "If we're going to meet the local dignitaries, we might as well look as formal as possible."

For the benefit of watchful eyes, Crockett made a very exaggerated slow of sealing the gun ports and locking the doors with an electronic remote. Phil waited patiently, then gestured toward the bat-winged doors. Crockett led his team inside.

If it hadn't been for the electric light fixtures and the bank of video monitor screens in the far corner, the saloon might have been mistaken for a watering hole on Earth six hundred years earlier.

The bar top, the tables and the floor were exceptionally clean, and brass footrails and spittoons gleamed with a high polish. From the distance came the faint throb of an electric generator. A long wooden-sided craps table occupied the center of the floor.

Syne, standing beside Crockett, said softly, "That is curious. "

"What is?" Quanah asked.

He pointed. "That."

Following his pointing finger, the four people gazed at the huge, metal-framed banner mounted on the wall behind the bar. It depicted in vivid hues of gold and red a round-topped triangle, bisected by a stylized lightning bolt with squared-off ends.

On either side of the symbol stood half a dozen figures of nude women and men. The artist had rendered them in bright varying hues of gold. They were all blonde, blue-eyed, smiling and exceptionally fit. Their sexual characteristics were exaggerated to a heroic scale, with bounteous breasts and pumped up penises. Blood-red words were imprinted beneath the symbol in confusing Gothic script: *Treu, Tapfer, Gehorsam, Reinheit.*

"It's German," stated Alex.

"What's it mean?" Crockett asked.

"Loyalty, Valiance, Obedience, Purity," a soft, hollow voice replied. "Words to live by…if you want to live in Loki's Rock."

CHAPTER SIX

The vision of the banner had taken everyone aback for a moment, so they hadn't immediately noticed the man sitting against the north wall. He presented a vision almost as startling.

The man's body was lanky, and very thin. Beneath a mane of backswept straw-yellow hair rose a remarkably high forehead. A drooping leonine mustache framed his mouth and chin. His eyes were in shadow, but a force swam in them that raised the fine hairs on Crockett's nape. It was a spark of self-centered dedication to a single goal, a single-minded drive to attain an inexplicable objective.

The man's hands were very long, and he had them steepled before his pursed mouth. He was dressed completely in black—black frock coat, black shirt, black string tie, black trousers and black boots. There wasn't a single speck of color anywhere on him, except for the scarlet satin sash around his waist. He sat in a large chair fashioned from heavy, dark wood with brass inlays. The hexagonal shape of the chair's back resembled the top half of a coffin.

Affixed to the top of the chair was a bleached, polished skull. It was that of an animal, but one Crockett had never seen. Feline in shape, it was twice the size of a human cranium and two great fangs, six inches in length curved down from the upper jaw. The sight of it raised the hairs on the back of Crockett's neck.

Phil stepped up to the black-suited man and ducked his head. He spoke to him rapidly in a low whisper for quite awhile, then gestured to Crockett to come forward.

Crockett approached the chair and the man suddenly waved a hand.

"Close enough, kindly," he said. "You are covered with road dust and exude a frightful odor."

Crockett didn't bother to swallow his irritation. "If I'd known you were so discriminating, I'd have bathed in disinfectant before coming in."

The thin man eyed him broodily. "You've an impertinent tongue. Did I ask you a question? No matter. Phil tells me your name is Crockett."

"That is true."

"And that you're from Earth...the Oldworld."

"Yeah."

"He tells me you're here on official Oldworld business."

"True again."

"What business is that?"

"Exploration, mainly. Loki has been cut off from the Commonwealth for a very long time."

"So why start inquiring about us now?"

"I get asked that a lot."

"What do you tell them?"

Crockett lifted a shoulder in a negligent shrug. "Better late than never."

The man smiled in an odd, cold way. "I don't think I believe you. I think you came here to make mischief."

Crockett returned the cold smile. "Oh?"

"There could be no other reason."

Crockett heard a shuffling from behind him, then a barely audible click. He spun, hand darting to his pistol. In a jagged fragment of a second he saw that the entire wall backing the bar had swiveled open, disgorging five security men from behind the banner. All of them brandished large-caliber hand cannons. They were of different makes and models, but they all looked brand-new.

The cold tip of a gun touched the back of Crockett's neck. He heard the sound of a round being jacked into a chamber and he froze, hand on the butt of the Hawken.

The thin man held up one narrow hand. "That bloodies the floor, as much as you'd enjoy it. There are other ways."

The black-clad man stared at him with shadow-pooled eyes. Crockett's mind sensed a whispering touch, like a wispy cobweb brushing him with ectoplasmic tentacles. His heart began to pound. The man was a psionic, a line-of-sight telepath. He had heard of humans with those gifts, but he also knew people who possessed true telepathic abilities were extremely rare.

The man's eyes suddenly seemed to swell, to grow gigantic, blotting out everything else. His eyes sparked blue like gems and they were gem-like in their hardness, as unwinking as those of a bird—or a serpent.

His eyes receded and the vague touch disappeared. Crockett heard Zeda draw in her breath sharply. The man in the black suit suddenly stiffened. Crockett guessed that the mind probe had been directed at Zeda and met unexpected resistance.

"Your Gypsy is a telepath?" the man demanded. He paused, then added in a meditative tone, "No, a Mind Sifter. But with formidable abilities."

"You're not so special after all," Zeda said sarcastically. "And I'm not his Gypsy."

"Then whose are you?"

When Zeda only glared, Alex stepped forward. "We found her yesterday, on the other side of the river. She was being attacked by shreekwings."

The man's lips pursed as if he tasted something sour. "There are no wild shreekwing flocks around here. There is very little prey for them."

Alex made a dismissive gesture. "Nevertheless."

Fixing his stare on Zeda, the man in black ordered, "Turn around, Mind Sifter. Let me see the back of your neck."

Crockett maintained his neutral expression, although his mind wheeled with surprise and conjecture.

"Why should I?" Zeda demanded.

"Because you have no choice. If you don't do as I say, I'll force you to cooperate. It will take longer and you may be hurt but the outcome will be the same as if you had simply turned around and shown me the back of your neck."

Balling her fists, Zeda glowered to her right and to her left, and then with a muffled curse, she spun around. Reaching up to the back of her head, she parted the feathery blue hair at the base of her neck. Silver glinted briefly and she whirled to face the man. "Satisfied?"

The black-clad man leaned back in his chair and chuckled. "For the time being. What Gypsy clan do you belong to, Mind Sifter?"

Crockett said, "You ask a lot of questions without providing any answers yourself."

A smile drifted onto the man's angular face. "Very true. My name is Django Bonner." His tone and attitude became much more relaxed. "Sorry about the coldness of the reception, but we can't be too careful with all the anarchist crazies and night-creeping Indians running loose in the Hellgrounds these days."

"Is that so?" Crockett inquired. He heard the person behind him breathing. The pressure of the gun bore was still against the back of his neck, and he considered disarming the bastard, but Bonner raised a languid hand.

"Hold on that, Pagan. I've scanned him. He is who he claims to be, so he's not an enemy. At least, not yet."

The pressure of the gun barrel was removed, and hearing the rhythmic clacking of boot heels on wood, Crockett turned slightly.

The tallest woman he had ever seen walked slowly around him, giving him the briefest of appraising glances. A black Beretta 85-T dangled from her right hand. She looked to be only an inch shy of Crockett's height. Her face might have been beautiful if not for the grave, joyless expression imprinted there and the gold-embroidered black patch covering her right eye.

She carried herself with an air of dangerous assurance, of knowing precisely what her abilities were and how superior they were to others. However, that quality, coupled with her manner of dress—skin-hugging dark red leather pants, knee-high jump boots and a tight black leather vest–didn't detract from the femininity exuding from the smoothly chiseled features.

Her cobalt blue eye glittered with surmise as it flicked up and down his body. The open collar of the vest revealed a lack of a bra. Her round, heavy breasts pressed against the material. Luxuriant wine-red hair fell to her shoulders. She fingered the hilt of a fourteen inch Bowie knife scabbarded crosswise across her belly.

The woman squirmed into a comfortable position on Bonner's lap, and he absently fondled her upper thigh. "This is Pagan, my warlord."

Crockett smiled slightly. "Shouldn't that be war *lady?*"

Pagan impaled Crockett with a blue glare. "I'm not a lady."

"Who would've guessed?" Alex whispered, but not loud enough for either Bonner or Pagan to hear.

Addressing the armed security men, Bonner ordered "Guns down. It's safe enough for the moment."

Crockett made introductions all around and removed his hand from the butt of the Hawken. He said, "I had the impression from your man Phil that you expected us."

"Not you personally," declared Bonner, "but offworlders in a big wagon. Eyes have been on you for the last few weeks, since you crossed the steppes. Word of your presence eventually reached me."

Crockett grunted. "Loki's Rock is the first settlement we've found since arriving here."

"Predominantly white settlement, you mean," Bonner replied, eyeing Quanah and Alex superciliously. His gaze flicked over to Syne. "And human."

Alex frowned. "Mr. Syne is human enough. Just different."

Bonner snorted derisively. "He's a synthetic. A mandroid. A product of genetic engineering. That's a little bit *too* different for me to consider him human."

Crockett tried to keep the jolt of surprise from registering on his face. "You know about genetic engineering?"

"Why wouldn't we know about it? We're not all uneducated barbarians out here in the Hellgrounds."

"It's interesting how you seemed be educated about the little piece of jewelry on Zeda, too." Crockett tapped the back of his neck.

"You might say I recognize the manufacturer."

"Do you mind sharing with us what it is?"

"Your manner is a little on the abrupt side, sir."

"Agreed," said Crockett. "But the question still stands."

"You're a very cocky cat," Pagan said. She had a pleasant, melodic voice, despite the overtone of menace in it. "But guess what can kill you?"

"Another cliche?"

Pagan leapt from Bonner's lap, cheeks reddening, hand raising the Beretta. Crockett drew the Hawken in one smooth motion. He had the bore on a direct line with her eye patch just as she centered the Beretta on his forehead.

Django Bonner snapped, in a surprisingly pettish voice, "Freeze on that, Pagan... Colonel!"

The woman froze, but she didn't lower her pistol. She reminded Crockett of a ravening beast of prey, preparing to spring. With a self-indulgent chuckle, Bonner reached up and drew the woman back to him by the wrist.

He patted her buttocks, and she slowly tucked the autopistol into a holster at her right hip. She leaned against the chair but she didn't take her eye off Crockett.

"You must forgive my warlord," Bonner said with a smile. "Pagan prefers a more active, physical type of debate rather than verbal one-upsmanship. She can be rather difficult when she's feeling testy."

Crockett started to say something, thought better of it and leathered his pistol. Quanah cleared his throat and asked, "Lord or lady, why do you find it necessary to have a war counselor at all?"

Bonner didn't seem pleased to be questioned by Quanah, so his answer was brusque: "Counselors of all kinds are necessary when you build an empire."

Alex's eyebrows lifted in a skeptical arch. "An empire?"

"You need to learn a lot more about us before you make judgments."

"That's why we're here," Quanah declared.

Bonner nodded. "Of course. All of you are invited to remain here as my guests. It might be that we can be of some use to one another."

In a scandalized tone, Pagan demanded, "You're not going to make them roll the bones?"

Bonner glared the woman into silence. Fluttering a hand through the air, he added, "Please avail yourselves of our hospitality. There are spare rooms on the floor above, and you're welcome to them *gratis.* I will make arrangements for our merchants to extend you credit so you may resupply your remarkable vehicle if need be."

The skin between Crockett's shoulder blades crawled. He still sensed the half-dozen pistol bores behind him. None of the tension was evident in his voice when he said, "Thanks. We'll be pleased to visit for a while. It should make for an interesting report to the Offworld Operations office."

"Yes," Bonner drawled. "Shouldn't it."

As Crockett turned toward the door, Bonner said cheerfully, "I have a feeling I'll be glad to have met you, Colonel."

Crockett paused long enough to give him a half grin, showing only the edges of his teeth. "If that's the case, you'll be one of the few, Django. One of the very few."

CHAPTER SEVEN

Crockett and his team took their gear from *Ambler* and stowed it in the two upstairs rooms reserved for their use. Syne volunteered to sleep aboard the APC. The rooms were small, but furnished with brass railed beds and chairs. A bathroom was down the hall, done in gleaming porcelain with chrome-plated fixtures.

After getting settled, they met on the street outside The Bitter End. Zeda was nowhere to be seen. Alex said, "As long as she doesn't need money, she said she was going shopping."

They took a tour of the town, letting the settlement flow around them. The mingled odors, the colors, the people and the strange music made by old instruments were interesting but also disquieting. Crockett sensed a throbbing pulse of strong but joyful evil, but he dismissed the sensation as being due to nerves.

By engaging a few of the street merchants in conversation, they learned that the permanent residents of Loki's Rock lived in an insular world, a universe completely separated from the rest of the ravaged continent. Their world was Loki's Rock. Changes, rebuilding processes, old and new settlements were of absolutely no interest, and, in effect, didn't exist for them. This was their microcosmic kingdom, and anyone desiring to live among them had to think like them, believe like them and be like them.

More than once in response to a question about living conditions in Loki's Rock, a citizen intoned, "Loyalty, Valiance, Obedience, Purity."

After bumping into the by-rote response a number of times during the afternoon, Quanah was irritated enough to demand, "What's all this crap they spout about purity and loyalty?"

Syne regarded him curiously. "You mean you don't know? You didn't recognize the symbol or the slogan on the banner in the saloon?"

"Should we have?" inquired Alex.

"Perhaps not. Nevertheless it is one of the slogans and symbols associated with the Ahnenerbe Institute."

Crockett frowned. "You said it was a research and development branch of GenTek."

"That was the Ahnenerbe *Foundation*...I speak of the Institute, which dates back several hundred years to the nation-state known as Nazi Germany."

Quanah matched Crockett's frown. "Explain."

"*Deutsches Ahnenerbe* was set up by Henrich Himmler in 1935. This was a secret society concerned with the anthropological and cultural prehistory of the Aryan race. The main tenet of their belief system was that the Aesir, the old Norse gods and goddesses such as Odin, Thor, Freya and Loki had once been real people...leaders of an ancient Nordic tribe. The Ahnenerbe became a vast think-tank with expeditions to Tibet and actual occult studies and medical experiments to prove that the mythological Nordic populations had once ruled Earth."

Alex nodded thoughtfully. "If I remember my ancient history, Himmler was the *Brigadefuhrer* of the dreaded SS, the *Schutzstaffel* which only recruited soldiers of pure Aryan blood."

"Hence their motto of *Treu, Tapfer, Gehorsam, Reinheit*," said Syne. "The Ahnenerbe and the SS were obsessed with creating a master race of pure-blooded Germanic superhumans to help them first win the second world war and then rule the world, as their forebears, the Aesir had done. They were the first genetic engineers."

"What does that have to do with GenTek?" Crockett asked.

Before Syne could answer, a man wearing a sleeveless leather jacket sitting astride a bullet bike wheeled it in a dust-spurting circle around them. His toothless mouth stretched in a lascivious grin as he stared meaningfully at Alex. Her expression did not change, but her right hand eased down to caress the butt of the rail pistol holstered at her hip.

The biker saw the movement, and he blew her a kiss before turning the bike up the avenue and away from them. All of them saw the Ahnenerbe emblem sewn on the back of the jacket.

"I had just assumed," replied Syne, "that the old division of GenTek simply borrowed the Institute's name because of the goals of creating a master human race were similar. It didn't occur to me there was an overt connection between it and roots in Nazi Germany."

"Let's hope you know better now," Quanah declared bitterly.

"With all the other fringe groups and cultures that settled on Loki," said Crockett, "a Nazi connected bio-engineering concern really isn't that much of a stretch."

Alex said contemplatively, "Perhaps if the Ahnenerbe Institute still exists in some fashion somewhere on Loki, they might be helpful in locating the Enclave station."

Crockett gave her a warning glance. "I don't think it's a good idea to let anyone in Loki's Rock know we have a specific objective. It could be giving them—Django in particular—a card to play against us."

"If Bonner is indeed a telepath," Syne said, "he might know about our mission already."

"He certainly didn't guess about Zeda's implant," Quanah commented, touching the back of his neck. "He knows what it is."

Alex's lips twitched in a humorless smile. "Which is more than we do."

A sudden commotion erupted from a large vendor's stall. Female voices shouted in a hard-edged cacophony of fury. Two girls came thrashing out into the street, swearing and hissing. One of them was Zeda.

With her right hand, she gripped a much larger girl by her coarse black hair while fending off fingernails clawing for her eyes with the left. The other girl wore a tattered shift of dingy gray, the monotone alleviated somewhat by the bright red silken sash wound around her waist.

Zeda had traded in her coverall for a white peasant blouse that hung half off of her shoulders. A calf-length skirt, slit at the side above her thigh, matched the blue hue of her hair, half hidden beneath a yellow scarf. She still wore the *Ambler-* provided combat boots and she kicked the other girl hard in the stomach with first the right one, then the left.

As the black-haired girl doubled over and fell to her knees, Zeda released her hair and pivoted to face the mustached man who wielded a Khanjarli, a dagger with a six inch-long double-curved, double edged blade. He made for an imposing, almost theatrical figure in his dark shirt decorated with pink polka-dots and bright green vest. Sunlight glittered from the golden hoop swinging from his right ear lobe.

Zeda backstepped away from the point of the knife but the girl on the ground grasped her tightly by the ankles, holding her in place. Zeda wrenched furiously to free her feet.

One long-legged bound put Crockett between the Zeda and the Gypsy man. "Hold it!" he bellowed, using a well-practiced tone of intimidation.

The Gypsy froze, hesitation flickering in his eyes for a split-second, then he lunged forward, dagger held for a disemboweling thrust. The edge of Crockett's stiffened left hand slashed down on the clump of ganglia on the inner forearm of the man's knife hand. He cried out in surprised pain.

Crockett locked the man's right wrist under his own left arm and heaved up on it. The knife fell from the Gypsy's nerveless fingers. Zeda leaned down and snatched up the knife, slashing it at the girl who clutched her ankles. The point scored a shallow scratch on the back of her right hand. Uttering a cry of pain, she released Zeda and rolled frantically away.

More Gypsies appeared around the vendor's stall, eyes seething with anger. They wore a complicated arrangement of garments—vests covered with old coins, baggy britches and an eclectic mixture of headgear, ranging from turbans to slouch hats decorated with feathers and fur. Crockett put his hand on the butt of his Hawken but didn't unleather it. He knew Alex had her hand on her own sidearm.

The mustached man demanded, "Who do you think you are, interfering in our business?" His voice sounded like sandpaper scouring the inside of metal wash-tub.

"What's your name?" Crockett asked.

The answer was as immediate as it was sullen. "Dondi."

"What's going on here, Dondi?"

"How could it possibly matter to you, Oldworlder?"

"It probably shouldn't, but since you were stupid enough to attract my attention, you also drew my interest."

Dondi rubbed his forearm and his wrist. "The girl you protect is a stafie."

Crockett squinted at him. "A what?"

The girl who Zeda had fought raked her hair out of her eyes, hawked up from deep in her throat and spit in the dust. Before flouncing away, she hissed, "Slinos!"

Alex murmured, "Apparently they think Zeda here is a dirty ghost."

"No," said Dondi in a guttural whisper. "Unclean spirit."

"What started this?" Quanah asked.

Angrily, Zeda said, "I dared to speak to them. I did not realize I was a stafie or slinos."

"You are not meant to speak to the Romani," snarled an old Gypsy man, pointing an accusatory finger. "You were driven from your own clan and your name, the memory of your birth expunged, wiped away!"

"Do you know who she is?" demanded Quanah.

Dondi's eyes flicked from Quanah to Zeda to Crockett. "Yes. She is no one."

Over his shoulder he uttered a few low words to the other Gypsies and they silently withdrew, drifting away among the crowd of passerby.

Alex said to Zeda, "Perhaps we should pursue this further...they're obviously lying about not knowing who you are."

Zeda shook her head, lips compressed in a tight line. "They will not speak of one who is as dead."

Crockett said to her, "I don't understand any of this, but I doubt you do, either."

"Why don't we find a place to get something to eat?" Quanah suggested. "Preferably a place where we can sit down at a table and not eat out of metal bowls."

Syne remarked, "I do see a café just down the street with a placard in front advertising fine dining."

Quanah linked arms with Zeda. "Since you're finally all dressed up, we at least now have a place to go."

Zeda gave him a fleeting, appreciative smile. She pocketed the knife.

The five people sauntered down the street, but they did not get far before shouts and the whine of turbines commanded their attention. A cloud of dust rose above the thoroughfare. They stepped to one side to allow a pair of hover cycles to glide past, their turbo fans and repellor jets keeping them three feet above the ground.

Lengths of rope stretched from the rear of the cycles. The ends were knotted securely around the ankles of a man so coated with grit and mud he was barely recognizable as human. Semi-dried blood shone in gummy splotches all over his body. His spade beard was full of dirt.

The onlookers hooted and pumped their fists in the air, chanting, "Crawfish catchers, crawfish catchers!" as the procession went by. The bikers grinned and waved at the people, as if they were heroes returning victorious from a dangerous quest.

"What's that all about?" Crockett wanted to know.

"They be trackers," muttered a woman standing slightly behind him. She was scrawny and rawboned with stringy gray hair. "Crawfish catchers, they calls 'em around here."

"Crawfish catchers?" he echoed.

She nodded distractedly. Her threadbare dress bore many crudely stitched patches. "They go after them what rolled the bones and then didn't live up to their end of the gamble. They crawfished on the bet and didn't pay Loki's Rock what they owed it."

Crockett inclined his head toward the man lying behind the hover cycles. "What did this man owe?"

The woman shrugged. "Who knows? Depended on the bones he rolled. Coulda just been a kidney."

Quanah stepped closer, eyebrows drawn down to the bridge of his nose. "What did you say?"

The woman suddenly seemed to think she had said too much and hastily side-stepped away. Quanah turned to Crockett. "Did she say a *kidney?*"

Pagan suddenly shouldered her way through the crowd, followed by Ken. She spoke in a low voice to one of the bikers and then strode over to the prone man. Between labored breaths he managed to husk out, "Almost made it, you psychotic bitch—"

Pagan smirked, prodding his ribs the toe of a boot. "Almost getting away means the same thing as almost getting pregnant, Willy Bill. Absolute shit."

She drew back her foot and kicked him twice in the side. The man cried out in pain and jerked in reaction to the double impact, but otherwise didn't move.

Pagan glared down into his raw, abraded face. "You rolled the bones same as everybody else, asshole. You had the same chance of winning as you did losing."

She kicked him again, bent down and snarled, "You could've jeopardized the trade agreement, you piece of shit. *Treau! Tapfer! Gehorsam! Reinheit!*"

She punctuated each German word by kicking Willy Bill in the ribs. She spat into his face and whirled away. To Ken she snapped, "I've tenderized him...clean him up for the cotillion."

When Pagan caught sight of Crockett, she stared at him with her single eye of cold azure. Tension knotted in the pit of Crockett's stomach like a length of slimy rope as she stalked past.

The two trackers put their bikes into gear and flew down the street, dragging the man behind them, his body cutting a red-stained trench in the dirt.

"I don't feel much like eating right now," Crockett said.

Alex swallowed hard. "Me either."

CHAPTER EIGHT

The five people returned to the principal market square and listened to the performance of a band of minstrels. They weren't very good, and the lyrics of the song nonsensical, but they drew nods of approval and applause nevertheless. The chorus repeated the same refrain: *Loki's Rock is where it's at, where it's at.*

At the end of the performance, one of the musicians humbly attributed the authorship of the song to Django Bonner.

"Multi-talented fellow, this Django," Alex commented dryly.

Crockett felt a tap on his shoulder. Turning, he looked into Phil's smiling face.

"Enjoying yourself?" he asked.

"To a point." Behind him, Crockett glimpsed Barbie in the crowd, glaring over Phil's shoulder. Evidently Barbie hadn't forgotten about the kicking incident. Crockett knew the man schemed a payback.

"Good," Phil said. "Django wanted me to tell you about a town function tonight, at midnight. You need to be in your rooms by then."

"Why?"

"Townies only. Everybody else off the street by nine."

As if no more could be said on the subject, Phil turned and disappeared into the crowd, Barbie joining him. Crockett repeated the message to the others.

"I say we pack up and get ourselves gone," Quanah stated.

Crockett eyed the dimming sky. "Be full dark soon. Too dangerous to navigate the route at night. Might as well grab a bite, turn in and leave at first light."

They returned to the eatery Syne had pointed out earlier. It was a small establishment, but seemed fairly clean. The proprietor, an overweight woman with leathery warts adorning her face, handed them handwritten menus. Before they could look the menus over, she said, "Serving only one dish tonight, folks. It's all we got, so it's the best we got."

"In that case," Crockett said, "give us the best."

The meal was on their table quickly, but after looking at it, Alex mumbled that she wouldn't have minded waiting a little longer.

The steaks were rump, and tougher than the old bull they came from. The vegetables—string beans, tomatoes and baked potatoes—were at least easy on the palate and the digestion.

The woman brought over a steaming pot and cups. "Take your time, let yourself out when you're done," she announced. "I've got to get ready."

"For what?" Quanah inquired.

"We got us a Crawfish Cotillion tonight."

"What's that?" asked Alex, a line of puzzlement deepening on her forehead.

The woman heaved her downsloping shoulders. "Hard to describe. But seein' as how I'm on the town council, attendance is mandatory. It's where it's at, you know."

With that, she hustled into a back room and disappeared from sight. From the pot, Quanah poured himself a cup of dark liquid. "In my experience, a cotillion is dance...a social occasion. Not that I've ever been invited to one."

He raised the cup to his lips, took a cautious sip and a sudden surprise shone in his eyes. "This is real coffee."

Zeda glanced at him in curiosity. "So?"

"As far as we know," Syne explained, "coffee was the one Terran crop that never prospered on Loki."

Alex filled a cup, tasted it and declared, "It *is* the genuine article."

Frowning, Crockett said, "Guns, fuel, electricity and real coffee. Can't think of a more undeserving bunch to have all these blessings."

When they left the little cafe, night had fallen and the streets of Loki's Rock were nearly deserted, except for a few merchants closing down their stalls. Dust blew in the streets, a cool night wind eddying it along in eye-stinging clouds. Carried by the wind came the sound of activity, northward of Loki's Rock's perimeter.

Crockett peered into the darkness. Pagan's thinly veiled threat about curiosity killing cocky cats came to mind.

"Let's get to our rooms," he suggested. "Wouldn't hurt to lock the doors."

"If Bonner meant us harm," Quanah said, "he's going the long away around the barn. He certainly would have disarmed us."

Alex said, "It's a good idea to stay on alert, no matter what."

Syne unlocked *Ambler* and passed out Commtachs to Crockett, Quanah and Alex. The little communication devices were small enough to be almost unnoticeable and allowed each member of the team to stay in contact with one another as long as they stayed within a five mile radius. Syne bid everyone good night and sealed himself inside the vehicle.

The four people entered the empty saloon and mounted the stairs to their quarters. Crockett felt his skin prickling as the passed the banner, fancying all the painted eyes following and judging him. Once in the room he shared with Quanah, Crockett chair-locked the door. Although he unbuckled his gun belt, he kept his pistol close to hand. He didn't turn on the lights.

He sat in a chair by the open window and lit a cigarillo, blowing the smoke outside. There was utter silence on the street below. Quanah lay on the bed, head pillowed by his hands. Quietly, he said, "This place is a black pit."

"It's a shit hole, all right," Crockett agreed in the same low tone.

"No. There's a something terrible lurking here."

"Real coffee notwithstanding?"

Quanah didn't laugh. "Makes me wonder...is it possible they've learned something about the Imperators?"

Crockett shifted in his chair uncomfortably. "There aren't any records of Imperator artifacts being found on Loki."

"We know the GenTek and Taktron corporations established facilities here...if they found anything they sure as hell wouldn't share that information with the Commonwealth."

"But they'd share that information with Loki's Rock?"

"No, but that doesn't mean Bonner couldn't have come across it on his own. There's something very off-model about this place. It's not just a frontier settlement."

Crockett tapped a growth of ash out of the window. "We'll be on the road at daybreak. If we're lucky, we'll never see Loki's Rock again."

"Could be Sam was talking about the Ahnenerbe Institute when he mentioned an old evil that's been resurrected here."

Crockett cast him a weary glance. "Let's keep our perspective. This group managed to get their hands on a few working pre-Catastrophe artifacts and some tech. I'm sure they're not the only ones we'll come across on Loki. Don't let Indian exaggerations spook you."

Quanah hiked himself up into a sitting position. "Right now, I'm *all* Indian. And something is making icicles up and down my back. That's no exaggeration."

Crockett exhaled a stream of smoke out the window. "Heap bad medicine. Ugh."

"All right," Quanah snapped. "I'm just telling you—"

The brassy bleat of a trumpet came in through the open window, startling them both so much that Crockett reached for his pistol and Quanah jerked upright in bed.

They sat quietly, listening for the sound again. When it came, Quanah rolled to his feet and joined Crockett at the window. By poking his head and shoulders out and craning his neck, he saw spots of distant torchlight beyond the limits of the town.

The wind carried a distant chanting—the voices of men and women singing a faint tune. It sounded familiar, but neither man could place it.

"Something's happening out there," Quanah said.

They heard the horn again, and as Crockett stared at the flickering pinpoints of light, an urge to see what was going on grew within him. It wasn't simple curiosity, or a tactical decision to recon a possible danger that tugged at him. It was a compulsion.

A quick rap on the door made him jump and smack his head painfully on the window sash. Quanah didn't laugh. Crockett stood up, swinging his Hawken toward the door.

"It's me," Alex said in a tense whisper.

Removing the chair from beneath the knob, Crockett opened the door and allowed Alex to enter. In the hallway stood Zeda, her eyes shining in the gloom. Both women looked keyed up and anxious.

"You hear that horn?" Zeda asked.

"Yeah."

"What do you think it means?" Alex asked.

"Probably the function we were told about."

Alex wasn't satisfied with the response. "I think we should check it out."

"I think someone *wants* us to check it out," Zeda said. She massaged the back of her neck with her fingers.

"Why?" Quanah asked, eyeing her keenly.

Her gray eyes narrowed, Zeda said, "Does anyone else feel a need to go out there?"

"Yes," Alex replied.

"Me too," stated Quanah, sounding mystified.

"I feel something pulling at me," Crockett admitted hesitantly.

Alex worried her lower lip with her teeth. "I suspect we're on the receiving end of a psychic beacon. Very subtle, but very insistent. If I we weren't all experiencing the same thing, I'd just discount the phenomena as impulsive curiosity."

"Bonner," Zeda stated flatly. "Bastard."

Alex turned toward the hallway. "What are we waiting for?"

"Where are you going?" Crockett demanded.

"We've got a lot of questions about Loki's Rock," she replied. "Time to get some answers."

"By doing what Bonner *wants* us to do?" asked Zeda doubtfully.

"If we don't respond to this invitation," Quanah interposed, reaching for his hat, "we may never get another one...except to a funeral, not a cotillion."

Crockett sighed. "All right, let's move out. Everyone on red alert."

Zeda rolled her eyes and muttered, "I do not even know what that means."

They left the saloon by the back door, moving stealthily, weapons in hand.

As it turned out, their precautions were unnecessary. No guards were posted and no one hailed them or barred their way. The streets were as empty of life as the Hellgrounds.

Attaching the Commtach to his right mastoid bone, Crockett activated it and hailed Syne in *Ambler*. "We're going on a recon. Stand by."

"A recon this late?" Syne's uninflected voice still held a dubious note.

"I didn't know recons had to be scheduled," Crockett retorted. "Just stand by."

"Acknowledged."

The sky was a deep blue-black, stars gleaming frostily around the weak moon. The stars and moonlight provided enough light for them to creep through the brush and scraggly vegetation without stumbling into holes or tripping over rocks.

They moved toward the glowing spots of torchlight until they reached the foot of a gentle slope. Crockett took the point, clambering up the deeply furrowed face to the crest. The others watched him peer over it, then drop flat. After a few seconds, he gestured for them to join him.

Alex lay down beside him and Crockett whispered in her ear. "I guess this is where it's at."

"Christ Almighty," Quanah murmured.

CHAPTER NINE

A glance at his wrist chron showed Crockett the hour of midnight was close at hand. "Looks like we're right on time," he whispered.

In the center of a natural bowl formed by several low hills reared a huge black boulder rising about six meters from the ground. The stone was carved in the likeness of a man's face, but a face of dark, classic beauty. Although the jaw was firm, the nose regular, there was something sly, even evil about the cast of the eyes and the tilt of the mouth, the sculpted lips curved in a subtle, mocking smile. Crockett realized he looked at the granite mask of a god, carved by a master hand.

"Loki's Rock, indeed," breathed Alex.

Atop the boulder, lounging in the coffin-backed chair and still dressed in funeral back sat Django Bonner. A flat-crowned, round-brimmed black hat sat at a rakish angle on his head. The only other addition to his ensemble were a matching pair of mother-of-pearl handled pistols, worn butts forward in the red sash. Crockett recognized them as Hawken 30s.

His lean body sat in a casual posture, but his eyes were penetrating and as keen as a hawk's. Crockett had the urge to duck his head, even though he knew it was impossible for Bonner to spot him and his friends.

A murmuring crowd thronged the area around the boulder. They wore strange, barbaric costumes. Many wore the hides of beasts, others nothing at all except body paint in multicolored patterns. Most of them wielded flaming torches. All of them had a feral, predatory look in their eyes. Born into a raw, wild world, they were accustomed to living on the edge of death. Grim necessity had given them the skills to survive, even thrive in the post Catastrophic environment. A six-foot deep trench separated them from the field.

Off to the right side of the boulder sat a small group of musicians. They tuned up a variety of instruments: violins, banjos and even a trumpet.

Bonner lifted a languid hand, and the murmuring of the crowd died away. Every eye fixed upon him, staring with an intensity that came close to adoration.

"I greet you, my brothers and sisters and children." Bonner's voice was like deep, compelling music and carried a great distance. The pitch, timbre and vibrations of his words seemed to caress Crockett's inner ear. He suspected it was a voice that could sway crowds to madness.

Crockett looked at the rapt faces of the people gazing up at him, and decided that Django Bonner was one of the most dangerous men he had ever seen. To the men, women and probably even the children of Loki's Rock, the rail-thin patriarch was already far along the road to divinity.

"We have survived. That's our key word. *Survival*. Loki's Rock has survived for over a century, even when the rest of the planet tore itself apart. Why? Because we are the chosen ones. We carved our own path, our way, just as Loki's face was carved into this stone. We took the land from those who misused it and we have prospered."

Absolute, uncompromising uniformity of purpose lay like a duplicated mask on all the faces turned toward him.

"We have seen the dawn of our success," Bonner continued. "We have risen like the fabled phoenix from the ashes, and we occupy the place that was kept from us years ago by the duplicities of false gods and old ways."

The listeners stirred, venting their enthusiasm in an ovation of "Loki's Rock is the heart of the new world!"

"Even if the world had not choked to death and spit up its own guts and burned itself out, we would *still* have survived. We outlived our enemies. Loki's Rock is the heart of the new world and from here we'll cut out the hearts of the old!"

"Loki's Rock is heart of the new world!" The throng went wild. Hoarse shouts and cries of hysterical delight resounded. "Cut out the old hearts!"

"I remember what it was like," Bonner went on. "When we first settled here we went hungry and thirsty...we watched our children die, crying for water and even for the smallest morsel of food. All we asked was the right to live but the old ways would not allow it. The old heart had no room in it for those like us...and then we found this stone, bearing the face of Loki...it inspired us to cut out the world's old heart and put in a new one."

Reverently, Bonner touched his chest. "Ours."

The crowd whooped and waved their torches.

"I can't believe this," Alex said in horror. "I really can't believe it."

Crockett knew what she meant. Bonner's presentation seemed so staged, so contrived, so childish, it was difficult to understand how anyone could buy into it.

"Loki's Rock is the heart of the new world!" Bonner thundered again.

The night trembled with wild acclaim and wilder screams. Everyone stamped their feet and shook their torches madly. Bonner's eyes roved over the faces of his audience.

Slowly the shouts and hysterical shrieks subsided into murmurs of heartfelt sentiment.

"But we who represent the new heart must ever be mindful that our own hearts remain true," Bonner continued. "We must not repeat the sins of the old. We know what is expected of us –and one of the sins we will not repeat is—we do not crawfish on wagers!"

The crowd muttered peevishly, shuffling their feet.

"All life is a gamble!" bellowed Bonner. "Once we roll the bones, we abide by the cast and the stakes of the wager. There can be only one judgment, one penalty."

"Cotillion!" roared the crowd in one voice. "Crawfish cotillion!"

Bonner grinned, showing the edges of his teeth beneath his drooping mustache. "Let's start the dance!" He gestured to the musicians. "Maestro, if you will—"

Fiddle, banjo and horn began producing a racket that Crockett could not recognize as anything but noise, let alone a tune. Quanah and Alex exchanged grimaces. Finally, they realized the band strained to play "Camptown Ladies."

"What the hell?" Quanah murmured. "They're going to dance to *that?*"

Zeda said curtly, "Not exactly. Look."

A section of the crowd surged forward and a naked, bearded man stumbled out into the field. He stood uncertainly, blinking around dazedly. Crockett recognized him as the man Pagan had called Willy Bill.

The crowd bellowed, "The Camptown racetrack's five miles long! Oh, de doo-da day!"

Although the man was no longer covered in grime, his body showed numerous contusions and abrasions. Fresh blood streaked his back, trickling from superficial cuts across his shoulder blades.

Pagan followed him out, a long black whip coiled in her right hand. Behind her, Crockett made out the outline of a wire cage. The whip lashed out, striking Willy Bill's buttocks. Crying out he began running, slowly and clumsily at first then with building speed.

From the onlookers came singing, punctuated by laughter: "Gwan to run all night/Gwan to run all day/I bet my money on a bob-tailed nag/Somebody bet on the gray!"

Pagan stepped back and swung open the cage door. Black, leathery-winged shapes poured through. A raucous chorus of high-pitched shrieks rose above the singing.

"Shreekwings," Alex said grimly. "So much for Bonner's claim that there was no prey for them here."

Stimulated by the vibrations in the air by the music and the shouted refrain of "Doo-dah" and driven to shrieking madness by the scent of fresh blood, the shreekwings swarmed directly toward Willy Bill.

The man glanced back once. His arms and legs pumped furiously as he sprinted across the field. He knew there was no hope if he ran toward the sides of the field since the trench would only trap him, so he single-mindedly raced toward the far end.

The band picked up their tempo and the crowd sang along enthusiastically. "Oh, the long tailed filly and the big black horse, Doo-dah, doo-dah, Come to a mud hole and they all cut across, Oh, de doo-dah day!"

The shreekwing swarm transformed into a whirling torus, orbiting Willy Bill in an ever tightening circle. He stumbled as he swatted wildly at the creatures. A cluster of the shreekwings detached itself from the torus, swerved and engulfed Willy Bill's head.

He howled in agony, clawing at the wings covering his face like leathery masks. He continued to run blindly. Wet crimson glistened briefly between the wriggling bodies.

"Goin' to run all night," bellowed the crowd. "Goin' to run all day! I bet my money on a bob-tailed nag, Somebody bet on the gray!"

Willy Bill tripped on an irregularity in the ground fell full-length. Little puffs of dust mushroomed up around his body. Even over the roaring "Doo-dahs!" they heard a high, gargling cry rising to a shrill pitch. It ended abruptly as if a hand were clapped over Willy Bill's mouth or his tongue torn out by razored talons. His writhing body disappeared from view under a layer of flapping wings and black-scaled bodies.

Spontaneous applause and cheers erupted from the crowd of onlookers as they thrust their flaming torches into the air and chanted, "Django! Django!"

Crockett hoped Willy Bill lost consciousness quickly. Dropping his gaze to the boulder, he saw that Bonner was still seated, tapping his long fingers on the butts of his pistols. He smiled, and he seemed to be staring past the throng to the ridge top hiding Crockett and his people.

Cold fear stole over him. Taking Alex by the arm, he backed down the slope. "Let's get the hell out of here."

As Quanah, Zeda and Alex followed him through the brush, Crockett tried to shake off the fingers of fear clutching at his mind and heart. The torment and death of Willy Bill was the concoction of a deranged mind. It served no purpose other than ceremonial slaughter. It was a sham.

"Still want to wait until daybreak to leave?" Quanah asked, jogging beside him.

Crockett shook his head. "Let's move out. If anyone tries to stop us, we'll roll right over them."

When they reached the outskirts Loki's Rock, Quanah volunteered to go on ahead, sneak through the rear entrance of the saloon and retrieve their gear from the rooms. Crockett and Alex went to prepare the ACP.

"You're welcome to go with us," Crockett said to Zeda as they stepped beneath The Bitter End's overhang.

"Welcome to go where?" she asked softly, her eyes downcast.

"Away from here first and foremost," said Alex. "That's a start, isn't it?"

Zeda nodded. "It is." She smiled in relief. "Yes, thank you. I will go."

Crockett activated the Commtach. "Syne, prep *Ambler* for immediate departure."

It took so long for a reply that Crockett nearly repeated the order. Then Syne responded in a flat, dispassionate tone. "That might prove difficult, Colonel."

Rather than question him, Crockett rounded the corner of the saloon, sprinting toward the parked vehicle, Alex running at his side. Zeda followed them. They ran only a few yards before Crockett rocked to such a sudden halt that Zeda nearly trod on his heels.

"*Bugger!*" Alex hissed.

Half-a-dozen men stood in a semi-circle in front of *Ambler*. They wore the criss-crossed bandoliers and mirrored sunglasses of Loki's Rock security men. Quanah kneeled on the ground in the center of the circle. The long bores of two hand-blasters pressed tightly against both sides of his head.

CHAPTER TEN

For a long, silent moment, the tableau held. Crockett slowly moved his hand toward the butt of his pistol. A man holding a gun to the left side of Quanah's head said mockingly, "Ah-ah-*ah*."

Crockett eyed the bruise darkening Quanah's cheek and asked. "You all right?"

Quanah said dispassionately, "They were waiting for me."

"Waiting why?" Crockett demanded, addressing none of the security men in particular. When no one answered the question, Crockett saw little point in continuing the queries. Nor was he comforted by the fact that neither he nor Alex had been ordered to disarm. That meant they didn't consider their weapons to be threats nor were they afraid the weapons aboard *Ambler* would be turned against them at point-blank range.

As casually as if he were commenting on the weather, Crockett said, "You realize my friend inside the vehicle will blow this town to hell if I give the word."

The man holding the gun against the right side of Quanah's head uttered a scoffing sound. "But not afore I blow this red nigger's brains out all over the street."

He twisted the barrel of the pistol into Quanah's temple for emphasis.

"Ancient racial invective," murmured Alex sarcastically. "And another piece of the Loki's Rock puzzle falls into place."

A security man suddenly came to attention, putting a hand to his left ear. He cocked his head slightly in an attitude of listening. He said, "Right away, Pagan."

Crockett exchanged a swift, surprised glance with Alex. The men were obviously equipped with com-links not too different from their own Commtachs.

The man gestured toward the Bitter End. "Django wants to see you, Colonel."

"Just me?"

"Just you."

Crockett hesitated, and then touched his Commtach. "Syne."

"Sir?"

"Tie all the automatic weaponry into the main fire control board. If you don't hear from me in fifteen minutes, hit the button and light up this town."

"Sir?"

Trying to keep the note exasperation out of his voice, Crockett said lowly, "Engage all weapons. Loki's Rock is the target."

Hesitantly, Syne replied, "I take it you haven't looked astern, sir. Not encouraging."

Crockett took several careful deliberate steps to the left, aware of gun bores following his movements. A man stood about ten yards from the rear of *Ambler*. A large cube-shaped object with rounded corners rested on his right shoulder. A hollow tube extended from the side facing the ACP. Little glowing power icons danced on the outer skin of the object.

"I've looked now," Crockett said.

"Then you might recognize a Taktron Pulse-Plasma Emitter," said Syne calmly. "Colloquially known as a Blitz Launcher. Although this looks like an early model, I'm sure the operating principles are the same as the ones currently on the market—the weapons accelerate electrons to fantastic speeds and eject them as coherent bursts of plasma energy. The discharges break down the molecules of the air and ignite sparks resembling lightning bolts. Anything they touch go up in flames."

"Including," Crockett said dolefully, *"Ambler.* And you."

"Yes," replied Syne. "We don't know if the Emitter is actually operable, however."

"I don't choose to take the chance."

"Nor do I. Thank you, Colonel."

A security man gestured impatiently with his pistol. "Don't keep Django waiting, man."

Crockett turned toward the saloon. To Alex, he said lowly, "Leave your comm channel open...at least you can hear my end of what's going on."

She nodded, her expression grave. "Understood."

As Crockett walked past Zeda, he whispered, "This might be a good time to make yourself scarce."

"Might be," she whispered back. "Might not be. So I'll stick."

"Good. Stay with Alex."

In the Bitter End, Crockett found Django Bonner seated in his coffin-shaped, skull-decorated throne. Pagan, still in her leather vest and boots, lounged against the bar, nursing a glass of red liquid that Crockett hoped was tomato juice.

Bonner beckoned to him with a gesture, and Crockett approached, trying to keep his face expressionless. Bonner's face was a bland mask. He linked his long fingers in his lap and leaned forward slightly.

"Few things ever change." His voice was no longer the strident roar of a few minutes before, but it contained a whispery note that lifted the hairs on Crockett's nape.

Crockett cocked an eyebrow at him, saying nothing.

"Even when building an empire that will transform the world, there are always low-order swine who cannot understand and wish to tear it down. Crockett, there is the stench of the sty about you."

Two men materialized out of the shadows and slammed into Crockett simultaneously, pressing him between them. They clawed at him, raking their hands over his body. A seam in his holster split and his Hawken Big 50 was gone. He was twirled about and thrown face first against the far wall. A quick frisk followed, with a knee positioned dangerously near his testicles. Then he was released and allowed to turn around. The entire process had happened so quickly that he hadn't even found time to blink.

Rearranging his clothing, Crockett looked around the saloon. Barbie and Ken smirked at him. He glimpsed the opening behind the banner and understood the sudden appearance of the two men.

Outwardly Crockett remained calm, but inwardly he raged at himself for being so gullible. Coldly, he asked, "What was the manhandling all about, Django?"

One of the men behind him grunted, but Crockett didn't bother to turn. He knew who had made the sound.

"I think you're here to interfere with me," Bonner intoned, "on the part of the Commonwealth so the Oldworld system can be rebuilt."

"You psi-scanned me, didn't you?" Crockett demanded. "Did you find anything in my mind that led you to this conclusion?"

"You've got a Sifter running interference," Bonner replied. "I can't be sure of the impressions I received. Besides, she's carrying a little gadget that makes me distinctly uneasy." He pointed to the back of his neck.

"The girl doesn't know anything about it and neither do I."

"Nevertheless, there's only one place on Loki that has that kind of tech."

"You're a Commonwealth spy, Crockett." Pagan spit. "Admit it."

"You're a maniac," Crockett shot back, his temper getting the better of his judgment. "Admit it."

Crockett caught a blur of movement from behind him and he wheeled, sucking in his gut just in time to only partially suffer the punch that was intended to pulverize his right kidney.

Still, the fist bouncing from his rib cage hurt, but so did the elbow he whipped into Barbie's windpipe.

The scar-faced man staggered back and dropped to the floor, gagging and clutching convulsively at his throat.

Ken swung at Crockett with the barrel of the Hawken. Crockett bobbed to one side and lashed out with a right foot that struck squarely on Ken's kneecap. The cracking of bone was loud and ugly.

Ken pitched forward, howling and plucking at his maimed leg. Crockett wrested the Hawken from the man's nerveless fingers and leveled it at Bonner just as Pagan lunged forward, her hand drawing the Beretta from her holster.

"Tell her to freeze," Crockett snapped.

"Freeze, Pagan," Bonner stated, a fraction of a second before Crockett squeezed the trigger.

The woman froze, her autopistol only half-drawn, but Crockett kept his weapon on Bonner all the same.

"You know what the worst kind of gamble is?" the black-clad man inquired. With exaggerated deliberation, he drew one of the pistols from his sash, but he did not aim it. "The kind that has no chance of paying off. Even if you manage to walk out of here, you're a dead man walking. Every hand in Loki's Rock will turn against you, and every one of those hands will have a gun in it."

"I don't doubt that," Crockett replied. "But you'll take that last ride to the boneyard with me."

Suddenly he felt the delicate, wispy brush of Bonner's mind reaching out to touch, or to ensnare his. Crockett focused his thoughts on a single vivid image: he visualized Bonner's head exploding in a spray of blood, bone shards and brain matter. He concentrated on a vision of the black blazer turning red and wet, of that long, lean body flopping lifelessly to the floor.

He powered the image with a vicious conviction, packing it with a ruthless, unshakable certainty that the image would come true, and that he, Crockett, would be more than happy to arrange it, regardless of the consequences.

Bonner leaned back in his chair with a jerk of his shoulders. His eyes opened wide, then they narrowed. "Get back, Pagan."

"He's just one man," his warlord snapped.

"Tell her, Django," Crockett suggested. "Tell her what one man can do."

"Goddamn you, Pagan," Bonner said shrilly. "Back away from him!"

Pagan removed her hand from beneath her jacket and retreated reluctantly, glaring venomously at Crockett. Bonner glanced unhappily at the pair of pain-racked men sprawled on the floor, then back to Crockett. He returned the pistol to his sash.

"I underestimated you," he said quietly. "Consider yourself lucky."

"You're the lucky one, Django. Most people who have underestimated me are reclining in a frozen grave on Io." He added helpfully, "That's a moon of Jupiter."

Bonner eyed him for a long moment, then with a hand clap he threw back his head and laughed. "You're a treasure, Crockett. Yes, you truly are. Loki's Rock needs a man like you."

Crockett's squinted at him. "I think I'd rather have you release my people and we'll be on our way."

Bonner laughed again. "Ah, well, that's the rub, isn't it? We need you, and you need your people...unharmed. Can't we help each other?"

Bonner grinned, and his face took on a cadaverous, skull-like aspect. "Because if you *won't* let me help, you and your people will die in a manner far less spectacular and far more agonizing than the late Willy Bill."

Crockett kept the Hawken trained on Bonner, even when four security men entered the saloon. They hesitated, hands straying to gun butts, eyes darting from Crockett to Bonner to Pagan.

The black-clad man waved to Barbie and Ken. "Never mind our visitor. Please attend to our injured brothers. The Colonel and I are merely discussing business."

The security men collected the groaning, cursing, coughing men from the floor and carried them outside. When Crockett was sure they were gone, he said, "All right, Django. Let's discuss business. I'll put my gun away, providing you keep that warlord of yours on a short leash."

Bonner nodded. "Very well, Colonel. Pray, take a seat."

Crockett tucked the Hawken back into its holster and pulled a chair away from a table. Spinning the chair around, he thrust it between his legs and sat in a position where he could see the passage behind the jukebox, the saloon doors and Pagan all at the same time. A glance at the monitor screens in the corner showed black and white images of Alex, Quanah and Zeda still held at gunpoint outside *Ambler*.

"You don't need to keep my people prisoner," Crockett said. "Let them go."

Bonner shook his head. "They're not prisoners, not yet. Let's call them... co-operation inducers."

"You telepathically drew us to Willy Bill's foot-race, didn't you?"

"Excellent. I'd believed my influence was so subtle you would never detect it as intentional. Your Gypsy girl no doubt detected the psionic summons."

"Why did you want us there?"

Bonner fluttered a pale hand through the air. "Various reasons, actually. I wanted to test the strength of your spines, and I wanted to provide you with a glimpse of the unity of the Loki's Rock."

"And," Crockett interjected, "to see if you could scare the shit out of us."

Bonner smiled. "That, too. Did we succeed?"

Crockett grinned derisively. "Django, in some places in the Spur, I've seen church services that made your little sadistic foot-race look like a folk dance."

The smile on Bonner's lips faltered for a moment, but it returned. "Good. If you were easily stressed out, we couldn't use you."

Crockett let that remark pass for the moment. "What about Willy Bill? What did he owe Loki's Rock?"

The smile fled Bonner's lips completely, and the messianic expression he had worn earlier settled on his face. "Willy Bill was once a trusted member of my inner circle, second only to Pagan. He violated our racial purity laws. He lay with an Indian woman and tried to conceal it from me."

Crockett thought about Barbie and several other mouth-breathing types he had glimpsed shambling around Loki's Rock but he decided against mentioning the apparently broad definition of racial purity to Bonner. Instead, he said, "I wouldn't think you'd be so particular about rape."

"Rape, during times of war, is encouraged. It's a sound psychological tactic. But Willy Bill fell in love with the red whore, and they even had a child. When I found out, he was brought here. He knew the rules, the penalties." He gestured toward the craps table. "He rolled the bones."

"And the dice weren't loaded?"

Bonner stiffened. "We play an honest game here, Colonel. It's the only way to maintain order. He rolled and forfeited his eyes. He got off easy, all things considered."

Crockett pursed his lips. "He didn't seem to think so. He cut and ran—crawfished, as you people call it."

The smile crept back to Bonner's face. "Yes, but it all turned out for the best. Instead of losing a pair of eyes, we now can harvest all of his organs...and those are far greater in value in the Hellgrounds than anything you can imagine."

His belly turning a cold flip-flop, Crockett asked, "How are they of greater value? I've seen the quality of your weapons and you obviously have access to gasoline and tech."

"All true." Bonner linked his fingers and leaned forward. "What do you know about the Ahnenerbe Institute, Colonel?"

"Only what my Mnemosyne reported."

"Which was?"

Choosing his words carefully, Crockett said, "It was a division of GenTek that got its start hundreds of years ago on Earth...in Nazi Germany."

Bonner nodded. "Yes. But it is far more than that now."

"'Is'?" Crockett repeated. "It's still around?"

Bonner smiled, grinned, and then laughed. "Oh, most definitely. Evidence of it is everywhere."

Crockett stared at him, wondering if Bonner was not only a psychic, but a psychotic, as well. "Here? Loki's Rock is the Ahnenerbe Institute?"

Bonner scowled. "No, not Loki's Rock... but it influences us, of course. Our philosophy of Loyalty, Valiance, Obedience and Purity is shared by the Ahnenerbe. Unfortunately, we're also dependent upon it. *Totally* dependent."

From her position at the bar, Pagan said icily, "He shouldn't be hearing this."

Without looking her way, Bonner hissed her into silence. "Our weapons, our vehicles, our fuel, much of our seed crop, even our electrical generators come from the Institute. But we don't have direct access to it. We trade dearly for what we have and what we have is doled out piecemeal."

"By whom?"

"It's rather a long story," Bonner replied. "Much of it is surmise rather than fact."

"Until you decide to let us go, I appear to have plenty of time."

Bonner chuckled. "I begin to like you more and more, Colonel. You intrigue me. However, I'll show you the Institute rather than tell you about it."

"Show me?" Despite himself, excitement pulsed within Crockett's chest.

"Sure. It's only a few hours ride. If we leave soon, we can reach it well before sunset."

"I want my people to accompany us."

"No," Pagan bit out.

Bonner directed a dark glare toward her and she averted her gaze. "I see no problem with that. Besides, your Mind Sifter may prove valuable in case we run across some dangers."

"Like what?"

"Like Indians," Bonner replied. "For some reason, they hate us."

Thinking about Sam, Crockett said wryly, "I can't imagine why."

Bonner grinned, his face lighting up with an almost boyish glee. "This could be fun, a real outing! I'll have a picnic lunch prepared for us. I'll order your people released, Colonel. Get some sleep and meet me back here at dawn."

Crockett stood up and stitched a friendly smile onto his face. "Understood."

He moved toward the door, glancing back once. Pagan stared at him reflectively, as if he were a bit of steak and she was wondering whether to devour him raw or rare.

CHAPTER ELEVEN

For over four hours the X-MAC had rumbled across the rocky plain, pushing deep into the Midnight Hills. Though the ride was much smoother than it had any right to be, Crockett was growing impatient.

When he'd first boarded the long, box-shaped X-Mobile Armored Control unit, he had been so impressed that the cumbersome maneuverability of the vehicle hadn't bothered him.

Alex had been in just as much awe, especially when the prideful Bonner pointed out the gun racks, the sixteen missile and CS gas grenade launchers and the eighteen weapons ports. The vehicle was twice the length of *Ambler* and the six-inch-thick triadium armor plate protected the interior against chemical weapons and conventional firearms.

Bonner explained that the X-MACs were virtual wheeled fortresses and had been used two centuries before as both personnel haulers and war machines. They combined the best elements of an APC, a ground assault vehicle and wheeled battleship.

The X-MAC was in perfect operating order, as though it had been built a year before, not two hundred. The big engine throbbed smoothly, the suspension didn't creak or squeak and the air-conditioning system kept the interior cool and comfortable.

"Where did you find this machine?" Alex wondered aloud

Bonner only smiled a mysterious smile and touched a forefinger to his lips.

Crockett, Alex, Quanah and Zeda shared the passenger compartment with Bonner, Pagan and eight security men, who were identically armed with spidery-looking, lightweight TR-90 automatic rifles. Crockett had decided to leave Syne behind in *Ambler,* just as a hole card, although they had been out of Commtach range for the last couple of hours.

A pair of bipod-mounted, gas-operated M-200 minicannons were positioned at gun ports on either side of the vehicle.

Two men were seated in the control cockpit, one driving and the other constantly checking their backtrack with a periscope-type device that rose from the roof of the X-MAC.

The vehicle had departed Loki's Rock at daybreak. As the morning dragged into early afternoon, the X-MAC rolled through scattered pockets of ruins—houses leaning in on themselves, roofs cocked sideways and the burned out shells of buildings rising like headstones from the arid landscape.

During the ride Bonner acted like the perfect host. He passed sandwiches and beverages around to everyone but the security men.

He maintained a steady stream of inane chatter about crops grown around Loki's Rock, the weather and some of the odd people who had passed through the town. His manners were impeccable, and his vocabulary flowery.

Still, his brittle conversation scratched at Crockett's nerves. He kept busy repairing the torn seam of his holster, but midway through the fourth hour of eating, drinking and listening, he was irritated enough to ask bluntly, "How long has Loki's Rock been in existence?"

Bonner broke off the anecdote about the pet smilodon he had once owned. "Feels like forever."

"Perhaps that's what it feels like," Alex said, as anxious as Crockett to talk about something more substantial, "but there are no pre-Catastrophic records about your town."

"It did not exist by that name," Bonner replied. "My followers and I found the remains of the village and we restored it. That is all you need to know."

"We can't help but be curious, you know," Quanah said.

"I'll answer what questions seem fitting when we reach our destination." Bonner's tone was cold, barely civil. He didn't look in Quanah's direction.

Crockett reflected that since Bonner apparently based his philosophy on the racist beliefs of the Ahnenerbe Institute, Quanah Parker's obviously equal relationship with the other members of the Offworld Ops team was a source of great offense to him.

Crockett glanced past Bonner, focusing on the panorama of broken hills displayed beyond the windshield. He knew if he looked at Bonner, he wouldn't be able to disguise the loathing in his face.

In the distance, a mountain seemed to grow. Towering and dark, the play of sunlight on the broken, eroded edges of butte rock seemed to form faces. Then the mountain receded as the X-MAC dropped down the side of a slope. Luxuriant grass carpeted the shallow valley, and a creek ran between a grove of trees. As the vehicle rumbled on, the walls on either side lifted higher, almost joining together at places, making a narrow pass.

Zeda suddenly stiffened, her eyes widening.

"Danger," she said in a clear voice.

Crockett and his group drew their side arms. Bonner didn't question her announcement, but called to the man in the front who peered through the periscope.

"What do you see?" he demanded.

"Nothing," the man responded, eyes pressed against the viewer. "Getting a three-sixty recon, but all I see are some birds— Oh, shit!"

The driver immediately lessened the pressure of his foot on the accelerator. Crockett moved forward, shouldering Pagan aside. He looked out the windshield, then lifted his gaze to the valley walls.

They sat on spotted ponies upon facing rims of the arroyo, perhaps two dozen, twelve on each side. White, blue, red and yellow paint distorted their faces into masks of naked, cruel hatred. They wore breechclouts and moccasins, with feathers in their long black hair.

The Lakota braced the butts of automatic rifles against their thighs, the barrels pointing upward. Their gazes were locked onto the vehicle as it rolled slowly beneath them.

At a word from Bonner, two of the security men left their seats and crouched behind the M-200 mini-cannons.

"They're just watching us," Crockett said.

Bonner hitched over in his chair and looked up. "Like I figured," he said bitterly. "It's that fucking Sky Wolf and his band of zealots."

Crockett thought it best not to mention that he had met Sky Wolf, but he did ask, "What can they do to us in here?"

Pagan looked at him contemptuously. "It's not what they can do, it's what *we* can do."

Bonner spoke to the security men at the machine guns. "Explain it to them."

With rattling roars, the pair of M-200s opened up. Gouts of dirt exploded from the facing rims of the arroyo, flinging up rock and grit in high fountains. Spent shell casings clattered to the floor of the X-MAC. Acrid smoke stung the eyes and the nose. Behind it all was the steady double hammer of the mini-cannons. Even inside the X-MAC, the whine of ricochets was audible, and they heard the patter of projectile-pulverized stone raining atop the vehicle.

The X-MAC continued to roll forward slowly, passing beneath the position of the Lakota.

The double streams of autofire kept on chewing up the edges of the arroyo, and Crockett saw that the Indians had disappeared from the rims.

"They're gone!" he shouted angrily. "You're just wasting ammunition!"

Bonner swung his head, spearing him with an icy glare. The two men locked gazes.

Without removing his eyes from Crockett's face, the black-clad man declared loudly, "Cease fire!"

The security men complied immediately, the weapons falling silent at precisely the same time.

"Keep a lookout," Bonner ordered the man at the periscope.

Then he said sharply to Crockett, "It's my ammunition to waste, isn't it, Colonel?"

"And it's our hair to lose," Quanah snapped. "It's a traditional trick of the

Sioux, to keep an enemy hosing their ammo around, shooting at shadows until all the blasters are drained. That's when they mount an attack."

"Ah, I see." Some of the sharpness left Bonner's tone. "Have no fear. We have enough ammunition here to wipe out the entire tribe, not just Sky Wolf's group."

Swiveling his head, he bestowed a gallant smile upon Zeda. "And thank you, my dear, for your perceptions."

Alex cleared her throat and asked, "So you are acquainted with that particular band?"

Bonner nodded. "Sky Wolf is a traditionalist. He thinks that the Catastrophe ceded the Indian lands back to him and his people through divine intervention. He regularly patrols this area, killing any non-redskins who might cross into it. He's a fundamentalist psychopath, completely unreasonable."

Alex raised her eyebrows in a "look who's talking" expression. She asked, "Why does he hold this area in such high esteem?"

"It's not esteem," Pagan said. "It's fear and hatred."

"Why?" Quanah demanded.

The X-MAC jounced as it climbed up a slope and out of the arroyo. As it topped the crest, Bonner gestured toward the windshield. "That's why."

The mountain filled the rectangular window, framed like a work of art. Although it was miles in the distance, Crockett saw that what he had first interpreted as an optical illusion combined with erosion was indeed a carved face on the mountainside—or what was left of one.

"Oh my God," Alex murmured, her eyes wide.

"No," Bonner contradicted her. "Adolph Hitler. Or it used to be."

Crockett surveyed the granite cliff looming above heaps of broken shale and scrubby trees. He said softly, "Now I know why it's called Mount Maleficent."

The eighty-foot-high head of *Der Fuhrer* had been nearly obliterated by groundquakes and rockslides. The top of Hitler's head had crumbled away, and one of his huge eyes was jigsawed by a network of cracks. Only his nose, sculpted mustache, thin-lipped mouth and chin remained completely intact.

Alex said flatly, "That's the Ahnenerbe Institute." She made a statement, she did not ask a question.

"It is," agreed Bonner.

"Why are we here?" Crockett demanded.

"To learn if my first assessment of your little band was correct."

"What assessment was that?"

"That you can be a help in my undertaking."

"You've mentioned that before," Crockett said suspiciously. "Maybe it's time for you to explain."

Bonner waved a hand in a dismissive gesture. "Perhaps I will. After a demonstration."

The man at the wheel steered the X-MAC toward a series of gentle grass-covered bluffs.

He navigated the big vehicle expertly over the top of one, then followed a winding course between two of them. Bonner didn't provide him with directions. Evidently the driver had come this way before.

He braked the vehicle at the foot of a slope that was only ten feet high, more of a dirt dune than a hill. He keyed off the engine. From a box attached to the wall, Pagan removed a hollow-bored Very pistol and a flare cartridge. Bonner gestured to the security man in the passenger seat and he arose, coming to stand beside him.

"Take his place, Colonel," the thin man instructed. "Man the periscope and watch everything that transpires with a close eye. Pay particular attention to *der Fuhrer's* nose."

Then, to the surprise of Crockett and his companions, Django Bonner stood in a smooth, lithe motion, not even bracing his hands against the arms of his chair. A pair of security men joined Pagan and the other security man as Bonner unlatched the side door and pushed it open and out.

"What about the redskins?" Quanah asked, with only a hint of mockery underscoring his tone.

"They never come this close," Bonner answered. "Some sort of tribal taboo. Or maybe they've got better things to do than get killed."

Crockett waited until Bonner and his group had stepped out of the vehicle, then he pushed his way forward to the empty seat. The man behind the wheel ignored him, and Crockett returned the favor.

He examined the periscope, noting that each of the hand grips bore two buttons. On the right hand grip was a button marked with a plus sign, and another button with a minus sign. The left hand grip buttons were inscribed with arrows, indicating directions.

Crockett placed the upper portion of his face against the viewfinder and focused on the graven image of Hitler. It was at least half a mile distant. He thumbed the plus button, and the great stone face swelled and enlarged until only the nose filled the viewer.

The right-side nasal passage looked different than its mate. It was a deeply shadowed depression, like a hollowed-out tunnel.

Hearing Bonner's voice, Crockett removed his eye from the viewfinder and saw that he, accompanied by Pagan and the three security men, had climbed to the top of the bluff.

At a word from Bonner, Pagan pointed the Very pistol skyward and pulled the trigger.

The magnesium and thermite flare smoked through the air, ascending higher and higher until it exploded in a flash of bright yellow.

The flare hung there in the blue sky, shining with a brilliant glow. As it slowly descended on a miniature parachute, Bonner turned toward the X-MAC and shouted, "Watch the nose, Colonel!"

Crockett pressed his face against the viewer again. Nothing happened for what seemed to be a long time. "I don't see anything," he muttered, more or less to himself.

"Just keeping watching," the driver said.

Suddenly he caught a flicker of movement in the hollowed-out nostril. Sunlight briefly gleamed off metal, then a shape appeared, seeming to crawl out of the nasal passage. It paused in the open air, just above the sculpted upper lip, and Crockett stared at it so intently and unblinkingly that his eye began to sting.

A mechanical device, barely two feet long, hovered above the stone square of Hitler's mustache. Its body was made of interlocking metal segments, like the carapace of an insect. A pair of membranous wings unfolded from the back of the device, extending outward at least five feet. They looked to be composed of an extremely thin blue alloy. They began vibrating. On the metal skin a photoreceptor shone red, like a cyclopean eye. Right beneath, Crockett made out the logo of the Taktron Corporation.

"Jones," Crockett called, not taking his face away from the viewer, "come here."

When she reached him, Crockett pulled her onto his lap. "Take a look. Tell me what you think."

Alex peered into the viewfinder and caught her breath. "Bloody hell."

"Ever seen anything like it?"

"No."

"Ever heard of anything like it?"

"Perhaps." Her tone was doubtful. "Some sort of servo-mechanism. By the end of the last century, robotic units were being used for a lot of different functions, including surveillance and construction. You can see what looks like the lens of a camera on it. But I've never heard of anything as sophisticated or advanced as that thing."

"We call 'em Blue Beetles," the driver offered.

"What's the motive power of the Beetles?" Crockett asked.

When the driver didn't respond, Alex said, "Taking an educated guess, I'd say it probably utilizes local gravitational fields for propulsion. The wings help it maneuver. Extremely efficient."

"That's for certain," Crockett said. "Who would've built it?"

Alex shrugged. "Hard to say. As you know, there was a lot of black tech being developed by various corporations like Taktron during the first century of Spur colonization."

"Could that be the same thing we saw in the sky the other day?"

"I don't think so...the radar registered a much larger signature. But-whoops! It's moving."

She got up, allowing Crockett to take over the periscope again. He adjusted the magnification and direction so he could focus on the beetle. Its wings a blur, the little device flew in a straight line for Bonner's position. Crockett estimated its speed at around five miles per hour. In a less than a minute the beetle came to an abrupt halt, hovering twenty feet above the bluff.

Crockett looked away from the periscope and out the windshield. A faint funnel of waxy light emanated from the beetle's undercarriage and fell upon Bonner's face. An amplified male voice demanded, *"What do you want?"*

CHAPTER TWELVE

Bonner's answer was smooth, relaxed and apologetic. "The harvest is requiring more time than I estimated, *Brigadefuhrer*. It'll be a few more days before we can make the delivery. I regret the deviance from the timetable."

"Is that all?" The voice was uninflected and well-modulated, but the underlying note of arrogance in it made Crockett's hand reflexively move toward his holstered Hawken.

"We spotted a war party of Indians on our way here. Have they molested you?"

"Isn't it your responsibility to ensure that they don't? We've supplied you with the means to place yourself in a superior posture to them. And much more besides."

Bonner bowed his head formally. "For which we are eternally grateful."

"Then live up to your end of our trade agreement. Is there anything else?"

"No," Bonner replied unctuously. "I trust I've not disturbed you."

"This communication is ended."

Soundlessly the beetle slid backward through the air, as though it were unwilling to turn its photoreceptor away from Bonner. After a hundred yards, it rotated quickly, ascended, and sped back toward Mount Maleficent.

Bonner, Pagan and the security men returned to the vehicle. Crockett went back to the passenger compartment. Bonner smiled, but it didn't reach his eyes. "Pretty impressive, wasn't it?"

"Very," Quanah said.

Bonner shifted in his chair so he could look at Crockett. "What did you think, Colonel?"

Crockett smiled wryly. "I think I've never seen a finer demonstration of the art of ass-kissing in my life."

Pagan spun toward him, lips pulling away from her clenched teeth. "Watch it, Colonel."

Bonner frowned, then forced the smile to return to his face. "You're right. But if you knew the power behind that beetle, you'd want to weld your mouth to its ass, too."

"Then why don't you tell us about it instead of making vague references?" Alex asked impatiently.

"In a little while." Bonner barked an order at the driver, who started up the X-MAC and steered it back in the direction from which it had come.

Crockett consulted his chron. "We'll never make it back to Loki's Rock before nightfall."

"I know," Bonner replied. "There is salubrious ground for a campsite a few miles away. Once there, we can relax and talk."

"What's wrong with here?" Zeda demanded.

"I want to put some distance between us and the mountain. I'm not sure of the range of the beetles, and I don't want them getting a premature peek at the four of you."

"Why not?" Quanah wanted to know.

"Patience, Dr. Parker. All things come to those who wait."

The vehicle rumbled back through the arroyo, and when it reached the small grove of trees near the creek, Bonner ordered the driver to halt. Everyone disembarked and pitched camp.

Small tents, made of a lightweight fabric, were set up easily and quickly. There wasn't much deadwood for a fire, but there was no need for it. One of the crew carried a metal cylinder from the X-MAC, which was three feet long by three wide. At the touch of a lever on the side of the cylinder, chrome legs slid out from beneath it, and metal rings at the end of foot-high stalks projected from the top. Bonner explained that the cylinder burned a gas that furnished a smokeless fire for cooking and heating.

The security men established a defense perimeter, assembling four tripod-mounted spotlights and alarm sensors around the campsite. Guards were stationed every twenty feet outside of the perimeter. By the time the sun began its slow descent, the area was bathed in a bright white light.

Neither Crockett nor his friends felt particularly safe. As Quanah pointed out, Bonner seemed to be extending an invitation for the Sioux to come in and lift their hair.

Alex agreed. "All he needs now is a full orchestra playing the *1812 Overture*—complete with cannonfire--to advertise our presence. This is *not* salubrious ground. A deaf, dumb and blind multiple amputee could find us."

"Everything checks out secure so far," Zeda said, although she looked around apprehensively.

"Yet," Quanah interjected. "The night is young."

"I thought Indians didn't attack at night," Alex said.

Quanah chuckled. "And I thought you studied all the Native tribes who had settled on Loki."

"Sociological groupings," Alex responded with some irritation. "Genotypes, cultural linkages in linguistics and the like, not whether they preferred waging war when the sun was up or down."

"It's true that Indians didn't attack at night hundreds of years ago," Quanah replied, "because dew would take the tension out of their hide-and-sinew bowstrings, or dampen the powder in the pans of muzzle-loaders. Sky Wolf's warriors we saw carried automatic rifles, and they don't have to worry about keeping their strings or powder dry."

"Thanks," Zeda said sarcastically. "I feel better now that's cleared up."

At least dinner was sumptuous, which helped to offset some of their anxiety. First, potatoes fried in fat, then remarkably tender and juicy beefsteaks followed by baked ears of corn. Dessert consisted of thick slices of apple pie, swimming in cream. The repast relaxed them, the strong coffee notwithstanding.

Bonner sat in a camp chair and ate with a gluttonous gusto that surprised Crockett. If the volume of food he consumed was a normal meal, it was astonishing how he had remained so thin. Pagan made several trips to the cookstove simply for him.

As they nursed their coffee, Bonner waved them over to him. "Gather 'round, boys and girls. Time to come clean and to speak of many things."

" 'Of ships and shoes and sealing wax, and of cabbages and kings'?" Alex inquired with a rueful smile.

Bonner's lips twisted in a strange, mirthless rictus. "Madam, you are more correct than you could know."

* * *

Contrary to the accepted dogma, Bonner said—the end didn't come as a nightmarish surprise to everyone on Loki. A select few of the original colonists realized it was inevitable that the world would rend itself asunder and took measures to survive. This elite group figured out a way to survive the apocalypse. They possessed the forethought, foresight and wherewithal to prepare for the worst.

It was only natural, inasmuch as this select few were inveterate survivors. They were representatives of the GenTek Corporation, a bioengineering firm formed in the 21st century and based upon absorbing every possible permutation of genetic engineering that had ever been researched on Earth.

The most radical permutation had been the research and experiments conducted by the Ahnenerbe Foundation in the years preceding, during and even following World War II.

The Foundation, under the command of doctor and *Brigadefuhrer* Karl Brandt, was internationally famous for eugenics programs which attempted to maintain a "pure" German race through a series of programs that ran under the banner of racial hygiene. Brandt served as Hitler's personal physician and his dedication to *der Fuhrer* and the Reich were intertwined with his fervent belief in the goals of the Ahnenerbe—to further the advancement of the Aryan race by adhering to the principles of *Treu, Tapfer, Gehorsam* and *Reinheit*.

Under Brandt, the Foundation performed extensive experimentation on live human beings to test their genetic theories, ranging from simple measurement of physical characteristics to the experiments carried out by Josef Mengele on twins in the concentration camps. During the 1930s and 1940s, the Nazi regime, following the Ahnenerbe guidelines, forcibly sterilized hundreds of thousands of people who they viewed as mentally and physically unfit

The Foundation also ordered the killing tens of thousands of the disabled through compulsory euthanasia programs such as Dr. Brandt's Aktion T4. The methods of execution developed in the euthanasia policy led directly to their widespread use in concentration and extermination camps, especially the use Zyklon B gas.

The Foundation also implemented a number of positive eugenics policies, giving awards to Aryan women who had large numbers of children and encouraged a service in which racially pure single women could deliver illegitimate children. Also "racially valuable" children from occupied countries were forcibly removed from their parents and adopted by German people. Of course, the Ahnenerbe's policy was also explicit in the systematic killing of millions of undesirable people, especially Jews and Gypsies. But the Foundation scientists also created a synthetic form of DNA—albeit in crude form.

When Hitler's thousand-year Reich fell somewhat short of expectations, the architects of the Ahnenerbe Foundation scattered across the world. Some of them faked their deaths and acquired new identities. Some of them became the founders of the GenTek Corporation.

From modest beginnings, GenTek expanded over the next two centuries, finding ways to cure diseases, end birth defects and even retard the aging process. But always behind the scenes, working in the basement so to speak, remained the fundamental goal of the Ahnenerbe—to create the pinnacle of human development through the spread of pantropy: new humans for new worlds.

GenTek was devoted to the spread of the human race throughout the galaxy, but only the *right* kind of humans. And so was born the Ahnenerbe Institute which maintained the trappings, slogans and beliefs of its twentieth century predecessor.

The minds behind it knew they would come into conflict with the other divisions of GenTek as well as Commonwealth laws and regulations. Therefore, when the Spur worlds were opened up for colonization, the Ahnenerbe Institute judged the planet Loki best suited their needs. It was far enough away from the most populous cluster and sufficiently unpredictable to attract only the most desperate, even poverty-stricken colonists. The Ahnenerbe Institute referred to this rabble as "useless eaters."

The Ahnenerbe Institute brought with it the genetic samples of many Terran life forms, including those long extinct, such as the mammoth, the smilodon, and the brontotherium.

They set about resculpting the face of Loki, to transform it into their vision of the perfect birthing ward for the perfect human.

The Ahnenerbe built an enormous facility—part corporate headquarters, part laboratory, and part home of a new race of godlike men. They called it Jotunheim, after the realm of the Frost Giants in Norse mythology.

It was a vast complex, with underground sewage plants, railways, and even sports arenas. Supplies of foodstuffs, weapons and anything of value were stockpiled, often times in triplicate.

Because of its size, Jotunheim was built inside of Mount Maleficent, the most massive mountain in the Midnight Hills region. The entire mountain was honeycombed with interconnected levels, passageways and chambers. From Jotunheim, they directed the redesign and reconstruction of the entire planet. Then came the first Catastrophe.

The magnetic poles shifted, the great glaciers and ice centers at them sliding into new positions. Enormous portions of the ocean floor rose, while equally tremendous land masses sank beneath the waves. The configuration of Loki radically altered.

When the first tremor shook the Midnight Hills, the Mount Maleficent facility had been in operation for only a few years. The safety measures kicked in, and everyone inside was safe and sound—or so they thought.

Despite all their precautions, the global earthquakes caused extensive damage to Jotunheim. The Ahnenerbe Institute had no choice but to remain in the facility in order to survive, and, hopefully, one day rule again. It took them several years to realize that they were just as much victims of the Catastrophes as those whom they contemptuously referred to as the useless eaters of the planet.

When this select few, this powerful elite, did realize it, they were upset. It wasn't part of their plans. They had assumed that in ten years or less, all of Loki would be theirs to rule. When they realized the actual timespan would be many times longer, they changed their plans, rather face slow death from old age and sickness, they had to buy themselves some time.

They embarked on a radical and daring plan. Cybernetic technology had taken great leaps in GenTek since the era of prosthetic limbs and artificial hearts, and the most up-to-date technology existed inside Mount Maleficent.

Surgeries were performed on everyone living in Jotunheim, making use of the advances in techniques in organ transplants and medical technology. The select few within the bosom of the mountain, over a period of several years, were turned into cyborgs, a hybridization of human and machine.

Of course, such transformations didn't solve all of their survival problems, nor were they intended to do so. Compensation for the natural aging process of some organs was very difficult to arrange. The Jotunheim inhabitants needed a supply of fresh organs, preferably from people who had died young with their bodies in generally good condition.

Because of the Catastrophes, this supply was severely limited, so they came up with the next best solution—cryogenics, or a variation thereof.

The temperature inside the facility was lowered just enough to preserve the tissues—not to such a low degree that the organs were damaged, but low enough to suspend the aging process. Combined with their cybernetic implants, the people in Jotunheim achieved a kind of immortality. But they had only temporarily halted Hel, Goddess of Death, not defeated her.

They had spent over a century in their little frigid world, looking out over Loki, over the Hellgrounds, forever prisoners of their own fantasies of power.

* * *

"That's the story," Bonner stated. "And who should know it better than I? All right, question-and-answer time."

"Who told you all of this?" Quanah asked suspiciously.

"Years ago, I met one of the original Oldworlders who had escaped or was exiled from the installation. He was dying and he didn't tell me everything, so I filled in some of the gaps myself."

"Then you're speculating," Alex challenged.

"Surmising. If you're a historian of Loki, you should know what is possible here."

"I for one certainly do," interposed Quanah. "I'm a doctor with a background in cryonics, and I know that for it to be effective the subjects have to be deep-frozen in liquid nitrogen at minus 196 degrees Celsius."

"They found a way around that," Bonner said.

"They, they," Zeda said acidly. "Keep saying 'they.' Don't these frozones of yours have names?"

Alex cast her a perplexed glance. "Frozones?"

"Slang for people who've been in cryonics," Bonner explained. "As far as names are concerned, I'm not on speaking terms with anyone up there. The only individual who has ever identified himself is a man who calls himself the *Brigadefuhrer.*"

Alex's eyebrows rose. "Not *Brigadefuhrer* Brandt?"

Django shrugged. "Possibly."

"That would make him nearly five hundred years old."

Django shrugged again, as if the matter were of little importance.

"How many times have you been inside the Institute?" Crockett asked.

"None. All of my communications have been conducted through the bee-tles, which they use as surveillance and early-warning devices."

"How'd you arrange a trade agreement with them, then?" Crockett de-manded.

Bonner tapped his temple with a forefinger. "A simple question of supply and demand. They demand certain products, and I supply them. I learned that from my father."

"Your father?" Alex echoed.

"Gustav Bonner. After the Catastrophe, his grandfather established Bon-nerville Flats...it was the only big settlement between the steppes and the Hellgrounds. It thrived for many years as a trading post and a supply station. When I was fifteen, it was wiped out by the army of Captain Caracortada. I was one of the few survivors. Before that, I had received what used to be called a 'classical education,' and though I was exceptionally book-smart and knew the pre-Catastrophic history of Loki and even of Terra, I had little practical knowledge of how to survive the Hellgrounds."

"It appears you managed," Quanah observed. "And very well, too."

"If you had met me ten years ago, you wouldn't have said that. For a long time I wandered and walked, learning the different cultures of Loki, the local dialects, the topography, the varieties of flora and fauna. I walked and walked. I must've walked the entire length and breadth of the Hellgrounds. The entire focus of my life was walking. That's why I hate to expend much energy on it now."

Pagan refilled Bonner's coffee cup and stood beside the chair, leaning a hip against the arm. She looked bored, industriously inspecting her nails.

Bonner took a sip of his coffee. "Where was I?"

"Making a short story long," Zeda said.

The black-clad man didn't appear to be offended, or, for that matter, to have even heard the young woman's words. "I knew I could never reclaim my own birthright of Bonnerville Flats, but I knew I could establish my own town, one so powerful that it could never be defeated. I was born to lead, to command, but there was one problem— I had no followers."

Bonner leaned back in his chair, crossing one leg over the other and clasp-ing the knee with both hands. He seemed to be enjoying himself immensely. "In my late teens, I discovered my latent psionic abilities. I found that I could sometimes sense what other people were thinking, and I assumed everyone had this ability. Eventually, of course, I learned otherwise. My power was undeveloped, truly a 'wild' talent. I found I could read some people all of the time, some part of the time, and some none of the time. I needed a method, a doctrine to employ, so I could zero in on those particular individuals my raw powers could influence. Then I remembered reading about Adolph Hitler."

"I remember reading about him, too," Alex said bitterly. "He was a sociopathic monster, a manipulator of the spiritually weak and desperate."

Pagan made a growling sound deep in her throat. "That's heresy, you Old-world bitch."

Bonner shushed her into glowering silence. "He was a very successful manipulator, nonetheless, since he very nearly conquered your world. Germany was crushed and beaten after World War I, yet in less than 15 years, he rebuilt it into the most powerful nation on Earth. I figured that if people bought his mixture of mysticism, ritual racism and paranoia centuries ago, they'd buy it again, especially with a new spin put on it."

"And," Zeda interjected, "especially if your mind influenced them."

"Quite true. The more I used my psychic gift, the stronger it became, like strengthening a muscle. I began encountering people whose minds were vulnerable to my own. I not only could sense what they were thinking, I could project my own thoughts into their minds, and in short, I controlled that mind on a modest scale. It's probable that Hitler himself possessed and exercised this power to a very developed degree."

"But," Zeda pointed out, "you aren't a Mind Sifter like me."

"No," Bonner admitted. "My talent is of a different order. I interact with brain-wave patterns. Precognition and empathy operate on emotional states. For example, Zeda here somehow intercepts the intent to cause harm, but she's not actually peeping into the future. Whereas I receive thought impressions, I'd guess that Zeda mentally picks up flashes of color, denoting emotions. Am I correct?"

Zeda nodded but said nothing.

Bonner reached up and touched the back of his neck. "I also suspect that your abilities have been augmented by the Institute...with the implantation of a control device."

"Possible," said Alex. "The Nazis *did* regard Gypsies as special, possessing advanced psychic gifts."

Zeda grimaced. "I don't recall any operation."

Crockett caught her eye and lifted a warning finger to his lips. Zeda affected not to notice, reaching for the coffee pot, but she said nothing else.

"At first," Bonner continued, returning to the primary topic, "my followers were the walking wounded, the flotsam and jetsam, strictly the dregs, the descendants of the survivors of the Catastrophes. But as I continued my wanderings, I found followers, especially among the Gypsies."

Zeda narrowed her eyes. "My people?"

"Not yours specifically, but the Romani. Through them, I managed to ac-quire a few decent heavy weapons but the nomadic life was wearing thin. It was too risky, especially after we drifted into this region of the Hellgrounds. We lost several people to shreekwings, and even more to the Indians. In fact, I rescued Pagan from the Indians during one skirmish, didn't I, Pagan?"

"Yes." She bit out the word, with no inflection or emotion attached to it.

"A little over four years ago, we arrived in this area, at the foot of Mount Maleficent. I'd heard about it from the old man I had met and I wanted to see it. We had barely pitched camp when a band of Sioux came upon us. We managed to kill quite a few, but racked up some casualties ourselves. That night, while we were tending to our wounded, the Institute—the *Brigadefuhrer* , in fact—made contact with me, via a beetle. The people up there had observed our fight and they wanted a trade."

"What kind of trade?" Alex asked.

"They wanted the bodies of the newly dead. They wanted the undamaged organs. I began a dialogue with them that built into a relationship. I persuaded them to supply us with what we would need to build a community nearby, and we would serve both as their protectors and their providers. I was told of a town that still stood and they gave me and my followers the means to march in take it. They also gave us seeds so we could plant crops, for them and us, and in return for fresh bodies, they traded us the means by which to provide them with even more fresh bodies."

"Let me guess this one," Crockett said, disgust thick in his voice. "You didn't want to kill members of the town since you were so few in number, so you viewed the local Indian bands as mobile organ banks."

Bonner laughed. "That's essentially correct. However, it's not as stone-cold as it sounds. It was also a matter of self-preservation. The Sioux wanted us and the people of the Ahnenerbe Institute out of this country by any means neces-sary. We would have been forced to kill them anyway, and at least their organs weren't just food for the worms."

"Why didn't you trade our livers to the Institute?" Crockett asked. "As out-siders, we were fair game."

"That you were, and indeed that was my original intention. I revaluated when I took a read of your mind and realized how you could provide a service to Loki's Rock."

"Loki's Rock has been around now for three years?" Alex asked.

"A little more," Bonner answered. "As the word about us spreads and more people join us, I estimate we'll be the most powerful township in the entire country in a few years. If, that is, we end our dependence upon the Ahnenerbe Institute."

"You want to take it over," Crockett stated. "To have all of the Oldworld tech—and freeze dried coffee-- to yourself."

"Wouldn't you, in my circumstances?"

"How can you get inside the place?" Quanah asked.

Bonner shrugged. "Up through the nose is the most obvious and most risky way. But there's another entrance."

"How you know?" Zeda asked.

Bonner reached behind him and rapped his knuckles on the armor plating of the X-MAC. "This wouldn't fit through the nose. No, they have some sort of railway system that can carry large merchandise through a network of tunnels. For example, I picked this up in a cave about two miles from here."

Interested despite himself, Crockett inquired, ""How do they receive your goods?"

"Simple. They lower a platform from the nose, and when it's loaded, they reel it back up again."

"If you covet their possessions so much," Alex said, "is there some reason you haven't staged a raid yet?"

"The best reason in the world. It would fail, our trade agreement would end and I would be placing the survival of Loki's Rock in terrible jeopardy."

"So why bring it up in first place?" Zeda demanded. "Are you just a lounge chair general?"

"Not quite," Bonner said softly. "A general needs soldiers, and I have them. But for this operation to have even a fractional success margin, I need very special soldiers. For instance, soldiers that can't be traced back to Loki's Rock or to me. Soldiers that aren't citizens."

Realization rushed through Crockett like a fountain of cold water. He fixed his gaze on Bonner, who met it with a thin, mocking smile.

"Khul!" Zeda declared, her spine stiffening. "I see red!"

One of the tripod-mounted security lights exploded in a blaze of blue sparks. A microsecond later, the sharp, snapping report of an automatic rifle split the night.

"Oh, my," Bonner said mildly. "I *do* believe the Indians are upon us."

CHAPTER THIRTEEN

The bulbs of the other three lamps shattered in rapid succession. Glass burst, sparks flared, and within a heartbeat and a half, the area was plunged into darkness.

Although Crockett and his people leapt to their feet, weapons in hand almost immediately, Bonner remained seated. Pagan shouted orders to the security men as they ran to and fro across the campsite. Crockett peered into the encircling shadows, trying to force his vision to quickly adjust to the sudden darkness.

With a sigh of ennui, Bonner arose from his chair and nonchalantly ambled into the X-MAC. He had just shut the door behind him when a bullet spanged off the vehicle's armored exterior, whining up into the night sky.

As Pagan shouted to the security squad to set up a fire zone inside the perimeter, Crockett and his team took cover beneath and to the rear of the X-MAC.

A bipod-mounted machine gun opened up with a staccato roar, smearing the darkness with bursts of orange flame. Pagan dashed to the security man behind it and dealt him a fierce kick in the ribs.

"Head shots!" she shouted angrily. "Head shots, you piece of shit!"

Crockett's eye grew accustomed to the gloom. The moon and the stars provided just enough light to make out the dim shapes of trees, brush and the sloping valley walls looming on either side. Another fusillade of shots stabbed from the shadows.

Crockett counted at least five rifles, firing more or less simultaneously. None of the bullets came near him or his people, but one of the security men howled and fell in a sprawl of kicking legs and flailing arms. The security squad returned the fire with their autorifles, triggering short, random bursts.

Quanah elbow-crawled up beside Crockett, his teeth bared in a humorless grin. "Maybe we should have taken Sam's advice when we had the chance."

"We don't know if it's the Lakota out there," Alex said.

A moment later, several undulating, high-pitched cries floated through the night sky. *"Hoka Hey! Hoka Hey!"*

"I guess you stand corrected—for once," Quanah told her calmly.

Another security man made a run toward the closed door of the X-MAC, but a storm of bullets struck sparks from its steel sheathing, and he was forced to dive beneath the chassis.

"If that's the war party we saw today," Crockett said, "then we've got about two dozen to contend with. We're outnumbered."

"But not outgunned. For some reason, they've got their weapons set on three-round bursts," Quanah observed. "Not full-auto."

"Less chance to waste ammo," Zeda said, gesturing to the security men raking the darkness with full autofire. "Not like these big karbaros-heads."

Alex laughed and quickly stifled it.

Crockett glanced her way. "What are karbaros?"

"Big penis heads."

He shook his head in weary exasperation. "Why did I even ask?"

Several full-metal-jacketed slugs ricocheted from the bodywork of the X-MAC, screaming off in different directions. A security man clutched at his leg and went down, howling a curse. From a prone position, he squeezed the trigger of his subgun, sending streams of flame and lead into the shadows. There was no return fire until the firing pin of his weapon hit the empty magazine with dry, audible clicks.

Then a single shot cracked, a bullet zipped out of the darkness and caught him in the forehead, punching a round hole between his eyes. The impact bounced his head hard against the ground, the back of his skull breaking apart. His legs kicked, then he was still.

"Now *that* was a head shot," Quanah remarked sourly.

Crockett reflected that if the Lakota were looking for scalps he and his people had full heads of hair of varying colors, lengths and textures, and they might present a terrible temptation. Zeda's blue tresses in particular would be a valuable prize. He hoped that if Sky Wolf was with the war party, he would recognize them. An instant later he hoped the opposite. The Lakota had warned him and his people about Loki's Rock, and he probably assumed they had thumbed their collective nose at his words of caution and, therefore, deserved everything that might come their way--including scalping knives.

Hefting his Hawken in a two-handed grip, Crockett said, "Lay down a firing pattern. We may not know where our targets are, but we've got a pretty good idea of where they're not."

Alex stared at him with wide, outraged eyes. "We can't kill them!"

"I don't want to and we'll do whatever we can to avoid it," Crockett said matter-of-factly, "but we have to defend ourselves."

A bullet whipped past Crockett's head, and he felt rather than heard the little slap of displaced air. It had missed him by no more than an inch, and it had come from behind.

Another bullet whistled past Crockett's face, splashing it with cool air, then flattened against the thick hide of the X-MAC over his head.

He twisted his body and pistol around, bringing the man-shape lunging from the darkness into target acquisition. The Hawken roared, spurting flame, and the rifle-toting figure back-somersaulted into the shadows.

Then the campsite was filled with running, shooting, half-naked men, shrieking out of the darkness from two directions. Not only did they carry automatic rifles, they wielded tomahawks, knives and even a few feathered lances. Their faces were painted with ferocious designs. They bounded and leapt too quickly for Crockett to get an accurate count of their number.

The defense put up by the Loki's Rock security squad was disorganized and sporadic. They retreated toward the X-MAC, halfheartedly fighting a rear guard action without watching one another's backs or even taking the time to aim their weapons properly.

Crockett and his team continued to crouch beneath the rear of the vehicle, watching several scenes at once: Pagan drilled one of the Lakota through the back of the head with her Beretta. She whirled on Crockett as he put a 50-caliber slug through the left shoulder of a warrior.

"Goddammit," she yelled. "I said head shots!"

At about the same time, a security man screamed as the flat razor point of a lance pierced his throat. The grinning Lakota withdrew it, and the security man dropped to his knees, trying to stem the geyser of blood fountaining from a severed jugular. Crimson droplets spattered over Alex's face and she wiped them away desperately.

"Colonel," she said tightly, "I think we should move. We seem to be in the epicenter."

He nodded. "Follow me...stay close together. Standard wedge deployment."

The three people followed Crockett from beneath the X-MAC The Indians used their rifles as bludgeons and fought hand-to-hand, uttering strident cries as they closed with their opponents. Crockett, trying maintain the point of the wedge, saw one of the warriors rush toward Quanah. He fired the Hawken point-blank, and the attacker dropped with a deep bloody cavity punched in his side.

Before he could shout for his team to watch their backs, a rush of bodies knocked him sprawling, and a heavy weight dropped directly onto his back, driving him face first to the ground.

Knees pressed into his buttocks and a pair of large hands closed about his neck and squeezed. Spitting out grit, Crockett heaved, bucked and twisted. He managed to roll over onto his back and look up at the hate-twisted, paint-distorted face bobbing over him. The Indian was by far the stronger, and he resisted each of the white man's efforts to throw him off.

Then he thrust a knife blade for his throat.

Crockett wrenched himself aside, and the edge of the blade skimmed the side of his neck, drawing a thread of blood. He fired his pistol at the Sioux, and a crimson spray erupted from the bridge of the warrior's nose. His grip loosened and he slowly fell forward.

Elbowing the deadweight from his body, Crockett rolled to one side and got to his knees.

A bullet plucked at his hair. He lurched forward, facedown, and felt the cool passage of another slug against his cheek. The campsite was screaming, bloody chaos. Guns blasted, lances lanced, knives sank into flesh and skulls were split with rifle butts. The security men were finally fighting back now that they were overrun, and they shot, slashed and clubbed.

He saw Zeda use a snapping right-arm toss to bury the Khanjarli dagger into the breastbone of a Lakota. The warrior staggered backward, wrenching the knife loose and dropping it to the ground before he toppled over himself.

Alex let loose with her TX5 rail pistol, picking and choosing her targets methodically, aiming for an extremity whenever possible. At one juncture she shot the rifle out of a warrior's hands, causing no more damage than temporarily numbing his fingers. An instant later her humanitarian impulse was ruined by a security man who blew the Indian's chest out with an uncontrolled burst from an autorifle.

A series of fat *pops!* reverberated through the air. Four cylinders spewing plumes of white smoke sprang from the launch tubes atop the X-MAC and bounced across the battleground. The cylinders rolled and hissed, and almost immediately the campsite was engulfed by blinding clouds of vapor. Shrieks of surprise came in the wake of the grenades.

War cries, yells of pain and shouted obscenities became incomprehensible as the combatants inhaled the gas. The smoke seared eyes, lungs, nostrils and bare flesh, and the warring parties staggered around the killing ground, groping for whiffs of fresh air, not for each other.

Crockett crouched, trying to get beneath the clouds of gas. He inhaled some of it, and for a moment he gagged himself blind. Through the jiggling, burning water in his eyes he caught glimpses of shapes moving through the billowing chemical vapors.

The Indians engaged in a slow, stubborn retreat back toward the shadows, hoping to melt into the night. They were obviously unwilling to give up the struggle despite the heavy losses they had incurred and the fact that they were all but incapacitated by the gas. Almost everyone coughed wept and gagged. Here and there came the choking gasps of people vomiting.

Crockett heard a female cry of pain from behind him and the thud of a body hitting the ground. He feared opening his mouth to call out for Alex, so he moved as quickly as he dared in the direction of the cry. Blinking hard, trying to focus through the fiery blur of his vision, through a part in the swirling vapors, he saw two figures at the far edge of the campsite.

For a heart-stopping instant, he thought it was Alex facedown on the ground, but after he knuckled his eyes, he saw a thin warrior kneeling on Pagan's back. One hand was tangled in the long burgundy fall of her hair. He pulled her head up and back, exposing the white column of her throat to the knife he gripped in one fist.

Crockett sprinted toward them, firing the Hawken's remaining four rounds so rapidly the shots were a single solid roar. The warrior sprang from the woman's body and into the shadows. Because tears blurred his eyes, Crockett wasn't sure if the Indian had been knocked away by the 50 caliber slugs or if he'd simply jumped.

Standing over Pagan, he reached down to help her up by one arm. She raked the hair out of her dirt-streaked face and looked up at him in astonishment.

"You helped me?" Her voice held an incredulous note.

"Actually, I saved you," Crockett said. He sucked in a lungful of untainted air. "Are you all right?"

Before she could answer, a bare arm darted from the darkness, hooked around Crockett's neck and jerked him backward. Instead of resisting the force, Crockett kicked himself off the ground, throwing his full weight against the body behind him.

He and the warrior fell and rolled clear of the brush, down a slight incline and onto soft grass at the bank of the creek. The Lakota had lost his knife, and his right arm locked in a death grip around Crockett's neck, while the fingers of his free hand pressed viciously against his larynx.

Crockett broke the hold by driving a powerful blow into the Indian's midriff with his elbow. The warrior grunted, and Crockett squirmed free and struggled to his feet. He clubbed down with the barrel of his pistol, striking the man between the shoulder blades.

From a kneeling position, the Lakota lunged forward and wrapped his arms around Crockett's legs. He fell forward, dropping the Hawken and toppling over the warrior. He managed to grasp the Indian by the hair and haul him into the stream with him. Both of them pitched into the water with a great splash.

The creek was shallow, barely waist deep, and the water felt shockingly cold, but it flushed the burning effects of the gas from Crockett's eyes and nostrils. The two men surfaced at the same time, gasping and blowing like whales. Crockett's closed left hand slammed into his adversary's jaw and knocked him off balance. He fell, disappearing beneath the surface.

The Indian clawed his way along the pebble-strewn bottom of the creek, using the gentle current as impetus to push him out of harm's way, but Crockett grabbed the Lakota by the back of the neck. He tried to rise, but Crockett held him down, using all of his upper body strength. The warrior heaved and kicked, thrashing the water into white froth.

Finally his struggles ceased. Crockett raised the man's head clear of the water and saw that his war paint had been washed from his face. He recognized the sharp, angular features of Sky Wolf, aka Sam. The lean-muscled Indian wasn't dead, though he was three-quarters drowned, his hair plastered flat to his head and shoulders, eagle feathers drooping and bedraggled.

Crockett allowed him to cough the water from his lungs and sneeze it from his sinus passages. The warrior was in no shape to continue fighting. Crockett slogged up the creek bank, hauling Sam with him. He dumped the coughing man onto the grass, noticing as he did so that Sam bore two superficial bullet wounds, a blood-oozing hole on the outside of his upper right thigh and a red-edged furrow across the small of his back.

After a few moments of groping, Crockett retrieved his Hawken, popped open the cylinder and reloaded with bullets taken from his cartridge belt. By the time he had accomplished that, Sam was sitting up, inhaling shuddery breaths, his jet black eyes narrowed and seething with hatred.

"Kill me, *wasicun*," he hissed, sounding half-strangled. "I deserve it for failing to kill you when I first saw you."

"Someone has already expressed the same opinion about you," Crockett said. "I'm not going to kill you unless you force me."

There was a sudden, surprised intake of breath, and Sam demanded, "Aren't you with Bonner and his psychotics?"

"We're with them, but we're not *of* them. Get me?"

Sam opened his mouth to answer, but Alex's voice, shouting Crockett's name, cut him off. She sounded very worried and hoarse, and her next call terminated in a coughing spasm.

Gesturing with the pistol, Crockett said, "Take off."

"What will you tell the others?"

"That you got away from me. That's the truth, isn't it?"

Sam didn't respond. He rose to a crouch and soundlessly merged with the darkness. Crockett climbed back up the slope and called to Alex. She ran to him, dark eyes clouded by worry and gas-induced tears. For second, she squeezed his forearm as if to reassure herself he was still alive. Pagan marched close behind her.

"You're wet," Alex said. "You're not hurt, not wounded?"

"No. The Indian got away when we hit the creek. He swam underwater, I think."

"You think?" Pagan repeated suspiciously. "That was Sky Wolf himself! You didn't make sure?"

Crockett stared at her stonily. "Normally I would have, except that I emptied my gun saving your life."

Pagan scowled, and then wheeled away, taking long strides back to the campsite. Alex and Crockett followed her. The area looked like an open-air charnel house, given an added unearthly atmosphere by the planes of drifting chemical fog. The gas had dissipated to some extent, but the survivors of the battle all looked and sounded miserable.

They stepped over the bodies of the slain and called to their friends. None of them were injured, beyond a few cuts and contusions. Zeda suffered the worst from the effects of the gas, and Quanah tended to her as she gagged, wept and dry-heaved.

Crockett did an automatic body count. There were eleven dead Sioux warriors sprawled on the ground, leaking fluids from a variety of wounds in a variety of places. Out of the ten security men, he spotted only four who were ambulatory and one cradled an obviously broken arm.

"Looks like you got big-time skunked," Crockett said.

The door of the X-MAC banged open and Bonner stepped out with a grand, long-legged flourish. He held a handkerchief over his nose and mouth. Pagan quickly approached him, saying, "We have five dead, one wounded. Zeon won't last through the night, so he doesn't count."

"The opposition?" Bonner's voice was muffled and nasal, as if he were holding his nose behind the handkerchief.

"Eleven, but only six are worth salvaging."

"And the value of our people?"

Pagan made an exasperated gesture. "Seven, if you include Zeon."

"A baker's dozen. Get to it. We'll attend to our own back home."

Pagan snapped her fingers toward the standing security men, and they bent over and began arranging the bodies of the slain. Bonner nodded in the direction of Crockett and his friends. "You and your group turned the tide, Colonel. My thanks."

The black-suited man eased himself down in his chair and fluttered the handkerchief before his face. "Whew! Pungent, isn't it?"

Crockett strode over to him, put a boot against the crossbar of the chair and shoved with all of his strength. The chair overturned, and Bonner fell unceremoniously to the ground, uttering a wordless cry of outrage and surprise.

The move had been performed on impulse, so Bonner had no opportunity to sense Crockett's intentions. As he gathered a handful of black frock coat and yanked the man to his feet, Crockett heard the clicking of rounds jacking into cylinders and hammers thumbed back. His people covered Pagan and the surviving security men. Quanah held the stock of an appropriated subgun to his shoulder and Zeda, still wheezing, aimed a pistol she had snatched from the ground.

Holding Bonner almost clear of the ground, Crockett shook him savagely. He weighed no more than a suit of clothes. "You son of a bitch, you knew this would happen. You *wanted* it to happen!"

A shadow of fear darkened Bonner's eyes, but there was also a monstrous anger. "You Oldworld prick, do you know how close to death you are?"

Crockett jammed the bore of the Hawken against Bonner's underjaw and cruelly forced his head back. "Nowhere near as close as you."

He heard the snapping crack of Alex's TX-5 and then a security man yelping in pain. "Just pierced his ear for him," Alex called. "He makes another move, and I'll pierce his testicles."

Forcing a laugh, Bonner spread solicitous hands. "Okay, Colonel. You're annoyed. I don't blame you. I understand it. But there was a reason."

Crockett stared at the man for another handful of seconds, and then released him. He stepped back, lowering the pistol but not leathering it. Bonner rearranged his clothing, uprighted his chair and sank into its seat.

To Pagan, he said, "Get on with it. We don't have all night." To Crockett, he said, "All right, Colonel. Point taken. I apologize."

"I'll need more than that, Django."

"And I'll offer more than that. Normally you would be put to a slow death for laying hands on me, or at the very least, sentenced to run the Doo-Dah. However, I must make allowances for this circumstance. Yes, I expected the attack, and to some extent I needed it."

"Why?"

"Two reasons: Firstly, I was curious to see how you people handled yourselves in a crisis. Very impressive, very professional. All of you kept your heads, which is more than I can say for my own people."

"Is that why you waited so long to use the gas, because you were testing us?"

"Yes."

"You sacrificed an entire security squad for a test?"

"That's what they're here for," Bonner replied.

"What's the second reason?"

Bonner hooked a thumb in the general direction of Mount Maleficent "You heard me tell the beetle that the harvest was delayed?"

"Yeah. So?"

With a hand wave, Bonner indicated the corpses spread out around the campsite.

"Behold the harvest."

Crockett's face twisted. "The organs. That's why Pagan was obsessed with head shots."

"Exactly. We need hearts, livers, lungs and the occasional pancreas. Infrequently, we need eyes. Since I spared you people from the harvester's knives, I had to arrange a new crop from someplace."

"You lured the Indians to you. How could you be so sure they wouldn't have harvested all of our scalps?"

"I wasn't. Hence the gas attack."

Crockett sighed, shook his head and said, "You know what's really sick about this, Django? It makes sense."

"I hoped you'd see it my way."

Quanah said grimly, "In the land of the ghoul, whoever has the most viscera wins."

A smile creased Bonner's lips. "Something like that, yes."

"You're overlooking one thing," Crockett said. "There's nothing to stop us from taking your machine, leaving you here for the Sioux to find among the mutilated bodies of their friends and relatives and going back to Loki's Rock to pick up our own vehicle."

Bonner shook an admonishing finger. "I'm surprised at you, Colonel. You're overlooking one thing. Only someone who knows the correct sequence can start up the X-MAC. If you fumble around, you'll blow it and yourselves to atoms."

"Lame bluff," Zeda husked out.

"Hardly. It's a standard security procedure to wire an antipersonnel device to the engine of a security wagon to keep thieves at bay. I'm sure your precious *Ambler* is equipped with something similar. Am I right?"

He was, and it grated on Crockett's nerves to acknowledge it. The Loki's Rock chieftain had them exactly where he wanted them. Different strategies cartwheeled through Crockett's mind. Even hijacking the X-MAC once it was underway would be a pointless exercise, since they would be forced to go in the opposite direction of Loki's Rock. And with a limited quantity of fuel and no idea where to obtain more, they would be stranded and vulnerable to the Lakota. He couldn't count on the sparing of Sam's life to save them from warriors seeking to avenge this night's slaughter

"You're right," Crockett admitted. "So what's the plan?"

"We'll harvest our crop and return to Loki's Rock at daybreak." Bonner frowned as he looked over the bodies of his security squad. "It appears that a few of our staff will have to be promoted sooner than expected."

"I'm surprised you don't want us to fill the vacancies," Crockett said sarcastically.

"Oh, by no means," Bonner replied cheerfully. "I have far greater ambitions in mind for you, Colonel. Believe me."

Crockett believed him.

CHAPTER FOURTEEN

Pagan and the battered survivors of the security squad worked the rest of the night and well into the early-morning hours, separating the victims of head and neck shots from those who bore wounds in their torsos.

Crockett was curious to see if they would remove the organs on the spot, but Pagan and her men employed another practice, no less grisly and bloody. Plastic body bags were removed from a rear compartment of the X-MAC, and three corpses were snugged inside a single bag.

Of course, the bodies were first decapitated and the arms and legs amputated in order to facilitate easy packing. The limbs and heads were tossed down the incline toward the creek. Once the torsos were crammed belly-to-butt-to-belly inside the bags and containers of dry ice emptied into them, the bags were closed with zippers and hermetic seals.

It was apparently an operation Pagan and the rest had engaged in many times before. Their skill with knives, bone saws and other surgical implements looked very efficient, born of long practice.

Quanah watched the sawing and chopping with a clinical eye. "The dry ice will burn the epidermal tissues, but it'll preserve the organs, and I suppose that's the whole point."

"Disgusting" was Alex's observation.

Crockett and his party claimed tents as far away from the scene of dismemberment as possible without leaving the safety of the X-MAC. But they were all too keyed up to sleep, and because their clothes still reeked strongly of gas, no one cared to share the close quarters of the tents. Crockett felt uncomfortable in his wet clothes, but fortunately the temperature didn't drop to an intolerable degree. Everyone sat and watched the organ harvesting and talked in low tones.

"We don't know if there's a bomb wired to the ignition," Zeda commented. "He could be bullshitting us."

"True," Alex said, "but Bonner doesn't strike me as the bluffing type."

"All bluff," Zeda declared. "Take away his ass-kissers and he's nothing but a coward."

"He's no coward," Alex objected. "He's a pragmatist, just like we are. If we weren't, we wouldn't be sitting here."

Crockett grunted. "Yeah, well, I'm not sure we should be. It might be better if we take them prisoner, try to deal with the Lakota for safe passage, or take them back to Loki's Rock and ransom them off."

"Both of those options have a certain merit," Alex said. "But I fear they appear to have similar outcomes, as well."

"With us being killed?" Quanah inquired.

Alex nodded sagely.

Around two o'clock, the torso packing was completed. True to Pagan's estimate, the wounded security man called Zeon was pronounced dead shortly thereafter. Bonner gave the order to wrap his and the other security men's bodies in canvas in preparation for the return to Loki's Rock, then he retired to the X-MAC.

Crockett drifted into a dreamless sleep, his head pillowed on his arms. He had gotten very little rest the night before, and the exertions and accumulated fatigue of the past two days caught up with him.

He was awakened almost immediately, it seemed, by Alex whispering into his ear, "Wake up, Colonel. Time to go."

Crockett opened his eyes. The blue-black backdrop of the sky was broken up by the pink and orange scraps of approaching dawn. He sat up, yawning. Alex sniffed, pinched her nostrils and said, "Phew."

"I smell bad, huh?" he asked.

Alex smiled wanly. "Well, you aren't up to Ken standards yet, but I can see the start."

The security men were breaking camp, laboring to disassemble the tents and carry the shattered lamps into the X-MAC. The one with the injured arm was hampered by a makeshift sling. Of the body bags there was no sign, but the Indian corpses that didn't fit Bonner's needs were left to lie where they had fallen.

The bodies of the slain security squad had been shrouded in canvas and were lashed to the roof of the vehicle. All of Crockett's team were baggy-eyed and disheveled. None of them had caught so much as a catnap, and Crockett experienced a momentary pang of guilt. As it was, he didn't feel the slightest bit refreshed. He felt rusty and mean.

One of the security men strode over to them. "Knock down your tents and pack 'em out."

Crockett rose stiffly to his feet. "You knock 'em down."

The security man's eyes were rimmed and netted with red. He probably hadn't gotten any sleep either. His growled retort was full of menace. "You heard me, Oldworlder."

"I've got a better idea," Crockett said. "How about I knock *you* down and pack *you* out," and he hit the man as hard as he could in the middle of the belly.

He doubled over, mewling. His hands clutched at his stomach convulsively, his breath fought to get back into his lungs. Sweat sprang out on his forehead.

"Let's get some breakfast," Crockett said, walking around the bent-over security man and toward the X-MAC. His friends followed him.

Bonner sat inside the passenger area, looking fresh and clear-eyed. He greeted them with a rousing, "Good morning, good morning!"

He gestured to a hot plate on a shelf where a pot of delicious-smelling coffee warmed and sweet rolls were stacked on a tray. "Help yourselves."

After washing down a roll with a cup of the coffee, Crockett felt a little more human, albeit a very smelly, short-tempered and unshaven one. Bonner didn't bother chatting with them, for which everyone was grateful.

After Pagan and what was left of her security squad boarded the X-MAC, Bonner assigned two of the men to the control cockpit. The man whom Crockett had belly-punched passed him, steadfastly avoiding eye contact.

The broken-armed man sat near one of the M-200 mini-cannons, and Pagan sat beside the other. Since there was much more room in the back on the return trip, Zeda stretched out across several of the chairs, her head in Quanah's lap. Alex, who appeared so exhausted as to be ill, lay down on the facing row of seats and fell asleep immediately.

"Let's roll," Bonner commanded.

The engine of the X-MAC caught on the second try, and though he tried, Crockett didn't see the driver's preliminary start-up sequence, which, presumably, prevented the vehicle from self-destructing.

13 Orionis rose clear of the horizon by the time the X-MAC rumbled from the mouth of the valley and onto the flatlands.

Without preamble, Bonner announced, "Colonel, I'm naming you a scion of the Loki's Rock. Your official function will be to serve as warlord and adviser."

From the corner of his eye, Crockett caught Pagan whipping her head around in astonished outrage.

"You will share the title on equal footing with Pagan," Bonner went on smoothly. "And she should not have any objections, inasmuch as you saved her life last night."

Bonner stared past Crockett's shoulder at Pagan. "I am correct, am I not? My eyes didn't deceive me?"

Pagan murmured in a subdued tone, "You're correct. It's all in order. *Treu, Tapfer, Gehorsam, Reinheit.*"

Crockett uttered a short, weary laugh. "I appreciate the honor, Django. However, I respectfully decline it."

"And I appreciate your candor, if not your ignorance. Unfortunately, you can't decline it without declining your life and that of your friends."

Crockett sighed. "I'm fed up with your threats, Django."

He made a move to pull his weapon, but Bonner threw up his hands in exasperation.

"Guns! Always with the guns! Put that goddamn thing away, Colonel--I'm not threatening you. By bestowing this rank upon you, I'm making you an untouchable, sacrosanct, blessed. You're protected, understand? If you turn me down and try to go on your way, you'll be fair game for every bladester, bulleteer and chopmonger in the Hellgrounds. Word will go out ahead of you. Your mission will end before it really begins."

Crockett opened his mouth to respond, but Bonner held up a hand. "I know what you're going say, but I'm sorry, but the traditions, the protocols of *Treu, Tapfer, Gehorsam* and *Reinheit* must be observed, or I place my position in jeopardy. I don't want to hurt you, Crockett--I want to help you."

"What do you expect us to do?" Quanah demanded. "Stay in Loki's Rock forever, so your population of scumbags won't come after us?"

Bonner shook his head. "Hardly. I have a business proposition for you."

Crockett guessed the answer to the question he put to Bonner, but he asked it anyway. It seemed to be expected. "Which is?"

Bonner shifted in his seat. "It's difficult for me to maintain the level of respect I deserve because I trade with the Oldworld frozones up Hitler's nose for everything we have in Loki's Rock. Some high-ranking citizens are a bit disheartened by the fact that our very survival depends on those holdovers from Earth."

Bonner's expression became vaguely disconcerted. "Believe me, the Brigadefuhrer and the other frozone swine up there are a much greater menace to restoring the health of this world than Loki's Rock could ever be."

Quanah snorted. "You're breeding a generation of kill-crazy maniacs. You're *not* a menace?"

Bonner ignored him. "I want--I need--those Oldworlders out of the way and I need you to help me do it."

"How so?" Crockett asked. "You've got a pocket-sized army at your disposal. They're fairly well trained and very well armed, aren't they?"

"Yes, but there has to be an arsenal up there in the nose. As far as I know, they may have guided missiles to nuke Loki's Rock from afar."

"What about a siege?"

"Same answer. From their vantage point, an assault force would be cut to pieces, and there would be no more trading."

"That's really what's worrying you, isn't it?"

Bonner tugged nervously at his mustache. "Of course it is. If we could stage a successful assault, we'd never have to trade again. Loki's Rock would have everything it ever needs. There's a vast treasure of Oldworld tech sitting up there, just out of reach."

"Do you have anything approximating a plan?" Crockett inquired.

Bonner pinched the air between a thumb and a forefinger. "A germ of one. For it to succeed, it requires courage, cunning and a warrior's intrepidity. Which all of you possess in enviable amounts."

"Assuming just for the moment, that we're inclined to go along with you," Crockett said, "what's in it for us?"

"You don't seem like a fool, Colonel, but you certainly can sound like one. 'What's in it for us,' he asks." Bonner thrust his head toward Crockett. "What do you think? You'll be rewarded beyond your wildest dreams of avarice. If you're successful and you care to remain with us, you'll enjoy a position in Loki's Rock second only to my own. If you wish to continue on your journey, I'll grant you a special dispensation. Everyone will be so happy with the new toys, they won't question any decisions I make. We'll be the most powerful settlement in the Hellgrounds, maybe even on the whole planet."

"And if we're not successful," Quanah said, "you can always claim we were wild-assed mercenaries in the employ of the Commonwealth, not connected to Loki's Rock at all, operating without your sanction or knowledge."

Bonner smiled. "The Oldworlders called it plausible deniability. Isn't that a lovely phrase?"

"The frozones in the nose may not believe you, lovely phrases or not," Crockett pointed out.

"That's an acceptable part of the risk."

Glancing over his shoulder, Crockett exchanged a quick look with Quanah who only shrugged. He turned back to Bonner.

"I'm too tired to give your proposition the consideration it deserves. Let us get back to Loki's Rock, rest up and have a chance to discuss it among ourselves."

"A fair proposal," Bonner replied. "From the moment we reach Loki's Rock, you have thirty-six hours to reach a decision."

"And if you don't like our decision?"

Bonner replied with a smiling face, but there was no humor in his tone. "Then I'll be forced to make one of my own."

CHAPTER FIFTEEN

They arrived back in Loki's Rock shortly before noon. The driver of the X-MAC maneuvered it into a gated, walled-in compound behind the Bitter End, parking the vehicle between *Ambler* and a pair of open-canopied dune buggies.

There was a fueling station with two gasoline pumps situated on a concrete apron in the center of the lot. Two security men armed with compact Tak-10 machine pistols walked sentry.

Everyone disembarked and trooped to the saloon. Pagan beckoned to the compound guards to help carry the bodies out of the X-MAC.

Upstairs, Alex and Zeda made it plain that baths were their first priority. Quanah opted for a nap. Crockett, who felt soiled and grungy, checked in with Syne at *Ambler*, collected a fresh shirt, pants and a razor then went to the first-floor bathroom.

The tub was old and deep, but it was equipped with running water. A cake of homemade soap the size of a ham sat on a stool. Crockett filled the tub with hot water, removed his clothes and eased his body into it. He sighed with relief. For a few minutes he occupied himself with the ordeal of shaving by feel. He nicked himself twice before he'd rid his face of the stubble.

He scrubbed himself with the soap until his skin prickled, then lay back, closing his eyes, hoping some of the tension and worry would ease from his muscles and mind. He was on the verge of dozing off when he heard the bathroom door click open. He reached for his Hawken on the stool.

"No need for that, Colonel."

Pagan, wearing a pink silk wrapper, the cuffs of the voluminous sleeves edged with brightly colored feathers, leaned against the door frame. With her long hair tumbling about her shoulders, she looked surprisingly feminine, despite the eye patch.

"What are you doing here?" Crockett demanded. Unconsciously his knees drew together.

With an easy smile, the woman replied, "I want a bath. No one told me this one was occupied."

"As you can see," Crockett said, "it is. Close the door on the way out."

"All right," Pagan said, but she didn't seem inclined to hurry.

Crockett angled an eyebrow at her. "Something?"

"That tub looks very accommodating. I think it might hold two."

"Let's agree to test that theory another time."

Instead, Pagan strode forward. She casually raised the hem of her wrapper, sat on the lip of the tub, swung her legs over the top and plunged her feet into the water.

"What do you want?" he demanded.

"If we're to share the title of Loki's Rock's warlord, we need to talk."

"I haven't made up my mind about accepting the appointment, yet."

"That's what we have to talk about, Colonel."

"Why?" he asked.

Pagan's face acquired a solemn, quiet expression. "I don't care to share my position with anyone, unless it's someone I can trust."

"Makes sense."

"And I can't trust someone who doesn't know where I came from, or how I came to be."

"Tell me, then."

"When I was twelve, I was crossing the Steppes with my parents, as part of an overland wagon train. We were heading for a fishing settlement on the coast. Turned out our guides led us into a trap. A gang of bandits swept down out of the hills and killed everybody."

"Except you," Crockett said.

"Except me. Since slavery was one of their sidelines, they figured they could trade me to Captain Caracortada."

"That's the second time I've heard that name," replied Crockett. "Who is Caracortada?"

"Pray you never find out." Pagan repressed a shudder and Crockett didn't feel it was feigned. "I tried to escape several times...the last time, I got this." She touched the patch covering her eye. "One of the bandits buttstroked me with his rifle. He was a little too enthusiastic, and I was instantly damaged goods."

"They didn't trade you to Caracortada, after all?"

The corners of Pagan's lips twitched in a small, bitter smile. "They didn't have the opportunity. The very next day a war party of Lakota swooped down. They butchered the bandits just like the bandits had butchered the people on the wagon train."

"Let the punishment fit the crime," Crockett intoned. "What did the Lakota do to you?"

"They took me with them. They knew I was a prisoner, so they more or less rescued me. They took care of me."

"How long did you stay with them?"

Pagan frowned. "Can't say for certain. Four years at least, maybe five. It wasn't a bad life, though we were on the move a lot. I learned their language, they taught me to hunt, to track, to use weapons. To kill."

"How did you hook up with Bonner and his crew?"

"We came across Django and his people struggling through a mountain pass in the winter. There weren't very many of them, and they were slowly starving to death. Django wasn't taking any food, but gave what little they had to the strongest members. They were even eating their own shoes. My band of Lakota took pity on them and allowed them to share the winter camp."

Pagan closed her eye, as if viewing the past. "Django and I made an instant connection. I knew, somehow, that he was a born leader, a messiah who would carve an empire out of Hellgrounds, one who would rule forever. I was shown that my white blood was far superior to that of the savages I'd been living with."

Disgust welled up within Crockett. He guessed that Bonner had psi-scanned everyone in the Indian village and found Pagan's mind the most malleable, the easiest to influence.

"Django and one of the tribal leaders, Sky Wolf, agreed to a pact," Pagan went on. "The Lakota would allow the whites to remain in this country as long as they didn't go anywhere near Mount Maleficent."

"The Lakota knew about the Institute?" Crockett asked.

Pagan opened her eye. "Oh, yes. It was a source of great anger to them. They viewed the frozones as undead monstrosities, surviving inside a monument to the Oldworld evils that they had hoped were forever destroyed."

"Of course," Crockett said with a mocking smile, "Django broke the pact at the first opportunity."

"And why not?" Pagan demanded, her eye suddenly shining with near-religious fervor. "Who are the red savages to order their genetic superiors around?"

"This is their land, for one thing." A thought suddenly occurred to him. "Was Willy Bill part of Bonner's group?"

"Yes," Pagan admitted reluctantly. "He fell in love with Sky Wolf's sister, Many Stars. When Django left the Indian camp, Willy Bill took Many Stars with him."

"And you went, too?"

"Of course. It was my destiny, wasn't it?"

"I think I understand now," Crockett said. "When Sky Wolf saw Django had made a beeline for Mount Maleficent, he feared that he would ally himself with the frozones up there. A war party followed you, a fight broke out, Many Stars escaped and the seeds of the hatred between Django and the Lakota were planted. Then, of course, by the time Many Stars gave birth, Loki's Rock was established and Willy Bill returned to the Indians."

Pagan nodded. "And eventually he was cast out. He returned to Loki's

Rock but Django would only have him back if he rolled the bones. He gambled his eyes and lost. But he ran off again."

"That's all very complicated," Crockett said dourly. "And ugly."

"That's all past, Colonel. We need to discuss your future with Loki's Rock."

"I don't see much of one, Pagan."

"You had better, or you won't have any future at all. That goes for all of your people, including your pet Gypsy Mind Sifter."

Forcing down his anger, Crockett took a deep breath and said, "I'm listening. What's your take on my future as co-warlord of Loki's Rock?"

Pagan leaned forward, her hand moving beneath the surface of the water to stroke Crockett's thigh. "After the ceremony, when your appointment is made official, you and I will enter into a contract. A bonding."

"Like a marriage?" He found himself responding to her touch.

"Somewhat. My life belongs to you now, Colonel. Together we will expand Loki's Rock's influence, especially after you win the tech inside Mount Maleficent. You, me and Django will be the most powerful people in the Hellgrounds."

"You're forgetting a few things," Crockett said, trying to get control of his body. "I have a mission to perform and a responsibility to my people."

Pagan lifted the corner of her mouth in a half-smirk, half-smile. "They'll enjoy a privileged status in Loki's Rock. That's equitable enough, isn't it?"

"No. Because whatever I decide, the arrangement you're talking about will never happen."

Pagan moved her hand farther up his thigh. Her fingers brushed his testicles, and her smile widened. "Don't let your pride lead you into making a foolish choice, Colonel. After you're with me for one night, you won't want any other kind of arrangement."

As her hand made a move to caress his penis, Crockett grabbed her by the wrist and yanked her arm, jerking her into the water. He used more force than was necessary, and she cried out in surprised anger.

"Get out of here," he said, his tone containing a deep, rumbling tone of menace.

She didn't try to wrest away from his grip. "Our lives are intertwined now," she said, a note of urgency in her voice. "Mutual destinies. Between us, we have three eyes and can see further than anyone. We'll share one vision. Don't you understand?"

"I understand perfectly. Your life is your own. And I don't need another eye to see the truth." He paused, then added, "You're a sociopathic, narcissistic bitch. Your idea of loyalty lasts only as long you benefit from it."

He released her. Pagan stood in a rush and stepped from the tub. "You've made an enemy today, Colonel. Maybe the last one in your life."

Crockett expected her to slam the door behind her, but instead she closed it with a quiet click. He swore and concentrated on regaining his sense of comfort. It wasn't easy. His mouth was dry, his heart beat fast and a part of his body still reacted to the touch of the woman—and not to his disgust and anger with her.

When the water turned cold, he was grateful for it. His body soon answered to his mind again. He climbed out of the tub, dried off and dressed quickly.

Back upstairs in his room, he found Quanah, Alex, Zeda and Syne all present, sharing coffee and sandwiches. "Good, you're here. I was going to schedule a tactical meeting anyway and there's no time like the present."

Zeda stood up as if to leave, but Crockett said, "I prefer you stay—if you've thrown your lot in with us, you need to know what you're in for."

"I'd like to know that myself," Alex said with rueful smile.

Crockett told everyone about his encounter with Pagan. No one made any jokes, for which he was grateful, but Alex's eyes narrowed.

"Do you figure Bonner sent her?" Quanah asked.

"I doubt it. She trotted out the old 'my life is yours' line, even though crawfishing on debts seems to be part of Loki's Rock's basic philosophy despite all the straight games Django cites."

Zeda intoned, "Never play cards with a man called Honest John."

Crockett smiled. "Exactly."

"What do you do?" Zeda asked. "Be the warlord?"

"It very much appears that is your sole option," Alex said. "Otherwise..." She drew a thumb across her throat.

"If I accept the offer," Crockett replied, "then we'll be bound to take on Bonner's mission to breach the Institute. Syne, do you know how much of Bonner's story about the installation can be matched up with actual history?"

Syne shook his head. "Some of it, perhaps none of it. Until we can find and access the database in the Enclave, there is no way to know. Since the technology existed to create human-machine hybrid organisms over two centuries ago, I don't find the concept of bionically altered Oldworlders living in a cryonically controlled stronghold all that improbable."

"If it is true," Quanah said contemplatively, "we could have access to possibly the only stockpile of advanced technology left on Loki. We could write our own tickets, anywhere on the planet."

"And Django Bonner can and will punch those tickets," Alex said grimly. "We can't trust him to keep his word."

"It is a rigged game he wants us to play," Syne said. "And there is only one way to win at a rigged game. That is not to play at all."

"Or rig the game in our favor," Crockett replied. "Any suggestions?"

"Kill Bonner," Zeda said.

"That'll be our final hand to play. No, I think our best tactic is to keep a low profile for the next three days. Maybe during that time we can find a hidden ace and stack the deck."

"And if we can't?" Alex challenged. "Then what?"

"Then I'll accept the appointment to warlord and we'll go from there."

Quanah shook his head in frustration. "I hope this teaches us to be more careful about paying attention to warnings we get from hair lifters we meet in the woods."

Crockett nodded thoughtfully. "That's one way of looking at it."

CHAPTER SIXTEEN

Crockett and his people saw and heard nothing from Bonner throughout the remainder of the afternoon or the following day. They walked around, sampling the sights, sounds and tastes of Loki's Rock, and tried to ward off the fingers of dread and apprehension clutching at them.

Zeda was the most impatient. She felt claustrophobic and more than a little trapped. She sorely wanted to jump in *Ambler* and tear out of there, with no regard for the consequences, shooting, slashing and slugging anyone who stood in their way. However, she was intelligent enough to realize that the five of them were enmeshed too tightly in Bonner's web to escape safely.

On the evening of the second day, Crockett was summoned to the Bitter End taproom by Django Bonner. Barbie gave him a sidewise glare as he passed. Pagan studiously avoided looking in his direction.

Without preamble, Bonner said, "At seven-thirty tomorrow evening I will have your decision. A war council has been called and your attendance is mandatory."

"What if I make up my mind before then?" Crockett asked.

"Then you'll wait until the council convenes, Colonel. I do not grant private audiences on war council days. You may go now."

Though he earnestly tried to conceive of a plan through that night and most of the next day, Crockett could not come up with a suitable strategy to delay making the decision.

The jaws of the Loki's Rock trap had snapped shut neatly and painlessly, but very securely.

He saw no other choice but to go through with the pretense of accepting the position of warlord. Gloomily, none of his companions could offer an alternative, either, except to engage in a firefight that would cost lives.

At seven o'clock, a little after twilight, Crockett checked over *Ambler* before going to the Bitter End. Pagan sauntered around the corner of the building and when she caught sight of him, a hesitant, almost shy smile played over the finely chiseled planes of her face.

"Evening, Colonel," she said.

Tension lizards crawled along the buttons of his spine, but Crockett returned the smile.

"Evening."

Casually he placed his right hand on his hip, just above the butt of the Hawken. If Pagan caught the movement, she gave no sign.

Taking a deep breath, she said, "I regret the incident the other day. I was out of line, expecting you to abide by customs that are new to you. I apologize."

Crockett said nothing.

"Django has finally decided upon a plan to get inside the Ahnenerbe."

"Good."

"Will you be a part of it?"

"I'll tell that to Django."

Pagan nodded, and as Crockett made a move to step around her, she said hurriedly, "Not all of our security force has assembled. We're missing one."

"Who might that be?" Instantly Crockett regretted asking the question.

"You know him. Barbie." Seeing his eyes narrow, she added, "He's addicted to a certain vice. He'll be up to his ears in it by now, and somebody has to get him in shape for the council. He respects you. Maybe you can see to it."

It was such an obvious attempt at entrapment that Crockett almost spit on the toes of her boots. "Why should I? I'm not a truant officer."

"You may not realize it, but your position in Loki's Rock is very precarious. Django doesn't trust you. If you bring Barbie in, he may alter his thinking and believe you're cooperating on your own free will. Besides, it's the duty of a warlord to look after the warriors."

Crockett stared unblinkingly into Pagan's single eye for a long silent moment. She stared back. He asked, "Where can I find him?"

Pagan hooked a thumb over her left shoulder. "Last house on the last lane." She smiled cryptically. "Be prepared to use your fists, Colonel. Barbie may not want to come."

Crockett smiled just as cryptically. "I'll do my best."

He walked around her, down the dusky, dusty streets of Loki's Rock. Going along with Pagan's flimsy story was a big risk, but he couldn't back down in front of her, nor could he resist the urge to find out what she had planned.

He followed a twisting side lane, passing a number of shoddy shanties at the far end of the path. He heard the faint whine of reedy music emanating from the last of the slapdash structures. It was little more than a lean-to, with crudely hewn clapboard walls and a door hanging crookedly from leather hinges.

As he approached it, keeping to the lengthening shadows, the door banged open and a man stumbled out into the lane. Crockett stepped back in the murk, not moving, hand resting lightly on his Hawken. The man passed within a few feet of him, and by the light of the rising moon and the setting sun, Crockett saw his face.

It was the face of a mindless brute. Crockett had seen more intelligence in the eyes of animals. The man mumbled to himself as he staggered, then barked out a snarl of a laugh. Drool-strings stretched from his lower lip.

With a thrill of loathing, Crockett realized that the vice Pagan had spoken of was Cannabis Lupus, the so-called werewolf weed. According to the reports he had read, it was a rare drug, hard to find even in the hinterlands of the Hellgrounds.

Composed of a mutated form of marijuana and various hallucinogens, the werewolf weed stimulated the hindbrain, causing an atavistic regression. It was at the same time an unpopular and popular drug. Its sole attraction for the user was to wallow in artificial bestiality for a time. Crockett had read that some bands of marauders appreciated its influence before a raid, since it made them fearless and predatory. Unfortunately they would just as soon turn on their own comrades as an enemy while in its brutal grip.

Crockett catfooted up to the shanty and peered into the open door. The yellow glow of a lamp was dimmed by a wall of hot, acrid smoke. A skinny man playing a wooden flute crouched in a corner. On the floor lay a number of naked men and women, limbs entangled as they engaged in various sex acts. Their faces were slack, they growled like animals, they clawed and bit and slapped at each other. He saw no sign of Barbie.

Stomach churning with sour bile, Crockett turned away and headed back up the path. A scuffling of feet from the shadows to his right drew his attention. He fisted his blaster and whirled.

A stooping, naked figure crept out of the pool of darkness. For a moment Crockett didn't recognize the slack-jawed, blank-eyed, gape-mouthed face. Then, with a surge of revulsion, he recognized the naked man as Barbie. Crockett stepped back. Barbie shambled forward, a grin splitting his foam-flecked lips.

"Stay back," Crockett warned. "I'll kill you where you stand."

Barbie didn't seem to hear or care. In his regression, he probably didn't even recognize the purpose of the Hawken aimed at him. He laughed, a deep, wet, slobbery sound.

Crockett backpedaled carefully, his finger on the trigger, even though he knew full well the repercussions of killing Barbie. Pagan had set a very neat trap.

If he, an outsider, killed Barbie, she would demand bloody retribution. It would be a legal execution, since Bonner hadn't yet officially named him a scion of Loki's Rock. And if he didn't kill Barbie, the man was sure to murder him. Either way he would be removed from the equation, and Pagan would be restored to her former status as the sole warlord.

Crockett considered shooting to wound, but he knew that powered by the drug, even a 50 caliber slug in an arm or leg would be only an insect sting to Barbie. There was really only one option.

Crockett pivoted and took to his heels, running full-out toward Loki's Rock. If he could reach the saloon so that Bonner could see Barbie pursuing him, there would be no question that he killed the man in self-defense.

But he didn't get anywhere near the Bitter End. He barely reached the mouth of the lane. Barbie was more than half animal now, and with his slobbering snarls sounding in his ears, Crockett heard him loping swiftly behind him.

Trying to force more speed into his pumping legs, Crockett increased the length of his stride. In less than a hundred feet, Barbie caught up to him.

One hand locked in Crockett's hair and the other gripped the back of his neck with an agonizing pressure. He tried to fight free, but he staggered, losing his balance on the uneven ground.

He went down heavily. His head struck the ground, and the Hawken clattered and bounced from his grasp. Still, Crockett continued to roll, throwing his body in a frantic somersault toward the lights of Loki's Rock.

Barbie landed on him with his full weight, his teeth sinking into the collar of his shirt. Crockett hammered at the frothing face pressed against his, not giving in to the impulse to cry out in pain.

Talon-like nails raked at his face, and knees jacked into his midsection, seeking his groin.

Barbie swarmed all over him, pounding, clawing and savaging. Snarls and thick-throated laughter filled his ears as Crockett struggled to shake him off.

Barbie grabbed handfuls of Crockett's hair and banged his head against the ground, once, twice, three times. Maybe more. Crockett was unable to count beyond the third time.

He tried to draw up his legs, hoping to get in at least one solid kick, but Barbie was all slavering madness, his steely fingers shifting from Crockett's hair to his throat. He struck in a blind frenzy of desperation, but Barbie did not feel the blows.

Crockett stretched out one arm, groping for his pistol and his fingers brushed a rough, pitted surface. His right hand closed around it and he heaved up a rock the size of a small pumpkin. Not even trying to gauge the accuracy of the blows, he smashed the rock again and again against the side of Barbie's head.

The man uttered a peculiar growling yelp, and the death grip on Crockett's throat relaxed a bit. With his free hand, Crockett slammed the steely fingers away. Barbie bounded up and away from him, using Crockett's torso as a springboard, and very nearly drove all the wind from his lungs.

Crockett scrambled to his feet, bleeding, sick and dizzy, while Barbie crouched on the ground only a few feet away. Blood streaked the side of his face and dripped down over his cheeks and mouth. A laceration in his forehead leaked twin scarlet streams down either side of his nose. He touched the blood with his fingers, sniffed it, then put his fingers in his mouth, sucking them clean.

Snarling, Barbie glared at Crockett, eyes gleaming balefully. His muscles tensed and coiled, then he sprang out of his crouch directly at Crockett's throat.

Instead of trying to avoid the leap, Crockett bounded forward, rock-weighted right hand swinging forward in a short, adrenaline-charged arc. The arc ended as the rock caught Barbie in the center of his scarred, sallow face.

He howled as the force of the blow drove him flailing ten feet across the ground. The force also crushed his nose, driving the bone splinters through his sinus cavities, then into what was left of his brain.

Barbie jerked, twitched and rolled in the dust. He came up to his knees, blood flowing from his nose. He opened his mouth as if to voice another howl, and a crimson torrent spilled past his lips, splashing on the ground. His eyes lifted to stare skyward, then he fell face first to the ground.

Crockett stood and watched as Barbie's death spasms slowly ceased. He gasped in lungfuls of air and probed gingerly at the raw abrasions on his face. Every tendon, every muscle in his body burned with pain. His head throbbed, in cadence with his pulse. The world tilted around him and he sank to his knees.

Then voices roared, shouted and cursed all around him. Rough hands hauled him to his feet. He blinked his eyes against the glare of torches and flashlights. Around him he could see the security men of Loki's Rock, their faces contorted with fury and outrage.

"The son of a bitch murdered Barbie!" a woman shouted.

" Hold him, gimme my knife!" shrilled a male voice that Crockett recognized as Phil's.

Crockett struggled against the hands and arms pinioning him, but he was held fast. Pagan, silhouetted by the flickering torchlight, came striding toward him.

"It's like I said," she shouted. "He's a Commonwealth spy, an insurgent, an Oldworld hired killer!"

"You're a liar," Crockett croaked. "Barbie was a drugged animal, and you set me up to kill him, you—"

The back of Pagan's hand smacked across Crockett's mouth. He reeled backward and spit crimson at her feet.

"Blood for blood!" Pagan shouted. "It's the justice of Loki's Rock, it is the way of *Treu, Tapfer, Gehorsam, Reinheit!*"

Then Bonner was there, his face hidden by the shadows, but light reflected from his eyes like a pair of tiny stars.

118

"What is going on here, Crockett?" he demanded.

Pagan began shrieking before Crockett could collect his wits. She began a furious tirade about how Crockett was deceiving Bonner and everyone in Loki's Rock, how he had been plotting to betray them to the frozones in Mount Maleficent, about how he was on a secret mission from the Commonwealth, how he had tried to convince Barbie to turn traitor, cold-bloodedly murdering the hapless security man when he was in a sedated condition, simply because he refused to be party to the treachery.

Crockett snapped, "She lies, Django... she hates me because I saved her life and then spurned her—"

Pagan's fist struck Crockett painfully and with terrific force in the belly, robbing him of all breath. He sagged in the grips of the men holding him. Bonner motioned for Crockett's captors to release him. He found that his legs wouldn't support him and he fell to his hands and knees, hanging his head and sucking in lungful after lungful of air.

Bonner patiently waited for Crockett to stand up again before he spoke. His angular face was expressionless, but he was in a bind, and Crockett saw the knowledge of it in his eyes.

He did not believe Pagan's accusations, and he still had a use for Crockett and his people. However, he had to assert his patriarchal status in the eyes of the citizenry of Loki's Rock.

"I want no more violence between you two. If you're making me choose between the pair of you, it'll have to be settled in combat."

Pagan said angrily, "He's an outsider! We kill outsiders who violate our laws. He hasn't earned the right."

"*Shut up!*" Bonner roared. He whipped his pair of revolvers from his sash and swept the bores over the crowd. They drew back and fell silent.
The unexpected fracture in his icy, controlled reserve startled everyone into shamed silence. "I'm ceding him the right! I'll put off the war council until this matter is settled."

Pagan ducked her head and murmured, "I beg forgiveness."

Then a smile crossed her face. She eyed Crockett with a murderous glee and declared, "A track stand."

Crockett didn't say anything for a moment. He remembered what he had overheard of track stands—two combatants, both astride bullet bikes, each armed with only a whip, a knife and the individual warrior's skill. He wasn't at all certain he was qualified. His experience with hover bikes was limited. He hadn't ridden one since he his teenaged years in Montana. Nor was he confident he could handle Pagan, a trained killer whose crazed ego demanded Crockett's life.

119

"Well?" Bonner challenged. "Are you up to it?"

Crockett wiped a thread of blood from his lower lip, surveyed the expectant faces all around him and said, "Name the time and place."

CHAPTER SEVENTEEN

Crockett awoke at dawn, feeling as if all the bones in his body were stitched together at the joints by wire. Everyone was awake, and they crowded into the room he shared with Quanah.

Alex brought him coffee, and Zeda handed over the curve-bladed Khanjarli dagger. "I've spent the last hour sharpening it," she said. "It ought to cut through plate steel."

"Or that bitch's throat," Alex said coldly.

Crockett and Quanah swung their heads toward her in surprise. She looked from one to the other and asked with feigned innocence, "What?"

Heavy footfalls sounded out in the hall, and a knock came at the door. Crockett opened it. Four security men, all holding Tak-10 machine pistols, stood there. Phil was in the lead.

"We're here to escort you to the track," he said in a clipped, businesslike tone "Everybody leaves their blasters here."

Crockett exchanged a long, warning look with Alex. Her finger tensed on the trigger of her TX5, but with a grimace, she tossed the weapon onto the bed.

Phil jerked his head toward the hallway. "Let's go."

"Is the escort a courtesy?" Quanah asked, putting on his hat. "Or a guard detail?"

"None of your fucking business, you red-skinned sack of shit."

Quanah smiled gently and tapped the side of his head with a forefinger. "I shall remember you said that, white boy."

A carnival air hung over the gathering in the large open field a half mile outside of Loki's Rock. Children squealed and chased one another, climbing over the mothers who were dressed in holiday finery. Most of the Gypsies were in attendance. There were scarves, headbands, shawls and quilted cloaks of every conceivable color and style. The men wore deerskin tunics, ruffled silk shirts and talismans of animal claws and mummified human fingers.

Crockett shivered in the cool air of early morning and inspected the field of battle. It was the same area where Willy Bill had been forced to run for his life a few nights before, but all signs of the ceremony had been removed. A dozen poles, ornamented with colored glass prisms and feathers, formed the boundaries of a giant circle, at least a hundred yards in diameter.

Two hover cycles were parked at opposite ends of the field. Syne identified them as Comet Model Bullet Bikes, manufactured by the Hiflite Corporation well over a century before. Both were clean and seemingly in good running condition. One was painted red, the other a deep black.

Phil indicated the red bike with the barrel of his Tak 10. "That one is yours, Colonel."

Syne gave it a quick inspection, checking the turbines, the fuel system and the transmission. "Looks in good shape, Colonel. So far, I think they're playing fair."

Bonner arrived, borne in his chair by a three-man detail. They placed him atop the boulder. The huge carved rock presented an obstacle as well as a viewing station. Bonner caught his eye and beckoned to him with a finger.

Alex led the rest of the team toward the throng at the sidelines and Crockett joined Pagan as she stood before Bonner. There were no words of encouragement, no lectures about the abiding by the rules. He merely studied them silently with his hooded eyes, and then he raised a hand. The eager throng ringing the field voiced a great wordless shout and the two combatants trotted toward their mounts.

Pagan jogged toward the far end of the field and straddled the seat of her hover cycle. She quickly kicked it into roaring life, and a man handed her a whip and her Bowie knife. She grasped the whip in her right hand and placed the long knife between her teeth.

Taking a deep breath, Crockett received the whip from a security man, coiled it in his right hand and slid the dagger halfway between his crotch and the bike's seat. He experimented with it until he had the weapon in a position where he could easily and quickly grasp the handle.

Bonner drew his pistols, pointing them overhead. After sweeping his cold stare over Crockett and Pagan, he squeezed the trigger of both revolvers simultaneously. The booming echoes of the twin reports were swallowed up by a gleeful roar from the crowd.

Crockett shifted his Bullet Bike into gear. At the opposite end of the field, Pagan engaged the rear jets of her own mount and rode toward him, the engine humming. He moved out into the field, testing the gears, heading toward his adversary at an oblique angle.

Pagan turned straight toward him, on a collision course, the whip lashing out. Crockett evaded the steel tip by ducking low and activating the rear rocket jets. He jumped the cycle out of her path. Pagan hurtled past, almost to the edge of the field.

Swerving expertly, lifting the nose up, she brought the bike around without the a break in her momentum. A volley of cheers and a medley of whistles broke from the spectators.

Crockett was impressed, but he wasted no time gaping at her. Throttling up, he crouched behind the control bars and swooped at Pagan before she could realign her hover jets and upshift.

She evidently expected such a tactic, because her whip flailed out and opened a rent in the left sleeve of Crockett's shirt. It stung like liquid fire, but the skin remained intact. As he turned the bars, abruptly changing direction, his cycle's bullet-shaped nose struck Pagan's machine a glancing blow. She swayed in the saddle but managed to keep her balance.

Whirling the whip over his head, Crockett snapped its weighted end toward her. She avoided the strike by leaning gracefully to one side.

The two hover cycles whirled apart, churning up a great cloud of dust. Pagan roared up the field. Crockett massaged his left arm and directed his Bullet Bike to follow in her wake. The observers shouted their approval.

The battle of skill went on as 13 Orionis rose higher over the horizon. The two machines and circled, feinted, raced at each other, hurtled at appallingly unsafe speeds around the field. Twice Crockett was nearly forced out of the ring by Pagan's bikemanship. Once, she nearly caused him to pile up against the base of the boulder.

Dust hung heavily in the air, like curtains of dirty lace. Crockett rolled through one of the curtains, which induced a short coughing spell. With his right hand, he tried to wave the grit and dirt particles away from his face.

Pagan chose that instant to ride up on his right side, lashing at him all the while, her hair flying in tangled witch locks around her head. The whip ripped Crockett's pants and the thigh beneath it. Another stroke raised a blood-edged welt across his rib cage. He managed to catch the snaking metal end of the whip. He gave it a yank, at the same time feeding the Bullet Bike more throttle. Pagan had to release the whip's handle or be pulled from her mount.

She relinquished it with a screamed obscenity, then pursued him with her Bowie knife held high. Sweat pouring down his face, the wind whistling in his throat, Crockett kept up the acceleration, roaring up, then down, then diagonally across the field, never giving Pagan a clear opportunity with her knife.

Pagan came abreast of him, on his left, and struck with her knife. Crockett managed to block the disemboweling thrust with the handle of his whip, but in doing so he was nearly unseated. He was forced to drop the lash and had to keep both hands on the bar grips to maintain his balance on the violently wobbling machine.

Pagan crowded him, backing the Bullet Bike to the edge of the field. She hacked at him with her Bowie, and he parried her thrusts with Zeda's Khanjarli. Although the knife had a broader blade, it was all Crockett could do to block Pagan's swipes and stabbing thrusts. A couple got through his guard and opened superficial cuts on his right forearm.

Trying to maneuver away from her, he felt himself slipping out of the saddle, losing control of the bike. All Pagan had to do was ride hard and bump his bike with her own,   and he would be sprawled out on the ground, helpless. Crockett fought to hang on, to keep the Bowie from spilling his guts all over the field.

She slashed at him again, the knife inscribing a figure-eight pattern through the air, and he felt the cold fire of a graze across his left shoulder blade. Ignoring the ticklish sensation of flowing blood, he raised the dagger to parry another thrust from the Bowie.

Steel hilt locked against steel hilt with a clear musical note. She maintained the pressure, pushing against his knife with all her strength, their sweaty, dirt-streaked faces only inches away from each other.

The strain against the force exerted by Pagan overbalanced him, and Crockett had no choice but to drop his weapon or fall. Letting go of the dagger, he twisted his torso to one side, and the Bowie blade skimmed past his upper arm, the point snagging and tearing the cloth.

Pagan was unable to react in time, and she nearly toppled face first from the saddle.

Putting both hands on the grips and twisting the nose to the right, Crockett cut back on the throttle at the same time.

The woman sped past him and Crockett slipped out of the trap, gliding off in the opposite direction. He regained control of his mount, wincing at the pain in his shoulder blade, concentrating on a new problem.

Pagan knew he had dropped his Khanjarli, and when she charged him again, she would be completely on the offensive, doing her best to slice, stab, eviscerate and decapitate him.

Crockett's quick assessment was correct. Pagan staged sortie after sortie, swinging her Bowie, her single eye ablaze with triumph and fury.

To evade her savage slashes, Crockett leaned forward, then backward, at one juncture almost lying prone while he rode his Bullet Bike in an ever-tightening circle. Pagan dogged him all along, her blade slicing and snicking through the air.

This went on long enough for Crockett to note that at the end of every stroke, the momentum of her arm pulled up her far knee and loosen the grip of her thighs on the saddle.

As Pagan veered toward him again, swinging the Bowie in a downward chopping arc, Crockett planted the sole of his boot against her rib cage. All things considered, it was more of a prod than a kick, and not very powerful since he had only the hover cycle to brace against. Nevertheless, his foot jolted her sideways. She shrieked, struggling to maintain her balance and keep her grip on the knife.

Crockett broke away from the circle, engaged the rear jets and rocketed in a straight line across the field. He leaned down, at full speed, and retrieved his fallen dagger. Even as he did so he heard her cycle roaring in pursuit. Spinning the Bullet Bike about, he turned to face the infuriated Pagan.

She rode toward him full tilt, throttle wide open, turbines moaning, knife held out like an accusing finger. Before Crockett could maneuver, the red and black Bullet Bikes collided with a screech of metal tearing into metal. Pagan struck at him, Crockett parried with the Khanjarli then both of them were hurled to the ground. The hover bikes, reacting to the sudden lack of hands on the controls came to dead stops.

Though he tried to shoulder roll, Crockett hit the ground with his head. The shock of impact caused the sky to grow dim for an instant. He rolled over just as Pagan, knuckling grit from her eye, arose and rushed at him, knife plunging downward.

Crockett threw himself to one side, and the Bowie bit into bare earth. At the same time, he flung up his right leg, and the toe of his boot sank into her lower belly. She jackknifed over his foot and fell, snapping desperately at air.

Crockett was on his feet in an instant, and as the woman started to rise, he side-kicked the hand that held the Bowie. A wrist bone popped, Pagan screamed and the long knife skittered across the ground. She gaped at him in horrified surprise, then lunged sideways, scrabbling with her good hand across the ground, reaching for the knife. Crockett brought the heel of his boot down on the back of her hand. She screamed again as he pressed down with all of his weight. When he heard the faint crunch of bones, he removed his foot. Pagan, hissing curses in an aspirated voice, tried to get to her feet again, using only her legs. This time the heel of Crockett's boot connected squarely against her forehead. Her one eye rolled back in her head, and she flopped flat on her back.

Crockett stared down at her, the dagger hanging from his hand. The on-lookers went berserk, screaming and shouting, "Knife her! Kill her! Kill the bitch!"

The screams whirled and spun in the air around him. His body ached, his shirttail was a sodden, soaking mass from the blood leaking from his shoulder wound, and he was expected to play to the crowd by killing an unconscious woman.

Crockett surprised the spectators. He slid the knife through his belt, turned and walked toward the boulder where Bonner sat. People swarmed out onto the field, yelling, laughing and shouting congratulations. Crockett looked around and saw Alex and Syne in the crowd. He hoped Quanah and Zeda were nearby.

As Crockett reached the foot of the boulder, Bonner waved a hand. "This is it, Colonel. Pagan is yours. Chop her to fish bait or take her as a slave. Your prerogative."

He glanced over his shoulder. Two men propped up Pagan and dragged her forward. Glancing back to Bonner, Crockett muttered, "The law of the jungle with a relish."

Bonner smiled in genuine amusement and tapped the boulder under him with a boot heel. "The law of Loki's Rock. She gambled and lost."

Someone handed him Pagan's knife. Crockett turned as the woman was dumped unceremoniously at his feet. She was conscious, though dazed and disoriented. She stared up at him as he stood over her. Her one eye gleamed with fear, but her lips curled in a sneer.

Crockett looked at her for a very long moment, from the soles of her dusty boots to the top of her tangled mass of hair. Finally he rested his gaze on her hands. Both were discolored and swollen. He figured his kick had dislocated the radiocarpal joint of her right wrist.

He stooped over, not averting his eyes from her face. He laid the Bowie knife beneath the heel of his boot, stamped down and yanked up sharply on the handle at the same time. The shank snapped at the hilt with a chiming sound.

Turning away, Crockett dropped the useless hilt on the ground and turned back to face Bonner, who smiled a faint smile of bemusement.

"Let's hear your decision, Colonel."

CHAPTER EIGHTEEN

Crockett and his companions were accompanied back to Loki's Rock by a jubilant crowd. There was no sound reason for their good humor, though the sight of blood and violence had obviously started their day on a high note.

Back in his room at the Bitter End, Quanah bathed, disinfected and examined Crockett's wounds, pronouncing them superficial. Only the shallow knife slash on his shoulder blade warranted stitches.

Crockett stoically sat through the operation.

Watching Quanah's deft movements with the surgical tools he had taken from *Ambler's* first-aid kit, Zeda asked, "What'd you tell Django?"

Crockett started to shrug, but a sharp spasm if pain made him turn it into a short nod. "I told him yes. He wants us downstairs by noon for the swearing-in ceremony."

Alex winced. "I hope there's no tattooing or ritual scarring involved."

Quanah snorted. "Quent's got so many scars on his hide already, one more won't make much difference."

"Bonner won't want to mark us as part of Loki's Rock," Crockett said. "If we're captured inside the Institute, we're not supposed to have visible connections to the place."

When Quanah was done, Crockett put on a new shirt, his last clean one. "We better request that our other clothes are laundered, or I'll be wandering around buck-ass naked soon."

"Who'd notice in this place?" Alex asked sourly.

"Perhaps a clothing allowance is one of the warlord's perks," Syne suggested.

At noon a security man fetched them. He ordered them to leave their weapons behind, since the theme of the ceremony was one of trust. Reluctantly they did as he said, trooping downstairs to the barroom. A dozen security men stood in sloppy "parade rest" postures aligned across the far wall. They all gazed stone-faced toward Bonner. None of them appeared to be armed.

Bonner greeted Crockett warmly and bade him to stand on the left side of his chair. In a whisper, Bonner said, "Since our time is short, we'll dispense with the public ceremony."

Crockett didn't ask why the time was limited; he figured Bonner would tell him sooner than later.

In a ringing voice—the same powerful, persuasive tone he had used at Willy Bill's cotillion—Bonner announced, "This is Quentin Crockett, a warrior of superior abilities. He has performed splendidly in the service of Loki's Rock, and he has upheld the principles of Loyalty, Valiance, Obedience and Purity.

Therefore, I name him a scion of Loki's Rock. I further name him warlord, the master of all of you. His every command is to be obeyed without question, without hesitation."

A murmuring broke out among the ranks of the security men. For a moment Crockett thought they were voicing their discontent, but he realized they were muttering, "Loki's Rock is where it's at, where it's at."

Still, a few pairs of gimlet-hard eyes bored defiantly into his. One pair belonged to Phil.

"It is done," Bonner declared. "You are dismissed. Be happy, be loving, and remember our watchwords."

As the security force filed out, Bonner called, "Phil, Clem, wait."

"Painless enough," Crockett commented. "Now what?"

"Now I'll brief you on the plan. We lost precious time because of that idiocy last night and the track stand today."

Bonner arose and strode toward the saloon doors. The pair of security men fell into step beside him. "Follow me, warlord and company."

They followed Bonner down the street to the eatery. A hand-scrawled Closed sign hung in the dust-streaked window, but the door was unlocked.

Bonner sat down at the largest table while Phil and Clem assumed sentry positions before the door. Crockett and his friends took seats around the table.

Zeda gazed at Bonner distrustfully. From inside his black frock coat, Bonner produced a large folded square of paper and spread it open on the tabletop. It was hand-drawn map, and Crockett could tell that an experienced hand had made the drawings. When he saw a dotted line leading west from a hilly area labeled MT. OLDWORLD, he realized the map depicted the region around Mount Maleficent

Bonner began talking quickly, without wasting a word. "I have no idea what lies inside Mount Maleficent, the layout of the Jotunheim complex or even how big it is. However—"his finger traced the dotted line that terminated in a series of wavy lines, "—the cave where we pick up our large trade goods is here. The distance between the nose and the cave is 2.3 klicks, so there has to be a tunnel system."

"I thought you said they brought in large items by rail," Quanah said.

"I assume there is some sort of concealed rail tunnel running through the mountain to the cave," Bonner replied. "Unfortunately we can't search the cave for it because of the beetles. The only way into the complex is up through the nose. Once someone gains entrance, the rail system can be located and used to transport an assault troops inside."

"Won't the *Brigadefuhrer* become suspicious if he sees an armed squad hanging around the cave?" Crockett asked. "You can't just sit around waiting and hoping that the railway system will eventually be under the control of your people."

"Of course not," Bonner responded. "I'll be in contact with the scouts who enter through the nose. I presume you have comms?"

"Small but exceptionally powerful ones," Syne said helpfully. "They can transmit voice or electronic signals over a five-mile radius."

Bonner nodded approvingly. "Still, there will be a time lag to put the assault force in position, so our scouts will need to remain out of the scanning range of the beetles."

"You stated you were unsure of the range of the beetles," Alex pointed out. "It could be less than five miles, or as much as ten."

"Part of the risk, Dr. Jones."

Quanah shook his head in disapproval. "Since you don't have a damn germ of information about what's up there, how do you figure your scouts will survive long enough to signal the assault force? Hell, for all you know, there's a legion of Secbots just waiting for an idiot to crawl up the nose."

Bonner squinted at him. "Secbots?"

"Security robots," Crockett answered, "programmed to kill intruders."

"Take care of any you might meet in the Institute, and you'll have nothing to worry about."

"How do you expect to get up the nose in the first place?" Alex asked.

Bonner stood. "Come with me."

They followed the man through the dining area, into the kitchen and to a heavy door sheathed in aluminum. Grasping the lever handle, he popped the latch and swung open the door. Mist and an icy draft wafted over them. Breathing the very cold air was difficult and dried out their mucous membranes. Bonner marched into the meat locker, pushing a path through the sides of beef swinging from hooks. He paused by a pair of large metal containers. They were about four feet deep and five feet long, three wide. They resembled utilitarian coffins.

He waited until everyone clustered around, and he raised the lid of one of the airtight oblong boxes. He waved away the cloud of vapors rising from it. Protected by transparent plastic wrappings, lying on beds of dry ice, were various human organs: hearts, livers, a set of lungs, even a pair of eyeballs.

Alex made a gagging sound and turned away. Even Crockett felt a quiver of nausea.

Smiling, Bonner shut the lid. "The other box contains what's left of the redskins we became acquainted with the other night. Since the frozones are expecting this shipment, you'll be able to gain entrance into the mountain with a minimum of fuss."

"How is anybody supposed to breathe in there?" Zeda demanded.

"You'll be equipped with small oxygen tanks."

"How many of these containers do you intend to ship?" Quanah asked.

"Just these two. Normally each container carries four organ trays stacked on top of one another. If two are removed from each box, then we've made sufficient room for a pair of you, one to a box."

Reaching behind the container, Bonner made an adjustment and the entire back panel lifted upward, connected by small hinges on the inside of the container.

"There's a latch on the inside. A quick and easy way to get in and out." He shivered in the freezing temperature and turned to leave. "Let's go."

As they followed him out of the locker, Alex said, "Only two, you said. Are you planning for the ones who don't go up the nose to be your assault force?"

Bonner waited until everyone had filed out and he had shut the door before answering.

"No."

Crockett exchanged quick, disconcerted glances with his friends, then they fell into step behind Bonner as he returned to the dining room.

As the man took his seat, he said, "Obviously, Colonel, you will be in one of the containers. You will be supplied with weapons and whatever ordnance you might need. I will leave it up to you to pick your partner."

"What about rest of us?" Zeda demanded.

"Oh, that's been covered," Bonner replied airily. "You'll remain here, in Loki's Rock. As my hostages."

Crockett and his companions reacted immediately, reaching for guns that weren't there. At the same time, Clem and Phil snapped up compact Tak-10 machine pistols that had been hidden beneath their clothing.

Crockett stood in baffled rage, fists balled, teeth clenched. "What kind of lousy deal is this, Django?"

Bonner steepled his fingers at his chin. "The only deal is that there is no deal. We reached no agreements, came to no terms. Your weapons have already been confiscated. Your vehicle will be impounded. Which ever one of you has the remote key and starter should give it up at this point."

No one moved. Crockett nodded brusquely to Syne who removed a small black ovoid from a shirt pocket. He tossed it to Bonner and said flatly, "There is more to the operation of the *Ambler* than merely activating the engine."

"I'm sure." The corner of Bonner's mouth lifted in a disdainful smile. "Did you truly expect me to trust you? You had to be coerced to accept the honor I bestowed upon you. Even without a psi-scan, I knew you were only playing along, waiting for your chance to escape. In any event, I wouldn't allow all of you to get inside the Mount. You know too much about us and could make your own deal with the *Brigadefuhrer*."

"I still could," Crockett bit out.

Bonner shook his head. "No, I think you'd rather do anything than put the lives of the people you leave behind in jeopardy."

"And what if we're captured or killed? What happens to them?"

"Then we'll turn them over to the Institute upon demand. I will state I heard of the plan to breach their stronghold and imprisoned them."

"They won't buy that," Quanah snapped. "Not if they learn that two of us were smuggled inside their complex by hiding in merchandise boxes."

"I'll have a Loki's Rock patsy ready," Bonner replied smoothly. "Pagan is a good choice—disenfranchised, stripped of her rank, embittered. She'll be the perfect scapegoat to pin it all on."

"Plausible deniability," Alex muttered.

"What if they still won't believe you?" Syne asked.

"I'm not under the delusion that they won't be suspicious, but as long as some culprits are caught and punished, they will be too worried about losing their organ shipments to cut off their trade entirely."

"Got it all figured out," Zeda sneered. "Big plans for big man. No matter how big, you can still die."

"Of course," said Bonner with a patronizing smile. "I trust you are aware of the reverse."

Turning toward Crockett, he said, "We leave tomorrow morning at first light. You have until then to choose with whom of your gallant crew with whom you wish to share the dangers."

Bonner pointed toward the door. "Meet me outside at dawn. Do not make me come looking for you."

The five people marched back to the saloon in such a fury that no one dared speak to them. None of them reacted with much surprise when they reached their rooms and found their weapons missing.

Crockett sat on the windowsill and surveyed his team. "Guess I waited too long to find that hole card."

"That's because Bonner is dealing from the bottom of the deck," Alex said gloomily. "We should have expected a double cross."

"Not that it matters," Syne said, "but I did. Colonel Crockett, I volunteer to accompany you into the lion's den, even though Daniel had only his faith to sustain him. I am, after all, your greatest liability and therefore the most expendable."

"You?" Quanah's tone was incredulous. "Sure you're up to a challenge like that?"

Before Syne could respond, Crockett said, "Dr. Parker is right, Syne." He threw the pale, hairless figure a smile. "I appreciate the offer, though."

"Whoever goes with you will need a grounding in cryonic science," Quanah said. He feigned a modest smile. "I wonder who, out of all of us, has those qualifications?"

Zeda said, "Guess I can sense danger, and that's more useful than knowing about Oldworld tech. Seems I can throw knives better than most hair-lifters, too."

As an aside to Quanah, she added, "No offense."

Alex started to speak, but Crockett held up a hand. Calmly, he said, "I've already made my choice...and I don't think you'll like it."

CHAPTER NINETEEN

The day dawned white and ghostly. The X-MAC rumbled across the barren plains, towing a four-wheeled trailer. Beneath a canvas covering were baskets and crates brimming with loaves of bread, ears of corn, wheat and even hand-loomed bolts of fabric. In the distance, across acres of thorny shrubs, towered Mount Maleficent.

Crockett glanced over at Alex. She tried a jittery, reassuring smile on him, but he was too tense to even try to return it. He knew she was more worried about the people left behind in Loki's Rock than what awaited them at their destination.

Bonner sat in the back with ten security men. He had dropped all pretense of the relaxed, friendly host. He snapped orders to the man driving and the one operating the periscope. Everyone's speech was faster and clipped, their movements tense, their eyes never still for an instant. They were like soldiers preparing for battle.

Crockett wore a calf-length leather coat. Beneath it was a combat harness, and from that hung four grenades--two were V-90 minis, and the other two were DZ-19 incendiaries.

Though the Hawken was snugly holstered at his hip, he had clipped a mid-sized Taktron MPL subgun to the harness. The perforated barrel spit out 550 depleted uranium rounds per minute. Four extra clips of the ammunition were stowed in his coat pockets.

Alex was similarly attired and outfitted, with the same kind of grenades. Though she still packed her rail pistol, she had chosen--at Crockett's recommendation--a lightweight and compact subgun, constructed largely of stamped metal parts and heat-resistant polymer. It took a 20-round magazine, and its eight-inch barrel was equipped with a noise and flash arrester.

As the journey continued, Crockett found himself drifting off, lulled by the rocking motion of the X-MAC. Too much tension, too much bloodshed, and even his endurance could drain away.

He kept replaying the scene with Quanah, Zeda and Syne the afternoon before, when he had told them Alex was his choice to breach the Institute. He had been prepared for a long argument, and when it didn't arrive, he felt a little let down.

His decision was logical, based primarily on Alex's knowledge of history, psychology and technology. Also, he felt certain the SIN officer was a good person to have at his back if the going got tricky.

After apprising Bonner of his decision, Alex and Crockett were allowed into the Loki's Rock armory to pick out weapons. There were hundreds to choose from, all in mint condition.

Bonner had commented on the irony of using the Ahnenerbe Institute's own traded-in firearms against its inhabitants. Crockett took silent note of the number of guards and the security measures around the place.

"You bored, Colonel?"

Crockett opened his eyes and gazed at Bonner. The man's face was strained, although he tried to smile. "No, just thinking."

"About what awaits you after you get up Hitler's nose?"

Crockett shook his head. "No. About what I'll do to you when I come back and find out you've mistreated my people."

Bonner's forced, stitched-on smile faltered. "A little premature, aren't you? Besides, there's no need to worry. Unless circumstances warrant otherwise, their status as guests won't change."

"That's good, that's real good," Crockett said. "But listen to me, Django, and believe what I say. Harm any of them, and all of the planets in the Spur won't hide you from me."

Bonner's shoulders stiffened. He glared at Crockett and opened his mouth to say something. Then he shut it and glanced away, shouting at the man at the periscope for a recon report.

Crockett settled back, repressing a smile. Although Bonner held the high cards, he was still unnerved enough by Crockett's self-confidence to take the threat seriously.

The X-MAC retraced the route of five days before, rolling through the valley and over the bluffs. They saw no sign of the Lakota whatsoever, and Crockett wasn't sure if he was happy about that.

Once the vehicle parked in the vicinity Mount Maleficent, Bonner took the Very pistol and accompanied by a trio of security men, left the vehicle and climbed to the top of the ridge. He fired off the flare and waited.

Looking out past the windshield, Crockett watched the Blue Beetle zip from the direction of Hitler's face and hover above and before Bonner.

"*You have the merchandise.*" The amplified, metallic voice wasn't asking a question, it made a statement.

"Yes," Bonner replied. "Everything you asked for and all of the freshest quality, too. What do you offer for it?"

The beetle pivoted slowly, wings vibrating, its glowing photoreceptor eye turning toward the X-MAC. Crockett ducked back out of sight.

"*We will make that decision once we examine your goods and ascertain if they meet our present needs.*"

"Then we shall remain in the area until you contact me with your offer,"

Bonner replied. "Is that acceptable?"

"If you withdraw back to the valley, then it is acceptable. Return to this spot twelve hours hence. Understood?"

"Understood. Will you now make preparations to receive the merchandise?"

"Yes. You are familiar with the procedure."

As it had done before, the beetle retreated across empty air, ascended, twirled and skated back toward Mount Maleficent.

Bonner entered the X-MAC, face glistening with a sheen of perspiration. He mopped his brow with a handkerchief and said to Crockett and Alex, "Almost time."

Crockett threw him a mocking half-smile. "Hot out there, is it?"

Bonner's lips compressed in a tight line. "Where you and that Oldworld mixed breed are going, you'll be praying for some hot."

The driver started up the X-MAC and rolled it over the bluff, heading for the boulder strewn base of Mount Maleficent. Above it, vast and exuding an ancient malevolence, towered the ruin of Adolph Hitler's head.

As the vehicle rumbled closer, objects dropped from the huge pit of Hitler's right nostril. Like streams of metallic mucus, four steel cables connected to a long, flat platform descended from the nasal passage.

"Rapunzel, Rapunzel, let down your golden hair," Alex murmured in a sing-song tone.

Crockett didn't bother asking her what she meant.

When the platform scraped rocky earth, two security men left the vehicle and pulled it away from the cliff side, while others busied themselves unloading the crates of crops and homemade goods.

Bonner announced, "Your transportation has arrived. Time to get ready."

Crockett and Alex ran a quick inventory of their equipment and ordnance. The pair of Commatchs were seated securely to their mastoid bones and they made sure the devices were tuned to the same frequency and the circuits were open. Then they walked to the pair of metal containers at the rear of the X-MAC.

"Hurry up and climb in," Bonner said anxiously. "I don't want to make them suspicious."

They slid into the metal-walled containers feet first. Each held a small oxygen tank, with a length of flexible hose extending from the nozzle. The hoses terminated in breathing masks, which fit securely over the nose and mouth.

It was an extremely tight fit for Crockett. He had to lie in a fetal position beneath the bottom tray that held human organs and dry ice. A security man pushed in the back panel of the box, and when Crockett tightened it with the inner latch, it squeezed against a flexible seal. It was dark and cold, but the air was breathable. Still, he felt a stirring of claustrophobia.

After what seemed like a long, cramped, cold wait, Crockett felt the container being heaved up and carried out of the X-MAC by at least four men, judging by the voices. He was dropped none too gently onto the platform, and he winced. The knife wounds on his shoulder and arm hadn't yet begun to heal, and the jolt set them to stinging. A few minutes later he heard a thud he assumed was Alex's container being loaded onto the platform beside his.

A jerk shook the container around him, and he experienced a giddy, rising sensation in the pit of his stomach. Faintly Crockett could hear the steady creaking of a winch. He could feel the platform swinging gently back and forth, and he tried not to think of what might happen if the container slid off into empty space, spilling him, dry ice and human viscera all over the rocky ground.

The cranking, creaking sounds grew louder, and a moment later they echoed hollowly. Crockett figured the platform had reached the nasal passage. Dimly he heard the steady throb of an engine.

The rising motion suddenly ceased. The platform swung forward, dropped a few inches, and he heard the crunching of rock as a heavy weight was dragged over it. The scraping of stone set his teeth on edge. The engine sounds abruptly ceased. When that sound stopped, Crockett held his breath, listening for more noise.

Suddenly a flat male voice intoned, "Barter and exchange report, record of the month of Octember, Orionis standard calendar."

The sound of the voice was human enough, but its colorless monotone motivated Crockett to grasp the butt of the Hawken.

The voice continued speaking, reciting a monologue concerning, barley, wheat, corn, surpluses, overages and shortages. Numbers were mentioned, over and over and for a very long time. Crockett considered showing himself and shooting the boring bastard just to shut him up.

The droning voice ceased, then he heard the sound of footsteps slowly receding. They seemed to have a peculiar echo. The footfalls faded away, swallowed up by a hissing noise. Crockett waited for a count of sixty, then touched the transmit stud on the Commtach.

In a very low whisper, he asked, "Jones? You with me?"

In an equally faint voice, she replied, "So far. I think we're alone."

"Me too. On the count of three, let's open up."

"Do you mean one-two, open, or one-two-three, open?"

Crockett couldn't help but smile. He placed his fingers on the panel latch. "One... two...three... open!"

Pushing the latch to its down position, he shouldered the panel up and squirmed out as quickly as he could. Fortunately his legs weren't as stiff as he feared they would be. As he got to his feet, he saw Alex rising from behind her container. They smiled at each other, then surveyed their surroundings.

A naked light bulb provided a dim overhead glow from a low ceiling. Feeble light filtered in from the tunnel in Hitler's nose. A few feet away yawned a doorway chiseled out of solid rock. A series of worn stone steps led up to a dull gray metal door.

The circular chamber wasn't very spacious. A large winch occupied most of the space.

Crockett noticed that it was powered by a generator. He also noticed that it felt very cold in the room.

Shivering, Alex pulled a pair of black leather gloves out of a coat pocket and slipped them on. "Must be around forty degrees Fahrenheit in here."

Crockett grunted. "Tolerable."

"If you enjoy winter sports."

Both of them spoke in whispers.

Turning toward the doorway, Alex said, "Time to see what there is to see. Keep a watch for those beetles."

Crockett unleathered the Hawken. "I'll keep a watch for anything."

As they eyed the metal panel, searching for a doorknob or latch, it suddenly rolled upward with the whooshing squeak of hydraulics. Both of them leapt for cover on opposite sides of the stone chamber. Crockett crouched down behind the cable-wrapped drum of the winch, and Alex melded into the shadows at the far corner.

A man strode into the chamber, walking down the steps with long, deliberate strides. He carried a clipboard in one hand. He was a pale, burly man of medium height, his gray hair so close-cropped that the scalp could be seen beneath it. His face was as craggy and as furrowed as the stone walls, with a complexion an almost translucent pallor that came from not being exposed to the sun for a very long time.

His attire was a uniform, the black tunic, jodhpurs and knee boots Crockett recognized as belonging to the *Shutzstaffel*, the dreaded order of Black Knights who pledged their loyalty to Hitler, not to Germany. It was covered in gaudy emblems, including the twin lightning strokes, silver skull and crossbones and the Ahnenerbe Foundation insignia.

Crockett noticed the cuffs of the tunic were frayed and the boot leather cracked. The Sam Browne belt crossing his chest and girding his waist showed greenish spots of mildew. Loose threads dangled from the shoulder seams.

The man wore a rectangular plastic-coated badge on his lapel that bore his likeness. There was only one word on the badge. It read simply: OTTO.

The man marched purposefully to the container that had concealed Crockett and opened the lid. Without hesitation, he plunged his free hand into the bed of dry ice and picked up a plastic-shrouded heart. He examined it closely, grunting a time or two. He hefted the organ in his hand like a butcher trying to gauge its worth by weight alone.

Replacing the heart, he shut the lid and moved toward the other container, the one that had conveyed Alex. As he did, he noticed the rigged back panel on Crockett's box hanging open a few inches.

The man didn't look alarmed, but he glanced quickly around the chamber, dark eyes wide and bright. He reminded Crockett of a very alert bird, trying to focus on the source of a mysterious sound. Those darting eyes swept over Crockett's hiding place, then just as quickly returned.

Rising up, Crockett leveled the Hawken at him, saying in a cold, clear voice, "Don't move. Just stand there."

The man stared at him in silence, an awesome disdain in his eyes. "I wondered when one of you perverted shits would try something like this."

He moved, unafraid, to a small metal panel inset on the wall beside the doorway. A halfdozen colored buttons studded its surface.

"Don't try it, Otto," Crockett said, the bore of his pistol floating along with him.

Otto granted him one glance of disgust and continued reaching. Crockett held the Hawken in both hands, straight out in front of him, brought the sights into line and squeezed the trigger. The weapon bucked in his hand.

The slug hit the man with the force of a sledgehammer, smashing him off his feet and ripping his right arm off at the shoulder socket and sending it pinwheeling across the chamber.Crockett stared, astonished. He had shot to wound, not to kill. He hadn't expected the man's arm to be ripped off. Then he saw why it had happened. No blood flowed either from the ragged shoulder socket or from the stump of the arm. Instead, Crockett glimpsed a gleaming tangle of twisted metal, cables and wires.

Otto glanced down at his arm, then back to Crockett. "*Damn* you! That construct alone cost the Institute two million dollars. You've ruined it, you fucking renegade!"

Lurching to his feet, Otto stumbled toward Crockett. The echoes of his footfalls resounded hollowly within the stone vault.

"I don't want to kill you," Crockett snapped. "Don't move."

Otto didn't seem to hear or care. Clumsily he rushed at Crockett. Sidestepping quickly, Crockett delivered a roundhouse kick to his belly. The man didn't cry out or even gasp as he folded over Crockett's leg. With the back of Otto's head exposed, Crockett brought down the barrel of his weapon against his skull.

Otto slid limply down Crockett's leg and fell face first to the stone floor. He made no movement afterward. As Crockett kneeled beside the man, he was joined by Alex. She peeled off a glove and pressed two fingers against the man's carotid artery.

"He's alive, but his pulse is weird," she said. "Very fast and irregular. His body temperature seems unusually low, too. Turn him over, will you?"

Crockett obliged so Alex could examine the stump of the shoulder. Within a raw orifice, color-coded wires intertwined and a complex network of circuitry glistened wetly.

Touching a fractured cylinder protruding several inches from the stump, Alex said, "Looks like a polymer socket."

A small transparent plastic tube corkscrewed within the hollow socket. A pale greenish liquid dripped from it to the floor, crawling across the stone. Crockett touched it, rubbing the oily fluid between thumb and forefinger.

"This isn't blood," he said. "A lubricant?"

Frowning, Alex dipped a finger into the spreading puddle, brought it to her nose and sniffed. "I think it might be some kind of chemical coolant."

Crockett's eyebrows rose. "A coolant?"

"Like nitrous oxide mixed with propylene glycol or something along those lines."

"What do you think of this outfit he's got on?"

"Seems to be historically accurate but it needs a little repair."

Alex undid the man's tunic, tugging aside the strap of the Sam Browne belt. His flesh was very pale, an unhealthy mushroom shade. A five-inch pink scar ran down his clavicle, marked on either side by a saddle-stitched pattern.

She grunted. "He's one of the zipper club."

"What's that?"

"Old medical slang. Means he either had open-heart surgery, like a bypass operation, or he's had a heart transplant. See if you can get his mouth open."

Mystified, Crockett did as she said, squeezing the hinges of the man's jaw until his mouth gaped open. To his surprise, Alex stuck a finger inside Otto's mouth, under his saliva slick tongue. After a moment she withdrew it, wiping her finger on her jacket.

"Why did you do that?" he demanded.

"Testing his body temperature. If it was normal, his mouth would be hot even if his epidermis isn't."

"Well, is it hot or not?"

"Not," she replied. "Very cool. In fact, probably not over seventy-five degrees Fahrenheit. It's almost as if the poor bugger is walking around in a constant state of hypothermia."

Alex stood up and went to retrieve Otto's arm. Crockett studied the badge pinned to the man's lapel. It bore very little information beyond his picture, his name and a red dot about a quarter of an inch in diameter. The dot looked as if it had been affixed to the card somehow, and it bore an odd reflective sheen.

Alex returned with the arm. Holding the limb by the wrist and the bicep, she bent the elbow back and forth. "This is extraordinary, Colonel."

"How so?"

"It's a bionic prosthesis, but it's about ten years beyond anything in use even now. Touch the hand."

Crockett poked the hand, pinched it and shrugged. "Feels like skin."

Nodding, Alex said, "Exactly. It's a synthetic, organic equivalent of flesh. Perfect in every detail, right down to the texture and implanted hair follicles, which is pretty amazing, considering a human hair is only sixty microns wide."

"How's it made?" Crockett asked.

" A synthetic skin this close to the original has to be developed by genetic engineering, maybe through a form of cloning."

"So," Crockett said musingly, "it looks like Django was telling the truth about this place."

"As much truth as he understood. Make no mistake—from what we've seen so far, and that's very damned little, I'd judge the people who live here are a hell of a lot more dangerous than the Loki's Rock crowd."

Crockett stood, prodding the senseless Otto with the toe of a boot. "Yeah, Django said that, too. What do you want to do with this guy?"

Alex tugged on her glove. "Your call. You shot him."

After dragging Otto to a far corner and laying him on his stomach, Crockett used the man's belt to bind him. It was difficult since he had only one arm, so Crockett bound his wrist to his ankles, bending his legs up behind him. He briefly contemplated dumping the man down the nasal passage but there was a tactical wisdom in sparing the man's life--he and Alex were the invaders here. Unwilling interlopers, maybe, but interlopers nonetheless. If there was even a marginal chance of reasoning with the Jotunheim residents, it made sense not to arouse their anger by murdering their own.

He returned to Alex and they approached the doorway. The panel was still up. The woman suddenly put a hand on his chest and said, "Wait!"

Eyeing the panel, she said, "I think there's a photoelectric sensor there. Just strolling through it might trigger an alarm."

Crockett produced Otto's ID badge and clipped it to the breast pocket of his coat. "Already thought of that. This dot looks like a pass-code cell."

140

Alex nodded in understanding. " Like an electronic passkey."

"Let's give it a try."

Hands on their pistols, they walked up the steps and through the doorway, past the wall panel. Nothing happened.

"You were right," Crockett said, relief in his voice.

"You thought of it first," Alex replied, sounding just as relieved.

They found themselves in a squarish tunnel. The light from two wire-encased electric bulbs glistened from the cold rock walls. The crude marks of tools showed on the stone.

Crockett pointed them out. "So far, this place doesn't seem to be the high-tech heaven Bonner made it out to be."

A musky but cloying odor took them by the throats and tried to force out coughs.

Crockett stifled his cough, walking steadily along the passageway, his Hawken leading. A powdery coating of dust covered the tunnel floor, and each footstep caused a small cloud to puff up beneath their boots.

"They wouldn't win any awards for good housekeeping, either," Alex commented, holding a finger beneath her nose to prevent a sneeze.

A wedge of light glimmered before them. They slowed their pace and sidled along the wall. The tunnel opened out into an enormous vaulted chamber, its ceiling almost lost high in the darkness. Both of them jolted to unsteady halts, forgetting the killzone they were braving. They had to blink and shake their heads, fighting to absorb what they were seeing. Crockett in particular wondered if it was indeed real and tangible and not a hallucination.

Alex opened her mouth, gaping, her staring eyes sweeping the chamber. "Mother of God."

Crockett didn't say anything. He seemed to have lost the capacity for speech. He caught his breath in awed wonder.

The enormous room was filled, almost as far as the eye could see, with crates, boxes, stacks of electronic gadgets, furniture, sleek and shining wheeled vehicles, paintings and even musical instruments. The huge room was a museum of mechanics, art, literature, seemingly of the entire Oldworld culture. There was simply far too much to absorb, much less identify.

Many of the objects and items were unfamiliar to Crockett, but he knew the thousands of items in the gargantuan vault represented the aspirations to build the ideal Terran society on a new world.

Crockett finally regained his voice. "What was that Django said? 'A vast treasure of tech'?"

Alex husked out a small, faint laugh. "He truly had no idea, did he?"

CHAPTER TWENTY

The sun rose in the east and streaked red ripples on the roof of the depart-ing X-MAC.

Dust floated in gray spirals from beneath the tires as it rumbled through Loki's Rock. Quanah, Zeda and Syne stood outside the vehicle compound and watched as the big armored vehicle shrank in the distance.

"Don't like this," Zeda murmured. "Not one bit."

Behind them, a security man swung the wire gate shut and clicked a heavy padlock into place. "Best move on, folks," he said.

As they turned and trudged up the street, Zeda whispered, "You get an eyeful, Quanah?"

"Yeah," he answered in a low voice, ducking his head. "If we can't get to *Ambler,* one of the Sandcats looks to be our best bet. Small, fast, maneuverable."

As the three people walked toward the eatery, no one else ventured forth on the streets. As early as it was, there should have been a few people, if only those staggering home from an all-night drunk.

Syne remarked, "From the oppressive atmosphere, it appears the Colonel's assessment was correct."

No one responded. All of them had stayed awake most of the night, talking in whispers, planning courses of action. The question that never arose among them was whether they should trust Django Bonner to allow them the run of Loki's Rock during his absence. They already knew the answer.

Therefore, they had devised an escape plan, with Crockett briefing them on the location of the armory where their weapons were stored and how much opposition they could expect.

They had also settled on an escape route, using Bonner's map of Mount Maleficent and the surrounding environs as a blueprint. For the plan to work, it was crucial that they all behave as if they suspected nothing, to maintain the facades of trusting souls, worrying only about their friends, off on a mission in the service of Loki's Rock.

They entered the eatery. The heavyset, wart-faced woman behind the coun-ter glanced at them with sullen eyes. She did not greet them.

"Breakfast!" Quanah said with forced good-humoredly."First and foremost, deliver to us a pot of your genuine coffee."

The three people took seats around a table, and cups and a steaming pot were placed before them. The woman didn't look them in the eye.

They ordered their food. The woman did not write down their requests, but her eyes suddenly flickered, casting an anxious glance toward the doorway.

Quickly she turned and slipped into the kitchen.

The four security men entered quietly, lining the counter, leaning against it lazily. A couple of them stifled yawns. Phil seemed to be the leader of the quartet. He met Zeda's gaze and grinned. "Got tired of breakfast in bed, little Gypsy queen?"

She returned the grin, reaching for the coffee pot. "No, I got tired of seeing your ugly face first thing every morning. But as long as you're here, fetch us some toast and butter."

Phil stiffened, brows drawing low over his eyes. His hand strayed to the butt of his pistol. "You Gypsy whore. I'll show you some fetchin'."

Zeda was in the process of pouring coffee into her cup. As Phil's fingers brushed the Tak-10, the pot and cup fell from her hands. Long before they struck the floor, she threw the curve-bladed Khanjarli dagger with a blurring snap of wrist and forearm.

The blade pierced the back of Phil's hand, the razor point slicing through the palm and pinioning it to his upper thigh. His splayed fingers contorted, like the fluttering wings of a butterfly transfixed by a pin.

Before the three other security men could react, Quanah, Syne and Zeda were on their feet, overturning the table. They flipped it toward the counter, smashing it against the four men, making a wooden sandwich with a human fill.

One of the security men managed to draw his weapon. His first few shots crashed through the window and killed a drowsy, unsuspecting merchant who was opening his stall across the street.

The security man's breath had been driven out of him by the table edge, and he tried to adjust his aim to find the proper range. Quanah threw his weight against the table, driving the crown of his head into the man's face. Cartilage crunched and crimson gushed from his flattened nose. He dropped his pistol.

Zeda. scooped the Tak-10 from the floor just as a security man, roaring in wordless fury flung the table away from him and closed on Quanah. He was either too drunk with rage or humiliation to draw his weapon.

Quanah ducked a roundhouse right that ruffled his hair, and he slashed savagely upward with the stiffened edge of his right hand. The security man spit a gurgle of pain and surprise, and he stumbled backward against the counter.

Clutching at his throat for a moment, his eyes went wide and wild. Dark vermilion erupted from between his slack lips, and he fell, first to his knees, then to his face.

Phil yanked the knife from his hand and clawed for his Tak-10. Fingers slick with blood, he could not gain immediate purchase on the grip.

As Phil fumbled, Quanah snatched up the knife and held it point upward.

"I told you I would remember what you said, white boy."

"Fuck you, canoe nigger!" Phil grated. His injured hand finally closed over the butt of his weapon.

Quanah lunged forward, the point of the dagger sinking into, and then quickly withdrawing from, the left side of Phil's chest. A stream of blood followed it. Grunting his disbelief, Phil covered the wound with his left hand. Scarlet squirted from between his fingers. He raised the Tak-10 with his right hand.

"You red son of a bitch," he croaked, his unsteady hand trying to put Quanah's body before the barrel of his firearm. "You've killed me."

"No," Quanah said, "but I let out a little of your overheated blood. You should recover."

Phil leaned against the counter for support. Syne smoothly reached out, wrested the pistol from his nerveless fingers and aimed it toward the final security man, who broke for the door in a panicked run.

Before Syne squeezed the trigger, Zeda. fired from the hip, holding down the trigger. The security man pitched through the doorway and into the street, his back perforated by half-a-dozen rounds.

Syne, dangling the autopistol in his hand, looked over the litter of bodies and intoned, "Pointless loss of energy and blood. Very foolish."

"And so are we if we stay here," Quanah said, swiftly snatching up a Tak-10 from the floor. "All we can do now is make a run for the compound."

The streets of Loki's Rock were no longer empty. People converged on the eatery from all points of the compass, some shouting questions, others looking only mildly interested.

Quanah and Zeda held them at bay with gun barrels and threatening scowls. They trotted up the street, trying to cover all directions with their eyes, ears and weapons. Their pace wasn't slow, but it should have been faster.

From ahead, they heard the tramp of security men running to cut them off, the creak of leather boots, the thud of footfalls and the metallic clink of weapons. There were over a dozen of men, racing from the direction of the vehicle compound. They fanned out in a circle, gun barrels bristling, eyes glinting with the desire to kill.

Quanah took it all in, surveying the autoblasters and the men behind them. "Time for a judgment call," he announced.

His Tak-10 dropped into the dust, and he placed his hands on top of his head. One by one, his companions did the same.

CHAPTER TWENTY-ONE

Alex and Crockett looked about them. The floor was surfaced with a highly polished light blue material, as were the smooth, curving walls. Bending, Crockett rubbed his hand over the floor, then looked at his fingers.

"Clean. You could eat off it. Looks like it's made of some kind of alloy. How do they keep it this way?"

Alex squinted at the floor. "A low-level electrostatic field, to keep the environment sterile. The field in here prevents dust and foreign particles from entering, pushing them toward the tunnel, like a giant whisk broom. That's the detritus we walked through when we came in."

She tapped her Commtach. "More than the likely the further we go, the more the field will interfere with our comms."

Although they looked for them, there saw no indication of spy eyes or surveillance cameras. The two people moved carefully among the boxes, crates, vehicles, sculptures and tables holding electronic parts and even more crates. There seemed to be an order in which the artifacts were stored, though none was cataloged by name or even number. It required all of Crockett's willpower to resist the temptation to stop and examine everything.

"Most of this stuff is a minimum of two hundred years old," Crockett said. "Some of it older, but it all looks brand new. Maybe the electrostatic field protects them."

Alex only nodded. As they wended a path through the artifacts, both noticed it was growing colder. The temperature seemed to have dropped by ten degrees. Crockett finally put on his gloves, ones with the index fingers snipped off to allow easy access to triggers.

"Any ideas on how they keep it so cold in here?" Crockett asked.

"Must be a huge air-conditioning system," Alex answered, "with giant circulating fans somewhere, like the blast freezers they used to have in food-processing plants. It has to be a terrific energy drain to pump air this frigid through the entire complex. There's got to be something else at work, too."

"They probably have nuclear power, maybe a mini-fusion reactor."

They passed several yellow four-wheeled contraptions outfitted with long, front-projecting prongs that Crockett identified as remote controlled forklifts.

"What happens to the people when we knock out the cold circulation system?" Crockett wanted to know.

Alex shrugged. "That depends."

"On what?"

"If their metabolic rates have been artificially reduced, through cybernetic

alteration and organ transplants, just so they can survive in such low temperatures, the result of raising the temperature could be catastrophic. Depending
on the age of their original soft tissues and organs they could begin to decay
almost immediately. That's what happens in conventional cryonics when a
subject is accidently thawed out."

They continued walking through the vast space, the floor and walls echo-
ing oddly to their footsteps.

Alex craned her neck, looking up at the ceiling. "The shielding in here must
be fantastically absorbent and insulating."

Gesturing behind him to a long, massively built vehicle bearing a chrome-
plated Taktron logo, Crockett said, "There's got to be a big cargo transportation system in here. There's no way a fleet of that many vehicles could have
gotten up here any other way."

Alex smiled. "Unless they packed them up part by part and assembled
them later."

"What we really need is a map of the layout of this place. We could wander
around in here for more than the twelve hours Bonner gave us."

Because he spoke in a whisper, he failed to hear the first footfall settle in
front of him, but he grabbed Alex by the arm before the second one had fallen.
They crouched behind a table and watched a man, dressed similarly to Otto,
sauntering between the aisle of artifacts. He walked directly toward them.

The man passed them without a glance. Crockett realized be was heading
toward the chamber inside Hitler's head. After a warning glance to Alex, he
crawled among the tables, the cargo containers and the stacked crates. He
couldn't allow Otto to be discovered.

Dodging between the antiquities, Crockett managed to reach a point to the
left and well ahead of the tunnel entrance. The man walked purposefully past.
Crockett glided behind him, his left arm crooking around his throat. The man
uttered a faint gagging sound of shock as he was dragged behind a large bright
red vehicle.

The man struggled for breath and clawed at his attacker's arm. Crockett
kicked his legs out from under him, and he fell heavily, banging the side of his
head on the vehicle's gleaming bumper. A small cut was opened in the pale
flesh. He put a hand to it and stared as Crockett showed him the Hawken.
He was middle-aged and slight of frame, with tiny eyes surrounded by puffy
pouches of wrinkled skin.

The man uttered a growl of rage. "Are you insane? Are you a fool? Get out
of here!"

Like Otto, this man showed no fear, only surprise and contempt. Curious,
Crockett pushed his hand away from the cut in his temple. It was superficial

and bleeding only slightly, but the blood oozed sluggishly. The color wasn't a deep red, it was more of a dark pink. He wore a badge like Otto's, which identified him as WELCH.

Grabbing the man's Sam Browne belt Crockett hauled him to his feet, put him in front of the gun and marched him back to Alex. He gave her a look as though he were regarding a pile of excrement on a breakfast table.

"You're from Loki's Rock," Welch said in a voice sibilant with spite. "Undisciplined mixed race maniacs, aren't you?"

The remark irritated Alex. She drew her pistol and pressed the muzzle against his forehead. "Not exactly. In Loki's Rock, murder is indiscriminate and meaningless. I have a method. You don't talk, you die."

"From my view strata," Welch replied, "your methodology of data synthesizing is reactive, rather than proactive. You've assumed a posture which is simplistic and adversarial, rather than cooperative, inasmuch as your rationale for trespassing on restricted property is based on an insufficient grasp of the legalities involved and the disposition thereof."

"What the hell did he say?" Crockett demanded.

Alex smiled sardonically. "Authentic corporate jargon."

Pressing harder with the bore of her pistol, Alex said, "In simple, unadorned language, I want you to tell us the layout of this place."

By threatening and poking and prodding with their guns in more delicate portions of the man's anatomy, he finally agreed to take them to a map. They marched him ahead of their weapons toward the nearest wall. With a grin, Alex whispered, "I guess not every one of Welch's organs is prosthetic."

Welch walked over to a blank wall. He stood and looked at it, saying, "Complex display."

Suddenly a three-by-three-foot square came alive with countless lines and dots of many colors. One of the dots throbbed steadily. Pointing to it, Welch said, "That represents my current position, indicated by the locator lozenge on my badge. Since I was the one who activated the display, the computer shows my position first."

Fixing their position in the confusing webwork of colors and intersection points and angles, Crockett and Alex saw that the central core of Jotunheim was indicated by a large pattern of blue lines and several big green dots.

Tapping Otto's badge on his lapel, Crockett asked, "Does the computer respond to your voice or to the locator lozenge?"

Welch was reluctant to answer. It required Alex poking his kidneys with her rail pistol for him to say, "The lozenge."

"Locate the *Brigadefuhrer*," Crockett said.

One of the dots in the central core suddenly flared brighter and began to throb.

"Locate the circulating and pumping station," Alex stated.

Nothing happened. Responding to Crockett's glare, Welch said, "It's only pro-grammed to locate the installation's personnel. It was assumed that everyone in here was supposed to be in here and would therefore know their way around."

Studying the map again, Crockett traced a network of glowing grid lines with a forefinger. "We're here, almost on the top level. The *Brigadefuhrer* is below us...looks to be—" he counted quickly. "—four levels. Where's the near-est elevator?"

Welch inclined his head to the left. "That way, about a hundred yards. Fol-low the curve of the wall."

Crockett pulled him away from the map. "Show us."

As they walked beside the wall, Crockett asked, "How many people are in this place?"

"Would you believe me if I told you?" Welch retorted.

"Probably not. But answer me anyway."

"Sixty-eight active, one hundred and twelve inactive."

"Inactive? Do you mean dead?"

Welch shook his head disdainfully. "I say what I mean. If I'd meant to say 'dead,' I would have said 'dead.' I said 'inactive.' Are you unable to compre-hend English, as well as simple survival-oriented common-sense measures?"

Angrily, Crockett rapped the back of his head with the barrel of the Hawken. "Are you unable to comprehend that I will make you *permanently* inactive if you don't cooperate?"

Welch did not even flinch, but he said sullenly, "I comprehend."

"What about security forces," Alex said. "Sentries and guards."

"At one time we had a special division for that sole purpose, but all of us now act in that capacity when necessary."

The wall curved lazily to the right and opened up in a low-ceilinged, colon-naded antechamber. They saw a metal pair of double doors topped by an arch bearing a long set of colored lights. Hovering before the doors, bobbing gently up and down on thin air, was a beetle, but a smaller model than the one they had seen interacting with Bonner.

Alex and Crockett froze, both of them grabbing Welch and pressing their guns into his back. They stared at the device. Its red photoreceptor eye stared back.

"What's it doing?" Alex whispered into Welch's ear.

"Scanning us, or rather, the locator lozenges on the badges," the man re-plied in a normal conversational tone. "Your companion and myself are noted and logged as known installation personnel. However, since you are not wear-ing a badge—"

148

An unnerving *whoop-whoop* of a Klaxon caused Alex and Crockett to jump and curse at the same time. The beetle drifted forward. "Make it back off," Crockett snarled, shoving the bore of the Hawken against Welch's neck.

Smiling, Welch said, "I can't. The automatic intruder-alert system has already been triggered." He crooked a finger over his lips and giggled. "She's been targeted for deactivation."

A needle-thin beam of white light shot out from a nozzle on the underside of the beetle, which touched the barrel of the gun in Alex's hand. Sparks flashed and showered.

Crying out, she stumbled backward, dropping her TX5. The mechanism swooped closer, needle beams stabbing with crackles of current.

Alex screamed and fell thrashing to the floor, covering her face with her arms. She tucked her legs up and shrieked, "Do something! It's electrocuting me!"

Crockett crashed the Hawken over Welch's skull, and even as he hurled the unconscious man away, he centered the pistol's sights on the beetle and fired five rounds in such rapid succession, the shots sounded like a single explosion.

The device fragmented under the .50 caliber assault, metal and circuitry flying in shards. Its power pack flared in an orange halo of flame. Spinning crazily on an invisible axis, the beetle listed to the left, then clattered to the floor, the red light of its photoreceptor eye fading. The Klaxon still whooped.

Bending, Crockett pulled Alex's arms away from her face. A red welt showed against the dusky complexion of her right cheek. She shook her right hand in irritation and pain.

"Are you all right?" he asked, helping her to her feet and handing her the TX5. It was undamaged.

She took a long, shaky breath. "I think so. Electric shock, considerable voltage. Good thing I protected my eyes." She kicked the shattered, smoldering remains of the beetle. "A damned nasty little toy."

The lights over the lift door were blinking. "We're going to have company," Crockett said, tugging the badge from Welch's lapel.

They sprinted back toward the storage area, hearing the hydraulic hiss of door panels sliding open behind them. Crockett reflected that the prospects of their surviving inside the complex were moving from poor to zero. All the odds were stacked against them, but that was nothing new in his experience.

The explosive report of a gunshot sounded from the rear, and a bullet whipped between them, The slug chewed off the corner of a varnished, ornately carved table on Crockett's right.

"You idiot!" bleated a male voice from somewhere behind them. "Don't shoot in here!"

Crockett and Alex exchanged tight grins. The frozones wouldn't shoot out of fear of damaging the relics, but since they were under no such obligation, they unlimbered their autoweapons.

Spinning, Alex and Crockett triggered the subguns at the same time. The weapons spit bullets into the space on either side of the trio of armed, black-uniformed men dogtrotting toward them in a flanking maneuver. A crate jumped and blew apart under the steel-jacked hail. They didn't bother to gauge the accuracy of their shots. They whirled and ran among a collection of life-size statues, several of them bearing the sculpted likeness of Adolph Hitler.

They changed direction twice, then sank down in the shadow of a giant electronics console. Male voices filtered to them, but they were too distant to be understood. The tones were undeniably petulant, like children ordered to perform an unpleasant task.

"There's got to be another way out of this rat's nest," Alex panted.

"Speak for yourself, Jones," Crockett replied.

"No, not us. Them. They're the rats. Hear them?"

"Yeah. They sound like bratty kids. And neither Welch nor Otto were afraid of us, almost like they couldn't believe what was happening."

"Exactly," Alex said. "My granddad liked to say, 'crazy as a shithouse rat' to describe mental illness. I think we're dealing with the equivalent here. If you pack rats too closely together in a nest for too long, you get homicidal rats, suicidal rats, cannibalistic rats, insane rats. Maybe not too different from the people in this place."

They stopped whispering when the sound of the voices grew louder.

"How's Welch?"

"How should I know? I'm not a medic. Where's Otto?"

"He was supposed to check out the merchandise. Somebody go look."

The voices drifted away, becoming distant and incomprehensible again. Crockett, suddenly realizing that he was very cold, repressed a shiver. It felt like he was squatting in the path of a frigid blast of wintry air. Wetting a fore-finger, he held it up in several directions.

"Air movement that way," he whispered, nodding ahead of them. "Damn *cold* air movement."

They crept in that direction and saw the shadowed, circular mouth of a hole in the floor about fifty yards away. Rising, they raced toward it, casting glances over their shoulders every few feet. It was more of a shaft than a tunnel. Icy wind blew up through a thickly meshed metal screen, stinging their faces, bringing water to their eyes and ruffling their hair. The frame of the hatch cover had a combination lock, but no handle or knob.

Beneath it they saw ladder rungs affixed to one circular wall.

Crockett took aim with the Hawken and emptied the cylinder at the lock. He stood fast as ricochets whined and screamed around him. The .50 caliber rounds smashed and shattered the combination lock, blasting the steel catch to scrap. He wrenched the hatch cover up and gestured to Alex. "After you."

She didn't protest, but quickly climbed into the opening. Crockett followed her, not bothering to shut the cover after him. The men would have undoubtedly heard the shots, so as he clambered down the rungs, he swiftly ejected the spent cylinder of the pistol, took a spare from the harness and fit it into the Hawken's frame.

The ladder rungs descended about fifty feet. At their end, Alex and Crockett dropped down and found themselves standing in the elbow of an L-shaped shaft. The shaft was not composed of rock, but of a lusterless, non-reflective metal, featureless except for ridges where sections of tubing joined. At intervals, wire-encased light bulbs glowed from the ceiling. It was narrow, not wide enough for them to walk side by side.

The shaft stretched out almost as far as they could see, and the cold wind was stiff—to move forward, they were forced to lean into it. Far in the distance they saw a white circle, about the size of an old penny. A muffled, rhythmic throb set up steady vibrations in the floor of the tunnel.

"Air circulation shaft," Alex gasped out, the wind nearly snatching her words away.

Crockett glanced upward and saw the head and shoulders of a man peering down into the mouth of the opening. He pushed Alex forward, just in case someone topside started shooting.

They jogged along the narrow tube, Crockett in the lead, both of them maintaining a steady pace so their feet wouldn't slip on the smooth surface. He wasn't sure how long they navigated the passageway before a rattling roar came from behind them.

The din of bullets crashing into, ricocheting off and striking sparks from the metal was terrific, almost deafening. Alex pointed the subgun behind her and fired a long burst, but the enemy fire didn't abate.

Fragments of slugs and chipped pipe shrieked through the shaft like angry hornets. Bullets buzzed all around them. Behind it all, they heard the drumming hammer of a machine gun, a light caliber by the sound of it.

The two people kept running forward, bent almost double so as to present smaller targets. Each time they passed beneath a light bulb, Crockett smashed it with the barrel of his pistol. It was a tiring effort, fighting their way through the frigid wind pressing against them broadside.

Crockett's free hand groped over the combat harness under his coat until it identified and closed around one of the minigrenades. Detaching it from the harness, he hooked his thumb into the pin and tweaked it away.

He shouted, "Fire in the hole!" and tossed it behind him, over Alex's head. Both of them increased their speed, running as fast as they could, not worrying about the bullets or losing their footing. Crockett counted to five under his breath. A score of yards later, they received violent blows on their backs that knocked them forward and off their feet.

The shock wave of the exploding grenade buffeted them to the shaft's floor, skidding them along for a few feet, bruising their knees and elbows. They lay where they had fallen for a moment, biting at the frigid air, listening to the fading, rolling echoes of the detonation and the feeble moans of the men who had been caught by it.

Rising a little unsteadily, Alex and Crockett resumed their run, at a much slower pace. Their eardrums still vibrated, and their heads throbbed. Both of them had opened their mouths to equalize the pressure of the explosion, so neither one suffered hearing impairment. Ahead glimmered a circle of brilliant light, and the cold wind increased in intensity and strength. The throbbing sound grew in volume until they could feel it vibrating in their bones.

They emerged from the shaft, squinted their eyes against the brightness of artificial light and took two steps before stopping and staring.

CHAPTER TWENTY-TWO

All things considered, Quanah reflected, it wasn't the worst cell they could have been imprisoned in, but it was a long way from being the best, too.

A single barred window, high in the adobe wall, was set at ground level on the outside. Heavy flagstone steps led upward to the single massive door through which the three of them had been shoved by the security men. It bore a small observation panel in the center, covered on the outside by a metal grille.

The cell was sparsely furnished with one bunk, made of crudely nailed-together two-by-fours and wooden slats. A thin mattress of sewn burlap bags lay upon it. A casual glance was enough to see that it was urine-stained and probably crawling with vermin.

Fortunately, the security men hadn't mistreated them, though it was apparent they sorely wished to beat them. Bonner had evidently only given the order to incarcerate them, without adding a codicil concerning brutality to the command. No one seemed to be in charge, and since they were afraid of reinterpreting Django's commands, Quanah, Zeda and Syne were merely herded into the cell.

Squeaking rats scurried about in the sour-smelling straw. A pair of ten-gallon galvanized metal buckets sat in a corner. One held brackish water, and a tin cup was attached to the wire handle by a small-linked chain. The other bucket was empty, intended to hold the prisoner's' waste. Syne tapped it with the toe of his boot.

"In retrospect," he remarked, "I suppose our lack of breakfast is a blessing in disguise."

Zeda walked around the walls, her movements feline smooth and graceful. She pushed here and prodded there. She sprang up to the window, grasped the bars, hung from them a long moment, then dropped back down to the hard-packed earthen floor. She shook her head in frustration.

The morning passed sluggishly. When no one else showed an interest in doing so, Quanah turned over the bunk's mattress and stretched out to nap, hat tilted over his eyes. Syne assumed a lotus position in a corner, sitting cross-legged, eyes closed, going through a relaxation exercise

Outside the cell, the everyday business of Loki's Rock went on. They heard merchants hawking their wares, raucous laughter, music and the roar of engines.

Zeda, who sat on the flagstone steps leading to the door, noted the quality of light through the barred window, said, "Getting hungry. Hope we get a midday meal."

Suddenly, unexpectedly, the small observation panel in the door opened.

A security man's face was framed behind the grillwork. "Everybody get away from the door."

Quanah awoke with a snorting start, but he didn't rise. He lifted his head and blinked as Zeda and Syne moved to the wall beneath the window. The cell door opened just enough to admit a single figure. In the room outside, they glimpsed two security men, Tak-10s at the ready.

The door banged shut behind her, and Pagan regarded everyone with an emotionless stare. Her clothes were in disarray, her hair a wild, unbrushed tangle. A purpling bruise showed on her forehead, and her lower lip was puffy. Her right wrist was encased by a wooden splint, and her left hand was thickly bandaged.

Syne stared at Pagan. "I take it your beloved Bonner snapped his fingers, and you were magically transformed from warlord to scapegoat."

Pagan didn't reply. She simply stood motionless, like a mannequin, not even appearing to breathe.

"Or," Zeda offered grimly, "he transformed her into a spy."

Pagan spoke, her voice hushed, like the rustle of coarse cloth. "I'm a prisoner, just like you. I was betrayed."

"Like you betrayed the Indians who rescued you from slavers?" Quanah snapped. "It's no sin to betray a betrayer."

"Or to kill a killer," Zeda said, a hint of menace entering her voice.

"Is that what you want to do?" Pagan asked calmly.

"Can you think of any reason why we shouldn't?" Zeda demanded. "You tried to kill Crockett. Twice, in fact."

Pagan didn't respond. She merely stood and stared. She was listless, as though her spirit had been more than broken. It had been stolen from her.

Shuddering, Zeda turned away from the woman. "Dead already. Soul dead."

"Is that true?" Syne asked.

Pagan's eye flicked toward him, but she didn't react.

"For if it is," Syne continued, "then you should have no objection to your material shell joining your astral self in the great ether."

Reaching down into his boot, he withdrew a flat, black-bladed throwing knife. Quanah and Zeda's eyes widened in surprise.

By way of explanation, he said casually, "I counted on being dismissed as a threat and so I wasn't searched."

He returned his steady gaze to Pagan. "If a spark of vitality still resides within you, we may yet offer you a way to fan that spark into a full blaze."

Interest stirred faintly in her blue eye. "How?"

With a quick flip of the wrist, Syne threw the knife into the earthen floor at his feet. He took note of how deeply the blade penetrated. "I

154

have," he announced solemnly, "an idea."

Quanah cast his eyes ceilingward and groaned. "I was afraid you would."

CHAPTER TWENTY-THREE

The chamber was immense, nearly the size of the storage area above them, but built in an unusual cylindrical design.

Shaped like a hollow cone, the apex funneled up high overhead. Two floors rose above their position. Banks of consoles ran the length of each. Brilliant overhead lights gleamed on the alloyed handrails, the glass covered panels and meters. Chairs were attached to slideways so the console operators could be ferried from panel to panel. A quick count told Crockett that both levels contained a dozen chairs. None of the chairs were occupied.

Beetles flitted over the consoles, extensor cables manipulating dials, keyboards and switches. Crockett quickly handed Alex the ID badge he had taken from Welch, but none of the gadgets paid any notice to them.

Six chrome-capped glass tubes, each one ten feet long and three feet around, were positioned at equidistant points on the top level of the cone-shaped chamber. The tubes were filled with a churning, bubbling green liquid, flexible metal conduits extending from their tops and bottoms. The conduits stretched from the bases of the tubes and disappeared into sleeve sockets on the deck.

The temperature felt very cold, well below freezing. The frigid wind roared up from beneath, where the chamber's diameter was at its widest. Gingerly Alex and Crockett peered over a handrail. Far below, perhaps a hundred feet, was a dark metal framework, surrounding six gargantuan fan units. Four of them spun, two did not, and Crockett estimated that the three fan blades of each unit were close to twenty feet long and ten wide.

Surveying the upper levels, they saw twelve open shaftways like the one they had used to reach the chamber.

Shivering and hugging himself, Crockett asked, "What the hell is this place?" The roar of the wind was so loud, be had to practically shout his question into Alex's ear.

"I'm not sure," she shouted back. "An air circulation station, but it can't be the only one in an installation this size." Eyeing the hovering beetles, Crockett said, "They haven't noticed us."

"They're probably not supposed to. More than likely their sole program is to maintain operations."

"Why are those things doing it, since this place was designed for humans?"

"Lack of manpower to spare, easier to automate, I can't say."

Taking another look at the fan units below, Crockett said, "A couple of grenades might knock those out and start warming this place up."

Alex shook her head and gestured to the tubes of bubbling liquid. "That wind is almost gale force. Unless you find something to weigh down the grenades, they'll probably be blown right back up here. Besides, those containers of coolant must be pumped into a conversion chamber below the fans. If we want to start a thaw, we need to prevent the flow of coolant."

Crockett lifted his Hawken, but Alex tugged at his arm. Her face was troubled. "This isn't right, Colonel. Our plan was to try and strike a deal with the *Brigadefuhrer*, remember?"

"Yeah, but his rats might gnaw us to death before we reach him. If this is only one of their stations, shooting out one or two of these coolant containers shouldn't putrefy the whole place, only show them what we can do."

Alex hesitated, biting her lower lip, then nodded. "Do it. We can't stay here much longer or we'll freeze."

Bringing the center of the nearest tube into target acquisition, Crockett squeezed the trigger of the Hawken. The report of the shot was completely swallowed up by the rush of the wintry wind, but the glass casing acquired a grayish smear. It didn't break or even crack.

He cursed and fired again, aiming at the same spot. He expended three more rounds before he saw a small network of cracks appear, and he fired twice more before a trickle of green fluid began sliding down the tube's exterior and crawling down the conduit.

Immediately an overhead light went from white to red, and the beetles' smooth, hovering motions became hurried and frantic.

"Their instruments have registered a drop in the coolant level," Alex shouted. "Time to go."

They chose a shaft at random and were grateful for the lessening of the cold and the thunder of the fans. Squeezing through the passage, the darkness grew almost absolute.

The lateral shaft terminated in another elbow joint, and Alex wasn't happy that it crooked downward rather than up.

"Makes sense, doesn't it?" Crockett asked, squatting at the lip of the upside down L and reloading the Hawken.

"I suppose so. The air has to be circulated to all levels of the Institute. I'm just not crazy about climbing down into God knows what."

Putting his feet on the ladder rungs, Crockett replied, "Can't figure that it's much different than climbing *up* into God knows what."

After a few minutes of hand-over-hand descent, the shaft terminated in another elbow, joining with a passageway branching off to the left. They were able to walk side by side along this one. As they did, they passed several smaller openings. Judging by the icy drafts that blew out from them, there were a number of other subsidiary shafts connected to more circulating stations.

Presently they detected a faint radiance ahead, and as they went farther down the shaft, the light grew brighter and they heard a series of noises. Crockett was able to distinguish the humming of generators and the murmur of voices. A metal-meshed grille stood in front of them. They approached it in a crouch and peered through the screen.

They looked down on a miniature city. They saw buildings with foundations of brick and concrete, narrow paths twisting and turning between the squat structures. None of the buildings looked like they could comfortably fit a child, much less a full-grown adult. It looked like the model of a city, shrunk in volume and reduced in scale. In the center rose an obelisk tower made of white stone, stretching upward about twenty-five feet. The obelisk had been fashioned to resemble a broadsword and the hilt bore the graven insignia of the Ahnenerbe Foundation.

Alex caught her breath in surprise, but she said nothing. The city, if it could be called that, was devoid of life, despite evidence to the contrary. Both of them had heard voices. Crockett pressed his face closer to the grille, looking from the left to the right.

Almost directly below them was a metal pole, and topping the pole was a rectangular green sign with white lettering. He read it aloud: "Wewelsburg Alle. Wewelsburg Avenue."

Running a hand across her forehead, Alex said, "Now I get it. It's a scale model of the city the Abnernbe Foundation intended to build to build on Earth...their utopia, so to speak...you could see part of it on the banner in the Bitter End."

After waiting a few minutes and hearing nothing, they decided to move. Feeling around on the inside of the hatch cover, Crockett found a slide lock and he pushed the bolt aside.

The hinges were stiff, and he had to launch several kicks at the frame before it creaked open. They were about twenty feet above the floor, but only five from the arched roof of a strange building supported by Doric columns. There was the statue of a standing man inside it, wearing the plate armor of a medieval knight. His hair swept across his forehead in a dramatic dip and his upper lip curled in a sneer beneath a square mustache

"A baby-sized Hitler Memorial," Alex said. "No surprise."

Both of them jumped to the roof of the miniature memorial and clambered down to the floor. They walked carefully down Wewelsburg Avenue, looking for any movement or signs of life, straining their ears and eyes. The sound of their footsteps echoed unnaturally loud. Evidently the city wasn't equipped with the sound-absorbent shielding of the storage level.

The ceiling rose to fifty or more feet, tapering upward to armatures holding electric light fixtures. Very few of the buildings were more than six feet tall, and Crockett and Alex felt uneasy striding among them like giants.

The city room was so long that its far end was indistinguishable in the shadows. Neither Crockett nor Alex saw doors or any way out. Suddenly, Crockett felt the fine hairs on his nape lift.

The cold, still air blazed with automatic gunfire. Bullets smacked into a building beside them, digging white pockmarks in the brickwork, shards scattering in every direction.

Crockett and Alex responded instantly, in lunging rushes for cover on opposite sides of the avenue.

Men in uniforms, brandishing handblasters and autorifles, bounded toward them from all directions. Ducking behind a four-foot-high building, Crockett fired the Taktron MP in a stuttering spray. He heard ricochets, screams and curses, and the snapping snarl of Alex's rail pistol.

A machine gun was unlimbered. The staccato hammering of the weapon was amplified, and echoes of the rapid reports were sent booming back and forth. Out of the corner of his eye, Crockett glimpsed a shadowy shape and heard automatic fire. He flung his body to one side as a shower of rock chips swept over him.

He saw the man running toward him between two buildings, a subgun held at waist level spitting flame, lead and noise. Crockett's Taktron loosed three rounds and the man flipped backward, his chest blown out.

Another stream of autofire thumped through the air over his head. Crockett tried to press his body into the building as the slugs stitched a red-hot path against the opposite wall of his refuge. Smoke and pulverized stone filled the air.

Suddenly the autofire stopped. Crockett didn't wait and wonder why. He sprang away from the office building, holding down the Taktron's trigger.

Only one man stood in the open, about thirty feet away. He held a slender silver wand in his right hand. Over two feet long, the tip vibrated. The man swung the wand in a semicircle, trying to catch up with Crockett's sidewise lunge. He heard a high-pitched hum and a corner of a building only inches to his left burst apart in an eruption of mortar.

Angling his body toward a collection of structures, Crockett dropped into a clear space between them. He drew the Hawken and put it next to him while he popped a fresh clip into the MPL. He didn't see Alex, so he touched the transmit stud on Commtach. "Jones, where are you?"

"About twenty meters to your right," came the crisp response. "You made a head count yet?"

"Not yet. You?"

"Rough estimate. I think there's about fifteen of the opposition, not counting any you've put down."

"As far as I know," Crockett said into the mouthpiece, "I've accounted for two."

"What's your score?"

"Two definites, two maybes." There was a pause, and Crockett heard the crack of the TX5.

Her voice filtered into his ear again, tense and worried. "Make that three definites. Listen, we're already pinned down, and pretty soon we'll be outflanked and outgunned."

"They've also got some sort of weird weapon—I don't know what it is, but it's pretty nasty."

"I saw it in use...I think it's what was known as an infrasound wand.... electricity converted to sound through a Maser. Ultrasonics." She paused and added, " Perhaps we should split up."

Crockett didn't answer for a long moment. It was a tough call to make, but each of them had to take fundamentally the same chances—both were important, and therefore both were almost equally unimportant, in terms of the risks to be faced by separating. It was the only way they really had a chance.

"Colonel?" Alex's voice was urgent.

"Agreed," he said. "We split up. We can stay in contact with the comms. I'll draw them away from you in a very flashy way."

"I'll give you covering fire if I can."

"Negative. Don't draw any more attention than necessary. Just wait for my next signal."

"Acknowledged," she replied tersely.

Crockett leaped from cover, sparing one split second to survey his surroundings, and then he raced through the miniature city, in a long-legged, yard-eating lope. He jumped over boulevards, pounded past the sword obelisk and sprang over a river in a single bound. Voices yelled to his right. He spied four men, less than fifteen feet away,

Rising from cover, fumbling to bring their weapons to bear, faces registering astonishment. Crockett swept them with a long burst from the Tactron. He didn't slow his pace, but he swerved back and forth, running in a broken-field fashion, trying to keep buildings at his back and sides at all times. Staccato pops filled the air, and bullets blasted chips of brick and masonry from the structures all around him.

Flakes of stone and fragments of concrete stung the back of his neck and the left side of his face. A dark-haired man ran to intercept him, a long-barreled pistol held in both hands. He assumed a two-handed combat stance, and with smooth, practiced motions drew a bead on Crockett.

The Hawken spit flame and two rounds centerpunched the man in the lower body. He staggered backward, dropping the pistol, arms windmilling as he tried to maintain his balance.

Another fusillade of shots chewed up the facade of a building only a couple of feet in front of Crockett. Without aiming, he pointed the Taktron behind him and fired a strafing burst.

The air suddenly shivered with a hum. He felt a shock of impact in the muscle of his right shoulder, and he spun completely off his feet. His head reversed position with his boots and his back thudded heavily onto the floor with such force he couldn't see or breathe for agonizingly long seconds.

He choked back the burning bile sliding up his throat, and he bit his tongue against the pain. Rolling over onto his left side, gulping the cold air, he looked behind him.

The uniformed man he had glimpsed earlier with the wand sauntered confidently toward him. Propping himself up on his elbows, Crockett steadied the Hawken in a double-handed grip. He worked the trigger.

The gleaming rod swept out, fanning the air in a blurred semicircle. The tip hummed, popped and Crockett heard the sharp clang of impact, then the whine of ricochet. The man stood unharmed and smiling a patronizing smile.

Crockett fired again, aiming for the smile. Again the wand inscribed a humming arc, the tip dancing from left to right. A loud *pop!* concussed the air as the bullet screamed away. Crockett realized the rod produced an invisible field of sound powerful enough to deflect bullets.

Crockett dropped his sights and planted a round in the man's ankle. He went down with a great yelp of pain and astonishment. He crawled frantically behind a flat-roofed building.

Getting to his knees, Crockett kept low and crawled behind the base of the obelisk. White-hot pain and nausea washed over him in a wave, but it passed. Gingerly he flexed his fingers, and though the movement tore a protest from his shoulder, the muscles, tendons and nerves still worked.

He seated the earpiece of the Commtach more securely and called Alex. He heard no reply, only the hiss of static. He repeated her name, and received the same response—static.

Refusing to speculate on the reasons why he couldn't contact her, Crockett opened his shirt to check the severity of the injury. Outlined in blue and vivid red against the bronze hue of his skin, a spiderweb pattern of broken blood vessels and ruptured veins spread from his shoulder across the top of his chest.

The blast of infrasound hadn't broken bones, but the wound hurt like bottled hell, and it throbbed in cadence with his heartbeat. Sensations became rubbery, wavering. His eyes remained open, but the miniature city blurred and receded in his vision. Footfalls and voices forced him to focus. He could hear men moving quickly toward his position.

"He's over there, behind the monument. Henrich nailed him."

"And he nailed Heinrich. Let's be exceptionally careful."

The mechanical sound of firing bolts being pulled back was audible. Crockett pulled one of the incendiary grenades from his combat harness, jammed it firmly against the base of the obelisk and pinched away the pin. He got to his feet and trotted away in a fast backpedal, making sure to keep the monument between him and the men stalking him.

A quartet of gun-wielding men crept around the monument, two to a side. One pair sighted Crockett and raised their weapons. The second pair saw the metal egg at the hilt of the giant sword. They uttered cries of alarm and fear, and tried to scuttle away as fast as they could.

The base of the monument erupted in a blaze of flame, smoke and debris. Crockett felt the cold slap of the concussion. The sword shivered, swayed, and with a groan and grate of stone, the entire length toppled majestically down across the city, crashing into and crushing several buildings. Plumes of smoke and dust rose in the air. Men screamed in pain and outrage, cursed in a homicidal fury.

Crockett turned and ran as fast as he could down another lane, sprinting low to keep his head down behind the buildings. Once, he was forced to squeeze into a very narrow alley and squat there as a column of dark-uniformed pursuers marched past along the street. He didn't shoot at their retreating backs, reasoning that if he hadn't done enough to draw the heat from Alex by now, there was no point in engaging in another firefight.

He tried and failed to raise Alex a third time on the comm unit, and then he arose and moved through the drifting sheets of dust and smoke, wending his way between the buildings until he came to a barrier. Two very ornate, very tall double doors, bound with thick braces of brass, towered over him.

Emblazoned in the very center of the doors were two bordered disk-shaped symbols that depicted, in gold and black paint, a stylized side-view eagle with outstretched wings. One clawed talon gripped a replica of the Ahnenerbe insignia, and the other held a blood-red swastika.

An inscription was printed inside the borders of the disks, and Crockett had trouble reading it, sounding out the words.

"*Blut und Ehre*," he muttered. "What the hell is that supposed to mean?"

CHAPTER TWENTY-FOUR

As far as Pagan knew, prisoners were fed only once a day, in the evening. She was not even sure of that, since most violators of Loki's Rock's laws were either immediately killed on the scene of the infraction or tortured to death. Actual jail terms were exceedingly rare, and based on little more than Bonner's whims.

However, she was familiar with the two security men acting as turnkeys, and she voiced a sneering opinion of their alertness and intelligence. Their names were B.J. and Lex, and she doubted either one would bother to check on them until mealtime.

Since she was the tallest of the inmates, Quanah directed her to stand on the top step, blocking the observation slit with her back. If B.J. or Lex asked why she was there, Pagan was to tell them that her cellmates had threatened her life if she dared step farther into their dungeon.

Quanah. and Zeda moved the bunk a few feet down the wall and knelt on the floor, watching as Syne carefully slid his knife blade into the earth, slicing out squares. Meticulously he lifted them out, keeping the hard topsoil intact and separated from the bottom layer of softer dirt. Zeda and Quanah pawed through the heap of straw, examining and discarding individual stalks.

As the afternoon wore on, the process came faster and easier with repetition. They removed more and more squares of the hard-packed floor. The cell heated up, and all of them except for Syne perspired freely.

By late afternoon they had dug a long square hole in floor, a little more than a foot deep. It looked like a shallow grave, wide enough to accommodate two corpses.

Syne, using the knife, shaved off the excess loose dirt from the bottom of the squares until each one was perfectly flat and only three inches in thickness.

Noting the dimming quality of light through the barred window, Zeda whispered, "Better hurry. Be dark soon."

Reluctantly, Quanah tossed his hat into a corner and lay down on his back in the hole. Syne handed him the knife, then laid down beside him.

Zeda gingerly picked up the squares of earth and placed them over the men's bodies, fitting them together like the pieces of a puzzle. She rebuilt the floor from their feet up.

When she reached their necks, she placed a hollow straw in each mouth. Before she lay the last chunks over their faces, she exchanged long looks with both of them, smiling reassuringly. Quanah mumbled around the straw in his mouth, "This had better work, little man."

"If it doesn't," Syne responded in a similar mumble, "then we'll be saving the gravediggers of Loki's Rock time and effort."

Zeda fitted the squares over their heads, making sure the straws jutted between the edges. Rising, she fetched the water bucket and used the tin cup to dribble water over the cracks and uneven edges. With her hands she rubbed and smoothed the earth, mixing in the excess dirt and kneading out the cut marks. She very carefully broke the protruding straws almost even with the floor.

After washing the dirt from her hands, she moved the bucket back to its place and resumed her position against the wall. Nodding toward Pagan, she mouthed a question. "Soon?"

Pagan responded with a short, terse nod. She whispered, "Somebody is coming right now."

Zeda bowed her head, as if she slept. There was a rattle from the heavy cell door. Pagan quickly moved away as it swung open. The two security men came down the stone steps. Lex carried a metal pail and a handful of wooden spoons. B.J. had his Tak-10 in hand. They froze at the sight of Pagan sitting on the bunk and Zeda on the floor. Dumbly they looked around them, mouths dropping open.

"Where are the others?" Lex asked.

Zeda opened her eyes. She looked drowsy, and a dreamy smile played over her lips. "They had to leave. But they said they'd be back."

Lex dropped the pail, and what looked like a watery soup splashed up and out of it. He drew his Tak-10 and pointed it at Pagan. "How did they leave? Answer me!"

Pagan pointed to the window. "How else, you silly bastards? Through the bars."

B.J., face blank and stupid with shock, ran to the window, leaped up, tested the bars, then skipped around the cell, kicking at the pile of straw as if the missing men might be hiding beneath it.

"This is ridiculous!" Lex snarled. "Just plain fuckin' crazy! They have to be here! You two bitches—on your feet!"

Pagan and Zeda stood and were herded out of the cell at gunpoint and into the adjoining room. It was small, barely more than a foyer, but a chained set of manacles dangled from a bracket bolted deep into the wall.

B.J. stood in the doorway of the cell, his back to it. Lex moved to the other side of the room. Both women were caught between gun barrels.

With a jerk of his head, Lex indicated the manacles. "Cuff yourselves," he commanded. "I want to hear them click tight."

Dark rust-colored streaks stained the floor beneath the manacles. People

164

chained to the wall in the past had obviously left their blood as silent remind-
ers of their suffering.

Still smiling a dreamy smile, Zeda put the iron cuff around her right wrist
and snapped it shut. Pagan snugged the other manacle around her left wrist
and sealed it with a loud click.

"Okay, you bitches," B.J. snarled, "where'd they go? Start talking, or we
start shooting pieces off you! Pieces you'll miss!"

A motion behind B.J. caught Zeda's eye. Metal gleamed for a fraction of a
second. B.J. made no sound, not even a startled gasp when the blade plunged
through his back. His eyes blinked foolishly. Before those eyes went vacant,
Zeda yanked her right arm forward in a short arc. The bracket holding the
chain tore from the wall in a burst of powdered mortar and adobe.

Her arm's arc ended when her fist connected with Lex's jaw. The whole lower portion of his face skewed sidewise. The point of his chin skidded around and
took up position beneath his right ear lobe. His teeth spewed from his mouth
like a handful of corn amid a torrent of blood. The force of the blow caused his
torso to pivot violently at the waist with a loud grating of cartilage. Life went out
of his eyes with the suddenness of a candle flame being extinguished.

As he fell, his face horribly out of shape, Zeda slid the thumb of her left
hand into the space between the manacle and her wrist and exerted pressure.
Muscles rippled up and down her bare arm. The cuff sprang open, twanging
like the bass string of a guitar.

Quanah, his hair full of dirt kernels, withdrew the knife from B. J., who
flopped face first at Pagan's feet.

Pagan gaped at Zeda with mingled awe and terror. Her eye was wide, the
azure iris completely surrounded by the white. The dreamy smile on Zeda's
face had vanished. Her eyes gleamed like opals. She advanced on Pagan, and
the woman shrank in fear.

Grabbing her by the forearm and digging her fingers under the iron manacle encircling Pagan's wrist, Zeda wrenched it open. Pagan cried out in pain as
Zeda flung the cuff aside. It clanged against the wall.

"That could just as easily have been your heart," she said softly, not releasing her.

Quanah retrieved his hat and pushed his way forward, slapping dirt from
his clothes. He reached out to touch Zeda, thought better of it and said ur-
gently, "She can help us reach the Colonel and Alex."

Turning her head, eyes glowing like white-hot steel, Zeda stared at Quanah
for a long moment. Then the blaze in her eyes faded to a pale gray and she said
quietly, "Let's get on with it."

Pagan and Quanah armed themselves with the security men's machine pistols. The door of the building was barred on the inside, but rather than bother with the unlocking mechanism, Zeda kicked the door off its hinges. Quanah cursed at the loud splintering of wood and the screech of screws ripping from the wall.

Luckily, the door faced away from the street and no one saw it sailing away or heard it hitting the ground. Quanah estimated the time at around eight o' clock. It was early yet for the denizens of Loki's Rock, too early for the riotous partying that seemed to go on every night.

As the four people made their way toward the armory, trying to keep to the darkness, the few people they encountered paid them no attention. Pagan led the way, with Syne bringing up the rear, checking their backtrack with quick, all-seeing glances.

Quanah eyed Zeda closely and tentatively reached out to touch the metal stud on the back of her neck. His fingertip brushed its surface and a little jolt of electricity shot up his hand. She whipped her head around and growled, "Don't."

Two men guarded the armory. One of them tried to light a hand-rolled cigarette, his Tak-10 clutched under one elbow. The other stood at the corner of the flat-roofed, windowless building, urinating into the shadows.

Because of a steady breeze, the security man had trouble getting his lighter to stay aflame. He cupped his hands around it.

By the time his cigarette was afire, his eyes swam with multicolored spots from the dancing flame. He didn't see Zeda's bold approach, but he felt her hand fit itself around his throat and squeeze.

The security man didn't gasp or cough or cry out. Fingers like bands of tempered, tooled steel closed around his neck, crushing his windpipe, his larynx, his esophagus and his top vertebrae all in a single clenching motion. The only sounds were a mushy crunching of flesh and muscle mashing against bone and cartilage.

His companion heard the crunch, but he wasn't startled by it. He zipped up his fly and turned. When he saw the blue-haired Gypsy girl gripping his tongue-lolling mentor by the throat, his eyes bugged out and his mouth opened wide. For an instant he forgot all about the handgun tucked in his belt slide rig.

By the time he remembered it, Pagan lunged around Zeda, and crashed the barrel of her Tak-10 against his skull. He dropped without making an outcry.

She and Quanah dragged the bodies to the side of the armory, hiding them behind a clump of brush. A padlock secured the door and neither of the guards had keys on them, so Zeda wrenched away the lock and a sizable portion of the door frame.

Pagan knew the location of the light switch, so they shut the door behind them and turned on the overhead lights. The interior of the storehouse was stacked nearly to the ceiling with wooden crates and boxes. Most of the crates were stenciled with the legend, PROPERTY GENTEK, AHN-ENERBE INSTITUTE.

They moved down the main aisle, taking a check of the contents of open containers. Assault rifles were neatly stacked in one, along with what had to be thousands of rounds of ammunition. There were semiautomatic pistols complete with holsters and belts, plus more than an ample supply of Tak-10s.

Farther on, they found hand-held missile launchers, heavy tripod-mounted machine guns and several crates of grenades. Every piece of it, from the smallest caliber hand-blaster to the big pulse rifles, was in perfect condition.

Syne murmured, "It would require days to catalog all of this ordnance."

"You've got about five minutes," Zeda said in a quavering voice. She groped behind her and sat down heavily on a box. A dew of perspiration had gathered at her temples, her eyes were glassy and her hands trembled.

"When is the next guard change over?" Quanah asked Pagan.

"Not for a couple of hours. But we can't assume someone won't pass by and notice the guards are gone."

From behind them came Syne's triumphant announcement of "Found them!"

While they had followed Pagan through the death-dealing wonderland, Syne had dropped back and fulfilled the original purpose of breaching the armory. He handed out weapons and belongings as well as the remote *Ambler* key. Quanah snatched a burlap bag from a wall hook and rushed deep into the storehouse, calling over his shoulder, "One minute."

True to his word, Quanah emerged from the aisles a minute later, carrying a bulging sack. It clinked and jingled as he walked. "Everybody make sure they've got a full load before we move out."

"What about me?" Pagan wanted to know.

"What about you?" Quanah asked. "Can you handle a weapon with the shape your hands are in?"

Pagan lifted her shoulders in a shrug. "I'd like to help, as long as I'm sharing the risks."

Eyeing her closely, Syne remarked, "You've certainly undergone an extreme change in attitude. Perhaps a bit too extreme."

Quanah rummaged around in his sack and came up with a paper wrapped cylinder six inches long. He handed it to Pagan, saying, "Hold on to this. When I give the word, break it in half along the dotted line."

Examining it suspiciously, she demanded, "Why?"

"Do it or don't."

Her eye narrowed. "I'll do it."

Opposite the armory stood a tin-walled prefabricated building. According to Pagan, it was a billet, the quarters of the security men. It appeared unoccupied, though the dim light of a kerosene lamp shone through the window. The four of them moved quickly through the streets, Zeda being helped along by Quanah She was nearly staggering from exhaustion.

"What's wrong with her?" Pagan demanded in an impatient whisper.

Quanah shook his head. "I'm not sure...my guess is that some sort of bionic interface triggered a tremendous increase in her metabolic rate, flooding her system with adrenaline, amplifying her reflexes and her strength. Now she's crashing."

They reached the shadowed rear of the saloon without being hailed by any passersby or seeing any security men. *Ambler* was still there, sitting on a concrete apron. The jukebox inside the Bitter End blared some discordant tune, full of wild guitars and heavy drums.

Syne and Quanah. studied the compound across the dusty street. The chain-link gate was secured by a padlock, and beyond it, two guards loitered around the fuel pumps.

"Now what?" Pagan whispered. "If we just stroll over, they'll recognize me, and the rest of you aren't exactly forgettable."

"Except for me," Quanah replied.

He handed his sack and hat to Syne. He tucked a short-barreled pistol into the waistband of his pants and pulled out his shirttail to cover it. Mussing up his hair, he said, "Everybody get ready to move. You'll know when."

He contorted his face into a vacant-eyed, imbecilic mask and started shuffling drunkenly across the street. He weaved, waved, stumbled, mumbled and cackled. When he reached the gate of the compound, he hung on to the interlocking wire links with his left hand and stared at the ground, muttering to himself and kicking at the loose dirt.

One of the security men sauntered toward him, leaving his companion with the walkie-talkie. When the shaven-headed man was less than a foot away, he asked, "What are you doing there, wetbrain?"

Slurring his speech, Quanah said, "Lost my ma's locket."

"What?"

"Lost my ma's locket."

"Where?"

Quanah jerked his shoulder in the direction of the saloon. "Back there." He saw the security man's partner respond to a call on a comm unit, holding it up to his ear.

The security man scowled. "Then why the fuck are you looking for it over here?"

"Because—" Quanah drew the pistol and poked the barrel through a link in the gate pressing it against the man's belly. In a quiet yet flint-hard voice, Quanah said, "The light is better over here. You have the key to the lock?"

Gulping, the guard nodded.

"Very, very carefully, I want you to unlock the gate. Act like you're having a nice conversation with the wetbrain."

The guard fumbled inside his vest, produced a small silver key, reached around the frame of the gate and inserted it into the base of the lock.

"Hey, Pooh Bob!" the man's partner bellowed from the compound. "Got an alert! Them Oldworlders escaped, killed Lex and B.J.!"

The man opened his mouth to bellow a reply. Quanah saw the fear in his eyes change to panic. His warning bellow became a grunt as Quanah squeezed off a round. The impact slapped him away from the gate, and before his partner could do more than flail around to bring his Tak-10 to bear, Quanah shot him three times, just below the rib cage, counting on the hydrostatic shock to paralyze, if not immediately kill him.

Unlocking the gate, Quanah pushed it open, hearing the running footfalls of his companions behind him. Zeda reeled, her boots dragging in the dust, clinging to Syne, who had one arm around her waist.

Quanah pointed the remote at *Ambler* and after an electronic chirp, they heard the click of doors unlocking. The instrument panels lit up. He opened the passenger side door and gestured impatiently. "Move it"

Pagan said anxiously, "They'll just come after us, you know. Run us to ground like deer."

"They can try," Quanah grunted.

Everybody piled into the ACP. Pagan and Zeda sat in the back.

Zeda sagged limply against Pagan, her eyelids fluttering with the effort to keep conscious. Quanah started *Ambler*. The engine sound was steady, and though not loud, it carried a note of restrained power. Putting the big machine in gear, he steered toward to the fuel pumps.

Syne opened the door and jumped out, using the edge of his knife to slash through the pumping hose at a point just below the nozzle. Under pressure, gasoline sprayed in all directions.

Syne leapt back aboard, and *Ambler* rolled toward the open gate. He kept the door open. Down the street raced a group of security men, about five of them. Quanah hit the brakes and half-turned toward Pagan. "You still have that flare?"

"Yeah."

"Break it and throw it toward the fuel pumps."

She looked a little shocked, then a smile spread over her face. She snapped the cylinder between her hands, and a blinding reddish-white light splashed her with an eerie luminescence. The security men yelled at them, unslinging their weapons.

"Throw it!" Quanah shouted.

Turning in her seat, Pagan hurled the burning flare in an overhead half-loop, back into the compound. The spilled gasoline ignited immediately, and before Quanah floored the ACP's accelerator, a foot-high flame trail flashed toward the pump.

A mushrooming orange ball of fire roared angrily upward. The explosion uprooted the pumps from the concrete apron and they rocketed into the night sky. The fuel storage tank beneath the compound detonated, ripping a ragged split in the ground as if a giant fist had slammed up from beneath. It triggered a violent chain reaction as the other vehicles in the compound were flung in all directions and overturned. The gasoline in their ruptured tanks leaked out, then erupted in secondary explosions.

The shock waves thundered across Loki's Rock, knocking people flat, pushing over merchants' stalls, shattering every front window in the Bitter End.

A pillar of flame punched a hundred feet into the black sky over Loki's Rock. The column of brilliant light spewed flying tongues of flame, and burning debris and vehicle parts rained onto the dusty streets and atop the nearest buildings. Hungry flames jumped from shack to hovel to geodesic dome to the rear wall of the saloon.

The security men had been slammed to the ground by the concussion. Lifting their heads, they stared at the roaring fires like hypnotized moths. One tried to shoot at the ACP as it swung past, but Quanah floored the pedal, sending the vehicle rumbling out of Loki's Rock.

The terrain inclined gradually as *Ambler* approached a gully, which slanted down to the old streambed they had followed into the town days earlier.

Quanah was checking their backtrack in the mirror and didn't see the vehicle rocketing into view over the crest of the ridge ahead of them until Pagan said tensely, "Night patrol."

The open-topped ATV had huge knobby tires and an extremely broad wheel base. An M-120 machine gun was mounted on the roll bar, giving the vehicle a top-heavy appearance. The four men, all armed with spidery-looking assault rifles, clung to seat straps as the machine jounced full-tilt over the terrain. All of them wore goggles to protect their eyes from dust, their lower faces concealed by bandanas. The ATV traveled at such a high rate of speed, its tires left the ground when it topped the rise. It flew for twenty feet until it hit the sand on a course that would intersect *Ambler's*.

The barrel of the M-120 spit a tongue of flame. Little spouts of dirt sprang up well to the right of *Ambler*. The overstimulated triggerman had fired before he had established the correct range.

Quanah used the heel of his hand to wrench the steering wheel in a hard half-circle, the big tires flinging up plumes of loose gravel and sand. The cloud of grit blotted them from the triggerman's aim for a handful of seconds.

Quanah wrenched the wheel in the opposite direction, and *Ambler* fishtailed, spewing up another wave of dust to blend with the first. As he hoped, the driver of the ATV slackened his speed rather than charge blindly into the choking cloud.

Pressing down the accelerator, Quanah sent *Ambler* barreling past the ATV. He glimpsed the gunner swinging the M-120 around. He could not clearly see at what he was shooting, but two lucky rounds scored *Ambler's* armored coachwork.

"They're not using AP or hi-ex rounds, at least," observed Syne.

The M-120 continued to hammer, bullets smacking into the rear of the ACP with flat clangs and little flares of sparks.

Pagan said grimly, "They're finding the range now."

"How long will they keep this up?" Quanah asked.

Pagan smiled without humor. "Until they catch us and kill us or until we kill them."

Syne said, "We have counter-measures."

Quanah nodded. "I'll leave that up to you."

With a nod of acknowledgement, Quanah spread his long fingers over the glowing keys of the fire control board. He glanced at the side mirror, waited a few seconds, and then tapped three keys in rapid succession.

Three bright yellow fireballs bloomed in mid-air at the rear of *Ambler*. The ATV drove straight into the explosions. The vehicle flipped, rolling end over end, strewing the area with metal fragments. The security team catapulted from the ATV like rag dolls flung from slingshots. The fuel tank ignited and engulfed the body in a mushroom of roiling orange flame. The ATV disintegrated in a shower of hardware, both of its axles wrenched loose and cartwheeling in opposite directions.

Quanah slowed *Ambler*, but he didn't brake. He gazed at the settling wreckage in the mirror and commented inanely, "Good counter-measuring, Mr. Syne."

"Flash grenades," replied Syne. "Meant to disorient."

"They did more than that," Pagan said sourly.

Grinning savagely, Quanah said, "I don't think anybody else is going to be running us down like deer tonight."

"No, not tonight," Syne intoned. "Very encouraging."

CHAPTER TWENTY-FIVE

Out in the city, a man groaned and cursed. Crockett pushed against one of the tall doors with his good shoulder, and it swung open silently on oiled hinges. Stepping over the dim threshold, he pulled the door back into place. He stood there, surveying the gloomy interior of the big, high-ceilinged room.

It was about fifty feet long, lined on three sides with bookshelves floor to ceiling. He saw comfortable armchairs, upholstered in red leather, scattered about, and a huge globe of Loki stood in one corner. At first glance, the room appeared to be a combined library and office. The carpet was a medium blue, and a replica of the seals emblazoned on the doors was embroidered in thick gold thread. Shaded lamps, cast a subdued illumination.. The only odd feature was a fireplace, logs glowing cheerily in the hearth.

An immense circular desk dominated the fourth wall. Blinking in the semi-gloom, Crockett saw a man sitting at the desk. He sat as motionless as a statue, not even reacting when the huge door had opened and closed.

He was dressed all in black. His eyes seemed to be deep-set in shadowed sockets and they were without movement or the spark of life.

Crockett stared at him, not speaking, a little demoralized by the hush and vastness of the room. The man stared back. Finally, Crockett raised both weapons and ordered, "To your feet. Hands where I can see them. Quick!"

The man complied, silently and smoothly, without so much as a squeak of leather or wood. Crockett started to step toward him when the wall on his left seemed to explode like a grenade.

Splintery fragments flew in every direction, and something clipped him a stunning blow on the left temple. The whole side of his head went numb, and he reeled drunkenly, lurching to one knee. He stopped himself from falling, but he dropped the Hawken in the process.

Bits of dirt and pain-haze clouded his vision. He brought up the machine gun, lifting his head, searching for a target, tasting the coppery salt of blood at the corner of his mouth. He felt it crawling down the side of his face.

Something heavy and metallic swung down from his right side, smashing across his left wrist with nerve-numbing force. His subgun skidded quietly across the carpet.

Crockett sprang to his feet, and found himself face-to-face with Welch. Behind him he saw a man-sized recess between the bookcases. The man held a silver wand. It hummed as menacingly as a nest of hornets. The shot of infrasound had blasted a hole in the wall next to Crockett's head, and he caught not only a sonic overspill but also a spray of splinters.

Crockett wiped his face on a coat sleeve and slowly dropped his hands to his sides. Welch stared at him impassively and said, "You asked about the *Brigadefuhrer's* location. You've found it."

The man behind the desk said, "Come here." His voice was very soft and completely flat. It was the voice of a man with few feelings and a lot of authority.

Crockett did as he was told, measuring each step. He didn't seem to have much choice, with Welch marching behind him and the tip of the infrasound wand humming. He noticed as he passed it that the fireplace was a fake, colored lights shining through molded plastic logs, strictly a decorative item. It cast no heat at all.

Facing the *Brigadefuhrer* across the desk, Crockett got a better look at him. He wore wide collared uniform tunic with silver and red piping running in tight lines along the shoulders and chest. The Ahnenerbe insignia patch on his bicep looked like a splotch of blood against the black fabric.

He was not particularly tall, but his shoulders were very broad. The man's high-boned face was very pale, with sharp cheekbones and a jutting chin. His unnaturally smooth, white skin held very few lines or wrinkles. His ears were very small and delicately shaped, nestled close to the skull. His close-cropped hair resembled a pale gray skullcap of feathery bristles. His eyes were invisible behind the dark, curved lenses of sunglasses. He looked more than just gaunt, he was cadaverous. His posture and attitude reminded Crockett of career military officers he had encountered.

The reflective lenses over the *Brigadefuhrer's* eyes regarded him with an impersonal impassivity. "Who are you?"

"Quentin Crockett."

"A citizen of Loki's Rock?"

"No. I came from there, though. Against my will."

"Welch tells me you have a companion, a woman."

"Yes." Crockett didn't ask if Alex had been captured or killed. He kept his face and tone composed.

"How did you get in here?"

"The nose."

"Of course. An unforgivable security oversight on the part of my aides. It has always been so." The words were delivered without heat, without change in timbre. "Why are you here?"

Crockett took a deep breath, wondering how much to tell him. "It's about your technology."

"Indeed. What about it?"

"Django Bonner wants it all to himself."

The *Brigadefuhrer* nodded, his expression vague and preoccupied. "I am aware of that."

He moved around the desk and extended his hands toward the fireplace, as if to warm them by the cold, colored light. "Why did he send emissaries such as you and your companion? Are you negotiators or are you assassins?"

Crockett sidestepped the question. "Bonner feels that you should share more of your bounty, and not hoard it all up here."

"No. Impossible."

"I'll convey that message to him, then."

"No, I'm afraid that's impossible, too. Your friends at Loki's Rock will never receive word of the goings-on in this Institute."

The *Brigadefuhrer* no longer looked vague or preoccupied. "You anarchist scum. You filth. You maggot. How dare you profane the sanctity of the Ahnenerbe with your person?"

Crockett made a move to step backward, and the hum of the infrasound wand increased in volume. He lifted conciliatory hands. "I mean you no harm. I have nothing but admiration for you and your Institute."

The *Brigadefuhrer* looked at him closely, with the detachment of a scientist examining an unfamiliar germ strain beneath a microscope. He gazed at Crockett steadily for what felt like a very long time.

Finally, he smiled. "Perhaps I've been a trifle hasty. I *am* curious as to why Django Bonner took such extreme measures to alter the terms of our trade agreement, and you may be able to advise me."

He reached up and pressed his ice-cold fingers to the left side of Crockett's head. He brought the hand away and studied the blood. "You've sustained an injury. Several, in fact. You appear to be losing a considerable amount of blood."

"It's not as serious as it looks," Crockett replied.

"Losing any of the precious fluids of the body is serious, Mr. Crockett."

"That's Colonel, actually."

"Is it indeed? A military man, are you?"

"Yes...from Terra. I'm attached to the office of Offworld Operations."

"Never heard of it."

"There's no reason why you should," replied Crockett. "It was formed barely a year ago. Our mission statement is to investigate colony worlds in the Spur. We're starting with Loki."

"This seems like a good place. Have you found the Terran Enclave station yet?"

Crockett's eyebrows rose. "No, we haven't. We're looking for it...as well as for evidence of the Imperator Tyranny."

The *Brigadefuhrer* turned away as if he had lost interest in the topic. "Go with Welch and he will see to your wounds. In the interim, we will try to locate your companion. Afterward, we will talk."

Crockett managed to keep the surge of relief from showing on his face. Alex had not been apprehended or killed and was still loose somewhere in the giant base.

With the vibrating tip of the wand positioned near his face, Crockett took off the combat harness of the remaining grenades and ammo clips and dropped them on the desk. Then Welch pointed him toward the door. He marched Crockett out of the office and back into the miniature city. The smoke and dust had dissipated. A few armed men were in view, but when they approached, Welch waved them away.

"You fucked up this place and our personnel pretty good, Colonel," Welch said petulantly. "You made a big mess that your betters will have to clean up. Same as it ever was."

"I liked it better when you spoke gibberish," Crockett replied. "As long as we're on the subject of gibberish, what does *Blut und Ehre* mean?"

Welch laughed derisively. "I can see that educational levels haven't risen among the lesser breeds. It's German, meaning Blood and Honor."

He directed Crockett away from the perimeter of the city. A beetle appeared, hovering silently behind and above Welch, following them like a bird dog. Crockett noticed that Welch was wearing another ID badge, identical to the one he had lifted.

When they reached a titanium alloy wall, Welch aimed a small remote-control device at it. There was a muffled, hissing sound. A large section of the wall moved forward, tilting back from its bottom edge. It slid out on pneumatic hinges, turning into an up-slanted ramp. Crockett was herded up the ramp and into a wide metal-walled tunnel.

They walked for what seemed like a long time. Crockett saw that one section of wall to his left consisted of a glassy, smoke-tinted panel. He glanced into it, and then halted. Welch did not object—in fact, he snickered.

Frightful life flapped behind the transparent panel. Within a darkened chamber recessed deep in the wall flitted a swarm of shreekwings. The chamber was a specially designed habitat, with branches to roost upon and prey to pursue and kill.

However, these shreekwings were larger than the creatures he had seen just a few days earlier. Their scaled black bodies were nearly a foot long, and their wing-spreads were more than three feet. They looked like depictions of demons he had seen in an old religious text.

Turning to Welch, he asked, "What's up with the shreekwings? The *Brigadefuhrer's* pets?"

"In a way. More like a project. We're working on a way to increase their size and reduce their birth mortality rate. The mothers tend to eat their young. That's one reason they're rare."

"Damn good thing. They're vicious predators."

Smiling a superior smile, Welch said, "We wouldn't be interested in them otherwise. The shreekwings are perfectly adapted to their environment. They're a pure breed of killer."

"That's my point. Why make them larger and more numerous?"

"Microcircuitry, Colonel, introduced into their brains, connected to the visual neural system. We'll be able to control specific behavior and they'll make an excellent offensive/defensive measure. They'll be completely expendable, too, since we'll always be able to breed more."

He gestured impatiently with the wand. "All of this is way beyond you. If the *Brigadefuhrer* wants to give you a tour of our bioengineering facility, that's up to him. Let's go."

They continued another hundred yards down the tunnel, then took a hard right turn and crossed a short catwalk that stretched over a cavernous workshop. Crockett saw jigs, tooling machines, drill presses and equipment he couldn't easily identify. Men handled pieces of metal of all shapes that were spread out on tables. Many of the metal pieces were frameworks that resembled the skeletons of human arms and legs. A number of others looked like the molds and casings of the beetles.

Crockett stopped to survey them, but was pushed forward by Welch's wand. They reached the end of the catwalk, walked into another stretch of tunnel and entered a room. The door frame bore a square-armed red cross.

The room was occupied by a bald, white-coated man. He had a kindly, smiling face, and he appeared to have been expecting them. He looked to be about Quanah's age, and he asked Crockett to take off his coat and shirt. He hesitated, and Welch gestured meaningfully with the wand. The beetle hovered before the open doorway.

Crockett took off his coat and shirt. He shivered. His bones felt bruised, his flesh numb, his head light. The man examined the wand inflicted injury closely, without voicing any curiosity about the knife wounds or his old scars.

With remarkably gentle fingers, he probed the laceration on the side of his head. Crockett allowed the medic to use an aerosol-can spray on his wounds. Wherever the spray touched, a film like a thin skin formed, adhering to his flesh.

"This liquid bandage contains nutrients and antibiotics and will nip any infection, Colonel. Its composition is very similar to real epidermal tissue and your body will absorb it as your injuries heal."

"Is that how you guys keep your youthful complexions?" Crockett asked.

"New skin from a can?"

"Of course not! Our technique is far more sophisticated, far more—"

"That's enough," Welch interrupted coldly. "Get dressed, Colonel."

Crockett did as he was told, noting that his knife and sheath had been removed from the belt. At least the Commtach still adhered safely to his mastoid bone. "Now what?"

Welch opened his mouth to reply, then cocked his head slightly, as though he were listening to whispered instructions. He pressed a spot at the base of his throat, just beneath his larynx, and said, "Acknowledged."

Crockett eyed him suspiciously. "You didn't answer my question, Welch."

Welch grinned and squeezed the handle of the wand. "Now, we'll find out if you can take it as well as you dish it up."

CHAPTER TWENTY-SIX

The city trembled with the reverberations of gunfire, screams and shouted profanities. The hue and cry passed Alex where she lay in the shadow of the Hitler memorial.

She grinned wryly. Reliable Crockett, who seemed to have a plan for every contingency, had drawn away the rat pack, his guns blazing like an action hero in old movies her grandfather had enjoyed.

She waited for a count of thirty, and then began moving in a crouched duckwalk, back toward to the ventilation shaft so as to make her way to another level, hopefully to the primary circulation station.

The psychologist in Alex despaired of ever reasoning with the Jotunheim inhabitants. The very existence of the cunningly crafted miniature model of the city indicated a severe dissociative disorder--it was obsessive-compulsive behavior taken to a frightening degree.

The people inside Mount Maleficent had lived too long in isolation to feel emotions beyond contempt for the outside world or anger if their wants were not immediately gratified. In that, they were very similar to the people of Loki's Rock.

A shadow flitted over her, and Alex froze in mid-scuttle, not daring to move or even breathe. A beetle skimmed slowly above the rooftops, not slowing as it floated past her position.

Welch's ID badge clipped to her coat had saved her from detection, but she realized it was a two-edged sword. The tracer lozenge on it could just as easily be used to pinpoint her location anywhere inside the complex.

After the beetle was out of sight, she began moving again. The heavy exchange of gunfire seemed to be tapering off to a sporadic crackle.

Suddenly, the air shivered with a violent concussion. Alex heard screams and saw the sword monument swallowed by a cloud of smoke and flame. At least Crockett was still active, hell following in his wake. Bits of grit and pulverized stone pattered down all around.

After the echoes of the explosion and the crash faded, a mausoleum silence fell over the city. She found the quiet more disturbing than the noisy shouts and gunfire that had preceded it. She crept to within sight of the memorial and saw three armed guards posted around it.

Carefully, Alex backtracked, wondering where another exit might be located and how she could possibly find it. She glanced down at the floor and saw a layer of dust and grit produced by the explosion. She picked up as much as she could, rolled it, worked it between her fingers, crushing the larger kernels to fine powder.

She pitched the grit into the empty air, watching it whirl, the heavier granules separating from the dust. As the smaller particles settled, they drew into a neat vertical strip of light gray powder, about three feet wide. The band of dust slid across the ground, moving over and around obstacles, still keeping its vertical shape.

Rising to her feet, Alex followed the strip of powder through the city, losing it a time or two when it blended with other ground cover, but always managing to find it again. Inside of a minute she had reached the outskirts of the city.

She had correctly guessed that an electrostatic field was a standard feature in every room and on each level of the installation. She had followed the invisible broom as it whisked the detritus toward a built-in dustpan.

The opening was about two and a half feet wide and two feet high, covered by a meshed screen. Kneeling before it, Alex gripped the rim of the cover and tugged. It gave an inch or two, then popped out, connected tiny hinges flush with the floor.

The duct was clean, made of smooth metal sheeting that looked new. It stretched straight ahead, out of sight in the darkness. Taking a deep, nervous breath, Alex removed a small pen-flash from a pocket, tested it and decided the machine gun would be an encumbrance in such a confined space. As it was, she feared the combat harness beneath her coat might slow her, but she didn't want to jettison the grenades or even the extra clips of ammunition. They could be crucial pieces of ordnance—if not to her, then to Crockett.

She took off Welch's ID badge, clipped it to the trigger guard of the subgun and flung it back toward the city, angling it away from the direction in which she had come.

Distantly she heard it clatter against stone.

Lying flat, she elbow-crawled into the duct, holding the penlight between her front teeth.

It was easier going than she imagined, due to the electrostatic field's reduction of friction. She felt her flesh tingling and prickling from the field effect, as if a multitude of tiny ants crawled all over her. It was not as cold in the duct as it had been in the ventilation shaft or even the city. There was no smell to speak of, beyond a faint whiff of ozone.

Half crawling, half sliding, Alex moved forward, the light in her teeth dimly illuminating the darkness only a foot or so in front of her. There was a darker darkness ahead, and she approached it cautiously, every sense alert.

She reached the edge of the duct, where it slanted down at an angle, disappearing into yawning blackness. She groped around in the gloom before her and touched nothing but smooth metal. Alex laid her head down and groaned, then cursed her ingenuity.

It only stood to reason that dust, detritus and other foreign particles would have to be swept somewhere, to a container very much like a high-tech dumpster. Crawling back out the way she had come wasn't an option, but the concept of creeping headfirst into the chute frightened her more than facing a flock of shreekwings.

Raising her head, she looked forward. The duct still slanted away into blackness. She placed both hands flat against the walls of the duct and pressed the sides of her feet against them. By pushing, it was possible to gain the leverage needed to keep from sliding uncontrollably down the chute, assuming, of course, the angle of the incline didn't become any steeper.

A few inches at a time, Alex wormed herself into the downslanting duct, expanding her shoulders, using her hands and feet to grip the sides. She slipped a time or two due to the reduced friction on the metal surface. Once, she slid forward a dozen meters before she could brake herself.

Sweat collected on her face and beneath her clothes. Her teeth bit into the plastic casing of the pen-flash, nearly breaking it. She kept at it, over and over with her hands and feet, losing all track of how far she had descended. Her feet and shoulder sockets began to ache, and then screamed in silent protest at the strain placed upon them.

She experimented a few times, allowing herself to slide along under the momentum of her weight, sighing in relief at the ebbing of the pain in her back, shoulders and legs.

When she began to pick up speed, she caught herself, came to a complete halt, then started the entire laborious process over again.

After the fourth moving rest stop, Alex realized she was having difficulty slowing her descent. The incline of the chute had sharpened. She slapped at the sides of the duct, spreading her legs, pushing with her feet to stop herself, but the braking effect was marginal. She couldn't get a grip, and her body picked up speed. Then she was sliding out of control, diving headfirst down the black duct. She saw nothing below her but thick darkness.

She couldn't repress a cry of fright and the pen-flash fell from her mouth. It bounced from all four walls of the duct, the light jumping crazily, like a wild comet following a mad trajectory through the black gulfs of outer space.

The duct walls vanished beneath her gloved hands. Alex clawed for a handhold, then she dove headlong into a sepia sea. She didn't dive very long. A shattering crash numbed her body from the crown of her head to the tips of her toes. The darkness momentarily turned the color of blood. She was dimly aware that she was tumbling head over heels.

By the time her thrashing tumble ended, the world spun madly around her, tilting to and fro, and she wasn't sure if she was sitting up, lying down or standing on her head. She wasn't at all positive that she was alive.

When Alex's senses finally regained control of themselves, she found she had landed against a soft heap of something gritty and lay in a half-prone, half-sitting position. Her head, her shoulders, her neck and especially her back all ached abominably. She tasted blood sliding warmly from a laceration on her forehead, down her face and over her lips. Her hands smarted from the impact on whatever she had landed upon. The air was heavy and cloying, and she sneezed, sputtered and coughed.

Groaning, she pushed herself away from the heap and wobbled to her feet. Amazingly, despite the waves of pain washing over her, nothing seemed broken. As she stood, she felt a slight sinking sensation, as though her footing wasn't solid. She couldn't see what lay beneath her through the impenetrable darkness.

Patting herself down, she made sure all her personal equipment was where it was supposed to be. She took a step forward, and something gritted beneath her boots with a crunch that sounded unnaturally loud. She sneezed, and that sounded frighteningly loud, too. Taking off a glove, Alex reached down and felt powdery granules, finer than sand, all around her. She stood in the central dustbin, the detritus dump of the installation Though the motes irritated her nose and eyes, they had cushioned her fall and probably saved her life.

Walking through the dust was difficult, like striding through packed snow. She had to lift her feet clear of the layer of grit and place them down carefully, or else a cloud of dust would mushroom up and send her into a paroxysm of coughing and sneezing.

Dabbing at the flow of blood from her forehead with a sleeve, Alex wetted a forefinger and tested the air currents. She detected a faint movement from her left and began a high-stepping shamble in that direction. She groped through the blackness, both arms extended so she could touch any hidden obstacles.

Then, far away, Alex saw a tiny white spark of light. It was very distant, but she headed for it, the crunch of her footfalls sending up ghostly, reverberating echoes.

Long before she thought she had come anywhere near the source of light, she stumbled and saw the spark almost at her feet. It was the pen-flash, lying half-buried in the acres of dust.

Gratefully Alex picked it up and fanned the light around. As she had expected, she saw nothing but gloom and dust. She continued sifting her way through the powder toward the air current. She walked only for a short time before she felt the flow of air growing stronger. She stopped, right before she walked into a black metal wall. By shining the penlight around and groping with her free hand, she found a metal bracket in a flattened U shape, like a ladder rung. There were several more leading up the face of the wall, beyond the illumination range of her light.

Alex swung onto the rungs and began to climb, ignoring the fires of pain the effort ignited all over her body. She estimated she had climbed less than twenty feet before the rungs ended at a narrow ledge, maybe two feet wide. She stepped out onto it, flattening her back against the wall, digging the fingers of her free hand into the uneven metal surface. She edged out in the direction of the air current. Affixed to the floor of the ledge, in regularly spaced intervals, were threaded strips of rubber. These helped her gain traction as the ledge angled upward.

The ledge made a sharp turn to the left after a few dozen steps, and its pitch descended steeply. Putting the pen-flash into her mouth, she crabwalked along it, hands gripping the wall tightly. Alex wondered how deep beneath the mountain she was, and realized she couldn't hazard even an uneducated guess.

The ledge suddenly widened, opened and led out to a metal railed apron, and she realized with a leap of relief that she had been traversing some sort of maintenance walkway.

There was still no sign of anything approximating a door. As she pushed against a wall, something brushed the top of her head.

Craning her neck to look up, she saw a length of heavy, rust-flaked chain, with a handle attached. She couldn't see what it was anchored to, but she grabbed the handle and tugged gingerly. Nothing happened, so, using both hands, she pulled harder, putting all her weight into it.

Alex's effort was rewarded by a loud, shuddery creaking, as of long-disused gears or pivots struggling to turn. Feeble light suddenly appeared, a thread-thin outline tracing a tall rectangular shape in the wall before her.
Hand over hand, she hauled on the chain, and a wide, flat slab broke away from the wall with a shower of grit and rust. Grinding, screeching noises accompanied the lowering of the slab as it slowly fell outward.

Blinking through the rust flakes swirling around her face, Alex saw the slab resembled the drawbridge of a medieval castle, only this one was made of thick sheets of welded and riveted iron.

With a shriek of metal clashing against metal, the slab stopped moving, jamming at a forty-five-degree angle. No amount of pulling, hauling or hanging on the chain would budge it further.

The surface of the slab was by no means smooth or featureless, so Alex half crawled, half climbed up it. Judging by the oxidized streaks, she was pretty sure it was a very old accessway, a maintenance hatch to the detritus dump. It probably had not been opened in nigh on to a century, perhaps considerably longer.

She struggled to the lip of the slab, grasping the edge and carefully pulling herself to eye level to get a quick recon of her surroundings. There was very little to see. Alex looked out into a small enclosed space, not much more than a module with convex, curved walls. It was bare, everything coated with a thin patina of dust that had seeped out of the dump over the decades. So much dust floated in the still air that the light from a ceiling fixture glowed only as a faint yellow blob. A spiral staircase stretched up from the floor to a dark opening. The small room appeared to have been unoccupied for a long, long time.

Alex pulled herself up, squirmed over, hung by her hands and dropped to the floor. She landed easily, dust puffing up from beneath her boots, but needles of pain stabbed through her lower legs. At least the room wasn't cold. In fact, it felt close to normal air temperature. She reasoned that explained why the module appeared to be in disuse. The cryonically altered people of Jotunheim would find it very uncomfortable.

She considered staying where she was long enough to warm up, but the dust irritated her eyes and clogged her nostrils. She could even taste it. Without much surprise she saw that her clothing was completely filmed by gray powder.

At the foot of the staircase, Alex peered upward. She saw nothing but a dim light, so she went up the steps, treading quietly and cautiously. The staircase curved up and around, like a corkscrew. A faint luminosity shone from above, and it grew brighter the farther up the staircase she climbed.

She felt pleasantly surprised when the last step brought her to a door with an ordinary, standard-issue, commonplace doorknob. Before turning it, she drew the TX5, crooked her finger around the trigger, turned the knob and inched the door open. The walls were white and dingy and not composed of the titanium alloy. The floor looked like dirty linoleum, with a black-and-white-checked pattern. This level was obviously part of the original construction, built at least a century before the Catastrophe. Though the air was crisp, with a hint of a chill, it wasn't the Arctic atmosphere of the upper levels.

A sign on the wall, written in faded red letters, read Know Your Emergency Exits! The same message in German was printed below that. An arrow pointed to Alex's right, so she followed it. The corridor curved toward a distant set of double doors that looked like an elevator stand, so she quickened her pace.

As she passed a door, she heard a sharp, hissing sound and she whirled around. A girl wearing a ragged, dirty shift stood framed in the doorway. She screamed at Alex, an incomprehensible torrent of angry words.

It required a second for Alex to recognize the ear-filling screech of consonants as Romani—and it required another few seconds to recognize the wild-haired, wild-eyed girl as Zeda.

CHAPTER TWENTY-SEVEN

The flames billowing up from Loki's Rock smeared the dark sky with a glow that could be seen for miles. Even after *Ambler* dipped down into a gulley, the orange stain could still be seen, like the Aurora Borealis.

Syne, checking their backtrack on the monitor screens, said blandly, "The whole settlement is going up."

"What about pursuit?" asked Quanah, tightly gripping the wheel.

"No sign as of yet. They're too busy fighting the fire."

Quanah switched on the headlights. The APC had been running dark for the past hour, relying on his tracker instincts to find and follow the X-MAC's trail.

Zeda and Pagan were still crammed shoulder to shoulder in the back seat. Zeda's head rested on Pagan's shoulder as she slept a sleep so deep it was almost a coma. The jarring and jouncing of the APC over the rutted, uneven ground failed to stir her.

Quanah figured to follow the X-MAC's tire tracks to a certain point, then cut over in the general direction of the cave. Trouble was, he wasn't sure how to find that certain point.

Worries swirled through his mind like a tornado. Though he hadn't seen one, the X-MAC could be outfitted with a long-range comm unit, and Bonner could have already been apprised of their escape. The closer they rolled to Mount Maleficent, the greater the odds of rolling into an ambush.

He wasn't sure if they could find the cave in the darkness, since he had only glimpsed its general location on Bonner's hand-drawn map. Pagan had never been allowed to visit the pickup point. According to her, it was a trip Bonner always reserved for himself and a couple of security men. The closest she had been to the cave was the mouth of a canyon that led to it.

Consulting his watch, then the position of the stars and the moon overhead, he judged they had about seven hours of sheltering darkness left to them, seven hours to navigate ravines, hills and dry creek beds to locate a cave none of them had ever seen.

Ambler raced across the rugged terrain, and they made good time, much better time than the X-MAC during their initial trip into the area.

Around midnight, Quanah stopped the vehicle briefly so everyone could stretch their legs and he could get his bearings. Zeda continued to sleep in the back seat as they others walked around the vehicle.

Syne commented quietly, "If Zeda's physical strength and reflexes are enhanced by a cybernetic trigger, that trigger might serve as a tracking element as well."

Quanah nodded. "The thought occurred to me."

Pagan glared at them. "Then we should leave her here. She's just a Gypsy."

"Shut up," Quanah said coldly. "If anybody gets left behind, it won't be her. Get back aboard."

They rode far into the night until they recognized the mouth of the valley that had been the site of their battle with the Lakota. Quanah quickly switched off the headlights. Half to himself, he said, "If Bonner's anywhere about, that's where he's laying."

Syne nodded. "I concur. He appears to be a creature of habit, and probably intends to camp in familiar surroundings, at least until morning. I suggest we reverse our course."

Steering the vehicle around a rock slide, Quanah said, "I think the cave is in this direction."

For several miles the trail sloped gently upward into the Midnight Hills, and it became necessary to turn on the headlights again. *Ambler* carried them swiftly up, then down into twisting ravines. It took more than an hour to navigate the APC through and around obstacles.

The sun slowly rose behind them, tinting the brush and stands of grass a russet red. Quanah kept pushing on As 13 Orionis inched higher, the heat rose in the rocky gorges and gullies around them.

According to the chronometer on the instrument panel, it was exactly six o'clock when the narrow ravine they traveled opened into a canyon. Sheer walls rose to nearly a hundred feet on either side, grooved with deep horizontal lines. Ledges jutted out where the softer layers of strata had been eroded away.

The canyon floor was less than two hundred feet wide, and it wended off to the right, to a cave entrance. The opening was a lopsided triangle, twenty or so feet tall, fifty in width. Boulders lay all around, except for an unnaturally flat clearing immediately in front of the yawning black cleft carved into the canyon wall.

Carefully, Quanah steered the APC close to the right-hand wall, beneath an overhanging ledge and behind an outcropping. *Ambler* would be shielded from Bonner's sight if he came down the canyon, and from any eyes inside the cave. The stony floor was too hard to show their tire treads, so they couldn't be tracked that way.

After turning off the engine, Quanah turned to Pagan. "Is the front way the only way in?"

She shrugged. "As far as I know."

Zeda awakened, dragging a hand over her eyes. "Where are we?"

"Hell, I'm not sure," Quanah replied gruffly. "But its location fits the general coordinates we saw, and unless somebody can prove otherwise, I'm going to assume this is the right place. Anybody have an objection?"

No one did. Disembarking, Quanah scanned their surroundings. Because Bonner had mentioned beetles guarding the place, a frontal penetration of the cave was out of the question. He saw a rough but scalable natural staircase curving up thirty feet from the canyon floor and swerving over and down to a point directly beside the cave entrance. After a brief discussion, they decided to climb it. Quanah carried his pulse rifle and Zeda took one of the lightweight TX-20 pump pistols appropriated from Loki Rock's armory.

As they headed up, Quanah was struck by the brooding majesty of the place. The canyon was totally silent, the only sounds the grating of their feet on rock, their labored breathing and the occasional murmured word. The towering rampart walls felt subtly charged with menace.

They had scaled perhaps half of the staircase's length, cautiously approaching a projecting granite slab they would have to squirm around, when Zeda tapped Quanah's shoulder.

The girl peered intently at the canyon's opposite wall. "Hear something," she whispered.

"Like what?" Quanah whispered back.

A splitting *crack!* shattered the silence, and a bullet sang past Quanah's ear, bouncing off the cliff face behind him.

"Like that," Zeda said calmly.

CHAPTER TWENTY-EIGHT

Crockett could only judge the direction of the small elevator by the rising and falling sensation in the pit of his stomach.

First it descended, then smoothly switched to travel along a horizontal plane. Welch maintained a smug smile throughout, and Crockett kept his face impassive, only once sighing with impatience.

"Don't try anything, Colonel," Welch warned. He touched a spot on the base of his throat. "I'm wired for sound. Got a communication system implanted in me. Mess with me and I'll have an armed squad waiting to blow your head off."

"Why did you let something like that be sewn up inside of you?"

Welch frowned, as if he had never contemplated the question before. "So I can be contacted when the *Brigadefuhrer* needs me. Why else?"

"Yeah, right," Crockett muttered. "Why else."

The doors slid open on yet another stretch of alloy-paneled corridor. The *Brigadefuhrer* was there to meet them. He greeted Crockett with a bleak smile that didn't indicate friendliness. Crockett studied the man's face. He saw no malice there, but nothing else either. The *Brigadefuhrer* had gone beyond emotions--either they were frozen out of him, or he never had them to begin with. There was no human warmth about him, probably not even in his blood.

In the brighter light of the corridor, Crockett saw faint pink lines on the smooth-skinned face that looked like old surgical scars.

"Continue the search for the Colonel's companion," the *Brigadefuhrer* ordered. "She somehow escaped the city. Your identification badge was found attached to a firearm. A check on the model, make and serial number showed it was one traded to Loki's Rock over a year ago. So far, the woman has misled the search teams. They're very annoyed about it, so go and take charge of the operation."

Welch hesitated. "Sir, I shouldn't leave you alone with this renegade."

The *Brigadefuhrer* draped a paternal arm around Crockett's shoulders. The arm felt like a beam of steel. "Nonsense. We're going to have a talk, that's all--your presence will inhibit our discussions. Be off with you now."

Welch scowled at Crockett, handed the infrasound wand to the *Brigadefuhrer* and then turned toward the elevator. The *Brigadefuhrer* led Crockett down the corridor.

"Do you know who I am?" he asked in a conspiratorial whisper.

"The *Brigadefuhrer.*"

"I mean my name."

Crockett hesitated, then said, "There is speculation you are Karl Brandt... but for you to be that man, you would have to be almost 500 years old."

"Yes," he said thoughtfully. "I would have to be. But, regardless of my former identity, I have taken the name of Fenris."

With the tip of the wand he touched an insignia patch on the high collar of his uniform. It represented the stylized image of a snarling wolf's head. "*Brigadefuhrer* Fenris. Does the name meaning anything to you?"

Crockett managed to keep his apprehension from showing on his face. "As I recall, it's the name of a wolf from Norse mythology."

The man waggled the wand approvingly. "Correct. But not just any wolf... Fenris was a son of Loki and was foretold to kill Odin on the day of Ragnarok—the last day."

Crockett eyed the man, wondering if he were joking or simply insane. "So you consider yourself a son of Loki?"

The arm tightened around Crockett's shoulders, and his infrasound-induced wound screamed in pain. "Why not? My body may not have been born on this world, but my spirit certainly was. Loki is where my soul fully manifested."

"I understand," Crockett said quickly. "It's a symbolic rechristening."

The arm relaxed. "More or less, yes...but not totally symbolic. This complex became the birthing ward of a new race of humans, designed to thrive on Loki. It wasn't easy, making this place the nerve center of the world. But careful design, meticulous attention to detail and good, sound Aryan craftsmanship paid off."

Nodding, Crockett asked, "How large is the complex?"

"The tunnels run all through the mountain, leading down beneath it. We have fifteen levels above ground. I have lived here for—" Fenris frowned slightly, as though he dredged his memory. "—for many years. I still find it inspiring."

"An installation this size must require a lot of care, a lot of maintenance to keep it in operating condition."

"Oh, quite. The problems are many, and we devote a great deal of time to repair and improvement. But the topic is far too technical to go into now."

"Why did you retreat here in the first place?"

"I did not 'retreat,' Colonel. My reasons aren't open for discussion at present."

"Why choose Loki for a colony?" Crockett asked. "This world isn't the most hospitable Spur planet."

"True...but it did have the saving grace of being so far from the settled Spur cluster that the Commonwealth didn't care about it...not to mention the original colonists were such malcontents, there was a 'good riddance to bad rubbish' philosophy at work."

"Undesirables, in other words."

Fenris nodded. "Exactly. An undesirable planet colonized by even more undesirable people. Who could ask for better protective coloration?"

Crockett assumed the question to be rhetorical, so he didn't respond to it. Instead, he took a breath, held it for a second, then said, "Since you know about the Commonwealth Enclave, there's no reason for me not to assume you know about the Imperators."

"No reason at all, Colonel. In fact, the primary reason we built Jotunheim is due to the Imperators."

"How so?"

The *Brigadefuhrer* did not respond. He turned toward a doorway and the panel slid aside at their approach. The room beyond was very large, alloy-plated and staffed by men wearing white smocks. They read clipboards, checked gauges and thermometers.

Inside glass cases and fluid-filled jars were human internal organs: floating livers, pumping hearts, eyeballs, loops of intestines, and in one large cubicle, the naked body of a man. A metal framework extended from where the right arm should have been.

Crockett was both repulsed and fascinated. In glass-walled vats floated arms and legs, hands and feet and torsos, wires extending from the blood-rimmed stumps of necks, arms and thighs.

"Before your trade agreement with Loki's Rock," Crockett ventured, "how did you acquire the organs and body parts you needed?"

"We managed to stockpile quite a number, primarily from personnel in nonessential positions. Spouses and children of staff members provided us with what we needed, at least for several decades. We began to deplete our supply over the last few years."

If Crockett's mouth hadn't been so dry, he would have spit. "Was it worth it, just so you could exist in this frozen prison?"

Fenris waved a hand around the room. "Hardly a prison, Colonel. This installation is my gift to this world. It is devoted to bestowing order upon chaos. You have no idea how many years I have worked toward this. It's been a long life, a full life, a rewarding life."

Nauseated and angry, Crockett said, "And now you're cyborg, a half-droid that never grows old?"

"Not precisely," the *Brigadefuhrer* replied. "I have a new heart—my third—a few joints are prosthetic replacements, but I'm hardly a cyborg. Nor am I immortal."

"But if you can replace every body part that wears out—"

"We can't replace the brain, Colonel Crockett. Major organ transplants are sometimes successful and sometimes aren't. As you pointed out, the low temperature in which we must live has definite drawbacks. We haven't conquered every vagary that preys on organic matter, though we've made a great leap in that direction."

As they progressed deeper into the laboratory, they passed more dismembered bodies in glass vats, and past tables laid out holding electronic components—odds and ends of microprocessors, thread-thin antennae and a cluster of tiny silver studs. They were identical to the one attached to the back of Zeda's neck. Crockett feigned disinterest, but he considered grabbing a handful of the studs as he walked by so they could be examined later.

In a niche stood a pair of vertical, Lucite-walled vats. Within one, floating in an amber gel, was a shaggy, four-legged shape Crockett at first took to be that of a dog. Then with a sense of shock, he realized the animal was a miniature woolly mammoth, its trunk curled in a question mark shape.

In the second fluid-filled vat floated small, malformed figures—distorted duplicates of wolves, apes and even a shreekwing with a four foot wingspan.

Noting Crockett's expression of combined surprise and revulsion, Fenris said, "GenTek made great advances in resurrecting extinct species—all we needed was a bit of the original genetic material and if we came across a broken sequence, we synthesized the bridge. Now, creatures from Terran prehistory roam Loki."

"Living fossils," Crockett intoned. He stared directly into the man's face. "Much like you."

Fenris did not appear to be offended. "You may be more correct than you know. Follow me."

He opened a door leading out onto a long, bare corridor. The footsteps of the two men rang hollowly on the alloy-sheathed floor, and the overhead lights cast a dim illumination. "I don't come here often," *Brigadefuhrer* Fenris said. "It tends to depress me."

They stepped through a tall, narrow doorway at the end of the corridor, and Crockett saw why the man did not care to visit here. The cold felt overwhelming, like a physical assault.

It bit at his nostrils, his lips, his eyes, anywhere there was moisture. He raised the collar of his coat and lifted his hand over his nose and mouth to protect them from the numbing cold. His eyeballs ached, and he was forced to take short, shallow breaths, worried the air would freeze his lungs.

The gloomy room was a crypt, where the living dead were entombed, frozen in time.

There were over a hundred of them. They stood in orderly rows, each one upright inside a transparent glass canister, arms crossed sedately over their chests. With a quiver of surprise, Crockett noticed that not all of the encased people were men. There were a few women mixed in, mostly young. They wore only a simple drapery, and their bodies had the appearance of pale turquoise, not only in color but substance. The eyes were wide open and they seemed to stare, all one-hundred-plus pairs of them, straight into Crockett's soul.

"Who are they?" he asked. His teeth chattered so violently, he was surprised his words were intelligible.

Even the *Brigadefuhrer* seemed affected by the deep cold, tucking his hands into his pockets and slightly hunching his shoulders. "My people, the ones who contracted incurable diseases or went mad, or who refused to participate in the cybernetic implant program. They are scientists, engineers, military officers, doctors."

"This is a punishment, a prison?"

"No, only a rest stop. They are in stasis and require no air, no food, no interaction with others. I doubt they even dream. But, as you can see, we take care of our own."

Crockett now understood what Welch had meant about over a hundred Institute personnel being inactive. "Why not just shoot them and be done with it?"

"They have valuable skills, important information, abilities crucial to our survival. They held key supervisory and design positions during the construction of our complex and have much knowledge that we can draw upon."

"When you need to ask them something, you thaw them out long enough to ask a question, then refreeze them."

"Yes...but this system of stasis has nothing to do with cryogenics. It's a technology that essentially suspends them—all of us here--in a state of zero time."

"How so?"

"This entire complex utilizes a technology which for all intents and purposes turns all of Jotunheim into self-contained deep storage vault. The process maintains a form of active suspended animation, almost as if we're enclosed by a bubble of space and time, slowing to a crawl all metabolic processes. For all intents and purposes, it's a form of immortality."

"I think you'd be better off dead."

The *Brigadefuhrer* nodded sadly. "Many of the personnel here think the same thing."

They went back along the corridor, and it took Crockett a long while to stop shivering. He said, "I'm not up on the science of two centuries ago, but I don't recall hearing about a form of zero-time stasis."

"That is no surprise, since it did not exist on Terra two centuries ago. We found it here, within this mountain."

"Imperator tech?"

Fenris halted before a heavy metal slab of a door. He pressed the flat of his right hand against it and the slab quivered then slid aside with a prolonged squeal. Stepping aside, Fenris inclined his head in a short bow and waved one hand. Crockett walked across the threshold and into a long passageway, dimly illuminated by a blue light strip stretching along the ceiling. The corridor was completely featureless, but he saw signs of long-ago construction—the marks of tools on the rock walls and arrangements of joists, timbers and beams shoring up the low roof.

Crockett hesitated. The tunnel had an oppressive sense of emptiness of about it, of having once played host to great power but now there was only an energy vacuum, a sensation of absence, of sterility, even of nonexistence.

Fenris said quietly, "Go on, Colonel. You asked about the science, the technology of the Imperators. I will afford you the exceptionally rare chance to see a sampling—or what's left of it."

The corridor opened into a vast, dark space. Metal frameworks and support posts were twisted and bent as if exposed to an extreme heat. The air, though cold and stale, held the faint, acrid reek of superheated metal.

"Where are we?" Crockett asked, unconsciously lowering his voice.

"It was here that the Imperators tried to tap the enormous power boiling at the core of Loki," answered the *Brigadefuhrer*. "And it was here we tried to do the same thing, using the machines they left behind."

A three-tiered fusion generator rose from the floor. More than twenty feet tall, it resembled three solid black cubes balanced atop one another at opposing corners. Crockett had seen them before—usually the top cube rotated slowly, but this particular one did not move, seemingly locked in mid-revolution.

The two people strode between a pair of four-meter high Y pronged voltage converter pylons. Both of them tilted to the left at thirty degree angles, a webwork of cracks deeply inscribed into their soot-blackened surfaces.

"This looks like the scene of an explosion," observed Crockett. "Or several of them."

"Or just one very large, very destructive one," said Fenris, "which then ignited a chain reaction all over the planet."

Crockett squinted at him through the gloom. "How could that be?"

Fenris put a hand on his shoulder. "Stop."

They came to a halt at the edge of a huge round pit that occupied most of the floor space. Crockett's first impression was that they stood on the rim of an impossibly huge well, at least a hundred feet in diameter. He had no doubt the colossal shaft was artificial, a construction. The walls were sheathed in a gleaming metal alloy. A wide ledge ran all around the well. Carefully, Crockett peered down. He could not see the bottom or much below the first hundred feet.

"How deep is it?" he asked.

"As I said…it sinks to the very center of Loki. The Imperators apparently believed the core was a source of an unlimited form of energy. They sank identical shafts in three other regions of the planet. The power points…what our geophysicists called Parallax Pits."

"What form of energy is at the core?"

Fenris shrugged. "We were never positive. Particles of nonbaryonic dark matter, we believe."

"You didn't run tests?"

"We tried." The man gestured to the destruction all around. "This is the result…not to mention the global cataclysm."

Crockett stared at him incredulously. "Are you saying you caused the Catastrophes?"

Fenris nodded. "We activated all four power points on Loki simultaneously. It was an accident, a mistake. But all things being equal, it turned out for the best."

"Millions of people died."

"Millions of them were useless eaters. Totally expendable. Now they're no longer a strain on Loki's limited resources."

Crockett struggled to tamp down his surging anger. "It was due to you that Loki's resources *became* limited."

"You claim to be a military man, Colonel. You know that sometimes an accident has beneficial results."

Brigadefuhrer Fenris turned smartly on his heel and marched back in the direction from which they had come. Crockett hesitated a moment, then joined him. He followed Fenris around a sharp bend in the walkway and was dazzled by bright light reflecting from plate glass and chromium fixtures.

"You know about Imperator tech to some extent," Crockett said. "What do you know about the Imperator culture?"

Fenris smiled. "Other than the fact they were a highly advanced, highly militarized race with a complex code of behavior and morals, very little. All we know is that they are native to the Orion Spur and erupted from their homeworld—we still haven't determined its location—some twenty thousand years ago. They embarked on a long and bloody campaign of conquest and colonization throughout the Spur. The only thing we really know about them is that 'Imperator' was never the term they used to describe themselves."

"That seems to be general consensus of opinion," said Crockett. "Except no one has ever seen one of the so-called Imperators alive or dead."

"True," admitted Fenris. "Not alive or dead. Perhaps a state in-between."

Crockett cast him a swift, sidewise stare. "Explain."

"I intend to."

They entered a long hexagonal room. The left wall was composed of sheets of frosty glass. Crockett glanced through one, down into a chamber below. It took his mind a moment to identify what his eyes saw, and when it did, he instinctively recoiled. His hand grabbed at his empty holster.

He felt a great fear welling up within him, but not a natural, rational survival mechanism type of fear. It was a mindless, xenophobic cringing from a sight that was utterly alien.

Below him, wrapped in a shifting, glowing mist, stood a very tall, excessively slender figure. After a few seconds, Crockett realized the figure was male, dressed in an elaborate armorial garment. The colors red and blue predominated. The long limbs were covered by a pattern of iridescent, interlocking scales.

A crest of golden feathers topped the elongated, narrow skull and ran down the back of the cranium. The face had a subtly reptilian cast—broad, prominent cheekbones and a pronounced brow ridge. Crockett saw no ears.

Projecting out and down from between the brows was a nose resembling a small scythe—extremely thin, sharply ridged, curving toward a lipless mouth like an eagle's beak. The large, almond shaped eyes stared blindly, black vertical slits centered in golden, opalescent irises. They were animal eyes, the eyes of a predator.

Long-fingered hands were crossed over the breastplate and the thumbs were tipped with curved talons, like a gamecock's spur.

He tried to back away, but the *Brigadefuhrer* put a hand against his back to keep him in place.

"Nothing to fear, Colonel." The man's quiet voice purred with amusement. "He can't see you."

Fenris reached up and snatched away the sunglasses from his face. His eyes were narrowed in amusement. Black, vertical pupils bisected golden irises. "But *I* can."

CHAPTER TWENTY-NINE

Alex cocked her pistol and her head at the same time. In Romani, she demanded, "Zeda?"

The black-haired girl shifted from one bare foot to the other. "Who is that?"

With a sinking sensation in her stomach, Alex realized that although the girl resembled Zeda closely enough to be her twin sister, her tangled hair was jet black and her big eyes were so deep a brown they were almost the same onyx hue.

"What is your name?" Alex asked, switching to English.

The girl's face twitched in surprise at her sudden use of another language, but she replied in kind: "Simza. What is your name?"

"Alexis."

"My medicine, you were supposed to bring me my medicine."

"I don't have your medicine," Alex said.

The girl blinked her eyes at her owlishly. "Then why am I waiting for you to bring it to me?"

Even with her nerves on edge, Alex laughed. "Logical answer. How long have you been waiting for medicine?"

Simza heaved her shoulders in a half shrug. "Since the whitecoat man told me somebody would bring me medicine. He told me my sister needed the medicine first, but I don't have a sister, not really. The whitecoat man told me I did...that they had made a twin sister for me. She was a better Simza so she got to have the medicine first." Her face twisted in anger. "They gave her all of my jewelry too...all my rings and bracelets."

Alex, staring at the girl, felt clammy sweat bead her forehead. "How long have you been here?"

"I don't know. A long time."

Alex cast her eyes up and down the girl's body. The ragged shift looked like the dirty remains of a hospital gown. She saw a faded label reading ZED sewn onto the left breast.

Clearing her throat, but not lowering her TX5, she said, "May I see your left arm, please?"

Simza's eyes narrowed a bit. "Why?"

"Humor me...then I'll help you find medicine."

Simza thrust out her left arm. Alex gave it a swift, visual examination but didn't see numbers or letters tattooed onto the flesh. However, she saw the marks of hypodermics, IV shunts and tiny scoop-shapes where tissue samples had been taken.

"Turn around," Alex said. "Let me see the back of your neck."

The girl scowled, but did as Alex requested, parting her hair. Stepping close, Alex touched the nape of her neck and gently probed the base of her skull. She neither saw nor felt anything unusual.

"Do you remember where you came from?" Alex asked as Simza turned back around to face her.

Simza's face screwed up in concentration, then she nodded. "My family...my clan came to a town."

"What town?"

"Something-something-rock, I think."

"How did you end up here?"

Simza's eyes glimmered with tears. "Don't remember...out walking...men on floaty bikes came up...one took me...I fought and he hit me...did something else to me, too. I fell asleep."

Alex mentally supplied images of Bonner's security men on bullet bikes surrounding the girl on the outskirts of Loki's Rock.

Dragging the back of her hand across her eyes, Simza stated hoarsely, "Woke up here, but don't know where here is. Do you?"

"I do...but I don't know how to get out. How is it you're wandering free?"

Petulantly, Simza answered, "The whitecoat man said they didn't need me for the program any more. So that's why I couldn't have the medicine first."

"What program were you a part of, Simza?"

"The ZEDSex program, what do you think?"

Alex smiled wanly. "Of course. What was the purpose of the ZEDSex program?"

The reply was immediate, as if recited by rote. "To be fruitful and multiply."

"How many of you are there here?"

"Just me now. My twin sister was taken away."

Alex said nothing but she could guess at the purpose behind the program. Since she hadn't seen any females in installation, she suspected the ZEDSex program was designed to provide the complex with a stable population of organ donors.

If Simza provided the base genetic material to create clones, then she and few others could guarantee a controlled supply of organs to be harvested. However, the Alpha-subject clone she had named Zeda was most likely the end-result of extensive genetic tinkering. Whether she had escaped the Ahnenerbe or was set free, she had no way of knowing.

Alex said, "I have to be on my way, Simza. Come with me."

Simza's eyes narrowed with suspicion. "To find medicine?"

Alex strode down the corridor. "I'll try."

"You can't go that way," Simza piped. "Door is sealed. There's only one way topside."

Hesitating, Alex scanned the girl's face, looking for indications of deceit. "Can you lead me out of this place?"

Simza ducked her head in assent. "I'll show you."

Alex followed Simza through a door into a room that was the exact opposite of the rooms she had seen above. It was filthy. Rusting pipes crisscrossed at all angles along the ceiling and walls. She saw a cracked and dirt-filmed porcelain toilet affixed to a wall. The floor tiles were layered with ancient grease and layers of grime, in the shape of treaded boot soles. A long row of dilapidated metal lockers lined one wall. A few of the doors gaped open, revealing rotting military uniforms hanging from hooks.

The place had been abandoned a long, long time ago.

Alex followed the girl through what had been a lounge or common room. She saw couches, vending machines and even a huge television set. The screen was perforated by bullet holes.

"Do you live down here?" she asked.

"Sure," Simza replied. "For a long time."

"Alone?"

"Sure, all alone." Simza sounded troubled. "When the program was over, a man in a white coat showed me the way down here. He wanted the program to go on, said it had been stopped pre-prema—what's the word?"

"Prematurely?"

"Yes. He used to visit me here, make fuck to me, bring me food to eat. Then he went away to get medicine and never came back."

"How long ago was that?"

Simza came to a stop, eyes half closing. She twirled a lock of black hair around an index finger. "Don't know. Long time. I waited a long time, and he never came back. Figured he was with my sister."

Her full underlip quivered and she whispered, "That bitch."

Alex felt a surge a sadness. She speculated that once the Gypsy girl's usefulness had come to an end, a termination order had been issued. Before it could be carried out, one of the installation scientists found other, more venal uses for her. She couldn't help but wonder if Zeda managed to evade an identical termination order because of the same scientist.

"How do you live down here?" Alex asked. "Where do you get food and water?"

Tittering, Simza started walking again. "Plenty of food in little sealed packages. Lots of water in the drains."

They entered another room, very long and dimly lit, illuminated inadequately by overhead neon fixtures. It was a workshop, filled with heavy tables, tools, chain vises, band saws and cumbersome drill presses. She came to halt.

"Where are you taking me, Simza?"

The girl stopped, staring at her from about ten feet away. then said reproachfully, "You can trust me. Won't hurt you."

"Is that a promise?"

Very seriously, very gravely, Simza made the sign of the cross over her chest, then kissed the little finger of its right hand. "Pinky swear."

Alex was startled into laughing, but at the same time she wasn't about to place her trust in the girl, no matter how pathetic and harmless she seemed. She adjusted her Commtach and heard the hiss of static. Though the circuit was engaged and open, Crockett didn't respond to her hails. She moistened dry, dust-coated lips and fought both the worry about him and the pain of her bruised muscles. She turned to Simza.

"Lead on."

They left the workroom and entered a similar, slightly smaller one. Simza led the way toward propped open elevator doors. There was no car. The shaft rose above it.

Paralleling the cables and running up one wall into the darkness stretched a metal ladder. Far above gleamed a faint luminosity.

Simza stepped onto the ladder and began to climb. Alex snugged the TX5 into its holster and followed. They went up in silence for more than a hundred feet until they came to an opening, the elevator doors jammed to one side by a length of pipe. The air felt colder and throbbed to the rhythm of engines and generators. Alloy plates sheathed the walls and floors.

Beyond the shaft, Alex saw three entrances to corridors. One stretched straight ahead, and the other two branched to the left and right.

Simza moved down the neon-lit central corridor. It took several sharp turns and twists, like a maze. Even though Simza claimed familiarity with the layout, she sometimes hesitated at the various forks and bends.

After several minutes the corridor terminated in a large circular hatchway, rimmed by several concentric collars of dark metal. Simza giggled and waved a hand in front of it.

The hatchway irised open. The clank of mechanisms grew louder, and the air grew chillier. Beyond the hatch extended a short, cylindrical tunnel that led them to an identical hatchway. Simza opened this one in the same way, by waving a hand over a concealed sensor. The throb of generators deepened, until the air vibrated. Feeling like she was breasting invisible waves, Alex stepped through the hatch and found herself perched like a bird on a wire over what looked like a factory.

She and Simza stood on a narrow gallery. Above and below she saw other galleries, and from them sprang a webwork of catwalks that spanned the vast area, all interconnected vertically by a system of caged-in lifts. The lifts and walkways were constructed to give access to all levels of the enormous central circulating station and moisture condenser that filled the place.

Giant fan blades roared, and greenish liquid coolant bubbled and flowed through a confusing network of transparent tubes. Huge square conduits rose like skyscrapers almost out of sight between a pattern of cooling coils. Water beaded and dripped incessantly from the metal surface of the condenser. It was very cold, very damp and dank.

Though the room was unoccupied, Alex could see the subtle marks of use. Control consoles and banks of dials and switches surrounded the base of the gargantuan machine, and the chairs in front of them had deep hollows in the faded seat cushions.

Despite its size, Alex could tell that the massive machine had been assembled in a rather piecemeal fashion. It wasn't symmetrical, and it was obvious that many of its working parts had been cannibalized from other machines. Evidently, when the decision to live in a near-freezing environment had been made, the original air-conditioning system was modified and reengineered. Though she couldn't see it from her vantage point, it was clear that the station was connected to a fusion generator. There was no other way such a massive machine could be powered.

Leaning over a guardrail, Alex peered down at the floor far below. It was made of concrete and covered by several inches of standing, stagnant water. It drained sluggishly toward huge open grates scattered like giant poker chips over the floor. Resting on an elevated platform above the water she saw a row of six cube-shaped fusion generators, filling the huge room with a penetrating subsonic song of pure power. Alex could feel the sympathetic vibrations in the metal railing under her fingertips.

She concluded that it would take hours to find a central switching console that controlled the generators. Besides, she was sure the station had back-up power sources and redundancies designed into it. To kill Jotunheim, she would have to take out the generators. But what she wanted was to orchestrate a thaw, not deprive the entire complex of power. She checked over her complement of grenades and wondered if they were powerful enough to do the job.

Turning to Simza she asked in a shout, "Is there another way out of here?"

Nodding, Simza pointed to one of the nearby lifts. "That one goes up."

"How far? " she yelled.

"I don't know," Simza yelled back. "Just up."

Studying the generators again, Alex eyed the thickness of their metal casings and gauged that all four grenades might just knock out two of them. However, arranged in a semicircle around the last generator stood a collection of clattering pumps, the armatures dipping up and down with a blurring speed. She recognized the rattling machines as air pumps, sucking oxygen from the outside and feeding it into the massive condenser. Her eyes followed the conduit and ductwork, and she recognized particulate filtration systems, coolant distribution and return networks built into them.

Before she took any action, she pressed the transmit stud on the Commtach and said, "Colonel, come in. Colonel Crockett, respond. Goddammit, why won't you respond?"

This time she received an answer.

CHAPTER THIRTY

Quanah rolled behind the outcropping and came up with his pulse rifle in firing position just as two more steel-jacketed wasps stung the canyon wall overhead. The outcropping was over seven feet wide at its base and provided enough cover for everyone, as long they sat scrunched up, knees folded against their chests. Unfortunately, it was barely four feet high.

Zeda cautiously peered at the opposite wall of the canyon, the only place for the shots to have originated. She ducked aside as another bullet ricocheted off the granite shield, but she had seen a glint of sunlight on a gun barrel. "Spotted him."

"An Indian?" Pagan demanded.

Zeda shrugged. "Only saw a gun."

Quanah brought rifle to chin level, settling the rubber-cushioned stock into the hollow of his shoulder. He peered through the image-enhancing scope and followed Zeda's direction to the reflected light. He spotted it and took slow aim, centering the CGI cross hairs, waiting for the sniper to show more of himself than just his gun barrel.

Zeda said, "I'll speed along."

She lifted her head until the top of her cerulean hair rose above the edge of the outcropping. Quanah glimpsed a dark arm and head through the scope and squeezed the trigger of the rifle. The report sounded like the hiss of snake, blended with a piece of wood snapping in two.

"Think you got him," Zeda whispered.

Almost at the same second, a dark shape slithered over the lip of the canyon wall and fell with a clatter to the stones below. Quanah saw it through the scope and identified it as an ST- 90 automatic rifle.

"It's Bonner's people," he said grimly. "Loki's Rock must have gotten word to him."

"He'll send men up on both sides to block us off in two directions," Pagan said fearfully.

Peering over the outcropping, Zeda said, "Two across from us, and I hear at least two more above us."

Syne craned his neck, looking up the canyon wall. "We have been cast in the roles of the proverbial fish in a barrel. They will not have to expose themselves to point their weapons down and shoot."

"Maybe," Quanah said, pulling the sack to him. "But fish in barrels don't usually shoot back."

He pawed around in the bag and pulled out an oval grenade, the thin metal walls encircled by rubber rings. He tossed it experimentally in his hand.

"What are you planning to do with that?" Pagan asked.

"Take care of the bastards above us."

"You'll have to arm it and throw the damn thing straight up," said Pagan. "There's no guarantee it won't just drop back down and blow up in our laps!"

Syne said calmly, "That is a DM-92 incendiary grenade. It has a push-button arming device, but detonation occurs when the casing breaks."

"So?" Pagan demanded.

Quanah tossed the grenade to Zeda, who caught it gingerly. He turned his back to the outcropping and leaned as far back as it would allow. He looked straight up, holding the pulse-rifle to his shoulder.

"Zeda, when I say 'now,' I want you to throw the grenade straight up, over our heads. Try to put a little effort into it so it'll land on the top of the wall, but it doesn't matter if you do. Just make sure you throw high and straight."

Quanah flattened himself against the rock and fitted his eye over the scope. He waited, watching and listening. When he heard a faint clink of metal against rock and he said softly, "Now."

Zeda lobbed the bomb up in a straight line. Quanah followed the grenade's vertical flight through the scope. When it lost its momentum and began to drop, he waited until the small object was level with the edge of the canyon wall before squeezing the trigger.

The blast of the detonating grenade echoed across the canyon and back like a thunderclap. A fireball bloomed, and tongues of flame curled in all directions. Everyone below felt the slamming concussion. As the echoes of the explosion still reverberated, clattering rock fragments and screams of agony added to the noise.

Shielding her eyes from the falling rock chips, Zeda looked up and said with a grin, "Flash fried 'em."

A pair of automatic rifles began chattering from the opposite wall, bullets striking and ricocheting from the outcrop. Quanah hitched over, saw the men on the facing edge of the canyon and fired the rifle at them. After one man fell, arms windmilling, and the other dived for cover, Quanah said, "Time to move. I'll lay down a covering fire."

As the three people broke from their granite hiding place, Quanah propped his rifle atop the boulder, reset the selector switch and depressed the trigger, sending a steady stream of plasma-powered bullets to chew up the topmost edge of the opposite wall. He kept the security man up there pinned down, afraid to raise his head, until Zeda, Syne and Pagan reached the bottom of the stone staircase.

Grabbing his sack, Quanah scrabbled out on the ledge, climbing, crawling and sliding. He heard voices from the mouth of the canyon, and he recognized one of them as Bonner's. Evidently, he had sent a scout force ahead, holding back the remainder of the security squad.

Pagan, Zeda and Syne had taken cover behind rock tumbles beside the cave entrance the moment they'd jumped from the stone staircase. Quanah slid down to join them, hopping from ledge to ledge. Although the exchange of gunfire and the grenade explosion had happened in a very short span of time, he feared that whoever or whatever lurked inside the cave had been alerted. He expected a swarm of beetles to swoop from it immediately.

At the very least, he expected Bonner and his men to charge down the canyon, weapons blazing.

Quanah joined his companions behind the rocks on the right side of the cave opening before either one happened. He didn't have to wait long before six shaven-headed men raced across the canyon floor, gun barrels flaming. The men fanned out and took cover, maintaining a cone-shaped firing pattern. Bullets whined from their stone shelter and exploded against the rocky wall over their heads, sprinkling them with dust and gravel.

"As long we stay down, we're safe," Syne observed. "But if we try to make a run for the cave, we'll make excellent targets."

A bullet dug a gouge in a rock very close to his head. The shot had come from above, and Zeda returned the fire with a double blast from her pistol.

Pagan and Quanah exchanged knowing looks. It was only a matter of time before the security men got in position to lob grenades at them, or the sniper above would pick them off.

Syne, peering out between the open spaces in the rocks at the men shooting at them remarked, "This situation reminds of a very old piece of cinematic entertainment. A movie, they were called on Terra."

Pagan stared at him as if the synthetic man had suddenly gone mad, but Syne continued. "The climax of the drama was a stirring scene of settlers beset by bloodthirsty Indians. When events looked their darkest, the gallant U.S. Cavalry led by the stalwart John Wayne charged in over the ridge to rout the savages and set things aright."

No one responded to Syne's story. Quanah had only the vaguest idea of who John Wayne had been, and at the moment he wasn't inclined to solicit Syne for further information about him.

A movement on the canyon rim caught his eye. The head of a sniper was silhouetted against the blue of the sky, and sunlight gleamed dully off the gun barrel as he brought it into firing position.

As Quanah raised his rifle, the sniper's head suddenly acquired a new and different shape. The autorifle in the man's hands clattered down the face of the cliff. The crack of the shot was lost in the echoes of the gunfire from the men on the canyon floor, but Quanah definitely heard the volley that followed it.

Bullets punched gouts of dirt from around the security men's cover, and they shouted in surprise and fear. Quanah scanned the towering walls and saw at least half a dozen copper-skinned men on horseback, men with feathers in their long black hair, paint on their faces and weapons in their hands. He recognized Sky Wolf among them.

Quanah stared at the band of Lakota as they poured a withering hail of autofire down on the security men from above. He turned to Syne and said, "That's not your John Wayne *or* the U.S. Cavalry."

"I'm not going to complain," Zeda said, smiling with relief. "Are you?"

Quanah wasn't going to complain, but he did wonder whether the Lakota, after killing the security men, might end up blasting them down just to be thorough. He doubted Sky Wolf's arrival was to pull their fat out of the fire. More than likely he was taking advantage of the opportunity to rid the Midnight Hills of white intruders once and for all.

Zeda and Pagan opened fire on the security men while they were occupied by the Lakota. They were spread out all over the canyon floor, and half of them shot back at the Indians while the other half blasted away at them. But most of their shots went wild, since they were trying to dodge and duck the death belching from the rifles above.

Seeing that the security force was occupied with the Lakota, Quanah said, "Let's hit the cave."

"No time like the present," Syne said, rising swiftly to his feet.

The four people climbed quickly over the rocks and sprinted for the cave opening. The few hasty shots directed their way kicked up dirt and rock, but none of the bullets struck uncomfortably close.

As they darted inside, Quanah risked a backward glance and saw the Lakota astride their ponies, swerving away from the edge of the canyon and galloping toward its mouth. If Bonner lurked anywhere back there, the Indians' pounding arrival would flush him out.

The cavern had a huge, irregular dome shape. The sunlight slanting into the canyon reached only a few yards past the opening. Beyond that, darkness was a congealed mass, and none of them moved toward it.

"Remember what Bonner said about the beetles," Syne warned.

They remained at the mouth of the cave, hunkering down on either side of it, not shooting, just watching, waiting and listening. The security men didn't fire at them. The group had to be aware of their situation, trapped in the middle between the guns in the cave and the guns of the Lakota, but they stayed where they were, behind cover.

204

"Quanah," Zeda called, "we should go further into the cave. I don't know why or how, but there's something familiar about this place."

"I don't want to bump into those flying mechanical bugs in the dark. Besides, we should stay and finish it with Bonner." He paused and added ruefully, "I'm a little nervous too about going back there blind."

Pagan snorted. "We may not have a choice, if our men make a charge."

"'Our' men?" Syne echoed, eyeing her suspiciously. "I was under the impression you felt thoroughly disaffected from your former fraternity."

"You're welcome to go out there and join them," Zeda said in a tight, cold tone. "If you think they'll let you. If they do, I'll kill you personally."

The roar of an engine floated up from around a bend in the canyon wall, and mingled with it they heard the crackle of automatic gunfire and yipping war cries. A few seconds later the X-MAC jounced into view, with hard-riding Lakota flanking it, shooting at its armored hide and uttering fierce screams. A warrior crouched on the roof, clinging to the periscope.

As the vehicle rumbled closer, Quanah recognized the Indian as Sky Wolf. Though the windshield was tinted, he assumed Bonner himself was behind the wheel.

The security men rose to their knees, believing the X-MAC was making a rescue run and would brake, allowing them to board it. The big machine didn't stop, didn't even slow. It sped past the security force, and they howled in anger and terror. The Lakota used the big armored vehicle as mobile cover, and when their ponies paralleled the security men's position, they directed their fire into them. The return fire was sporadic.

Although a two of the Indian warriors pitched from their saddle blankets with bullet wounds, the remainder leaped from horseback and grappled hand-to-hand.

The X-MAC kept rolling on a straight course for the cave entrance, bouncing over loose stones. Quanah and Zeda triggered their weapons. Ricochets sparked from the front bumper guard. The windshield acquired a few stars, but it didn't break. Nothing less than armor-piercing rounds could wound the vehicle

Snatching a grenade from his sack, Quanah armed it and flung it in the X-MAC's path, trying to place it beneath a tire. A red-yellow bouquet of flame bloomed beneath the MCP, and the dulled thunder of the detonation echoed loudly. Still, the exploding grenade did little to impede the vehicle's progress.

Whirling around, Quanah shouted, "Move!"

He began to run into the blackness, hearing his companions sprinting beside and behind him. The engine roar filled the cavern. He heard a woman shriek, very briefly, and he cast a glance over his shoulder.

The X-MAC rocketed through the cave opening, and the driver cut the wheels sharply to the right, stomping the brakes at the same time. The resulting skid wasn't controlled, and the rear end swivelled around in a 90 degree turn. A wave of sandy soil crested from beneath it, the vehicle thrown off balance in the loose dirt when the brakes were applied.

The swinging rear end slapped against Pagan, swatting her off her feet and flinging her to the right. The rear of the X-MAC hit the rock wall hard, with a shrill squeal of metal grinding into stone. It lurched violently to a halt.

The one-eyed woman was pinned between the armored machine and the stone wall of the cavern. There was no need to dwell on the sight; the life had been crushed out of her body in a microsecond.

Quanah and his friends kept running through the dark throat of the cave, and within a few dozen yards they couldn't see their hands in front of their faces.

"Everybody link hands," Zeda said.

Syne produced a small pen-flash from his pocket, and after the human chain was hastily assembled, he took the point. The light was hardly more than a needle of white incandescence, piercing only a few feet of the cloying blackness. The cavern widened, and the ceiling grew in height. Irregularly formed stalactites hung from above. The light glinted off mineral deposits embedded in the fissured walls. The walls were also decorated with faded, crude paintings and carvings, representations of bizarre figures and shapes. They were obviously very old.

"Petroglyphs," Syne whispered. "Now I see why Sky Wolf didn't care to enter this place. To him, it is a holy spot, even if these marks were made by non-humans."

The *clink-crunch* of stones came faintly from behind.

"Bonner isn't worried about holy spots," Quanah said softly. "If he gets a bead on us with one of those subguns, he can cut us to pieces without getting close."

"Turn out the light," Zeda urged, staring behind them. "Wait until he gets into range. Kill him big time."

Syne complied and they were plunged into absolute blackness, which lasted only for a moment. In the gloom before them shone a fiery red orb, casting a blood-colored luminescence over their faces. Blue-tinged metal gleamed behind it.

"Not encouraging," Syne managed to husk out.

Then Crockett spoke.

CHAPTER THIRTY-ONE

Crockett stared into the face of Fenris, examining the faint interlocking pattern of scales ringing his hairless brow ridges, extending over and meeting at the bridge of his nose.

"I can see you've been playing around with DNA yourself," Crockett said, striving to sound casual. He gestured to the body of the Imperator. "His DNA?"

"Genetic engineering is a program we began on Loki well over two centuries ago," the *Brigadefuhrer* said quietly. "Have you ever heard of pantropic science?"

Crockett nodded. "It's a specialized form of bioengineering."

"Yes...it's a primarily theoretical science devoted to reproducing a strain of humanity designed to live in different environments. After the Catastrophes the science took on a new meaning. It was no longer theoretical or impractical. The challenge was to adapt and modify humanity to survive in the new environment. We experimented with human and animal subjects to create life-forms that could thrive in any physical condition, immune to radiation and other adverse environmental factors. The Gypsy clans roaming the Hell-grounds proved to be excellent subjects."

"And you experimented on yourself, too?"

Fenris nodded toward the body in the canister. "He possessed all the raw material I needed. I created a viral mixture from his nucleic acids and the virus replicated, infected and finally transformed my cells. The process nearly killed me, but within a few months, my genetic code had successfully melded with that of the Imperators."

Crockett frowned. "But what *is* its genetic code? He looks humanoid, but not the same species as *homo sapiens*."

A macabre grin split *Brigadefuhrer's* face. "Isn't that obvious? He is of the same species that gave rise to the legends of the Feathered Serpent among the Maya and the Aztec...Quetzalcoatl, Kulkucan...perhaps even gods such as Thoth and Horus. The creatures we call the Imperators once walked among humans and guided the human culture of Earth. There is no reason why they cannot do so again, here on Loki...at least through a proxy."

"So you think you share the genetic code of a race of gods?"

"Why not? My optic nerves are improved and though more sensitive to high light levels, I can see into the ultraviolet and infrared ranges. My longevity has been extended...I calculate I will live another century, barring accidents or assassination."

Crockett glanced into the face of the Imperator, staring blindly into eternity. "You found him in stasis here, inside the mountain?"

"Yes, right where he is now."

"If he put himself stasis, then he must expect to be released from it eventually."

"That is my surmise, as well. However, he has yet to awaken, even though we've been able to breach the zero-time field sufficiently to collect tissue and blood samples. But for now—he waits."

"Waits for what?"

Fenris shrugged. "To be found, to be rescued. To be relieved. To die. It doesn't matter. What is time to the Quetza?"

"Quetza?"

"My name for his race...for him. So far, he's not corrected me."

"He might if he's ever revived," Crockett pointed out. "What happens if the installation loses power and the stasis field drops?"

Fenris gestured negligently with the wand. "All the main generators would have to go off-line at once, before the redundancies kicked. The odds of that happening are astronomical...just like the odds of you ever carrying tales of what you've seen here back to Loki's Rock...or to that fabricated Office of Off-world Operations of yours."

Not bothering to hide his disgust, Crockett demanded, "Then why bother showing me this?"

Fenris fixed his inhuman gaze on Crockett. "To prove to you beyond a shadow of a doubt that the perverted, primitive kingdom of Loki's Rock cannot hope to trick us, cannot hope to break our trade agreement and cannot hope to overcome us. We hold all of the power in this new world. Loki's Rock exists only at our sufferance, at our whims. We can create new life. Loki's Rock can only take lives."

"Yet you rely on that perverted kingdom to supply you with human organs," Crockett snapped. "Without Loki's Rock, you probably would have died long ago, gone the way of all the other little power-mad tyrants who tried to set up dictatorships here."

Not responding to the comment, the *Brigadefuhrer* asked, "What is the population of Loki's Rock?"

"I don't know."

"How high are you placed in its hierarchy?"

"I'm not placed at all. I'm here against my will. Bonner is holding friends of mine hostage. I don't want to be here any more than you want me to be here."

"I don't mind your visit, Colonel, despite the damage and disruption you have caused.

A minor crisis, easily contained, can sometimes be stimulating. Did Bonner send you to assassinate me?"

"Not exactly." Crockett smiled without humor. "Though after meeting you and seeing this place, I don't find it such a bad idea. You've outlived your time."

The *Brigadefuhrer* regarded him blankly, and then shook his head. "How can I possibly make you understand? You, a landless, lawless renegade."

Crockett looked at him keenly. "As far as I know, a renegade is someone who betrays a cause or a faith or a group of people who trusted him. You are responsible for destroying most of this world and most of its population. You prey on your people in this installation, refusing to grant them a dignified death. I don't think I'm the renegade here."

The *Brigadefuhrer* didn't react, didn't reply, didn't respond. With the infrasound wand, he pointed to a door at the end of the hexagonal room, and Crockett walked in that direction. The door slid open on a gangway that bridged a fifty-foot gap of empty gloom. Glancing over the guardrail, Crockett saw an enormous, artificial cavern cut from the bedrock in the shape of a pentagon. Above a certain height, the walls were of unfinished stone but below they were sheathed in polished alloy.

Many of the shapes scattered about the vast floor were recognizable—Crockett identified digging machines outfitted with huge drill bits, as well as wheeled ATVs. He experienced only a distant quiver of surprise at the sight of the two aircraft. Both of the craft were sleek, compact and streamlined, painted a matte-finish black. The pair of stubby wings positioned amidships terminated in round VTOL turbine engines. Crockett instantly recognized them as the fast-attack craft nicknamed Skeeters because of their speed and ability to make sharply angled turns at virtually any speed. Manufactured by Hiflite Industries, the Skeeters were believed to be the pinnacle of atmospheric avionic engineering—two centuries before.

Tilting his head back, Crockett saw a spider's maze of catwalks strung from metal cables surrounding a bowl-shaped roof. He followed Fenris past a small elevator cage, but he noted that the shaft went only to the landing bay floor. At the end of the gangway, a transverse corridor ran to the left and right, as far as Crockett could see in either direction.

Nodding toward the Skeeters, Crockett commented, "My party and I were surveilled by one of those a few days ago."

"We occasionally send a pilot up to track one of our test subjects," Fenris said disinterestedly.

"Test subjects who escape or who are permitted to leave?"

A grim smile lifted the corners of the *Brigadefuhrer's* lips. "No one is allowed to leave, Colonel. And no one escapes. You should have guessed that by now."

The inward wall was pierced by an elevator stand, and *Brigadefuhrer* Fenris directed him toward it. They stepped into the nearest lift and it propelled them smoothly upward, but only for a short distance. It stopped, and the door panel opened onto a vault-walled chamber.

The *Brigadefuhrer* led him into it, past workers manning computer consoles, consulting printouts, all of them looking very industrious and intent. Circuits hummed and panel lights blinked. A bank of closed-circuit monitor screens ran the length of one wall. Only a few screens displayed images—dim, flickering black-and-white scenes of empty rooms and corridors.

One screen showed the interior of a cave, looking out toward an irregularly shaped entrance. Beyond the opening was rock-littered ground. Because the image was in black-and-white, Crockett could not tell the time of day.

Fenris led him along a narrow walkway that paralleled a monorail track. A flatcar coupled to a small shifter engine rested on the rail at the opening of a perfectly round, metal-collared tunnel. Crockett repressed the urge to ask where the track stretched, but he guessed it went to only one place--the pick-up point in the cave Bonner had briefed them about.

The *Brigadefuhrer* put hand on his shoulder. "This way, Colonel. The tour of Jotunheim has come to an end."

He directed Crockett across the room to a door. The door hissed open, and the man waved Crockett in. They stood together in a very small elevator as the door closed behind them. The lift fell very quietly, and for only a short distance.

The door opened, and they stepped out between a pair of bookcases and into the *Brigadefuhrer's* office. Fenris didn't say a word. He went to his desk and sat down, placing the infrasound wand before him. He stared at Crockett intently. Crockett stood in front of the desk, staring back.

"Have you nothing to say, Colonel?"

"What would you like me to say?"

"That you are impressed, intimidated even. That you have met your master."

"Is that what you are?"

"I am, but I'm interested in hearing you say it."

"Why? Will that save my life?"

The *Brigadefuhrer* shrugged. "I am afraid not. I toyed with the notion of simply releasing you, so you could carry the tale of your experiences back to Loki's Rock, perhaps even to the Commonwealth at large, but once we locate your companion, she will fill that function adequately. No, I believe I will have

210

you remain here with us."

"As a subject for your genetics experiments?"

"Perhaps."

"Or as an organ donor?"

"Again, perhaps."

"Or someone you can turn into a cyborg? Another one of your tools?"

"What else is man *but* a tool?" the *Brigadefuhrer* asked. "He has no other value. Humanity is self-destructive, suffering from anarchy of mind and spirit. Free of the moral deterioration that paves the road to decadence, can you imagine the marvels humanity could accomplish?"

"I've seen some of your marvels," Crockett said grimly. "Shiny toys and freak shows."

The *Brigadefuhrer* affected not to have heard him. "In fifty years, maybe less, this world will cease to be a planet of strife and disorder, wallowing in bloodshed. It will be secure."

"The security of the grave," Crockett replied with bitterness, edging forward. "Nearly two centuries ago your lust for order nearly destroyed Loki and left the survivors to pick up the pieces."

"The Catastrophes were actually blessings," Fenris continued. "You have no idea of what it was like here. Loki before the Catastrophes was totally out of control, populations of useless people were expanding, chaos overwhelmed all attempts to build political systems."

"So you don't care about all the suffering, the horrors, the destruction. It was best for the world to be destroyed–because you managed to survive?"

"Visionaries are needed. And there are things far beyond your understanding. The seeds planted a long time before are getting ready to take hold of this world, preparing for a new future."

"Like a world ruled by the old gods? Horus, Ibis, Quetzalcoatl?"

"That would be a fine world. Unfortunately–"The *Brigadefuhrer* lifted his face and his eyes bored into Crockett's own. "–it is a world you will never see."

He reached across the desk toward a row of inset buttons. Crockett lunged across the desk, his hand closing around the handle of the infrasound wand. The hand of Fenris grasped the tip of the wand, yanking it to one side. Crockett tried to wrest it away, but it was like wrestling with an iron vise. He strained against the man's grip, but he was unable to even move his hand.

The *Brigadefuhrer's* expression remained calm, almost serene, his inhuman eyes placid. "Killing me will serve little purpose. My death will not affect this place. The work will go on."

For an instant Crockett believed him, and he almost stopped trying to free the wand from the man's grasp. Then a boiling anger came fountaining up out of him, and erupted in a flaming, murderous fury. Still keeping his grip on the wand, Crockett threw his entire weight against the desk, shoving the edge hard into *Brigadefuhrer's* midsection.

Not relaxing his grip on the wand, Fenris fell over backward in his chair. He dragged Crockett over the top of the desk with him. Crockett's left fist smashed with all his weight behind it into the man's pale, unlined face. Blood sprayed from his nostrils and the man's grip on the wand loosened.

Crockett wrenched it from his hand, turned it and touched the right side of the *Brigadefuhrer's* head with the humming tip.

The skull of Fenris collapsed where the point touched. There was a sound as of a wet paper bag bursting and the *Brigadefuhrer's* body settled to the carpet, his head punched out of shape. He lay as Crockett had seen many corpses lie—boneless, mouth partly open, eyes wide and glazing over, an expression of shock frozen on his face.

Pushing himself to his feet, Crockett surveyed the office in a sweeping, searching glance, He saw his weapons, his grenades and ammo clips stacked in a corner behind the desk, within easy reach if he had known they were there.

The arrogance of power never failed to astonish him. Those who wielded control always seemed to lose their objectivity, rigidly believing that their authority could never be challenged. They grew blind to other possibilities, to random factors, to wild cards. The *Brigadefuhrer* and Django Bonner were so alike it was nearly comical. Or sickening.

Stepping over the body, he grabbed the subgun, thumbed new rounds into the Hawken and attached the grenades to the combat harness he still wore beneath his coat.

From the corner of his eye, he caught a shifting movement behind him. He whirled, the pistol leading the way. One of the tall double doors slowly opened, pushed from the outside.

CHAPTER THIRTY-TWO

Before the door had opened more than a few inches, Crockett bounded across the office toward the recess between the bookcases. Putting his back to the elevator doors, he held his breath and waited, the Hawken held in a two-handed grip.

Welch strolled past him, his attention on the desk. His pace slowed when he saw no one at the desk, then it quickened. Peering around the edge of the bookshelves, Crockett watched the man reach the front of the desk, look around, then do a violent double-take. A gasp of horror escaped his lips and he rushed clumsily around the desk, kneeling down to check the *Brigadefuhrer's* corpse.

Crockett crossed the carpeted floor on the balls of his feet, sacrificing a certain amount of stealth for speed. He got behind Welch just as the man straightened up. With both arms he secured a chokehold and cinched down with all of his strength.

Welch husked out a half-gagged curse and his hands came up, locking around Crockett's wrists, prising his arms away from his neck. Crockett felt his flesh and tendons being ground against bone, and it was all he could do to bite back a cry of pain.

Still gripping Crockett's wrists, Welch turned, faced the double doors and suddenly bent forward at the waist. Rather than resist the maneuver and risk having his arms dislocated or even torn from their sockets, Crockett kicked off from the floor, landing on his back but cushioning the fall with the soles of his feet.

Welch staggered forward, off balance from the lack of resistance. He had no choice but to release Crockett's wrists or fall face forward.

In the instant Welch's upper body was still bent forward, almost parallel with the floor, Crockett performed a backward half-somersault, kicking up with both legs, the soles of his boots slamming into Welch's face. The man straightened, half-blinded from the blood springing from his flattened nose and split lips. He staggered back and fetched up hard against the desk.

Crockett continued rolling, ignoring the pain in his shoulders, and came to his feet with his left fist driving into Welch's belly with all his strength behind it. The man bent over, clutching at his stomach, and Crockett slammed the barrel of the Hawken behind Welch's left ear.

If he had been a normal man, Welch would have died. But he was only half-stunned and struggled to pull himself erect. Crockett jacked his right knee against his forehead, and pain exploded up and down his leg, from ankle to thigh.

Welch fell facedown. While Crockett bit his lip to keep from groaning, the man forced himself over, fighting to get into a sitting position. His face a mask of dark pink blood, his expression twisted into one of dazed, confused hurt. Crockett moved behind him and put the bore of his pistol against the back of his head.

"The woman," he said, voice quavering with the effort to repress the pain in his knee and his wrists. "Did you find her?"

Welch buried his face in his hands. He began to sob with dry, shuddering heaves that racked his body.

"Answer me," Crockett pressed the pistol harder into his skull. "The woman!"

Voice muffled by his hands, choked with grief, Welch stammered, "Couldn't. Didn't. Don't know where."

Welch fell silent and inhaled a quavering breath. Slowly, he lowered his hands and he twisted his head around to glare at Crockett with homicidal hatred. Teeth bared, he said, "When we *do* find her, we'll have a lot of fun with her before we cut her up and use the pieces of her body in some of our experiments. We'll do the same to you."

"You're getting a little ahead of yourself," Crockett said.

The man's eyes blinked rapidly. His shoulders shook. Faintly, hoarsely, he whispered, "Dear God...I can't believe it. The *Brigadefuhrer* is finally dead."

Crockett said flatly, "And so are you."

He squeezed the trigger of the Hawken. The .50 caliber round broke open the back of Welch's head, but it didn't exit from the front. The gun bucked, the unexpected blowback nearly snatching it from his fingers. The force of the shot slammed Welch's upper body forward, face hitting the floor between his knees. Metal gleamed in the mixture of clotted brain matter, synthetic flesh, hair and blood.

Letting out his breath, Crockett knelt, quickly examining the body. Though partially deflected by the metal plate in his skull, the bullet had still done enough damage to kill him. As it was, he doubted that anything less than a point-blank shot would have accomplished the job. He took the man's ID badge from his lapel and climbed to his feet. He felt no twinge of regret and he wondered why.

After attaching the badge to his coat, Crockett adjusted the setting of his Commtach. Through a hash of static, he heard Alex's voice say, "—won't you respond?"

"That's what I'm doing, Jones."

"Colonel?" Her voice filled with elation, but there was a throbbing roar in the background, and it sounded as if she were shouting.

"Yeah, it's me. Are you all right?"

"You have to speak up."

Adjusting the comm-link's settings, Crockett asked again, "Are you all right?"

"More or less. You?"

"The same."

"What?"

Impatiently Crockett demanded, "Where the hell are you?"

"I don't know exactly, but I've found the primary cooling and circulation nexus. Where are you?"

"On the level where we split up. I've got Welch's ID badge and you can find me by the locator lozenge."

Voice troubled, Alex replied, "I don't think there's a computer tie-in down here. I'll have to go up, get my hands on a badge so I can access it. Listen, I can take out the generators down here, probably knock out the power and perhaps start a thaw. At the very least it'll be a diversion."

"Do it," Crockett said. "On the level directly above me is some sort of a central control room. I'll wait for you up there."

"What about Quanah and the others?"

"I don't know—yet."

Alex's response was so long in coming that Crockett almost called her name. Then her voice filtered over the earpiece. It was unsteady.

"If they're still in Loki's Rock, what are we going to do?"

"We'll think about that later. First we have to get out of here. Blow the generators."

"When?"

"As soon as you can. I won't make my move until you've made yours. I'm sure all sorts of alarms, bells and whistles will go off, and that'll be my signal. Acknowledged?"

"Acknowledged. You know something?"

"What?"

"We need to put more thought into planning our field trips."

Crockett smiled. "Understood. Standby."

He waited until he was sure she'd signed off before allowing himself the luxury of a groan. He sat down on the edge of the desk to wait, trying to massage the pain from his wrists and knee.

CHAPTER THIRTY-THREE

Turning toward Simza, Alex shouted, "You have to go back. It's not safe in here."

Simza narrowed her big eyes. "Why not? I've been here plenty of times."

Waving toward the row of generators below, Alex answered, "I'm going to blow those up. There's no telling what will happen."

Staring first at the generators and then at Alex, Simza said, "I don't understand."

"You don't have to. Just get back below, where we met. I think you'll be okay. I'll give you a minute to get started."

Her dark eyes moved from Alex's face to the generators, then back to her face. "What about my medicine?"

Alex swallowed hard, feeling pity well up like a lump in her throat. "You don't need it. You're just fine. Now go!"

Simza moved a few faltering steps toward the round hatchway, then turned, beaming broadly. "Come back when you're finished, okay?"

Alex nodded. "I'll do my best. It might be awhile...until then, do what you have to do to stay alive."

"I'm good at that." Simza flipped her a quick salute and scuttled through the hatch opening, swinging the heavy cover closed.

Alex counted to sixty under her breath, trying to give the girl as much time as possible to get away from the area. As far as she or Crockett knew, destroying one generator might trigger an atomic chain reaction that would result in a do-it-yourself Catastrophe.

Alex moved around the catwalks, heading for the optimum position from which to throw the grenades. Though her hand-eye coordination was excellent, she didn't possess the muscle strength or the experience to throw one of the deadly explosives very far. Her best bet was to get right over the generators and drop them straight down.

She was able to reach a point on one of the walkways that was almost directly above the generator connected to the pump array. Best of all, it was only a couple of long steps to a lift cage. She examined the control box inside of the cage and saw that it was a simple lever--to go down, she would push the lever down, to go up, she would pull it up.

Alex undipped two grenades from the combat harness, an incendiary and a fragger.

Leaning as far out over the vibrating railing as she dared, Alex held both grenades in her right hand. She armed them by pulling away the trigger spoons.

She opened her fingers, letting both devices fall away toward the rows of generators fifty feet below. Then she bounded for the elevator, slamming the gate shut and grabbing the lever. Before she could jerk it up, the brutal sound of detonating high explosives and ripping, rending metal filled the vast room.

The lift cage shook violently, rattling and clattering. Water, chunks of concrete and metal flew upward in a fiery column, battering the underside of the catwalks. Alex received a blurred image of a layer of fire clinging to the handrails and grillwork. The double concussion slapped against her eardrums.

The angry, deafening shrieking of ruptured metal replaced the thunder of the explosion, and blinding clouds of white vapor spewed up from below, billowing and rolling like heavy fog. It doused the flames and coated all of the walkways with a patina of frost.

Alex inhaled just a bit of the supercooled air, and for a moment she gagged herself blind, the soft, wet tissues of her throat afire with agony. She slammed the cage lever as far as it would go in the up position, and with an electrical whine, the elevator shot upward. It rose, rattling and shaking, past level after level.

Once, she hazarded a look over the gate and saw nothing but an expanse of white clouds, as though she were rocketing high in the air, far above the earth. Then, over the hum and the rattle, she heard the warbling and wailing of alarm Klaxons. Quickly, she drew her rail pistol. She had no idea where she was going to end up, but she was at least on her way.

The lift clanked to a jolting halt. Pushing aside the gate, Alex stepped into a small alcove fronting a tunnel from which a group of men emerged. They wore white coveralls and were frantically donning breathing masks. They stumbled to unsteady, fearful stops when they saw Alex and her pistol. She almost shouted "Freeze!" but thought better of it and commanded, "Don't move!"

The man in the lead wore a badge identifying him as MIKE. He sputtered and stammered behind the mask. "Pl-please, we've got to get down to the station!"

Snatching the badge from his coverall pocket, Alex said, "First things first, Mike. Show me the nearest computer tie-in."

Mike pushed his way through his companions, moving toward the rear of the tunnel. Alex said, "The rest of you can go about your business."

They made a concerted rush for the lift cage, and Mike stopped in front of a wall panel. "Here."

"Complex display," Alex announced.

The wall panel flashed with light, and a diagram of the complex appeared. "Where are we?" Alex asked.

Mike pointed to a pulsing green dot.

"Locate Welch."

Another dot began to throb. Counting the levels, Alex saw she was far below Crockett's location. "Where's the nearest lift, Mike?"

"Out the doors, a hundred feet to your right. To get to Welch's level, all you have to do is say into the tie-in, 'Welch.'"

"Handy. You may go now."

Mike bustled away, and Alex went through the doors at the end of the tunnel. She called Crockett on the transcomm and told him, "On my way."

"Good," he responded. "I think I know a way out of here."

"Are you sure?"

"No. Watch your back."

"Watch yours."

CHAPTER THIRTY-FOUR

When Crockett heard the first alarms, he picked up the subgun and the Hawken and walked painfully toward the private lift between the bookcases. Pushing the red button with the barrel of the pistol, the door panels rolled open and he stepped inside.

A push of the button on the inside wall closed the doors and started the elevator sliding upward.

When it sighed to a gentle stop, he poked the button, the door panels opened and he stepped out into a scene of utter, screaming panic and pandemonium. He stood for a moment, permitting himself a grin, relishing the energy of dazed, almost stupefied terror crackling throughout the control room.

He did a quick scan of the chamber, his senses on full alert, his instincts tingling from the waves of tension coursing and cresting through the place.

Men ran to and fro, back and forth, going from computer terminal to readout station to dial-and-button-studded consoles. All of them were screaming and shrieking to be heard over the rising and falling banshee notes of the Klaxon.

Crockett picked up snatches of shouts and yells.

"Coolant core breach! We've lost two generators—"

"Why aren't the backups on line—"

"Goddammit, my board shows a total circulation failure!"

"Main pumps and conduits are gone! Reserve processors and the temperature and humidity controls are locked—"

"Where's the *Brigadefuhrer*? The temperature will rise to critical levels in five hours—"

Crockett stepped into the control room, walking around the running, panic-stricken men, as he strode toward the monorail. He almost reached it with no one noticing him. A man bending over a flickering monitor screen glanced up and snarled. He shouted something, but no one heard him. One of his hands fumbled at his waist and came up gripping a long-nosed automatic made of blued steel.

Simultaneously Crockett brought up his Hawken and dispatched a 50 caliber round into the man's stomach A group of men spun in his direction. Already on the verge of mindless flight, it took them an instant to identify him as an intruder, as a danger.

Crockett kept walking, swinging the subgun toward them, and holding down the trigger. He sprayed bullets into the middle of the group and could hear their screams above the warbling of the alarm.

The burst of autofire was the signal for the men in the control room to go berserk. They milled around mindlessly, ducking beneath consoles and panels, some stampeding madly for an exit. The few who were armed were bowled over by their terrified comrades.

A short, stumpy-legged man bolted around a console, trying to run past Crockett, who reached out and grabbed the man's collar, swinging him around in a wide arc. The man clawed desperately at Crockett's hand, his face ashen with terror.

Crockett released the collar and the man floundered backward, toward the console and fell against it. Crockett rammed the muzzle of the Hawken under his fleshy chin, forcing his head back at a painful angle. His ID badge proclaimed him to be HOWARD.

"Are there beetles in the cave, Howard?" he snapped.

"Only one," the man gasped. "Programmed for surveillance and defense."

"Can you override the program from this console?"

Howard stared at him as though he were insane. "Why?"

"Answer me!"

"Yes, there are manual overrides here."

Crockett turned the man around to face the console. "Show me."

Quanah's face stared at him from the small screen in the center of the panel. Behind him, Crockett could make out Zeda and Syne.

Howard fiddled with a button or two and announced, "The beetle is controlled from here now."

"Can you speak through it from here?" Crockett demanded.

Howard's trembling finger touched a square grid. "Talk into that. The communication channel is open."

"Quanah," Crockett said loudly, "can you hear me?"

On the screen, Quanah and Zeda's expressions went blank, then lit up with relief. Both of them started talking at once, so Crockett had to say, "Is everyone all right?"

"Yes, "Syne crisply replied. "Where are you?"

"In the Ahnenerbe Institute. Can you see anything like a monorail switching station in the cave?"

"No," Quanah answered. "The place is as black as the middle of the Coal Sack."

Turning to the terrified Howard, Crockett said, "Where's the monorail track in there?"

"Only a few hundred yards ahead of them. You can guide them to it with the beetle."

"Do it."

"We copy that, Colonel," Syne said. He glanced behind him. "I think Bonner is on our heels, however."

"Forget him."

"Where is Alex?" Zeda asked "Is she with you?"

"Not yet," Crockett replied.

Quanah's lips compressed. "What do you mean?"

"We'll talk about it in a few minutes. Follow the beetle to the monorail and wait."

"Wait for what?"

Crockett blew out a weary sigh. "For the planning session for our next field trip, what do you think? Just do what I say."

He watched both the screen and Howard's hands, as under his ministrations on the controls, Quanah, Syne and Zeda followed the beetle to a metal rail that stretched out from a tunnel. It was the exact double of the tunnel opening in the control room.

"No controls here," Quanah said as they reached it.

"They're up here," Crockett responded. He glared at Howard. "Aren't they?"

Howard nodded several times and flipped up a cover on the console. Beneath it, inset into the surface, Crockett saw a set of buttons and tabs. He said, "Send the train to the cave, then bring it back."

Howard hesitated for only the briefest of moments before keying in a sequence. With a faint hum, the shifter engine and flatcar glided into the tunnel. "Transport is on its way," Crockett said.

"Standing by," Syne replied.

Crockett watched the screen, through the beetle's electronic eye. In less than a minute, the engine emerged from the tunnel. Quanah and Zeda eyed it suspiciously, but Syne swiftly climbed aboard, settling himself in a cushioned seat.

"What are you two waiting for?" Crockett demanded. "For the refreshment car to arrive?"

"I don't even know what that means," Quanah muttered, getting into the passenger compartment behind Syne. Zeda sat down beside him.

Howard tapped a button and the train slid backward along the rail into the tunnel. Plaintively, he asked, "Are you done with me?"

Crockett ignored him. Glancing over his shoulder, he saw Alex sprinting between consoles. Face caked with dried blood, her clothes were covered by what looked like gray dust. Her hair was a wild, Medusa-like tangle.

She came to a stop at the edge of the console. Breathing hard, she looked Crockett up and down and said, "You look like shit. Sir."

Crockett's lips quirked in a half-smile. "You should stand where I am."

With an electric hum and hiss, the train emerged from the tunnel opening. Syne, Quanah and Zeda climbed out, peering around at the control room. The alarm Klaxons fell silent, and the abrupt quiet was almost as nerve-scratching as the warbling tones.

"What's the plan?" Zeda demanded. "Take over this place, give up, or what?"

"I hope it's 'what,' " Quanah muttered, blowing on his hands. "I do not find the climate congenial."

Syne vigorously rubbed his upper arms. "Nor do I."

"We're going to get the hell out of this frozen nightmare," Crockett declared. "We can commandeer one of their aircraft and fly out of here." He gestured to the floor. "The hangar is below us."

"What'll keep the frozones here from following us?" Zeda asked.

Crockett shook his head. "Let's hope they have other matters to occupy them."

As he spoke, movement flickered across the monitor, transmitted from the beetle in the cave. Django Bonner stood before the monorail track, holding an automatic rifle in his left hand and one of his pearl-handled Hawkens in the right. Blood flowed from a wound at his hairline.

Crockett spoke into the speaker grid. "Django. Wondered when you'd show up."

Bonner's reaction was almost comical. He skipped around, glaring wildly up at the beetle, face contorting. His mouth worked for a long second, with no sounds coming from it. Finally he bellowed, "Crockett? *Crockett!* You deceived me! You betrayed me!"

"Sorry, Django, but after thinking it over, I'm afraid I must refuse your job offer. The hours stink, and the pay is lousy."

Bonner began to tremble, eyelids flickering, spittle collecting at the corners of his mouth. In a voice that shivered with the intensity of the emotions he was struggling to control, he said, "You stupid bastard. You stupid, suicidal bastard. You don't know what you've done."

Crockett snarled out a laugh. "I know *exactly* what I've done. I've cut off this sick trade between you and this monument to insanity. You're cast back out onto the Hellgrounds of Loki, to survive or to die on your own. My money is on you dying."

Bonner stood frozen, his body quaking violently, a thousand changing sparks of light dancing in his dark eyes. Then he threw back his head and screamed, a howl of agony, terror and rage torn from the roots of his soul. Saliva sprayed from his mouth, one hand clawed at the side of his face, the long nails tearing gouges in his skin.

"I'll track you down, Crockett!" he shrieked. "I'll find you and I'll keep you alive for years, in constant, unending pain! You'll promise me anything, give me anything, do anything, just so I'll kill you! And if you die before I find you again, I'll dig up your stinking corpse and spend my days pissing in its mouth! Your punishment begins *now*, Crockett! It will never end!"

The tone, the crash of his strident voice, the unregenerate, unforgiving madness in his eyes almost caused Crockett to drop his pistol in surprise. To witness Bonner losing his iron control and flaming up in a torch of demented fury was a more fearful picture than he had imagined. For a moment he contemplated taking the monorail to the cave and finishing his business with the patriarch of Loki's Rock.

Teeth bared, Bonner raised his revolver. The bore swelled in the little monitor screen like a hollow, cyclopean eye. A blaze of orange flame filled it—then the screen went black.

"Colonel!" Zeda shouted. "Come on, dammit!"

Crockett heard the slap of running feet on the smooth alloy flooring, rushing up from behind. He half turned, sweeping the ranks of the business-suited men with a prolonged burst from the Taktron. They screamed as the hail of rounds ripped through them. The few who weren't drilled scrambled for cover, flinging ineffectual pistol fire in his general direction. Everyone ducked.

"Colonel!" Alex's voice was high and tight with tension. "If we're going to go, let's do it!"

Crockett ran toward the elevator. "Follow me."

The five people crowded into the small lift. With the barrel of his pistol, Crockett punched the button and the elevator dropped smoothly. The doors opened at the end of the gangway spanning the hangar bay. Crockett left the car first, the others following him without a word. Hand over hand, he climbed down the ladder that extended from the gangway to the floor below. He looked around and saw a yellow control box attached to a thick cable stretching to ceiling.

He pressed the green button with a thumb and the two great leaves of the hangar roof swung upward on a complex arrangement of pivots and hinges. The sky above shone with brilliant, early morning daylight. As Alex joined him on the hangar floor, she demanded, "Colonel, do you know how to pilot one of those machines?"

"No," he said, nodding toward Syne. "But he should."

Alex glanced at him quizzically. Syne's placid expression did not change, but he returned Crockett's nod. "I do."

The five people rushed across the bay to the nearest Skeeter. To Crockett's relief, locating the canopy release catch for the aircraft's cockpit was not difficult. As he raised it, he heard shouting voices and saw a group of armed men fanning out across the gangway above. Wreaths of mist curled around them.

Crockett took Alex by the arm. "Get aboard."

She hesitated, and then the crash of gunfire echoed through the vast room. Bullets smashed into the floor, striking a pattern of white pockmarks. Swiftly, she slid into the Skeeter, followed by Zeda and then Quanah. Crockett and Syne took the pilot and co-pilot's seats. The people struggled to strap themselves in, but there were only four seats so Zeda was forced to sit on Quanah's lap.

Crockett lowered and locked the canopy into place. The instrument panel was surprisingly simple, consisting of a control stick, altimeter and fuel gauges. Syne flicked two switches, pulled the stick back slightly, then pushed it forward. The hull began to vibrate around them, in tandem with a whine that grew in volume pitch. The blades of the enclosed wing turbines spun—slowly at first, then the speed increased until they became blurred shadows.

Syne said, "VTOL launch system enabled."

Crockett retorted impatiently, "Then what are you waiting for? Launch us."

Syne pulled back on the control stick and with stomach-sinking swiftness, the Skeeter lifted upward. The engine whine became a droning hum as the aircraft rose smoothly to the open hangar roof. Despite the situation, Crockett couldn't help but be impressed by Syne's expertise.

Looking out the canopy toward the gangway, Crockett saw roiling plumes of fog, as the installation's cold air met the warmer air drifting in from outside. The armed men were only shadows in the mist.

Leaning forward, Alex said, "Looks like the spring thaw has come early."

"You should know," replied Crockett. "You gave it the nudge."

As the Skeeter rose higher, he glimpsed a tall, shadowy shape moving through the wreaths of fog below. The figure walked with a steady, swift and almost sinuous grace. The skin between his shoulder blades tightened and the short hairs at the back of his neck tingled.

As the aircraft floated between the open leaves of the hangar, the figure stepped to the guardrail at the edge of the gangway, staring up at the Skeeter with golden eyes. The crest of golden feathers running along the center of his skull glistened with droplets of moisture.

Crockett bit back a cry of shock His stomach turned a cold flip-flop as he recognized the Imperator whom Fenris had named Quetza.

Shifting in his jump seat, Quanah demanded, "Who is that?"

Crockett didn't answer, forcing himself to look full upon Quetza's face. He saw pride stamped there as well as a dark wisdom. He sensed that Quetza was old, so old that his soul wearied of trying to dredge up memories of youth. Dimly, Crockett understood that Quetza believed he was the last of his kind and that the world of Loki was his and his alone.

Quetza glanced sharply to his right and stepped swiftly back into the roiling vapor. Following the direction of his gaze, Crockett saw a uniformed man push up against the handrail, the butt of a Taktron Pulse-Plasma Emitter resting on his shoulder.

"Syne—" Crockett said tensely.

"—I see him, Colonel," Syne replied.

Syne slid the control stick all the way forward and the Skeeter surged upward, banking the ship a few degrees to starboard. Almost at the same time, a jet of blue flame spit from the hollow bore of the Blitz Cannon. The Skeeter shuddered with a bone-numbing shock as the plasma projectile impacted against its undercarriage.

No one cried out, but the aircraft slewed around in a one-eighty and electronic alarms began buzzing, ringing and beeping. Smoke and the smell of metal turning molten filled the cramped cockpit.

Quanah coughed and shouted, "Put us back down before we blow up!"

Syne did not reply. Only the compression of his tight lips indicated he felt any emotion remotely like fear. He kept his hands on the controls and the Skeeter continued to ascend, wobbling violently.

Trailing streamers of spark-shot smoke, the Skeeter rose above the hangar doors, made a wide, slow turn and skimmed over the craggy peaks of Mount Maleficent. 13 Orionis blazed brilliantly in the deep blue sky.

Syne engaged the ramjets and sent the aircraft arrowing away from the mountain. The Skeeter's trajectory declined quickly. He said, "I doubt I will be able to achieve a vertical landing."

"I don't care," snapped Crockett. "Just get us down."

"That will most definitely happen," Syne retorted. "Regardless of your orders."

The Skeeter skimmed over the rock-strewn ground, shearing off the tops of a few scrubby bushes on the way. The craft hit the ground on its belly, bounced twice like a flat stone skipping across the surface of a pond and crashed through a brush cluster. The Skeeter's wings dug deep trenches in the sandy soil before both turbine-fan housings were torn off.

Crockett's body strained the harness and then slammed back into the seat. The Skeeter sledded along the barren ground, leaving a wide, scoured path in its wake, loose soil piling up before its nose.

The airship careened to a stop. The canopy was jammed shut inside its warped frame. Unbuckling the safety harness, Crockett shouldered it open and dragged Zeda across the seats, then helped Alex, Quanah and Syne to climb out before he scrambled to safety. From the undercarriage of the Skeeter boiled a mixture of white, gray and black smoke.

The five people moved quickly away, in case unknown combustibles in the aircraft exploded. They stepped to the rim of a gully, inhaling fresh air. At Quanah's demand, everyone took inventory of themselves and found no injuries more serious than a few contusions.

"Where's *Ambler?*" Crockett asked.

Syne nodded in an eastwardly direction. "Several kilometers or so thataway."

" 'Thataway'?" Crockett echoed. "Not very precise."

"Best I can do under the circumstances, Colonel."

They looked up at the graven image of Hitler's head. Dark, oily smoke poured from the fissures and cracks all around it, masking the face.

Crockett said, "Jones, whatever you did in there, you did it up fine."

Quietly, Alex quoted, "And did the Countenance Divine shine forth upon our hills...and was Jerusalem builded her among these dark Satanic mills?"

"Are you asking me or telling me?"

She smiled slightly. "Neither. It's a stanza from a poem by William Blake. It seemed an appropriate moment to show off."

Quanah chuckled. "I guess you've earned the right...as long as you don't make it a habit."

Staring at the columns of smoke slowly corkscrewing into the sky, Crockett realized he was not satisfied with the carnage. The Ahnenerbe Institute still stood, a symbol of everything vile, depraved and self-serving that had fled Earth to find a new home in which to fester.

He knew he would never be satisfied until he clawed the mountain stronghold down, stone by stone, crushed it into rubble and stomped it flat. But for now, that would have to wait.

As if reading his thoughts, Alex leaned close and whispered into his ear, "We need to go back. I learned something in there—"

"—So did I, Jones," Crockett broke in more harshly than he intended. "And we *will* go back...but not today."

Alex nodded and said nothing more.

Stripping off his heavy coat, Quentin Crockett surveyed the sun-scorched, rocky terrain all around them. In many ways, Loki was a more beautiful world than Earth. Back home, man's greed and stupidity had raped the deserts and polluted the oceans. Here, there was a still chance for the planet to recover and return to a pristine state. He also knew that exploration for its own sake was a luxury few men of his age were afforded. There were plenty of worlds in The Spur, and he meant to make the best of the opportunities.

Crockett turned to his crew, met their expectant gazes and smiled slightly. He hooked a thumb over his shoulder. "We still have a lot of Loki to cover so it's best we get started. Thataway."

DON'T MISS THE NEXT BOOK IN
THE SPUR SERIES:

THE SPUR™

HELLDORADO

COMING SOON!

About the Author

MARK ELLIS is a novelist and comics creator whose many credentials include *Doc Savage: The Man of Bronze*, *The Wild, Wild West*, *The Justice Machine*, *Death Hawk*, *The Miskatonic Project*, *Ninja Elite*, *Star Rangers* and *Nosferatu: Plague of Terror*.

In 1996 he created the best-selling *Outlanders* series for Harlequin Enterprise's Gold Eagle imprint, writing under the pen-name of James Axler. He is the author of 50 books, and with his wife Melissa Martin-Ellis, co-wrote *The Everything Guide to Writing Graphic Novels*. He has been featured in *Starlog*, *Comics Scene* and *Fangoria* magazines.

He has also been interviewed by Robert Siegel for NPR's *All Things Considered*.

www.MarkEllisInk.com
www.Cryptozoica.com

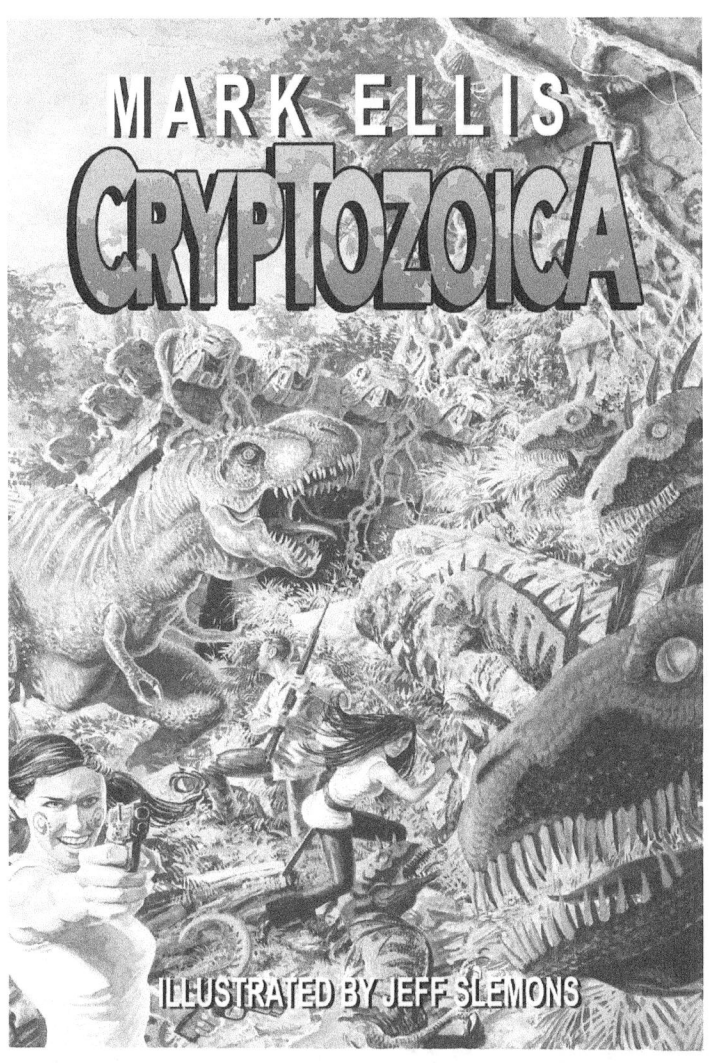

From Mark Ellis, the Creator of OUTLANDERS & THE SPUR!

"CRYPTOZOICA is a novel for those who really want to sink their teeth into something engrossing to the finish. For a modern take on pulp adventure, you would be hard-pressed to find one that delivers like this!"

-Bookgasm

Available in trade paperback at all online booksellers, and as an ebook exclusively at Amazon.com